Critical acclaim for
Kathleen Givens
and her epic romantic novel
ON A HIGHLAND SHORE

"An outstanding story! ON A HIGHLAND SHORE is like watching a grand movie epic unfold. . . . The story is brilliantly written with characters so real and scenery so vivid, you feel like you're standing in the middle of each battlefield. . . . A masterpiece."

—Freshfiction.com

"Breathtaking and absorbing. . . . An adventure, a romance, a historical of epic proportions."

—Marsha Canham, award-winning
author of *The Pride of Lions*

"The Scottish Highlands have rarely been more inviting."

—*Dallas Morning News*

"Givens brings the rugged, beautiful historic Highlands to life in a grand and sweeping adventure."

—*Romantic Times*

"Adeptly intertwin[es] history with romance. . . . The chemistry crackles. . . ."

—*Publishers Weekly*

"Powerful . . . full-bodied historical fiction."

ON A HIGHLAND SHORE

KATHLEEN GIVENS

POCKET STAR BOOKS

NEW YORK • LONDON • TORONTO • SYDNEY

A Pocket Star Book published by
POCKET BOOKS, a division of Simon & Schuster, Inc.
1230 Avenue of the Americas, New York, NY 10020

This book is a work of fiction. Names, characters, places and incidents are products of the author's imagination or are used fictitiously. Any resemblance to actual events or locales or persons, living or dead, is entirely coincidental.

ISBN-13: 978-1-4165-0991-2
ISBN-10:   1-4165-0991-7

This Pocket Star Books paperback edition June 2007

10 9 8 7 6 5 4 3 2 1

POCKET STAR BOOKS and colophon are registered trademarks of Simon & Schuster, Inc.

Illustration by Gregg Gulbronson
Woman by Donnie Rosse/Getty Images

Manufactured in the United States of America

For information regarding special discounts for bulk purchases, please contact Simon & Schuster Special Sales at 1-800-456-6798 or business@simonandschuster.com.

This book is dedicated to

Maggie Crawford, Aaron Priest, and Lucy Childs,
for their unflagging support,

and to

Gavin, John, Kate, Kerry, Michael,
Mikayla, Patty, and Baby C,
who are there in sunshine and in shadow,

and to

Russ, always and forever my love

For death and life, in ceaseless strife,
Beat wild on this world's shore,
And all our calm is in that balm —
Not lost but gone before.

Caroline Elizabeth Sarah Norton

**SCOTLAND
1263**

Ketelsay

*Orkney
Islands* • Kirkwall

• John O'Groats

Cape Wrath

*North
Sea*

HEBRIDES

Lewis

*Moray
Firth*

Dunvegan • *Skye*
Harris

• Inverness

SCOTLAND • Aberdeen

Somerstrath
Inverstrath • • Brenmargon

*Atlantic
Ocean*

Stirling • *Firth of Forth*

• Glasgow • Edinburgh
  Berwick •

N
W **E**
S

Haraldsholm
ANTRIM

ULSTER • Belfast

FERMANAGH

ENGLAND

0   20 miles
0   20 kilometers

*Isle of
Man*

Irish Sea

PROLOGUE

LAMMAS NIGHT AT THE EDGE OF THE WORLD
AUGUST 1254

The sky was still blue this August evening, the gray sides of the towering mountain peaks of western Scotland were still lit by the sun, but the long day was at last ending. To the east the light was fading in the deep glens and forests, the wind sighing through the branches, lifting drops of water from the tumbling streams onto nearby ferns, where they would linger through the short summer night. The sun moved ever downward in the west, changing the sea from blue to molten silver, and the cobalt of the offshore islands to a muted gray. Waves hurried to claim the shingle, lacy white foam flying from their crests to join with the descending evening.

The young girl who hurried up the headland saw none of it; she saw only the old woman ahead of her moving steadily away, and she increased her speed anxiously. Seals lifted their heads from the water and shorebirds dipped down to get a closer look at the two figures below. But the young girl did not look.

She wanted to see the future.

She was a beautiful child, with long bones and glossy dark hair that waved around her oval face and framed her blue eyes and even features. But it was her determination that one saw, the glint of steel showing in those lovely eyes, usually hidden under a layer of courtesy and training, but now, unwatched except by the creatures of sea and air, her jaw was set and her gaze unfaltering.

She thought of herself as Scottish, but in truth her blood was mixed. She'd been formed by fiery Picts, ancient Caledonians, and ferocious Norsemen on her father's side, triumphant Normans and passionate Celts on her mother's. She knew of their intermingled histories, had heard the stories of the old days and the battles for dominance, of foes who had come from the south and from the sea, of courageous people who had held the Romans at bay and fought off the Vikings. But all that was in the past, and she gave it little thought. It was what was to come that interested her now, and only the old woman could help her to see it.

She'd seen much already this evening, had watched as the rituals of Lammas Night, the first of the harvest festivals, were carried out, the storing of the seed corn and the ceremonial lighting of the bonfire that illuminated the sky. She'd watched the clanspeople her father led devour the Lammas feast and had tasted the Mass Loaf, made from the first flour ground after the harvest. And after the meal, when many of the others were worse for drink, or lost in the wonderful music, she'd watched her father clasp the hand of his latest mistress and slide from the hall. And watched her mother's eyes darken as she saw them go.

She'd seen her younger brother Rignor let an innocent servant take the blame for the cup he'd spilled and no one chide him for it, though both her parents had seen the incident. But why should she expect otherwise when she'd seen the same kind of thing repeated all of his life? She'd seen Dagmar, from the next village, only a few years older, but much wiser in the ways of the flesh, rearrange her skirts and flash a smile to the man she'd just entertained in the gardens.

She'd watched the priest bless the harvest and pray over the seeds that would be stored during the long winter. And, standing at the priest's side, enthralled, she'd watched while the old woman read palms and predicted the future, her tone solemn and accent foreign. The priest had frowned, but he'd listened as intently as the others. The old woman had predicted a good harvest for this year, and a new child for the girl's parents—hardly surprising considering her mother's swollen middle. But she'd told the girl nothing.

The girl already knew much of what lay ahead for her. She was the oldest child of the laird of Somerstrath and she knew her duty. She'd been betrothed to Lachlan Ross since early childhood and knew that eventually she would leave Somerstrath and live her life as his wife. But she wanted to know more than that, so she followed the old woman up this headland that faced the west.

There the woman paused, at the edge of the world, looking across the water, holding the golden star she wore around her neck between her long bony fingers. She turned when the child joined her. "You've come for a reading?"

The girl thrust her hand forward. "Please, if ye would, madam."

The woman's expression softened. She'd half hoped she could leave without the girl's noticing, but was not surprised that the girl had followed her. Now there was no hope for it but to warn her. Margaret MacDonald's life would not be peaceful. She, like her country, would be gravely tested in the years ahead. Scotland, the woman was sure, would survive, despite the forces that would threaten it and the challenges young King Alexander III would face. Margaret MacDonald would come of age in the midst of it all. The old woman sighed. How to tell an innocent what lay ahead? The old woman took the girl's hand, studying her palm for so long that the child shifted her weight impatiently.

"You are well named," the old woman said, looking up at last.

Margaret smiled, not sure what that meant, and the woman laughed gently.

"Look," she said, holding Margaret's palm between them. "This is your heart line and this your life line." She looked into the girl's eyes. "You will face dragons."

Margaret's smile was strained now. Dragons, she thought. Father had been right; there was no magic here, just an old woman hired for entertainment.

"You don't believe me," the woman said, leaning back and giving the girl an appraising look. "Do you know who St. Margaret was?"

"Oh, aye," Margaret said. "She was the queen of Scotland, King Malcolm's wife. I'm named after her. She wasn't a saint then, but . . ." She stopped as the woman shook her head.

"Not her, child. The first St. Margaret. Do you know her story?"

"No."

"Ah. Well, you should. St. Margaret was a beautiful young girl, not unlike you. She lived in Antioch, a long way from Scotland."

"Is that where ye're from, Antioch?"

The woman's gaze grew distant for the fleetest of moments. "No, child, but closer to Antioch than to here. Someday perhaps you'll hear my story, but not today. I will tell you of my life when next we meet. For, Margaret, I do think we shall meet again." She smiled, her gaze now sharp and tone brisk. "As St. Margaret grew older all admired her beauty, and she caught the eye of a Roman prefect, who wanted to marry her. When she refused, he threw her into a dungeon and left her to die. But she did not die."

"What happened?"

"The devil came to her, offering her freedom for her soul."

"But she dinna take it," Margaret said.

"No, of course not. The devil was so incensed that he turned himself into a dragon and ate her alive."

"Then how did she not die?"

The woman's smile widened. "She did what every self-respecting saint does, Margaret of Somerstrath. She held up the cross of Christ, and the dragon spit her out and died himself."

Margaret slumped, disappointed. She was quite sure no Roman prefect would seek her hand in marriage, that no dragon would threaten her.

"Look," said the woman, tracing a finger down the girl's lifeline. "See this break? You'll be torn from your home, and you'll face dragons. If you choose the right partner, you'll slay them together. And together find the love of legends."

"And if I dinna choose the right partner? What then?"

"You'll perish."

Margaret fought against the sudden chill that claimed her and forced herself to look into the woman's eyes. "I dinna believe any of that."

The woman laughed, the sound chilling Margaret even more.

"We do not choose what God sends us, child, any more than we choose our own names. Margaret you are, and Margaret you will be, and your life will be formed by that. You will face dragons. You need to prepare yourself for it." She started away, her progress surprisingly rapid for one so aged.

Margaret watched for a moment, torn between disappointment and curiosity, then ran after her. "But how will I ken the right partner? How will I ken it's him?"

The old woman stopped. "You will know him. He will be unlike any other man you've known. He will be golden. He will bring life after death."

"But how will I ken?"

"Listen. There is a voice within each of us. Listen to it."

"What will happen to me?"

"Before you leave this earth, Margaret MacDonald, you will see the birth of a people formed from many peoples, made of steel and fire and magic and mist, a people who will travel the world and change it forever."

"But how . . . ?"

"I can tell ye nothing more. Go home, child. The darkness is coming."

ONE

June 1263
An island off Scotland's shore

The dawn breezes stroked the water as the Norseman helped lay his father's body next to the mast of the long-ship. The first rays of the sun were reclaiming the island, but he did not turn to see the treeless landscape behind him, nor at the people who lined the shingle. He did not want to see their grief-ravaged faces. He felt no grief.

His father had been an old man; it was time for him to die. The Norseman had waited years for this day, when he would at last rule over this island, would lead its people into the future. Into glory.

Soon the pretense would be over. In the days since the old man's death, the Norseman had ignored the mutters of the people, their comments that it was passing strange that Thorfinn, the dutiful eldest son, was not here to bury his father. The Norseman had said nothing in reply, not even when he'd seen his younger brother Ander's glowering expression, and knew what Ander suspected. He'd kept his silence, and Ander had retreated, as Ander always did. And at last the people had agreed that, even in Thorfinn's absence, his father must be buried.

The funeral would be just as the old warrior had requested. Nothing had been overlooked. The Norseman had seen to every detail, had watched the old man's ship being readied, had packed the base of the hull himself the night before. He'd overseen the preparations for the feast to celebrate his father's life that he would host this evening in his father's longhouse. And then stay, sleeping in his father's bed, a symbol of the transfer of command. It was time. The last few years had been lean, the harvests poor, the winters overlong. All that would change under his leadership. Tonight, when the people were sated with food and ale and wine, when all the words praising his father had been said, he would tell them of his plans for the future. And none would gainsay him.

They worked in silence, he and Ander and Ander's young son Drason, filling the rest of the hull with tightly packed peat and sticks, covering his father's body and the base of the mast with the mixture so that no wool from his cloak showed through, no glint from the sword and axe that lay at his side could answer the sun's greetings. They placed the oars against the mast to help speed the flames, raised the red sail, and climbed from the ship.

The priest spoke then, his prayers and the responses of the people flowing out over the harbor accompanied by the waves lapping at the shore. But the Norseman did not hear them, listening instead to his own thoughts. He clenched his fist tightly and endured the priest's ceremony, giving the correct responses when necessary, nodding when appropriate. He kept his eyes lowered, as though overcome by emotion, thinking of what the people saw as they watched him. His bright hair would catch the sun, his eyes, a brilliant blue, would be sorrowful. He was tall and strong, his shoulders wide, his courage and daring well-known. And no one knew his thoughts.

At the end of the service the priest blessed the dragonship as if it were a vessel of God's, and the man whose body lay upon it as if he were a hero. The people wiped tears away, talking quietly to each other, saying that it was a fit burial for an old Viking. The Norseman thought otherwise. His father had been a failure in life and now in death. Instead of leading his people to prosperity and glory, he'd been content to keep things as they were. Instead of dying in battle, he'd died in his sleep. There would be no Valhalla for him, only this histrionic and unnecessary sacrifice of a good ship, burnt for an old man's vanity.

But even that sacrifice had been well utilized, for in the hull of the ship was the body of his elder brother, Thorfinn.

He'd had to remove Thorfinn. His brother was the eldest and would have succeeded their father. And would have kept things as they were, which could not continue. He'd had no choice, he told himself as he helped Ander and the village men ease the ship into the water, stepping back as the sea claimed it.

"Your father is with God now," the priest said.

Ander thanked the priest, then turned to talk to others. The Norseman did not answer, simply nodded.

With a concerned expression, the priest placed a hand on the Norseman's shoulder. "I know this is a difficult day for you."

The Norseman did not answer, but opened his hand slowly, showing the priest the dagger that had been clenched in his fist. The blade had split his palm.

"My son!" the priest whispered. "You have blood on your hand!"

The Norseman smiled. He pressed his hands together, smearing the blood across both of them, then opened them and showed the priest. Blood on his hands. He looked into the cleric's eyes, saw them widen, and tried not to smile.

"Thank you, Father," he said, then moved to join Ander.

The priest looked after him, fear in his eyes.

When the ship began to move on its own, they tossed flaming torches into it and watched it glide, borne on the ebbing tide, toward the mouth of the harbor. The fire caught quickly, orange flames leaping from the belly of the ship and flaring up the mast, turning the water around it amber. The canvas of the sail, even oiled as it was, lifted itself out of the reach of the flames and hurried the longship westward, toward the open sea.

Ander leaned close, his whisper harsh. "I know that you killed Thorfinn."

The Norseman met his brother's gaze for a moment, then lay a steady hand on Ander's arm. "It is time for change. Be part of it, and you will prosper. Fight me and . . ." He looked from Ander to Ander's wife Eldrid's pale and worried face, then to the stripling Drason. Then back to his brother. "Who knows which of us will be the next to die?"

He turned back to the sea then. Ander did the same, but Drason continued to watch his uncle. The Norseman considered all that might mean.

There were gasps from the people when the ship paused at the edge of the harbor. The sail burst into flames and the blazing vessel turned, silhouetting the proud profile of the dragon prow, as if to bid them one last farewell. And then turned again, to face the dark water beyond. The Norseman blinked, squinting as the sun suddenly danced on the water, gleaming so brightly that he had to turn away. When he looked back, the harbor was blue once again, the sea beyond cobalt. And empty. He stared at the horizon, his heart thundering in his chest.

It was a sign, an omen. He'd been right to be so bold. His plan would work.

Somerstrath, Ross
Western Shore of Scotland
June 1263

Margaret MacDonald raised her face to the sun and leaned back against a stand of rocks on the shingled beach, sighing with contentment. She was blissfully warm. The dark winter had been overlong, the spring wet, the summer late in arriving. The breeze caressed her face, the water softly lapped at the shore, and the rock was smooth behind her. Crisp white clouds scudded overhead in a brilliantly blue sky. On the shingle below, the water slid onto the rocks, then retreated with a soft hiss. And at her side her best friend Fiona leaned forward, arms wrapped around her knees, looking out to sea.

The peace would not last. Soon her sister Nell would arrive, bringing their four younger brothers—and chaos—

with her. There was no escaping it; their mother, who had already borne ten children and was now heavy with the eleventh, expected Margaret, the eldest of the seven who had survived, to bear a sizable portion of the child-watching duties. Most of Margaret's days were filled with caring for her younger siblings. Nell, at twelve, was a help, but the boys, aged four to ten, were always into something, and it took most of Margaret and Nell's attention just to keep them safe. She'd hurried on ahead of them to have these few quiet moments with Fiona, leaving Nell to watch the boys linger over every interesting rock, which they would then climb or examine. Or throw.

This might, she realized, be the only calm moment she would have before her wedding, certainly one of the only times she and Fiona would have a chance to talk alone before she left. Next month she would marry Lachlan Ross, and her life would change forever. She'd leave Somerstrath, and her old self behind as well. No longer would she be one more of Somerstrath's children; she'd be the wife of a cousin of the king, the wife of a wealthy and handsome man.

She'd been a babe in arms and Lachlan just a few years older when their fathers made the marriage contract allying the Rosses and MacDonalds yet again. The betrothal was as much a part of her as the color of her hair, and as unchangeable: the contract could not be undone except by the king. Which was as well, for she was eager to marry, anxious to leave childhood and this small stronghold on the western shore. And eager to discover what life as a married woman might mean. Lachlan had always been pleasant to her, but recently she'd seen the gleam in his eyes when he looked at her. She knew he found her pleasing, which pleased her as well. She slanted a look at Fiona.

"I canna believe I'll be gone soon," she said. "Three weeks is all that's left."

Fiona tossed her light brown hair over her shoulder. "Lucky ye, marrying and leaving all of us behind. Ye'll have yer own household full of servants, never lift a finger again. And ye'll go to court and make new friends and replace me in a fortnight. D'ye ken how fortunate ye are?"

Margaret looked at her in surprise. There was a note of envy in Fiona's voice she'd never heard before. She felt a twinge of guilt. Life must seem very unfair to Fiona, whose father was a weaver, respected, but far from wealthy. Margaret's father was the laird of the clan, a landowner, a rich and prominent man in western Scotland, her mother the sister of William, the Earl of Ross. Fiona had never been farther from her home than the next clan and, if her father had any say in it, would soon marry one of the Somerstrath villagers and spend the rest of her life within a stone's throw of her birthplace. Margaret had already been to King Alexander III's court twice, and would soon live there, at the center of everything. She'd been taught sums and could read and write in Latin, French, and Gaelic. Fiona could count on her fingers, but never learned to read or write. For most of their lives these differences had never mattered, but now her life and Fiona's would diverge sharply, never again to merge.

"I do ken how fortunate I am," she said quietly. "And I'll miss ye. Ye could never be replaced."

Fiona said with a wry smile. "Thank ye for that."

"I wish ye could come with me." Margaret leaned forward, wondering why she'd not thought of it before. "Perhaps ye could, Fi! I'll have no one with me from here."

"What would I be, yer lady's maid, help ye dress?" Fiona's tone was brittle.

"Ye could be my companion!" Margaret cried. "It would be so nice to have ye there. Surely Lachlan wouldna mind having ye along."

Fiona gave a short laugh. "Would that no' be something?"

"Perhaps we could even find ye a husband among Lachlan's men so we'd be together always!"

"I'm in no hurry for a husband."

Margaret nodded thoughtfully. Fiona's choices were few—the handful of unmarried young men, or the widowers with children—none inspiring. Unless she was successful in bringing Fiona with her, Fiona would eventually marry one of the local lads and live a life just like her mother's, a life of hard work and repetitious tasks. And the terror of childbirth, which had taken Fi's mother, and which threatened every woman. Margaret was suddenly filled with determination to change Fiona's fate.

"I'll talk to Mother about ye coming with me," she said fiercely.

Fiona shook her head morosely. "She willna agree. She's asked me to help with the others after ye're gone."

"There are others who can do that. I'll talk to her. Think of it, Fi! Ye and I among all those English ladies."

Fiona's eyes widened. "English ladies! Are ye going to England, too?"

Margaret paused before answering. She'd met the players at court, knew their histories and those of their families, often back several generations. But Fiona had been isolated here at Somerstrath and knew none of that.

"Our Queen Margaret," she said, "is the daughter of

King Henry of England. When she came to Scotland to marry our King Alexander, she brought many of her ladies, and many of their husbands. Almost half the court is English now, or has strong ties to England. They all speak French, of course."

Fiona nodded, as though she'd already known that. "Of course."

"So ye'll have to learn French, too," Margaret said. "And we'll have to get ye all new gowns!"

"Like yers?"

There was that note of envy again. Margaret looked at her finely tooled leather shoes with their painted designs, discarded now in the sand, then at Fiona's bare feet. Their clothing showed the differences in their stations as well, Margaret's soft linen and wool in stark contrast to Fiona's coarsely woven gown. The weaver's daughter wore his mistakes; the laird's daughter his finest work.

"As my companion ye'd have to dress well. And our hair! Wait until ye see how everaone wears their hair. Ye'll be unwed, so ye could wear yer hair loose. I will talk with Mother about ye coming with me."

"Not yet. Wait until yer parents are no' so angry with Rignor."

Margaret sighed. "Aye."

Her brother Rignor, only two years younger than she, often needed to be watched more closely than the little ones. His wild antics and volatile temper had earned their parents' disapproval often enough, more so recently. Her father often loudly despaired of him; her mother said he just needed a few more years.

"Is he still saying he's going to marry Dagmar?" Fiona asked.

"Oh, aye, the fool. As though he'll be allowed to."

"Yer father canna be pleased with that, and who can blame him? She's naught but the daughter of yer da's tacksman from the next glen, willing to lift her skirts for any man."

Margaret nodded, remembering all the times she'd watched Dagmar lure a man to a quiet corner, returning shortly with her clothing askew and her smile smug.

"Dagmar's hardly a suitable wife for the heir of Somerstrath," Fiona said crisply. "Can ye imagine her as the lady of Somerstrath?"

"How would we ken who fathered her children?"

"Someone should tell Dagmar she'd best set her sights elsewhere."

"Someone has. My mother was quite emphatic."

Margaret sighed, thinking of her mother's irritability in the last few months. Surely it was only because of the babe she carried, but Mother, always quick-tempered, had been especially difficult lately, her moods unpredictable, her annoyance with Margaret obvious. And frequent. Margaret couldn't wait for her wedding. She'd escape Mother's moods, go to court, and be part of its glittering world. Be the mistress of her own home, which she was determined would be filled with laughter instead of constant strife as Somerstrath was. And she'd have a husband who was both charming and devoted to her.

They turned to other topics, their conversation slowing, then stopping altogether. Margaret closed her eyes, telling herself that she needed to enjoy the sunshine, and after a few moments, she slept.

* * *

"Margaret! Wake up!"

She gasped in surprise and opened her eyes when four-year-old Fergus threw himself atop her with a gleeful cry. She smiled and clasped the little boy to her chest. Nell was right behind him, but the other boys ran down to the water instead, chasing the shore birds into the air with hoots of delight. Fiona laughed and shook her head.

"Ye were asleep, Margaret," Fergus said. "In the day."

Margaret laughed. "So I was."

Nell's mouth was pursed as she sank next to Margaret. "Mother is in one of her moods. Nothing makes her happy. She's constantly cross."

"She's tired," Margaret said. "Ye ken what she's like in the last few weeks. Everything wearies her."

"I," Nell intoned, "will never have children."

Fiona rolled her eyes. Margaret fought a smile and brushed Nell's light brown hair back over her shoulder. She remembered being twelve, remembered the struggle she'd felt she'd waged to be treated as an adult. Her sister was voluble, quick to love, quick to anger, quick to forgive. Impatient. Headstrong. And the most loyal ally Margaret could imagine. They were very close. She told Nell things she wouldn't even tell Fiona. She would miss that. As she'd miss the little boy curling now against her, the smell of sunshine and earth in his hair. She smiled at Nell. "No children? Not even if they were like Fergus?"

Nell shook her head and heaved a great sigh. "No, not even then."

"I get tired, too," Fergus said, dropping his head to Margaret's shoulder.

"Of course ye do," she told him. "We all do."

"Mother should take a nap," Fergus said. "Like ye did."

"She should indeed."

"Father's cross as well," Nell said, "and he's not even having the child."

Margaret looked into Nell's green eyes, seeing her sister's confusion. Their father was cross because he was worried. The wet weather had prevented the crops from being sown on time; the harvest would be lean. The cattle had found little to eat on the sodden hillsides when at last the men had led them to their summer grazing fields. And their mother was near her term, which always made her father worried and his moods unpredictable. But Nell was too young to realize all that; she would learn the fragile nature of life soon enough. And Margaret's thoughts were far too serious for such a lovely day.

She rose to her feet, pulling her brother up with her. "We're not cross, are we? The sun is out and we have no work to do right now. We're happy, Fergus, are we not?"

Fergus laughed. "Aye, Margaret. We're happy!"

Nell's expression softened as she reached for the child's hand. "Come, wee one, let's go see the lads," she said and led him down to the water, where the other boys were running out on the sand, then darting back as the waves tumbled in.

"Och, will ye look at them?" Margaret said, half-exasperated, half-entertained as her brothers, drenched to the knees, ran back from the water. She should tell them to be careful. But it was summer, the day was lovely, and this was one of her last days with them. "Remember being that age?" she asked Fiona. "When a summer was an eternity and we thought life would always be like that?"

Fiona looked wistful for a moment. "I do. We thought

nothing would change, didn't we? But we were wrong." She stood, then, her tone brisk again. "I wish I could stay, but I'd best get back before Father misses me. Come down after yer meal, aye?"

"I will," Margaret said, then watched her friend head back to the village. She would convince her parents to let Fiona come with her and never hear that note of envy in her friend's voice again.

She joined Nell and the boys then, dancing with the water and laughing, lunging forward, then hanging back to let the waves catch a foot or a dangling skirt. Overhead the birds joined the game, calling to each other, as though they, too, were savoring this hour. After a while Margaret stood back with Fergus while the others continued playing. The day was cooling; clouds were moving toward the sun. Farther down the beach something bobbed in the water, now visible, now hidden, finally tossed onto the sand by the waves. The boys, weary of their game, ran to see what it was. Davey reached it first and let out a shout.

"Look!" he cried, bending over it again.

Nell, just a few feet behind him, screamed and backed away. "Margaret!"

Margaret hoisted Fergus onto her hip. "What is it?"

"A head!" Davey cried, waving Ewan and Cawley toward him.

Fergus turned to stare at Margaret.

"It's probably just a clump of seaweed," Margaret told him as she started forward, "or a seal's head, or their idea of something funny to tell us." But when she saw what had washed ashore, she stopped laughing.

Davey was right. It was indeed a man's head, long

blond hair still attached to the skull. He appeared to be in his middle years, his face broad with flat cheekbones and lips drawn back in a grimace. Skin still clung to his cheeks. Which meant he'd died recently and probably not far from here.

Margaret's stomach heaved, but five young faces watched her, their eyes wide with fear. She pushed aside her sudden sense of foreboding and took a deep breath. "Poor soul," she said, keeping her tone calm and trying to still her heart.

"How did it get here?" Davey asked.

Margaret looked across the water, half-expecting to see more heads bobbing in the waves, but the sea was empty. "Perhaps a ship got caught in a storm. Remember how hard the wind blew last night? Perhaps he fell off the ship."

"And the wind cut off his head?" Nell asked.

Margaret frowned at her.

"Maybe a monster ate him!" Davey cried.

"Or there's a war!" Ewan said.

"It's probably nothing so dreadful," Margaret said. "There are no monsters. And Father will ken if there's a war."

"We should take it to him!" Davey said. The younger boys echoed his words.

"I'm not carrying it!" Nell cried, stepping backward.

"None of us are," Margaret said. "We'll push it higher, away from the water, and tell Father about it."

She glanced up at the sun, feeling a chill of apprehension. One man had died; it was nothing more. Ewan gave the head a kick, bouncing it away from the water.

"Leave it!" she snapped. "Let's go home."

* * *

Margaret herded her charges before her across the low hills of rock that separated the beach they'd played on from their village, relieved when she saw the keep rising starkly above the clansmen's homes clustered at its base. The four-story unadorned stone structure was neither beautiful nor graceful, but fearsome. Built to protect its own and discourage visitors rather than welcome them, it lay at the heart of Somerstrath, overlooking the houses and the harbor below. Margaret had always thought it ungraceful and bulky, but now it looked beautiful to her. And the sight of the stone walls that enclosed the village, the ones that she'd so often considered confining, she now found comforting.

She began to relax as people waved and called cheerful greetings to the children. Men were returning from the inland fields. Down in the harbor the fishing boats were being unloaded, the men's laughter drifting up the hill, and near at hand a plume of smoke rose from a cottage and danced on the breeze. She was being absurd. The head that had washed up on the beach was not an omen, not a sign of unrest across the waters or conflict within their borders, not a portent of the future. It was simply the head of some poor unfortunate soul lost at sea, washed ashore at the whim of the tide. *Missing his head?* She pushed the unsettling thought aside.

She let the others run ahead, waiting alone for Fergus to finish examining the worms he'd found, a battered flower clutched in his hand.

"Come, laddie," she said, bending over him.

He held up a worm for her inspection. "Look."

Margaret smiled. Someday she might have a child of her own as wonderful and full of life as this little one and his brothers. "Let's let the worms live, shall we?" She scooped them back into the hole. "Put him with his friends. Aren't ye hungry?"

Fergus looked from the worm to Margaret, then nodded and dropped his captive into the hole. She brushed him off as best she could, then took his hand and hurried him through the inland gate, where she collected the others and they made their way to the keep. The boys ran across the courtyard and barreled through the ground-floor storeroom that doubled as the guardhouse, then, punching each other, scrambled up the spiral stairway to the passageway that led to the great hall. They waited there, for Margaret and Nell and Fergus. She straightened their clothing and tidied their hair, then gestured them into the hall.

This was her favorite room in all of Somerstrath. The hall was not large compared to the structures she'd seen at Stirling and Edinburgh and in the mighty castles now being built in the Norman fashion all over central Scotland, but it was big enough to hold rows of polished pine trestle tables with their well-worn benches. And the stone-hewn fireplace at the end of the room was magnificent enough to grace any castle she'd seen. Her mother had warmed the room with tapestries, and her father had lined the walls with stag's heads and the occasional boar's head, which had inspired the boys to invent stories.

Several of her father's men were gathered in a corner, talking among themselves. Her father and Rignor sat separately at another of the tables. Margaret's mood sank when she saw their expressions. Father's color was high, which meant he and Rignor had been arguing again. Father slammed his fist on the table as the boys approached, not even seeing their startled expressions. He leaned forward, glaring at Rignor.

"I am weary of yer excuses and yer complaints," Father shouted. "Ye should have done it before midday, not ask someone to do it for ye. There is no job too small for the leader of a clan! It's time ye stopped making yer own life easier and everyone else's more difficult. Ye'd better start learning how to lead, lad, else I'll be looking at the younger ones to replace ye when I'm gone."

"Ye'll have no say in it when ye're gone," Rignor shouted.

Father's face mottled. "Say that once more, lad, and I'll see it done."

Rignor stormed out without sparing his siblings a glance. Father shook his head and stared into the distance while Margaret met Nell's gaze. Would there ever be peace between her father and brother?

They were alike in so many ways, both tall and dark and powerfully built. Both had quick tempers, but her father's behavior was usually measured, while Rignor's was impulsive. Her father put the clan's needs before his own—most of the time. Rignor rarely did. Her father listened to what he was told, and weighed it. Rignor was exhaustively garrulous and deaf to any comments that did not please him. Rignor rarely pleased his father, but where Rignor was concerned, Father was often unpleasable.

Her father's expression lightened as he turned to them and pulled Fergus into his lap. "Into the mud again, aye, laddie?"

"Father!" Ewan said. "We found a head!"

Father smiled. "Will ye have to be sharing? Should ye not have six heads amongst ye and not just one?"

Ewan shook his head. "No, no, Da. Really, we found a head on the beach!"

"Found a head? What d'ye mean?"

The boys all talked at once. Father frowned as he listened, then met Margaret's eyes over their heads. "Get yerselves upstairs now, laddies," he said when they finished. "Ye too, Nell."

"Is it a war, Father?" Ewan asked.

Their father shook his head. "I've heard nothing of one. Off with ye now."

Nell sighed as she gathered the boys, her long-suffering glance at Margaret letting her know that Nell resented being told to leave with the children. There was silence in the hall as the sounds of the boys' excited chatter faded up the stairwell, then Father, his expression darkened, turned to his men.

"Find the head. Bring it to me." He waited until they'd left, then turned to Margaret. "Tell me again what happened." He listened silently, with his arms crossed over his chest and his eyes dark, but made no comments.

When at last the men returned with the head, her father unwrapped the bundle and stared at it for several long moments. He touched it only once, to rub a strand of blond hair between his fingers before he pushed it away.

"It's a Norseman, isn't it?" Margaret asked.

Father nodded. "Bury it," he told his captain, then called for his war chieftain and stalked across the hall and out the door, his men in his wake.

Margaret waited, and as expected, Rignor returned, slumping to sit opposite her. He took a deep drink of Father's whisky.

"What was it the two of ye were arguing about this time?" she asked.

"He says I'm not doing enough to learn how to be a chieftain."

"Did ye tell him ye'd try harder, Rignor?"

He glowered at her.

"Ye've only to try," she said, leaning forward. "Ye'll be a good chieftain when the time comes. Just tell him ye'll try."

Rignor grunted and rose to his feet. "I'm weary of him always telling me I'm not good enough. And of ye agreeing with him. Some sister ye are, not even defending me. Like when they tell me not to marry Dagmar. Ye dinna help me at all! I'll not be dissuaded no matter what they say. And dinna tell me I need to look elsewhere, or that we need any more alliances with the Rosses or another clan. I've heard it all a'ready. He's talking about the Comyns now, as if the most powerful family in Scotland would need a marriage with us! I'll not talk to ye of Dagmar and who I will marry."

"I wasna going to say anything of it," she said, and in truth she was not. Her parents had exhausted the subject, telling their oldest son many times of his responsibility to the clan to marry well, that they would never accept Dagmar as his wife.

Nor was Margaret about to say what else she knew, that several attempts at betrothal between Rignor and a desirable match had been quickly terminated by some rash action of Rignor's. He'd insulted the father of one of the most important MacDonald families, a disaster that had yet to be remedied. And had been found in the bed of a maid of another possible match. Father had tried to make light of it, but the father of the lass under consideration had not. There were no further discussions.

Rignor had, like she, been betrothed shortly after birth, and again a few years later, but both lasses had died in childhood. There was talk among the clanspeople that Rignor had been cursed, that he would never have a wife, and there were times that Margaret wondered if they might not be right.

"Rignor," she began, but he interrupted her with a wave of his hand.

"They love Lachlan Ross, of course. Everyone loves Lachlan. And ye're happy to marry him."

"I am," she said, but again he did not let her continue.

"But Lachlan is not the prize they make him out to be, ye ken," Rignor said, leaning forward. "I've heard of the complaints of his people, that he neglects them, that he spends all his time at court and all his coin on clothing for himself. It will be difficult for him to find room in his life for a wife, Margaret."

"That's not true!" she cried. "He's always been kind to me. And to you. He went hunting with ye last visit."

"And what was it he caught, aye?"

She frowned at him. "What is that supposed to mean?"

"I dinna like him, Margaret. That's what it means."

He left the hall again without a backward glance. Margaret sighed.

Her father ordered the patrols around the borders of his land increased, sent word to the neighboring clans of the find, spent hours in deep conversations with his war chieftain that halted when anyone else came near. He told the rest of them nothing. No other heads were found. No news of unrest came from the runners who arrived from other clans, and people stopped looking over their shoulders and worrying. All of Somerstrath waited, but as the days passed without incident, everyone calmed. Except for Margaret, who continued to feel unsettled, as though her body had felt a shift in the air that her mind had not yet recognized.

She told herself it was simply bridal nervousness, that she was uneasy because these were her last days at Somerstrath. She'd done some traveling; she'd been to the MacDonald and Ross holdings, and to visit her Aunt Jean's family, the Comyns. She'd feasted with nobles and clan chiefs and a king, but most of her life had been spent here, on her father's small part of the Clan MacDonald lands. Her discomfort, she told herself, was nothing more complicated than that she was leaving everyone and everything she knew. As eager as she was to wed, part of her heart always would be here at Somerstrath.

She would not be here to see the winter storms come in from the west, to feel the wind lift the salt spray high above the water and sweep it into the keep, would not be here to see the rainbows that curved from the mountains or disappeared behind the blue islands offshore. Would not be here to listen to the stories told on winter nights, of mighty Somerled, from whom her family descended. Of the great warriors gone before who had risked all for honor or for love, of selkies and banshees and giants. She would not be here for the birth of her new brother or sister, would not know the child at all, would not see her brothers grow and change. She'd be married, living inland, surrounded by luxury and mountains and burns that mimicked the sea, but far from home and family. Of course she felt unsettled.

But she shouldn't, she scolded herself. It wasn't a

stranger she was marrying, it was Lachlan. Their life together would be splendid. She could visit Somerstrath; Lachlan did often enough. Nell and her brothers could visit her. And Fiona would be with her, for she'd convinced her parents of it. And she still had time here, a fortnight, before everything would change.

In that, she was wrong.

TWO

My lord."

Gannon MacMagnus looked up from the letter he was writing to Patrick Maguire, his stepfather, and leaned back in the chair provided by the croftholder in whose home they'd spent the night. He'd been about to write Patrick that all was well on his western lands, that the perimeter ride Gannon and his younger brother Tiernan had been on had proved uneventful. But one look at the man who now stood in the doorway made Gannon suspect that those words would never be written.

It was Alban Maguire, his brother at his side. Both men were tacksmen of Gannon's stepfather's and Gannon had known them for years. Alban's face was lined with grief, his manner shaken. His brother was pale and grim.

Whatever this was, it was serious. Across the room Tiernan looked up from the bridle he'd been examining and the brothers exchanged a glance.

"What is it, Alban?" Gannon asked.

Alban twisted his hands together before him. "My lord, d'ye remember me telling ye just yestereen what happened when my daughter went to Sligo, that the man offered for her, and she turned him down?" At Gannon's nod he continued, his voice shaking. "They must have kent that ye'd been at our home and left, for in the night, almost at the morning, they came." He paused to take a shuddery breath. "They killed my wife, sir. And took my daughters, both of them. I tried . . . I tried, my lord, but I could do nothing to stop them. I told ye, do ye remember, that he'd threatened his revenge on her? But I never thought . . ." He put his face in his hands and could not continue.

"Aye. I remember," Gannon said. He'd not been surprised that the man from Sligo had offered for her; she was very lovely. But he'd also not been surprised she'd refused him scornfully; she'd always had a high opinion of herself. Most men suffering such a rejection would have been bitter. But not violent. Gannon rose to his feet, gathering the papers together, feeling his anger rise.

"He came to me at dawn," Alban's brother said, gesturing to Alban. "And I told him to come to ye. I canna believe men would behave so, to kill a woman and steal my nieces. God only kens what's happened to them already."

Gannon thrust his paper and quill into the wooden writing box, letting the top close with a thud. "Ye want us to go and bring them back, aye?"

Alban's brother looked at Tiernan and the four other

men in the room. "No. There's not enough of ye. But we thought, kenning as ye are cousin to the great Rory O'Neill, laird of all Ulster, that ye could send word to him and ask him for help. He'd like as not send some men if ye were to ask him . . ."

"That would take three days," Gannon said. "How many of them are there?"

"Fifteen, my lord, all large men, and fearsome."

Gannon raised an eyebrow. "There are six of us, sir, and two of ye. And I assure ye we are far more fearsome than they are. D'ye ken where they went?"

"We tracked them to a glade not far from here, my lord, but, sir, ye canna think to take them on without help."

Tiernan came to Gannon's side. The brothers exchanged a look, then Gannon nodded. He turned to his men. "Get yerselves ready, lads. We've a task to do. Let's go and get the bastards."

Gannon leaned down closer to his horse's neck, whispering to the stallion, whose ears flickered in response. The horse, as highly trained as its master, kept silent. Gannon turned his head then to look at Tiernan, astride next to him, both of them dappled with shadows from the trees that surrounded them. In the glade before them the lasses huddled together, the younger one sobbing. The older one stared into the distance as the Sligo men tended the horses or talked with each other and passed a wineskin. They'd obviously been drinking. And more, from the looks they threw the lasses.

He gestured for Alban to come forward and signaled for him to be quiet. When Alban had joined him, Gannon parted the leaves. "Are these the ones?"

Alban nodded, his fear visible. "But, my lord, ye'll never . . ."

Gannon put a finger over his lips. "We'll get them back," he whispered.

He turned to the men behind him, gesturing for two of them to flank the glade. Then he nodded at Tiernan. His brother nodded in return and raised a hand to signal their men. Gannon gave his men a moment to get into position, then straightened and slowly drew his broadsword from its sheath, careful not to make a sound. He'd give the bastards one chance. He lifted his reins and rode into the glade.

The Sligo men leapt to their feet, a few reaching for weapons, then pausing, watching him. Gannon gave the men who stared at him now a moment to see his raised sword, letting his horse dance in a tight circle while he looked them over. Hardened men, most of them, hired, no doubt, for this attack. They looked at him with a mixture of contempt and amazement.

"Ye are accused of stealing these lasses and killing their mother," Gannon said. "I am here to bring ye to justice before Patrick Maguire."

"Alone?" one of the men asked with a sneer.

"Will ye come?" Gannon asked.

"Like hell," the man said, and started toward Gannon.

Gannon was waiting. The man fell at once and Gannon turned to the next one. Behind him he heard Tiernan's shout and the sounds of horses smashing through young trees as his brother led the charge into the camp, the others behind him roaring their battle cries. Most of the Sligo men never lived to grasp an axe or sword, but some fought madly.

Gannon mowed his way through a small cluster of them, then whirled his horse to plow across the camp again. One of the men thrust Alban's elder daughter before him, using her as a shield. The noise around him disappeared as Gannon looked into the man's eyes, then at the young woman with tears streaming down her face. There were marks on her neck already, bruises showing where she had been abused. She clutched her torn tunic across her breasts and closed her eyes, cringing in terror as Gannon raised his sword. He never touched her. The man behind her fell writhing to the ground and a moment later stopped moving. Gannon did not spare him even a glance, but turned to see how Tiernan and the others were faring.

It was over. Across the glade Alban was embracing his younger daughter. Their uncle met Gannon's gaze and nodded fiercely.

They spent the night in the walled village where Alban's brother lived, where they listened to Alban's brother and Gannon's men tell the story of rescuing the women, embellishing it each time. Gannon did not mind. He drank their whisky and accepted their thanks, but tried not to look at Alban and his daughters, whose suffering was tangible. The bed the villagers provided Gannon was warm, the woman who shared it more than willing, and he was grateful to have both.

He dreamt of water closing over his head, of limbs too heavy to raise toward the light that beckoned above, of sinking, slowly, toward the depths. Of knowing that he'd failed and that death was at hand. He could feel the water seep beneath his clothing, heartless liquid fingers that sucked the breath from his lungs and caught at his legs and pulled him relentlessly down, down, while the life left in him floated to the surface. He looked up at the light one last time.

And then there was nothing.

Gannon woke with a start, tremors still running through him, to find his hands clenched, his heart pounding, and his body soaked with sweat. It was a dream, he told himself. Not a memory. Not a foreshadowing. Merely the aftermath of the day's events. He slipped from the bed, careful not to wake the woman, and walked quickly from the house into the night. He stared into the sky, calming himself by naming the constellations. Leo, the lion. Draco, the dragon.

The whispers, then the dreams. It was always the same. The whispers arrived first, sounding like wind rustling through the trees, speaking words that he could almost hear, faint fragments of sentences. He'd be riding through a wood, or standing on the shore, thinking of something far different, and the whispers would find him, telling their half tale, bringing memories he'd suppressed. And then the dreams, nightmares so real that he could swear he was there, seeing the deaths, or witnessing his own, the images still lingering in the air when he woke. Next came relief that death had not claimed him, swiftly followed by the realization that one day it would.

He was not afraid to die. He was afraid to fail, and in the dreams he always failed. He'd wake each time, his body in turmoil, and think himself calm again by reminding himself of who he was, of all he'd learned, of the blood he carried in his veins. All men faced death, and someday he would as well. He could not change that any more than he could change the tide.

The whispers and dreams were warnings, he knew, that the time of his testing was at hand, the time that he'd always known in his bones would come, the time that he was born for. He would face whatever was coming. And he would triumph. There was no other choice. Change was coming, and he was ready.

It came sooner than he'd expected, for he and Tiernan had only just returned to their stepfather's stronghold when the summons came.

Nell MacDonald hummed as she swayed her skirts, watching their shadows on the plastered wall of the room she shared with her sister. She'd grown too quickly, her mother had complained when they'd hunted for something for Nell to wear at Margaret's wedding and found nothing was long enough, as though Nell could control her own height. Or anything about her life.

She'd received her new gown yesterday, both skirt and overskirt of a lavender silk, and a new bodice of a slightly darker shade. Together they made an exquisite, extravagant, elegant gown. She'd been trying it on constantly ever since, proud of her growth, proud that her body was changing, that she was leaving girlish clothing behind. Margaret was marrying an important man, a man who would take Margaret to court—and perhaps her sister— and simple clothing would no longer do. And although no one had told her, she knew there'd been talk recently of her own betrothal. It was time to look like a woman. Like Margaret, who'd had all of Somerstrath busy making her new clothes, bodices of silk and side skirts held back with ribbon, a woolen cloak lined with soft fur. At last Margaret's wardrobe was complete, and attention had been turned to the rest of the family, and Nell was most pleased.

Margaret's wedding was almost upon them, and her mother was all abuzz with the preparations, with trying to make her home and her family look their best for the guests. Nell had told her mother that no one would mind if things were not perfect, but her mother had irritably waved her words away and told Nell she didn't understand. Which was certainly true. It was supposed to be a happy occasion, but one would not know it from her mother's demeanor. Nell hoped her mother would be calmer when it was Nell's turn to be married. Whenever that would be. To whomever that would be.

"Watching yer skirts again, are ye?"

Nell spun around at Margaret's voice, then swirled her skirts again. "Laugh at me if ye will, but I'm going to enjoy it before I grow out of this one, too."

Margaret did laugh. "I came to tell ye that Mother's sending me to the shielings instead of going herself."

Nell nodded. Every summer her mother went to the shielings, the small huts in the foothills, to check on those clansmen who lived there year-round, and to make sure the unlived-in huts were ready for the villagers who would spend their summer there, taking their children and other animals with them, fattening their cattle on the lush pastures, not returning until the Lammas feast in August. But this year Mother was heavy with child; it was only sensible that Margaret went in her stead.

"Rignor's going, of course," Margaret said. "D'ye want to come as well?"

"Oh, aye! I'd love that." Nell smiled, delighted. A day

with Margaret, away from the village, even with moody Rignor, would be wonderful.

"Good. Now all we have to do is convince Mother. I'll have ye try that. I dinna seem to have much success pleasing her these days."

Nell nodded. Their mother was sharper with Margaret than with anyone else. It was, Nell had told herself many times, simply that Mother wanted everything so perfect for Margaret. Her sister went to stare out the tiny window, her expression so serious that Nell stopped for a moment and watched her.

"Margaret? Mother will be happier soon, when the wedding's over and the baby's here. She'll be herself again."

"But I willna be here to see it, will I, Nell?"

Nell felt a lump rise in her throat. "Are ye sad about that?"

Margaret turned, her eyebrows raised, dark crescents against her pale skin. "No, no, of course not. But I'll miss ye, Nell. More than anyone here, I'll miss ye. Ye'll have to come and see us, aye?"

Nell smiled, thinking of the clothes and shoes and fascinating people she'd meet. Her smiled faded as the door banged open and their mother entered, her face creased with frowns.

"Are the two of ye deaf? Did ye no' hear me calling ye? Get that gown off, Nell. Ye'll have it ruined before the day's out. Come, the both of ye. I canna do everything. Margaret, ye've been gone half the morning. Yer brothers are underfoot again. I dinna ken why yer father canna ever take them with him instead of leaving them here for me to deal with, and me trying to get this keep looking like a palace, not that it ever would no matter how much time I spent, and yer brothers undoing everything the moment I have it done. Och, will ye look at the mess of this room? Ye need to set it to rights."

"It's only a few things," Margaret said.

"A few things! Is that what ye call all the lovely clothes we've prepared for yer wedding? A few things!"

"I meant only that it'll be simple to clear them, not that they aren't lovely."

"Aye, well, see that ye care well for them. There's no more coming for ye, lass, and I dinna want ye disgracing us when ye're at court, though how we could be expected to compete with all those women with their fancy clothing when we're out here at the edge of the world I'll never ken."

Nell interrupted before her mother's tirade grew more heated. "When Margaret and Rignor go to the shielings, may I go with them? Please, may I go?"

Mother shook her head. "Ye'll watch Fergus. Ye'd only be in their way."

"I'd be a help."

Mother snorted. "Ye'd be glad of a day in the hills rather than staying here and working as ye should, wouldn't ye? Dinna pretend it's otherwise. Ye'll stay here and watch Fergus."

"Inghinn can watch Fergus. She never minds."

Her mother's eyes narrowed. "Ye'll stay here. Margaret, comb yer hair, Lachlan's just arriving."

Margaret's pleasure was obvious. "Again?"

"Ye should be pleased to have yer betrothed so attentive," Mother snapped.

"I am, I am. Just surprised that he's back so soon."

"Mother, please let me go . . ." Nell began.

Mother shook her head. "If ye ask me once more, Nell

MacDonald, I'll set ye to minding the geese. Come downstairs. I've work for ye to do." She spun on her heel and let the door slam behind her.

Nell sighed, then rolled her eyes at Margaret. "See, it's not just ye. I wish this baby would come."

"It dinna help that ye mentioned Inghinn."

"Oh, aye, just pretend she's not here at all, like Mother does?" At Margaret's surprised expression, Nell continued. "I'm not a child, ye ken, although everyone treats me like one. I hear her crying, I hear their arguments—we all hear their arguments. I know what Inghinn is to Father."

Margaret sank to the bed. "I guess ye do. I guess I was trying to believe ye dinna ken all that. I'm sorry that ye do."

"I know everything that happens here. Everyone ignores me. They talk in front of me, like I dinna understand." Nell sat on the bed next to her. "And dinna tell me I'll understand when I'm older or I'll scream!"

"I remember being yer age. That's how I felt too. I just thought perhaps ye dinna need to ken quite yet . . ."

"Inghinn says her babe is Father's."

Margaret sighed heavily. "Aye."

"Perhaps Father finds other women because Mother is always yelling at him."

"Perhaps Mother is always yelling at him because Father finds other women."

"Will it ever get better between them?"

"I dinna think so." They sat in silence for a moment, then Margaret straightened her back. "Off with ye before she comes back for us."

Nell left morosely, leaving Margaret thinking of her parents' marriage, then her own, wondering if she and Lachlan would be happy. How had her parents come to such a place as they were now? Peering into her tiny but precious hand mirror, she sighed, resolving that she and Lachlan would be different. She combed her hair and pinched her cheeks before going downstairs, hoping she looked better in person than in her reflection.

Her betrothed sat with Rignor in the hall, a cup of Somerstrath's fine ale in his hand. Lachlan was quite wonderfully handsome; everyone said so. She felt a wave of pride in his sophistication, in his tall, lean form, in his arched eyebrows and thin, patrician features. He was, as always, beautifully dressed, his dark hair pulled back by a ribbon woven with gold, his linen tunic edged with embroidery.

He rose to his feet when he saw her, his smile wide and his hands outstretched. "Margaret! Ye look bonnie, as always."

She curtsied. "Thank ye, sir. What brings ye back to us so soon?"

"What else but that I have missed yer company? I bring news. King Alexander will send two of his own musicians to our wedding as his bridal gift. Is that not fine news?"

"Ye told us that last time," Rignor said.

Lachlan's smile faltered.

"It is very fine news, my lord," she hurried to say, although Rignor was right; Lachlan had told them that on his last visit. He was using the news as a ruse to see her again. Which meant that he'd ridden for three days to come here. He must have missed her terribly. She smiled her satisfaction. "I'm sure they will be wonderful."

"Would King Alexander have anything but the best?" Lachlan asked.

"The king sends his musicians," Rignor said.

She heard it this time, the unmistakable note that meant he was spoiling for an argument. She drew Lachlan away, but Rignor raised his voice to follow them.

"Oh, aye, the king sends his musicians," Rignor said, "but does not deign to join us himself. Ye'd think he would, would ye not? Is Margaret not the niece of William, the Earl of Ross, one of the most powerful men in Scotland? And is our uncle's wife not one of the Comyns, another important family? And is Lachlan not one of the king's own cousins? Does this marriage not benefit both Alexander and William by allying their lines once again? William is coming to see ye wed, but the king willna be here. It's an insult!"

"The king canna be everywhere," Margaret said, throwing a stern look at Rignor. "I'm just as glad he willna be here for the wedding. Mother's worried enough without having to house and entertain a royal party."

"She'd love it," Rignor said.

"She'd hate it."

"It would have been an honor, of course," Lachlan began, "but the king . . ."

"Has more important things to attend to," Rignor finished.

"Of course he does!" Margaret glaring at her brother. "And we'll be seeing King Alexander often when we're at court. There's no need for him to come here!"

Rignor shrugged and Margaret moved Lachlan quickly away. She and her brother would talk about this later. Or perhaps not, she thought, taking Lachlan's arm. She was leaving. Rignor and his moods would stay at Somerstrath. She was off to see the world.

Lachlan smiled. "Come, let us find yer father."

Margaret nodded, pleased both that Lachlan was not angry and that a walk through the village would give her a chance to exchange a word with Fiona. "I thank ye for yer forbearance, sir."

Lachlan led the way down the spiral stairway to the ground floor, through the room there that served as both guardhouse and storeroom, and into the stone-floored courtyard, where her father's men stood with Lachlan's in small groups, trading news. She heard snippets of it as she and Lachlan threaded their way to the gate. Something had happened in the north. There had been some unrest in Ireland. *The head on the beach*.

"Is there news?" she asked Lachlan.

He shook his head. "Naught that affects us."

"Did Rignor tell ye about the Norseman's head we found on the beach?"

"Aye. But, Margaret, Norsemen sail past ye every day on the way to Skye and Man. Someone fell overboard is all."

"Aye," she answered, content to let the subject drop. Lachlan was here, and that was what mattered.

They turned right, toward the harbor. Next time, as a wedded couple, they would turn left, would take the path that led through the upper village, through the glen and the mountains and eventually across Scotland. Soon, she thought, pressing his arm to her side.

"How lovely to have ye back again, Lachlan," she said.

"I couldna stay away," he said, his smile warm.

"Only a few more weeks, sir, and I willna let ye out of my sight."

"Aye, 'tis almost here."

"Will we have any time before we go to court to . . ." She felt her cheeks flush. "To become more fully acquainted?"

He laughed. "I assure ye, Margaret, that we will become completely acquainted."

She tossed her head. "I wish to learn all there is about becoming a wife."

"Do ye?" His tone was amused. "And I'll be pleased to teach ye. But ye do ken that I will often have to be away on the king's business? And ye canna always accompany me." His gaze drifted to her mouth. "Much as I would want it."

"Aye, ye've told me. I shall have to find other ways to amuse myself when ye're gone."

"Most wives do." He smiled again and kissed her cheek. "I just want ye to remember that ye're mine, no matter how many men try to turn yer head with their compliments." He stroked her cheek. "Ye are verra beautiful, Margaret, and there will be men pursuing ye at court. Ye ken that."

"I will see none of them."

"See to it that ye don't," he said, and smiled widely.

She smiled in return. When she'd been at court she'd heard the love songs, the chansons that the French bards sang, full of lovers who sighed at the mere sight of their beloved, of men who did rare and exciting deeds to prove they were worthy of a woman's love. She thought of Aunt Eleanor, whose parents had arranged her marriage. She'd been a reluctant bride, but a happy wife whose face had lit up whenever her husband walked into the room, as did his whenever he saw her. Margaret had watched them, knowing that whatever it was that Eleanor and her husband shared, it was strong and heady and she wanted the same for herself. She glanced at Lachlan. She was sure they would have it.

Most of the houses of Somerstrath lay between the keep and the sheltered harbor. Lachlan was greeted cordially and stopped several times to tell the news from the east, of the king's latest visitors, of the unrest in England and how it distressed Scotland's Queen Margaret, who worried for her father Henry, King of England, and her brother, Prince Edward, who now led the English army in her father's stead.

At the weaver's house Fiona was waiting on the doorstep with a ready smile. Lachlan greeted her and her father warmly, saying all the right things when Fiona's father displayed his latest creation, a finely woven length of lichen green wool that would be his bridal gift to them. Lachlan and Margaret praised it, and Fiona's father beamed, showing Lachlan the recent improvements he'd made on his loom.

Fiona, standing with Margaret, sighed as she watched Lachlan and her father deep in conversation.

"Are ye no' truly the most fortunate of women, Margaret?" Fiona asked, her voice low. "Is yer betrothed no' the most handsome man ye've ever seen?"

Margaret smiled fondly. "Ye'd tell me the same even if he had only four teeth and one eye, would ye not?"

Fiona laughed. "That's true, I would." Her smile widened as Lachlan joined them. "Welcome, my lord. I'm hoping yer visit means that there will be music and dancing in the hall this night."

Lachlan's eyes were merry. "Somerstrath always entertains me well. I'm sure we'll all enjoy ourselves this day."

"I look forward to it," Fiona said.

"We all do," Margaret said with a smile, letting Lachlan lead her away.

That evening the hall was filled with music and laughter. Her father was always a warm and generous host, and, as usual, all of the villagers and half the clan outside the walls were in attendance. The meal was noisy, the people crowded at the long benches and tables, eating venison and the fish caught that day as well as soup and summer's fruit, accompanied by ale and the wines her father imported from the Continent. Trenchers were filled and filled again, shared with smiles. Iron chandeliers glowed with candles, the soft light illuminating the tapestries her mother had lined the walls with, tapestries that only a wealthy man like her father could afford. In the corner a harpist played softly, a prelude to the wilder music to come. Underfoot the rushes were clean and fragrant with herbs and the summer flowers strewn among them, and more flowers graced each table, leaning from their pots to touch the scrubbed pine surfaces.

Margaret was pleased to see that Lachlan's men seemed to appreciate the splendid hospitality her father was known for, and told herself that she would host evenings like this in her own home, full of music and laughter, meals more lavish than this hastily arranged one. She'd fill Lachlan's hall with comforts and the finest of things. And someday, children. She threw him a glance. She was, as she'd told him, ready to learn every wifely duty. Handsome man, she thought, watching him laugh at Rignor's jest. Not everyone liked Lachlan—certainly Rignor often made disparaging remarks—but tonight she was pleased to see her brother and betrothed laughing together.

"Ye look so pleased, child," Mother said.

"I'm thinking of the future," Margaret. "And enjoying this night."

Mother nodded absently, her attention already on to something else. Margaret did not mind. She watched the sennachie gathering the children for a tale of the old days. The priest had blessed the meal and said a prayer in which all joined, but more than one made the blessing gestures of the old gods, the spirits and deities of sea and shore, of trees and burns and the creatures who lived there. Christianity might have been the recognized religion here for centuries, but the old ways were still practiced in every glen. Above the hearth the crossed antlers of red deer shone white against the stone, a reminder of the land they shared with God's creatures. And of the ancient days, when a king might rule for only a season, then be sacrificed for the good of his people. When shapeshifters roamed the earth and trolls and fairies lived among men instead of underground. When seeing too much or venturing into the wrong place could result in a spell or a curse that would haunt generations.

It was those stories that the sennachie told now, her younger brothers among the children gathered before him. Tonight it was the tale of valiant Somerled, from whom they were all descended. The mighty warrior, known for his valor, love of peace, and for founding an empire in Scotland and its islands. Margaret stepped nearer, listening, although she knew the words well enough to tell the tale herself. Somerled, Lord of the Isles, who married the daughter of a king, who fathered Angus, whose descendants ruled nearby Moidart, whence her father's family had come. And fathered Dugall, from whom sprang the MacDougalls. And Ranald, who himself fathered Donald, whose deeds were so dark that he'd had to go on pilgrimage to Rome. The bard went on to explain her family's patrimony for ten generations, a history that the boys were meant to learn and pass on to their own children. As she would someday pass it on to hers.

The music changed now, the harpist retiring, replaced with the Scottish drums and whistles, and the lute from the Continent. Which meant the dancing would soon begin. She would dance, she was sure, but for now she sat with her parents and Nell and Rignor, listening to Lachlan's news of the world.

"There's trouble in Ireland," Lachlan said. "Problems on the Antrim coast. I dinna pay much attention to it, but I'll discover what it is when I go back."

"There's been trouble there for a while," her father said. "They canna decide who to follow, the old Celtic families, or the Norman lords with the lands and titles."

"Caithness is in an uproar," Lachlan said.

"Those Norsemen canna ever keep peace amongst themselves, can they?" Mother said, and all agreed.

"Which is why ye found one of their heads on the beach," Father said to Margaret. "They're always fighting amongst themselves."

"The most important news," Lachlan said, "is what's happening in England."

"The struggle between King Henry and Simon de Montfort?" Margaret asked.

"The war ye mean," Lachlan said. "It's come to that."

"De Montfort and King Henry are brothers-in-law,"

Margaret said, looking at Rignor. "Imagine waging war on yer own kin."

Rignor made a face at her. "Aye," he said. "There are times . . ."

He and Margaret laughed together.

Lachlan smiled and went on. "And, of course, everyone's worried that France will jump into the fray and back de Montfort to try to wrest the throne from Henry."

Mother shook her head. "The French," she said. "Always causing trouble."

"We thank ye for the news, Lachlan," Father said, "but none of this touches us, does it? We've got peace here in the west and we're determined to keep it."

"God willing," Lachlan said, then drained his cup and turned to Margaret. "Dance with me, lass? One more time before our wedding day."

She linked her arm in his, laughing as he whirled her across the floor, and again when he pulled her against him.

"Mine," he said, his eyes gleaming, pressing her to him. "Tell me that ye're mine, Margaret."

"I'm yers, Lachlan," she said breathlessly.

He kissed her then, bending her against his arm, continuing the kiss even when the music stopped and the applause began. At last he lifted his head and grinned at those watching before bringing her upright.

"That should hold ye," he said, releasing her. "I'm off to play dice with Rignor. Go dance with yer wee brothers."

She sent him off in Rignor's direction with a smile and did as he'd bid, dancing with Fergus and Davey until she could not dance another step. She came to stand with her mother and Nell then, smiling as she heard Rignor's laughter rising above the other voices.

"Sounds like Rignor is winning," she said, looking over at the men gathered around the table. Her father leaned back against the wall, laughing at something his son said. "But where is Lachlan?"

"He needed some air," Mother said.

Nell looked at her mother in surprise. Mother put a hand on Nell's shoulder.

"Air?" Margaret asked. "It's raining outside."

"He'll be back. Och, look at yer brothers. Can they never behave?"

Margaret turned in surprise. Mother had barely looked at Ewan and Cawley in weeks, and they were doing nothing terribly wrong, simply pummeling each other in time with the music. She glanced at Nell, whose eyes had widened, then back at her mother.

"D'ye ken where he went?"

"He'll return. He went out for a bit."

"Out for a bit? What d'ye mean?"

"He left with Fiona," Nell blurted out.

Her mother shook Nell's shoulder. "Nell!"

"They left together," Nell said. "They were holding hands and laughing."

THREE

Margaret looked from her sister to the men playing dice. Lachlan leaving with Fiona? But why? It made no sense. She touched her mouth, where the memory of his kiss on the dance floor still lingered, then looked around the hall. Fiona's father was there with Margaret's father, both laughing, as Rignor shook the dice. Lachlan was not with them. Margaret looked around again, willing Fiona to be here among the clanspeople. But Fiona was gone as well.

"No," she said loudly. "No. This canna be!"

Her mother clasped her arm, her voice low and tense. "Let it go. It's ye he'll marry, ye who will bear his children. People are watching ye. Smile. Let none of them see yer distress. Ye're not the first woman to discover her man fancies another. Be quiet now and smile."

Margaret pulled away, but her mother tightened her grip, her tone and touch harsh. Margaret had seen this woman a few times before, this fierce, unrelenting woman who had somehow in the last few years replaced the loving mother of her childhood. The concern in her mother's eyes was not for Margaret, but that others might hear them.

"Where are they?"

"Ye'll no' shame me by following them, Margaret MacDonald. Swallow yer pride. Fiona's a lovely lass. She was sure to catch someone's eye."

"Did ye ken this, Mother? Did ye ken and not tell me?"

"I kent ye'd discover it soon enough. What difference does it make?"

"What difference? It changes everything!"

"It changes nothing, Margaret. Look away, ye willful child."

"I canna . . . I willna!"

"Aye, ye will," Mother hissed. "Think on all that rests on this marriage and not just about yerself. Why should ye be any different than the rest of the women in the world? He willna be faithful to ye, not now, not after yer wed. Ye best set yer mind to accepting that. Look away. I did."

"I am not going to suffer in silence while my husband plays me for a fool!"

Her mother recoiled. "Like me? Is that it, Margaret? Ye willna do as I did? Well, if ye think ye can do it better, then ye're the fool, lass. Ye'll be sharing yer man. Accept it."

"I will not accept it! How can he do this to me? How can Fiona? She is my friend!"

"Inghinn was once my friend. Before she became yer father's mistress. She was not the first of his women, nor will she be the last. It is the way of men, and it's time ye learned that. Now smile, Margaret, and dinna disgrace me! People are watching."

"Let them watch!" Margaret ran down the stairs and through the guardroom.

She was halfway across the courtyard when Nell caught her.

"Mother wants ye to come back!" When Margaret did not reply as she passed through the gate, Nell followed, her voice rising with worry. "Margaret! Ye must come back!"

"I need to see if it's true."

"It is true. Everyone's kent for weeks . . ."

Margaret spun around. "And no one told me! Did ye ken?"

"No, no! I would ha' told ye."

Margaret nodded tightly, then stalked through the village, ignoring the rain, ignoring the guards who watched her, ignoring Nell, who hurried just behind her. She slipped once on the wet stones, caught herself, and plunged ahead, pushing her sodden hair out of her eyes. At the weaver's hut, light spilled from under the door.

"Dinna go in there," Nell whispered. "Let's go back."

Margaret opened the door. The room was lit by the fire in the corner and by the candlestick on the table, the one that had been in Lachlan's room. Her mother had brought the silver candlestick with her when she'd come to Somerstrath as a new bride, and now her mother's precious beeswax candle illuminated the small space, flickering in the wind that swirled past Margaret into the room.

Lachlan's shoes were by the door, his shirt nearby. And on the narrow bed on the other side of the room, Lachlan, naked, writhed above Fiona. Fiona clasped his shoulders, her head thrown back against the coverlet, her legs wrapped around his. Margaret watched, frozen in shock, her breaths coming in huge heaving gasps, as Lachlan bucked one more time, then fell against Fiona, his breathing audible. Nell's stifled cry and the wind from the open door caught their attention at last and they turned, Lachlan's eyes wide, Fiona's expression horrified as she saw them.

Lachlan rose, grabbing the blanket from Fiona to cover himself. "How dare ye follow me!"

Fiona scrambled to sit up, clutching her discarded clothing, fear in her eyes.

"I told myself it wasna true," Margaret said. Her voice shook. Her whole body shook. "When I heard ye'd left together, I told myself there must be some mistake, they must all be wrong, that neither of ye would betray me this way, that it was someone else they were speaking of. But it's not." Her breath caught on a sob, then another. "How could ye do this to me?"

"It has naught to do with ye," Lachlan said. "She's nothing to me."

Margaret ignored him, staring instead at Fiona. "I trusted ye! Every day of our lives! I told ye all that was in my heart and believed ye were my friend. And all along ye were playing me for a fool! This morning, when we came by, ye talked . . . did ye enjoy that, yer little game, planning this in front of me? Was that fun for ye? I canna believe this, that two of the people most dear to me have betrayed me this way. Fiona!" The name came out in a wail. "How could ye?"

"I dinna mean to . . ."

"Dinna mean to! Ye looked me in the eye and lied to me, Fiona."

"I had no choice!"

Margaret looked in horror at Lachlan. "Ye forced her?"

"No! No, of course not." Lachlan shook his head vehemently. "Tell her, Fiona! Tell her how ye flirted and told me she'd never ken. Tell her!"

Margaret stared at her friend. "Did he force ye?"

Fiona's voice was a whisper. "No. But ye dinna understand . . ."

"No, I dinna!" Margaret looked at Lachlan then. "And ye . . . !"

"Margaret!" Her father's voice boomed from the doorway, drowning her words. "Get ye home. Take yer sister. I'll deal with this. Now!"

Her father yanked her out into the path and slammed the door. She did not remember how she got back to the keep, nor how the hall was emptied of the revelers, nor how she managed to climb the narrow spiral stairway and finally throw herself onto her bed. She let the tears come then, not acknowledging her sister when Nell sat on the edge of the bed and stroked her hair. She did not speak when Nell at last left her alone again.

Later, after she'd cried for what seemed like hours, she was summoned to the hall. Rignor waited for her on the landing just above the hall, his face creased with worry.

"I'll kill him if ye wish it, Margaret," he said vehemently.

She gave him a wan smile. "I may yet ask that of ye."

"Just tell me when."

"Thank ye."

"And I'm sorry I was right about him. I have never liked Lachlan, and I suspected he was too friendly with Fiona, but I dinna see this coming. I would ha' warned ye."

She kissed his cheek. "Thank ye for that. It's good to ken ye're with me."

"I am," he said.

She nodded and thanked him again, then straightened her back and went down to the hall. Her brother followed.

* * *

Her father sat at his accustomed place at the table, her mother at his side, arms crossed over her belly. Nell, hovering near the fireplace, gave her a tremulous smile. Lachlan, who had been pacing in front of the table, stopped as she and Rignor entered. The boys were nowhere in sight, nor was anyone else. Rignor moved to stand with Nell, his arms crossed over his chest. Behind Margaret the heavy wooden door closed, the sound reverberating from the stone walls. Her parents watched her as she came to stand before them, her father's expression stern, her mother's smug, almost triumphant. Lachlan moved closer. Margaret ignored him, still shaken by what she'd seen in her mother's eyes.

"He has something to say to ye, Margaret," Father said.

Lachlan took her hands in his. Margaret withdrew them.

"I am truly sorry, Margaret. I must have been mad. It will never happen again, I swear it. I will be a faithful husband to ye."

Her father put his hand heavily on the table. "See that ye are," he said, as though that settled the matter.

Margaret shook her head. "Ye canna expect me to marry him now."

Her father's jaw was firm. "I do. Ye will."

"No."

Nell put her clasped hands to her mouth.

"Margaret!" Lachlan cried. "I swear this will never happen again. It was Fiona who tempted me, ye ken. She was so welcoming . . ."

"Dinna blame this on her! Ye chose . . ."

"Enough!" her father roared. "The contracts have been signed. Ye've pledged yer troth. He's apologized. That is the end of it. Ye'll marry as planned."

Margaret stared at him. "Ye canna mean it."

"I do mean it," her father said firmly. "I'll see the two of ye wed."

"To a man who cares only for his own pleasures, who breaks his word?"

"I dinna promise to be faithful to ye before we wed, Margaret," Lachlan said.

She turned to meet his gaze. "No," she said, putting all the contempt she felt for him in her words. "No, I suppose ye dinna." She turned back to her father. "How can ye think to marry me to a man who neglects his properties and his people? Who buys new clothing instead of repairing his home? Did ye ken his tenants have complained to Uncle William?"

"How do ye think ye ken all this?" Lachlan shouted.

She met Rignor's eyes, saw his plea for her silence. "I listen, Lachlan," she said. "I turned away from it, thinking we'd change all that together, but I listened. I willna marry ye."

It was her father who answered, his tone stern but not angry. "Margaret, surely I dinna need to remind ye of what ye already ken. We marry to make the clan stronger, to increase our lands and our power, not for our own pleasure. Ye've been betrothed to Lachlan since ye were a bairn. I've given my word to yer uncle William and to the king that ye'll marry, so marry ye will. That's the last of it."

Lachlan took her hand again. "I swear on my life that it willna happen again, Margaret. I swear it."

"I willna marry ye. There has to be more than this."

"There is not more," her mother said. "Ye've been dreaming of something that doesna exist." She threw her husband a glance. "Ye'll marry Lachlan and be glad of it."

"No."

There was silence in the room.

Mother glared at Father. "Tell her! Tell her she must marry Lachlan!"

"I ha' done that," he said wearily.

"I willna marry him," Margaret said.

"So I've heard," Father said. "Go to yer room, Margaret. When I've decided what to do I'll come to ye."

It was evening of the next day before Father came for her, knocking quietly at their door. Nell, who had kept Margaret company the long day, answered. Father stood for a moment, looking at his daughters. Ewan and Fergus peered around their father's side, but he waved them back.

"Go now, laddies. This is no' for ye," he said.

Her father's tone was somber, and Margaret winced. It was this tone that frightened her more than his shouting, for this tone was what he used when he delivered bad news or set decrees that were unalterable. He closed the door behind him. Nell retreated to stand by the window. Margaret sat on the edge of the bed. After a moment her father joined her, rubbing his hand along his thigh, then straightening the wool of his feileadh.

"Margaret," he said, "ye'll be going to the shielings as planned. Nell will go with ye. Then ye'll be going to the Abbey at Brenmargon for a night or two, until yer uncle William comes to fetch ye. And then ye'll go to court."

"To court? But, Father, why?"

He met her gaze. There was regret there, yes, but this

was the gaze of the clan chief and no one, even a daughter, could gainsay him. She felt her heart sink.

"Ye need to make yer choice, lass. It'll be marriage to Lachlan or the convent for ye. There are no other choices."

"There are other men, Father, other families . . ."

He held up a hand to stop her. "That's it, Margaret. Ye'll marry Lachlan and live a life of luxury with him. Or ye'll spend yer days in the cloister. I'll give ye the choice and hope you're not foolish enough to dig yer heels in."

"He lied to me, Father."

Father sighed again. "Aye, he did. But I've given my word, and ye've given yers. A contract is a contract, and we'll live up to our half."

"Father!"

He stood. "Tears willna change it nor will shouting. Ye should ken that after listening to yer mother for all these years." He started for the door.

"Why is it, Father," Margaret cried, "that Rignor remains unbound and I have to marry where I dinna wish to?"

Her father turned back, his eyes aflame now. "Yer brother remains 'unbound' as ye call it, because no one will have him. I've had four families refuse him. Four! Each time he destroys what I've built! I dinna ken where I'll try next. Nell's betrothed died. I've been avoiding that task for years, but now I've got to find someone for her. That's why yer marriage is more important than ever, Margaret. Without strong alliances we're just one isolated clan on the western shore; with them we're part of Scotland. Without them we face our enemies alone. With them we have allies on which to call. I'll not have ye, nor anyone, prevent me from doing what's best for the clan. I've no patience left for a lass who only thinks of herself, so make yer choice, lass. Marry Lachlan or spend yer life in the abbey."

"And if I chose the abbey?"

"Then Nell will marry Lachlan, and we'll rarely see ye again. So ye choose, lass, and live with yer choice. Which of ye will marry Lachlan?"

The door closed behind him. Margaret and Nell exchanged a startled look.

It had been two days since she'd found Lachlan with Fiona, one day of Lachlan's following her incessantly, pleading his cause, begging her forgiveness, then a morning of arguing. Two days of her father's refusing to discuss it, and her mother's bloodlessly giving only the most necessary commands, not one kind word or tender look. So be it. Margaret was beyond weary of the topic. Nothing had changed. She would not marry the man. But then she'd glance at Nell and sigh. If Lachlan was not a fit husband for her, how could he be any different for Nell? What were her responsibilities, to her clan and her family—and to her sister, just on the brink of womanhood? She had no doubt that their father would make good his threat and marry Nell to Lachlan in her stead.

How could she marry him? How could she not?

Lachlan left at last, assuming the demeanor of a disappointed man, his brows drawn together and mouth petulant. It was a fine act, but one that left her unconvinced. From her perch in her room she'd seen his head rise as soon as he cleared the gates of the courtyard, when he thought her father could no longer see him. And instead of turning to the left, to go through the inland gate and to the paths that would take him eventually to Stirling, he'd turned right. Toward the lower village and the harbor. Toward the weaver's house. Toward Fiona. Fiona, who had had the guards deliver her pleas to talk. Margaret had sent them back with the message that there was nothing Fiona could say that she wanted to hear.

Today she and Rignor and Nell would leave as well, riding out with a handful of guards to the shielings, then to the abbey and to court. How many times had she stood at her window and wished she could choose her future? And now she could, but the choice brought little comfort. She closed her eyes and let the wind flow over her. Snapping wind, she thought, opening her eyes and turning from the window. That was what her brother Davey called the kind of wind sweeping in now from the sea, bringing havoc with it. It fit her mood perfectly.

She looked around the small room she shared with Nell, appointed with every comfort Somerstrath could provide: rugs on the floor from faraway places, silk coverings for the bed they shared, a chest in the corner that held clothing and small things. A candle so they did not have to fumble in the dark. And a small window, a luxury in itself, an arrow slot really, overlooking the courtyard below and village beyond, but affording a view of the trees that ringed the base of the mountains, then the mountains themselves. She and Nell knew when the sun came up, knew when it was raining or the wind blew as it did now. Could she live in a cell in the abbey with no vision of the outside world? Could she kneel and pray for the rest of her life? Never run along the beach again, never feel the sunshine on her bare head? Could she leave the world forever?

The wind swirled around her, lifting a lock of her dark hair and laying it across her face, bringing her back to the present. Today would be full, and that would distract her. Some of the shielings, the huts they would visit, were clustered together, some separated by a burn or even a glen, but the riding would be easy. The sky was clear, the air already warming, promising a bright day. She'd get to visit people she liked. It would be a long journey, but with Nell's company, it should be a pleasant one, despite Rignor, who would no doubt still be bruised from last night's argument with their father. She'd heard the shouting even here, in her room. The wind snapped the draperies of the bed, and Margaret's mood lifted. She couldn't wait to leave.

Her good-byes were perfunctory. Her mother put a hand on each of her shoulders and leaned toward Margaret, but her lips did not brush Margaret's cheek, as they briefly did Nell's, or as they did Rignor's, lingering there while Mother whispered something to her eldest son. Margaret turned away, to meet her father's gaze, surprised to see tears in his eyes. And was that regret she saw there as well, quickly suppressed? His embrace was solid, his kiss on her cheek comforting.

"Promise me ye'll think long and hard on this, lassie mine," he said softly.

She nodded, unable to speak.

"That's all I ask of ye," he said, and released her. "Safe journey, then."

She thanked him and hurried to her pony, stopping only to hug each small brother, each laughing as he threw his arms around her. Fergus gave her a flower, grubby from his hand. Ewan and Cawley told her that they would drive Lachlan away so she could find someone else. She thanked them for the thought. Davey simply hugged her tightly, his dark eyes filled with shadow.

"What is it?" she whispered to him.

"I dinna want ye to go," he said.

"I ha' no choice, Davey."

"Aye." He nodded, his lips pressed together.

"I must go," she whispered. "But I'll be back. I swear it."

"Dinna go, Margaret. It'll be so long until I see ye again."

She smiled, touched by his affection, then kissed his cheek, his skin smooth under her lips. In a few years he'd not allow her this familiarity.

"Be careful," he said.

"I will. And ye in my absence," she said, smiling into his eyes.

"I'll miss ye."

"And I ye," she said, suddenly struck that no one else had said he would miss her. No one. She threw her arms around him again and kissed the top of his head, releasing him before he could protest. "God keep ye safe until we meet again," she said, using the old phrase of parting.

"And ye," he answered.

She'd almost escaped the village when Fiona caught her, running alongside her pony, clasping Margaret's ankle and asking her to stop.

"I never meant to hurt ye, Margaret! Surely ye ken that!"

Margaret did not look at her.

Fiona tightened her hold. "I never meant to hurt ye!"

"What did ye think would happen when I found out?"

"I dinna think ye'd find out."

"And when we went to Lachlan's? What then? How did ye think I'd not ken?"

Fiona's face twisted. "Lachlan told me . . . he said we would be discreet."

"When he would be married to me? The two of ye thought ye could continue this? How could ye do this to me, Fiona? How could ye attend me during the day, then slink away to share my husband's bed? How could ye?"

"I dinna think ye'd discover us, Margaret!"

"And that makes it all right? Ye'd betray me and tell yerselves that what I dinna ken cannot harm me? Is that it?"

Fiona's face flushed. "Ye dinna ken what it's like for the rest of us. All yer life ye've been cared for and cosseted. Ye kent from yer earliest day that ye'd marry a wealthy man. What did I ken, Margaret? That I'd marry some Somerstrath man and bear his children and be fortunate to live through it. Ye dinna ken what it's like to dream of a life like yers, to have a man like Lachlan give ye things. He's been kind to me. He loves me."

Margaret blinked, trying to reconcile this new Fiona with the girl she'd known all her life. "Do ye love him?"

Fiona's voice was hushed, but her words were clear. "Love? No. That's for the likes of ye. He was my way into the world."

Margaret pulled her ankle from her friend's grasp. "Not anymore. Ye'll die here in Somerstrath, Fiona."

Fiona's eyes hardened. "We'll see."

"Mark my words, Fiona. Ye'll never leave this place. Ye'll die here." Margaret kicked her pony forward. She guided it through the upper half of the village and through the inland gate, following Rignor and the guards up the narrow path to the ledge, which was wide and flat and afforded a view of all of Somerstrath. They paused there, but Margaret did not look into the village, did not want to see Fiona again. She kept her eyes on the sun's rays lighting the top of the keep, wondering if this would ever be her home again. She would not think of the future; she'd think no further than this lovely summer day just beginning. She turned her pony and rode into the trees.

She'd gone just a few feet when her pony shied, and she herself ducked out of the way of a raven that flew directly at them, croaking its message before disappearing into the pines. She calmed the pony, but had a harder time with herself. Everyone knew that to see a raven flying at one or to hear it croak at the start of a journey was among the most ill-starred omens. She shook off her sense of foreboding. How ridiculous to believe the old superstitions. Next thing she knew she'd be throwing salt over her left shoulder.

Rignor was, as she'd predicted, both sullen and silent, but Nell, blissfully unaware of last night's argument and wisely not mentioning the one with Fiona, chattered to him all the way up the steep hill that led inland. Rignor, to his credit, neither complained nor moved away from his young sister, but he did give Margaret several baleful glances, which she pretended not to see. They would ride for two hours before reaching the first shieling, and she was content to let Nell spend all of it talking to him.

The wind kept them company all day. Above them the sunlit mountains, blanketed with purple heather, kept the clouds from passing too quickly overhead, then reluctantly allowed them to continue on their way east. They were warmly welcomed by those who were already inland,

and ate their midday meal on the edge of a meadow high in the foothills. While Rignor told the clanspeople all the latest happenings in Somerstrath, Margaret let her gaze and her mind wander. She watched the shadow of the clouds move quickly across the hillsides, deepening the colors, then releasing them into the sunshine again. In a few weeks this meadow would be dotted with russet Highland cattle. By autumn they'd be fat and quite contented, and those who summered up here in the hills would come home browned and cheerful.

Nell stretched her arms high above her head. "I may stay here forever."

"Would that we could."

Nell threw Margaret a sidelong glance. "Are ye still angry with Lachlan?"

Margaret paused. Angry? There was not a word strong enough to describe what she felt for Lachlan. She took a deep breath and let it out slowly. "Aye, I am still angry, Nell. I keep growing more angry."

"What will ye do?"

"What would I like to do? I'd like to string him up by his toes and leave him to rot in the cellar. And bring Fiona in to join him."

"He's apologized."

"Oh, aye. Words."

"What about the abbey?"

"I dinna think I was meant for that life. No, I have to find a way to make Father and Mother change their minds. Or, failing that, find a way to have the contract revoked." Margaret grinned. "What I'm going to have to do at court is find a man who will marry me and be an even better alliance than Lachlan. And then find one for ye."

"How will ye do that?"

Margaret laughed. "I dinna ken yet. It'll come to me."

Nell gave a whoop of delight. "Ye can do it!"

"I will do it. Watch me and learn!"

Margaret watched the sun rise from her perch outside the small shieling in which they'd spent the night, the dawn filling the sky with flaming color. She sighed as she watched it. They'd have rain before sunset. Could not this one day have dawned gray so their weather would be clear? She'd not slept well, tossing on the tiny cot she'd shared with Nell, then rising in the dark to sit outside, her cloak wrapped around her, while she thought. There was no solution but the ridiculous one she'd already come up with—of finding two men, of appropriate families and character, to whom she and Nell could be wed. She'd have a very short time in which to find them, for their visit was to last less than a fortnight. Her chances of success were poor. If she married Lachlan, she would fulfill her responsibility to the clan and to her family, but she'd never be happy. And she was afraid that she would be no happier if she lived her life in the abbey. And if Nell married Lachlan in her stead, she'd blame herself forever.

She sighed again. She'd talk it over with Judith, the abbess at Brenmargon, whom she knew well. She'd been to the abbey before, had spent the night there several times while traveling and always enjoyed her visits. Judith, of English descent, was the cousin of one of Margaret's father's most trusted tacksmen, Rufus, who lived in the glen just south of Somerstrath. Rufus was a steadfast man, honorable, slow to anger, quick to ignore the exploits of his only child, Dagmar of the easy virtue and insatiable appetites. His cousin Judith was quiet, devout, and shrewd as they came.

Judith and Rufus's family had come north when the Normans invaded England a hundred years before, mixing their blood with the Scots but keeping their own names, and bringing with them a fierce priest who had, by his relentless efforts, done more to drive out the ways of the old Celtic Christian church than anyone in this part of Scotland. By the time he'd died priests were not allowed to marry and their sons did not inherit the post; bishops came from Glasgow and Edinburgh and Stirling and the ancient ways, the old religion that predated Christianity, had to be practiced secretly, or melded into the Christian tradition. Springs and burns that had had their own gods became wells of St. Bridget; banshees had become a form of Satan, or simply the wind. Trees were a manifestation of the divinity rather than spirits to be worshipped. Stories of giants who ruled the north were replaced with tales of Columba's missionary works.

And yet the old ways were not gone, despite all the efforts of the Church. The people still believed, and many of their habits had ancient roots. The pain of a woman in labor would be cut by placing a dirk under the bed. Herbs were sprinkled over the doorway to dissuade evil spirits from entering. A new father ran three times, following the sun's path, around his home to protect his family. Witch's brooms were always made of birch twigs, but a birch tree near one's home offered protection from the Evil Eye, or from barrenness. Everyone knew that a rowan tree planted by one's door could protect from witchcraft, and that one never sat under a hawthorn tree on May Day or Midsummer's Eve, or All Souls' Eve, when fairies were known to be abroad. Simple things. A guttering candle meant death would soon threaten the household. Spells and chants offered protection; charms were even more potent protection. Not to recognize the forces of nature meant one risked becoming their prey.

Which brought Margaret to another matter: that of her own faith. Had she been looking at her life and fate incorrectly all these years? Her dreams had been haunted by the old woman's words about the golden man: "He will be unlike any man you've known. He will bring life after death." Had she misunderstood the prophecy by assuming the golden man was flesh and blood? Had she been brought to where she was now because she was meant to choose a life of contemplation away from the world? Was being a bride of Christ her true destiny, her golden man a molten image of a dying Jesus? Had Lachlan betrayed her because she was not meant to marry any man, but to join Judith at Brenmargon Abbey and, using the power of prayer, slay the dragons of sin in the world?

She could not be more confused.

FOUR

It was Rory O'Neill himself who came to get Gannon and Tiernan. It was a bright summer day when the chieftain of all Ulster, Ireland's northernmost province, arrived at their stepfather's fortress with a large retinue. And dressed for war. Rory O'Neill was a large man, broad-shouldered and barrel-chested. He looked the same as Gannon had remembered him, though it had been years since he'd seen his mother's cousin. His chestnut hair was streaked with gray, but his dark eyes were as bright and clever as ever. He burst into Patrick's courtyard with his men and greeted Patrick, then, pulling off his helmet and running a hand through his hair, turned to Gannon, wasting no time with niceties.

"God above, Gannon, I would ha' kent ye anywhere as yer father's son! Ye look enough like Magnus to make one think of spirits rising from the grave."

Gannon nodded. He'd heard it all of his life.

Rory continued with hardly time for a breath. "I've come to take ye and Tiernan back to Haraldsholm. Yer uncle Erik has asked for my help. If he needs me, he needs the two of ye. And it's time anyway, lads. Yer mother's been gone the year."

Gannon saw Tiernan's surprise, but felt none, only an acknowledgment of what he'd know was coming. Change. "What has happened?"

Rory shook his head. "Dinna ken all of it. That's what we're going there to discover. There's trouble is all I ken for sure. Pack yer things, lads. We'll eat some of Patrick's fine food and get back on the road. And ye'll no' be comin' back here, the two of ye. Ye need to be with yer own people. From here on ye'll either be with Erik, or ye'll be with me." He laughed at their expressions. "Ah, family ties. Are they not marvelous?"

Gannon took a deep breath as they left the forest. The perfume of the pines was fading and he could smell the sea, could hear their horses' footfalls on the rocky road, now clear of the carpet of needles that had covered it under the trees. Ahead, Rory O'Neill rode with several of his men; more rode behind Gannon and Tiernan. The terrain was changing as the land leaned toward the sea. The wind lifted the edges of his clothing, heavy with the promise of rain later, but for now the sun shone, and he lifted his face to meet the light. He was pleased to be returning to the coast, whatever the real reason was for their travel. The sea called to him in a way that no inland water could. It was in his blood, he thought, this love of the shore.

His blood.

He was the son of Magnus Haraldsson, who had been born and raised on the northeast coast of Ireland, but who could trace his line back two hundred years to King Harald Hardrada of Norway. Magnus had been proud of his blood, explaining to his sons that they were descendants of the Vikings who had first come to Ireland to pillage and steal, but who stayed to marry and farm and raise families.

It was a familiar story. For hundreds of years, first the Danes, then the Norse, had attacked, claiming a great deal of land in Ireland, England, Wales, and Scotland, settling what they'd captured by force, mixing their blood with the people who lived there until those who called themselves the descendants of Norsemen lived with those they'd once fought, accepting Christianity and much of the local cultures. They became powerful political figures in the lands they'd settled. In Antrim, in the northeast of Ulster, at the edge of the sea, as in so many other places, the Norse allied with the Celts to form a strong union against all outsiders. It was only in Orkney—and on the western islands that lay between Scotland and Ireland— that the Norse had stayed Norse, were still under the control of King Haakon of Norway.

Magnus had taught his sons that their heritage was one of courage and valor, and Gannon, the oldest, had loved to hear his father's stories, reveling in the bloodlines that had come to him. Until the day his father died. From that day on, Gannon had turned his back on his Norse blood, had no longer called himself Gannon Magnusson, but instead the Irish form of the name, Gannon MacMagnus. He'd tried to forget why they'd left Haraldsholm, of his life before coming to Maguire's Bridge, but now he was about to face it again.

Tiernan came alongside him, throwing Gannon a sharp glance. "Are ye going to be silent the entire journey?"

Gannon smiled. Tiernan was ever one to wear his heart on his sleeve. If he was worried, all knew it. If angry, there was no mistaking it.

"Not the entire journey," Gannon said. "Perhaps just the most of it."

Tiernan laughed, then gestured at the road ahead. "What d'ye think happened that's got Rory O'Neill himself going to Haraldsholm?"

"Something important." Gannon suspected it was something very important indeed, that death was once again roaming the northern shore. And that this time it would not go unavenged. Rory O'Neill was not a man to arm himself without reason, and the chieftain and his men were both well armed and wary. "I keep asking, but he keeps saying nothing more than before."

"How long has it been since we were at Haraldsholm?"

Gannon gave his brother a glance. "Fourteen years." A lifetime when one was Tiernan's age. A lifetime for him as well, for so much had changed.

"Wonder what we'll find," Tiernan said.

Gannon shrugged. That was but one difference between them. Tiernan couldn't wait to discover the future. Gannon was mistrustful enough of it to let it unfold as it would.

"If we dinna like what we find," he said, "we leave. If we do, we stay. We've nothing to hold us anywhere. We'll make our own future, Tiernan."

Margaret felt her mood sink as the ponies descended down to Brenmargon Pass. They'd left the crofthouse where they'd slept shortly after dawn, the world still damp from the dew and the ponies not thoroughly rested because the darkness was so short. Their journey was made more difficult by the lowering clouds that opened at midday and drenched them. She covered her yawn.

She'd been awake for much of the night, lying in the dark, thinking of the decision she would soon have to make. Nell no more wanted to marry Lachlan than Margaret did. What a horrible choice Father had given her. How foolish she'd been to think that he might love her as more than simply one of two marriageable daughters. She was nothing more to him than a cow, one as like another to the farmer who killed it. And yet . . . she remembered the tears in her father's eyes when they parted, his warm embrace and kiss.

None of which helped her to sort out her emotions.

They arrived at the abbey in pouring rain, shivering and soaked to the skin. They climbed from their ponies in the walled courtyard, handing the reins to the two young lads who waited for them. Judith, standing in the doorway of the long wooden structure with a wide smile, hurried them inside, helping to remove their dripping cloaks, which were handed to waiting nuns. Margaret shook out her skirts, brushed her wet hair back from her face, and gave Judith what she hoped was a bright smile. Behind Judith lay the main hall of the abbey, with its spartan tables and benches, a large crucifix on the wall the only decoration. Several nuns clustered there, waiting for Mother Judith to introduce them.

"I wondered if you would find us in the storm," Judith said, leaning to kiss Nell, then moving to Margaret, her lips papery on Margaret's cheek.

"Another hour and we might not have," Rignor said sourly. "We'd have spent a night on the wet ground."

"I'm glad ye won't have to," Judith said serenely. "We have food and beds ready. Yer men may sleep in the stable. Rignor, ye'll be in the apartment over it. I trust ye will find it comfortable."

Rignor nodded with a frown, and Margaret knew he'd forgotten that men were always housed in the apartment; the handful of lads who worked at the abbey lived there as well. The women lived in the main structure, a few with a genuine calling for the Church, the rest widows or unwed daughters with nowhere else to go. It was their money that kept the remote abbey, home to forty women, solvent. The Church paid it little attention except for the bishop, who was a frequent visitor and did not hide his enjoyment in the food the abbey supplied. And Judith's company, some said, but that was hardly surprising; he was her brother-in-law. Judith, a widow herself for years, had married his brother shortly after the bishop had been ordained. It was his influence that had made Judith a candidate for abbess when her husband had died.

It had been years since Margaret had seen her. Judith had aged. Her cheeks were more sunken, her skin a finer texture than in years past, her bones more prominent. But she was still tall and regal, capable of a sudden smile that lit her face and made her seem almost girlish. That smile was hidden now, as Judith embraced Margaret and, placing a hand on each of her shoulders, turned Margaret so her face was lit by the wall torches.

"I was surprised when I received yer father's message, that ye were on yer way. And why. How are ye, child?"

Margaret felt dangerously close to tears. How was she? How could she tell Judith that she was heartsick, that she'd cried endlessly over Lachlan and Fiona's betrayal? That it had taken these two days of being away from Somerstrath for her to begin to get a sense of what had happened. And as for her mother—what had she done to deserve that? She looked over Judith's shoulder, to the crucifix on the wall, the golden carving of Christ gleaming.

"I am well," she said.

"Are ye, lass?" Judith said softly, her eyes seeing far too much. "We'll talk." She turned to clasp Nell's hand in hers. "And Nell, such a lovely child, now a lovely young woman. Are ye excited to go to court?"

Nell nodded, her eyes sparkling. "Oh, aye, madam. I've heard ever so much about it. I canna wait to see it for myself."

Judith smiled. "I hope it lives up to yer expectations. Now, come, all of ye, I've warm food and ale and wine for ye, and the sisters are anxious for news. Tell me all that is happening at Somerstrath."

It was long after Rignor had braved the rain to go to his bed, longer still since Nell had let herself be led off to the room she would share with Margaret, and after the rest of the nuns had retired, that Judith led Margaret into her own room. The abbess's chamber was larger than the usual cells the nuns occupied and full of furniture from her past life as the wife of a wealthy landowner. At one end was a box bed made of sturdy oak, carved with vines and flowers, its bedcoverings brocaded and hangings silk. In front of the warm fire, another luxury rare in an abbey, stood the two wooden chairs, their legs curved and crossed over each other, that Margaret had been told had been brought back from the Holy Land. Judith led her to the chairs, settling into one and folding her hands on her lap.

"Talk to me, Margaret," she said.

Margaret did, telling her all that had happened, about the head on the beach and Lachlan's betrayal, about Fiona's defiance and the old woman's forecast of a golden man, about dragons and marriage. Judith listened silently, her lips pressed together tightly, her derision obvious.

"A seer, Margaret? A woman, not of God, who roams from town to town telling people what they want to hear, that their lives will be dramatic and meaningful, that everything she tells them has significance? That she can see the future? Ye listened to such a woman? Ye'd have been wiser to pray."

"But she . . ." Margaret began.

"Was hired," Judith said. "But she doesna matter. It was a long time ago. Do ye have a calling to be in God's service?"

"I . . . I'm not sure," Margaret answered.

"I wasna either. At first I came here to retreat from the world, but soon I realized that this was my correct path. Tell me what yer parents have said about all this."

Margaret talked then about her mother's anger, about the choice Father had given her. Judith's expression was thoughtful, then she gave Margaret a half smile.

"A lot has happened since I saw ye last. Now talk to me of yer faith, lass, and tell me why ye're even considering a life here."

"The old woman . . ." Margaret began, but Judith shook her head.

"Not the old woman's beliefs, child. Yers. Has there ever been a moment before all this happened when ye thought of being a nun?"

Margaret thought of the peace she felt in the abbey, of the songs the nuns sang as they worked, of the calm manner in which they went about their tasks. "It might be wonderful," she said.

"And it might be all wrong for ye," Judith said, her tone more astringent than Margaret had ever heard. "I was a woman of the world for many years, lass. I've seen much and suffered much, and this abbey affords me the peace I seek. But ye—no. I see some of Nell's excitement in yer eyes when ye talk of going to court. I see the lads, few as they are here, looking at ye, and ye looking back, as lasses will, nothing wrong with that."

Judith fingered the cross around her neck, then looked to the crucifix on the wall. "Ye no more belong at Brenmargon than Rignor does. Ye must seek yer golden man and dragons elsewhere, child, or, better still, forget the words of an old woman who received gold for her fortune-telling. Life has mystical moments, aye, but dinna change yer life to suit a handful of words that like as not were thrown out without thought. Dinna confuse her words with prophecy, which only belongs to God." She held up her hands to still Margaret's protests.

"Dinna mistake me. I would welcome yer company were ye to join us. We're an aging group now. Ye'd liven up this quiet place and bring youth back. But I'd be wrong to encourage ye to do so. Ye might find it a refuge at first, but soon I think ye'd regret it, and not thank me for taking ye from the world. There are worse things than discovering that yer husband is unfaithful."

Margaret gasped, and Judith smiled wryly, holding up her hand to still Margaret's protests.

"I'm not belittling what ye've experienced," she said. "I'm merely telling ye that it would be wrong for ye to come here; ye're a lovely lass, and a spirited one, and ye shouldna be living the rest of yer life behind these wooden walls." She paused, threading her fingers and straightening her back. "And then there's yer duty to yer family. I'm sure ye've heard of all the tensions of the last ten years or so, between the Comyns and the Durwards. Yer Aunt Jean's family is presently verra powerful, but they need every weapon in their arsenal to stay that way. Ye, with yer beauty and yer liveliness, would be a welcome addition to their side. They're no doubt counting on ye to charm the king and queen and bring more favor to the Comyns. And there's yer mother." Judith sighed heavily. "I dinna need to tell ye that she's counting on ye to pave her way back to court."

Margaret stared at her. "Mother? At court?"

Judith nodded. "I've kent yer mother for much of my life. She was a wisp of a lass when we first met, small and lovely and one of the most unhappy people I've ever kent. Her parents doted on her, as did her brother and yer father at first—ah, I see in yer eyes that that's no longer the case. But it once was. And still it wasna enough. No one could give yer mother all the attention she wanted. She thought yer father would take her back to court. But his duty was to keep the western coast strong, so he stayed at Somerstrath and did just that. I dinna need to tell ye that didna make her happy."

She paused again, tilting her head to study Margaret. "And now, here ye are, beautiful and bright, the one chance she has for getting back to the life she thinks she belongs to, and ye're turning yer nose up at it because the man ye're bound to has been unfaithful before ye've even wed. And is that not the very thing—an unfaithful man—that she's endured all this time and lived through and ye willna tolerate? No wonder she's displeased with ye."

"It's almost as though she hates me," Margaret said.

"Aye, well, what happens when an already unhappy person is thwarted yet again? She has to have someone to blame, Margaret, and we both ken it'll never be herself. She's jealous of ye, and resenting that ye're throwing away the very life she's wanted for so long."

"But she's my mother . . ."

Judith laughed. "For some women that would change things, but not all. And not yer mother. Dinna think it's just ye, child. Nell, should she dare to defy her as well, will receive the same. She's too lovely to escape yer mother's wrath. I wish I could tell ye I'm surprised that yer mother's acting the way she is, but I canna. I pity her." She looked into the distance, then back at Margaret. "So much was given to her, and none of it is enough for her. She drove yer father away from her, then is bitter when he finds someone to console him. She has two daughters she should cherish, whose beauty and intelligence should be a source of pride, not jealousy, for her. Add five fine sons to that and a home that is the envy of much of the west. Most women would be content. But not yer mother." Her voice quieted. "Ye'd be wise, Margaret, to find a way to forgive Lachlan and make a new life for yerself, for despite what ye might want, yer time at Somerstrath is over."

She sighed heavily. "Now I must tell ye something that ye'll not wish to hear. I canna consider ye coming here without thinking of what that might mean for us. Lachlan has the ear of the king, and I dinna wish to make an enemy of him. We rely on the good graces of those who endow this abbey. I canna risk the lives and welfare of the women under my care for one lass, even one I am so fond of who would gladden this old woman's remaining years. I'm afraid that if I give ye refuge, I'll anger powerful men, and I'd not be wise to do that, would I?

She rose to her feet. "Now sleep, lassie, and when the time comes, use both yer heart and mind and not anger to make the decision. Life is often strange. I certainly never expected to end up here. Who kens what lies ahead for ye. But I will do one thing that might help yer decision."

"What?" Margaret asked, her hope coming alive again.

"I'll write to yer father and remind him that should ye choose a life with us, I'll be expecting yer dowry to accompany ye. Perhaps if he realizes he'll have to pay for the privilege of punishing ye, he'll reconsider."

Margaret forced her disappointment down and thanked her.

"The Lord will guide ye, my dear," Judith said. "Now off to bed with ye." She ushered Margaret into the hallway. "Good night," she said softly, closing the door.

Margaret looked at the door for a moment, then lifted her candle and made her way down the hall. After all the talk, after baring her soul, she'd received nothing but more rejection and a kind dismissal.

You'll face dragons.

The words were so clear that Margaret spun around, looking to see who had spoken. The hallway was empty, but she could still hear the echo, as though the spirit of the old woman had come simply to counter Judith's words and guide Margaret to a different path. Margaret hugged herself and hurried to her room. Dragons, she thought. Not within these walls.

She attended matins the next morning, praying for guidance in the small dark wooden chapel crowded with nuns. She watched the nuns go about their daily tasks, washing clothing and scrubbing floors, and listened to their lovely singing, the hymns taking on new meaning when sung so simply. In many ways life here was no different than at home: meals needed to be prepared, rooms cleaned, and plants tended. At the evening prayers, she bent her head low over her hands, trying not to cry, trying to feel a calling to this life. But no peace came. She still rehearsed things that she might one day say to her father, to Lachlan, to Fiona, things that she knew she would never say to her mother but still echoed in her mind. Her anger had not lessened, her sense of outrage had not waned. Even with all her prayers, her rage had not abated. She worried that she was more like her mother than she knew, holding her anger to her like a companion. She feared for her very soul, for if one could not find peace in such a setting, perhaps one could not find it anywhere.

The nuns seemed to have found it. Their movements, often hampered by the coarsely woven habits they wore, were calm, their expressions often serene, or thoughtful, as though they heard a voice she could not. And perhaps they did, for their faces lit with joy when they knelt before the crucifix, and while she felt both repentant for her sins and virtuous for her repentance, she did not feel elation as she gazed on Christ on the cross. How was she to find joy in His suffering?

They were at Brenmargon a day and a half before Uncle William joined them, his troop arriving in the early afternoon, large and noisy, the sound of male voices strange to Nell after hearing so many women's tones. Her uncle had not changed; he was still tall, lean, the same dark eyes and hair as her mother, not surprising since they were siblings. But his manner was far different than Mother's. William, now stripping off his gloves as he strode purposefully into the hall, was a direct man of few words and, unlike Mother, few emotional indulgences. He seemed preoccupied now, almost brusque as he entered, although he did linger a moment to kiss Nell and Margaret, smelling, Nell thought, wrinkling her nose, of horses and sweat. But William's smile was wide and genuine as he greeted his nephew and nieces, and again when Judith asked after his wife Jean and his sons.

"They're growing by the day," William said, with obvious pride, "and keeping their mother and me busy with their antics."

"Ye'll stay for a meal?" Judith said.

"Aye, we will, and I thank ye for it," William said. He handed his gloves to his waiting man and swirled off his cape, turning to Margaret. "Now, what's all this about ye and Lachlan? I'm told ye need accompanying to court, which I will do. I canna stay long, but I need to talk with the king myself."

When none of them answered, he gestured for Margaret to sit opposite him, which she did with reluctance, glancing at the audience of William's men and Judith's nuns.

"Well?" he asked, nodding his thanks to the nun who brought him a mug of ale. "I received a cryptic message from yer da, telling me ye're deciding whether to marry

Lachlan or to take the veil." He drained the cup, then looked at Margaret speculatively. "Have ye suddenly found God, or is there something else? Tell me quickly now, or tell me as we ride. I want to get through the pass before dark. So, lassie, what is it?"

Margaret's face flushed. "He lied to me, Uncle William. He was . . . he betrayed me with one of the Somerstrath lasses."

"Fiona," Nell said. "D'ye remember her, Uncle William? The weaver's daughter?"

William shook his head. "No, lass, I dinna remember which one she is."

"Margaret found them together," Rignor said. "I wanted to kill him."

"Did ye?" William said, shifting his gaze back to Margaret. "And ye?"

"Not at first," Margaret said. "That came later."

Nell saw the beginning of a smile in William's eyes, and an answering one in Margaret's, which quickly died at his next words.

"Ye ken the contracts have all been signed?"

Margaret nodded, sparing a glance at Nell as though to say, "I told ye."

"And how important this alliance is?" William asked.

"Aye."

"And yer father told ye to decide whether to take the veil or marry him?"

"Aye. And that if I dinna marry Lachlan, Nell will have to."

William's eyebrow rose at that, but he nodded. "It's a solution. She's young, but that is changing every day." He pushed himself to his feet.

"I willna marry him, Uncle William," Nell said heatedly.

"It's not me asking ye to," William said, with a pointed glance at Margaret.

William stayed for the midday meal, then immediately bundled up his men and nieces and nephew, thanking Judith for her hospitality and promising news of the court on his return. Margaret embraced Judith, hearing the words behind her words as Judith told her to enjoy her visit to court. She left with a heavy heart, knowing that her choices were narrowing. On the road, William set a fast pace that allowed little conversation, but once through the pass and onto the flatter eastern lands, he slowed to join Margaret, Nell, and Rignor, turning to Nell with a smile. "First time at court, eh, Nell?"

Nell nodded brightly. "Aye, sir."

"Ye need to ken some things before ye arrive." He glanced at the others. "Ye need to listen as well. First, Nell, tell me what ye ken of the king."

Nell took a deep breath. "King Alexander is Alexander III, son of Alexander II, and has been king since he was eight years old, but he began to rule on his own just two years ago."

William was pleased. "Good. And . . . ?"

"And we've had years and years of peace in Scotland."

"Not exactly. There's been no war, true, but there have been years of quiet competition by the Durwards and the Comyns for the king's ear. The Comyns have his ear now, and, allied as we are to them, so do we. We dinna intend to lose it. What else do ye ken?"

"That Queen Margaret is the daughter of King Henry

of England. And that Henry and Simon de Montfort are disagreeing about . . ." Nell faltered, not remembering.

"Doesna matter what started it," William said. "Ye're correct. But it's become much more than a disagreement now. And de Montfort has brought in the French, which complicates the situation since we have alliances with the French. And . . . well, ye can see we'll have to play this one carefully."

"And," Rignor said, unable to resist joining in, "King Alexander tried to buy the Hebrides from King Haakon of Norway, but Haakon refused."

William nodded. "Which is one of the things I'll discuss with the king."

"Why?" Margaret asked.

"There's been unrest in the north," William said. "Most of Caithness is Norse, as ye ken. We dinna want them uneasy up there." He gave Margaret a long look from under his brows. "All of which is why ye trying to end yer betrothal is no' likely to be the first thing on the king's mind. What did yer da have in mind to send ye to court?"

Margaret shook her head, but Rignor answered with authority.

"Father thought that if Margaret saw all Lachlan could provide her and how powerful he is at court, she'd change her mind."

"Lachlan is cousin to the king, Margaret," William said. "And a wealthy man."

"I ken all that. It's not enough," Margaret said.

"It might have to be." William spurred his pony forward.

* * *

Their journey was uneventful despite the treacherous marshland through which they rode, for William's men knew the safe paths. William was talkative again as they neared Stirling, where the king's court now resided, pointing out the genius of placing a fortress castle where Stirling lay, atop a massive rock formation that commanded views of much of central Scotland. To its west lay the marshes of the River Forth through which they now traveled, its bogs and frequent floods dangerous enough to prevent a large force of men from moving across it. To the northeast and southwest the fortress was surrounded by fearsome hills. There was no way to travel through the center of Scotland without passing the foot of Stirling; whoever controlled this land controlled the passage from Lowland to Highland, and as a result, there had been a castle, or stronghold, here for as long as men could remember. Hundreds of years ago Kenneth mac Alpin besieged this rock on his way to becoming King of the Scots. In the last century Alexander I dedicated and endowed a chapel here, and died within the castle walls, as did William the Lion fifty years ago. Now Alexander III had set his court here for the summer.

It was to Stirling that Margaret had come before, here where she'd spent a summer with the court. She'd told Nell a great deal about that visit, but still Nell had questions. Where would they sleep? Would she meet King Alexander and Queen Margaret and be allowed to attend court, or would she be shuffled off with the children? Could she see the Princess Margaret, a child of less than two years? Her questions were quickly answered, for William and his retinue were cordially greeted at the first guardhouse and escorted up the steep stone pathway to the castle itself.

Nell stared in wonder as they passed through the stone walls, which were being constructed around the already massive walls of timber and earth, and through the tall wooden gates that marked the entrance to the castle proper. They waited, still seated on their ponies, while word of their arrival was sent to the king. After what seemed an eternity, William was summoned to the royal presence while Rignor, Margaret, and Nell continued to wait in the outer close.

It was not William who came to them with the invitation to enter, but Lachlan, richly dressed in finely woven wool and silk, a golden brooch at his shoulder, a golden necklace at his throat, and golden rings on his fingers. His dark eyes skimmed over Nell and Rignor and lighted on Margaret, who turned slowly as though she'd felt his gaze. Lachlan lifted his arms to assist her to dismount.

"Welcome to court, Lady Margaret," he said, putting a hand on each side of Margaret's waist. He placed her on the ground before him and released her, turning at once to Nell.

Nell slipped to the ground unaided, drawing a quick glare from Lachlan before he turned back to Margaret, leaning close to her, his voice quiet.

"Dinna shame me here," he said. "Dinna try to talk to the king."

Margaret looked into his eyes, her anger visible. "I will ask the king to nullify our betrothal, Lachlan. I will never willingly marry ye."

Lachlan watched her for a moment, then smiled mockingly. "Who are ye to have the ear of the king, Margaret of Somerstrath? Have I not been here since I left ye? Who is he more likely to listen to, a lass from nowhere or his cousin?"

"But I will ask him nonetheless," Margaret said.

"If ye do," Lachlan said, his tone glacial, "ye'll pay the price for it."

Nell expected Rignor to protest, but her brother said nothing, watching with a wary expression as Margaret and Lachlan glared at each other. Nell stepped forward. "Dinna threaten her!" she cried.

"It's the truth, Nell," Lachlan said, glancing at her, "not a threat. But here is one just for ye: stay out of this."

Nell trembled with anger. "Do ye ken that if she doesna marry ye, I am to?"

Lachlan threw his head back and laughed. "No, Nell, ye willna. I can assure ye of that. I'd sooner wed yer brother."

Both Margaret and Nell began to answer him angrily, but their voices were drowned by William's voice booming from the doorway.

"Enough!" her uncle cried. "Come in. All of ye."

William led them into a large stone foyer, obviously part of a great hall still under construction, for stone-workers were shaping stones at one end, and the sound of chisels on rock could be heard behind the tall wooden wall that shielded the rest of the building from their sight.

"I'll have none of this!" William said, his voice tight with anger. "Lachlan, she has a right to ask. And Margaret, he has a right to be insulted by ye asking. It's a hell of a way for the two of ye to start a life together! Now, come, the lot of ye. Rignor, ye'll sleep in Lachlan's apartments. Margaret and Nell, ye'll share the Comyn women's quarters, and ye'll mind yer manners, the both of ye. Not one word about Lachlan, aye? Have some pride, for God's sake!"

He threw a baleful glance at Lachlan. "And dinna look so smug, laddie, or I'll ask the king to end the betrothal myself. Arguing in the close for all the court to hear! Ye'll be the talk of supper, I guarantee ye that." He waved at two servants, who apparently waited to take them to their chambers. "Now, go and get the dust off ye and prepare for the meal."

The first evening was a blur to Nell, the court a whirl of color and noise, words spoken in French and Saxon English, and Latin, accented Gaelic, and the strange mix of it all that the Lowlanders spoke. She sat quietly beside Margaret, while Rignor chatted with Lachlan and his companions as though they were the best of friends. Margaret hardly spoke, which suited Nell. There was so much to see.

She was fascinated by the gowns the women wore, their bright overgowns sleeveless and worn without a belt or girdle, some with open side lacing, some with short overtunics, heavily embroidered, skirts contrasting with laced-in sleeves of different materials. All the married women wore headdresses, some a simple wimple of silk caressing their cheeks, their hair drawn back into a net. Or a barbette wound over a hat and wrapped around the neck. Some were adorned with fanciful headdresses, high and jeweled. The unmarried girls wore their hair loose, or caught back in a weave of plaits and ribbons that matched their clothing, or held by a simple circlet. But the shoes! She was astonished by what the women wore—long, pointed shoes, some with beadwork, some carved from wood and painted with amazing patterns. She could have looked at the shoes for hours.

The men were dressed almost as colorfully. Some wore robes of velvet or silk, others tunics with buttons and laced-in sleeves and dagged hemlines over woolen trousers tucked into gleaming leather boots. Some wore soft leather shoes, painted like the women's, obviously not made for travel or work or war. They wore embroidered caps or coifs or left their hair loose, or caught under a hood, and some were as bejeweled as the women, their gems flashing from rings and belts and brooches, or buttons made of silver with a gem inset.

The Highlanders were easy to spot: their tartan clothing, colored by plant dyes, drab against the plumage of the courtiers, their hair loose or tied back simply with a leather thong. Many of the Highlanders wore gold and gems as well, some as ornately adorned as the king's retinue and visitors, while others were so simply dressed that they looked like clerics.

In this rich mixture of color and texture and style, she and Margaret looked like foreigners from a benighted land. Margaret's new clothing was well fashioned, but of a much older style, and while the sisters wore their best jewelry, it paled in comparison with that of the ladies of the court. Rignor, in his simple tunic and leggings, looked like an outsider. He seemed not to notice, but Nell saw Margaret observing the same things she did, the women and how they moved in their fine clothing, their sense of belonging obvious, their assurance daunting. Nell had never felt so insignificant. How did Margaret think to sway the king? She could hardly see King Alexander and Queen Margaret from where they sat halfway down the hall, far from the door, far from the king. Above the salt at least, she saw with a sigh, and actually well placed, for they sat close to Uncle William and two other Scottish earls, all well attended.

The meal was lavish by Somerstrath standards, with so many courses that Nell lost count. There were birds so small that they could be eaten whole, and some so large that a wing was larger than Nell's hand. There were whole fish served, eyes and all, which had always turned her stomach, and whole beeves brought in on huge silver platters that had to be carried by four men. There was fruit she had never seen, sweet and full of juice that dripped down her chin, and sweets laden with honey. And this, she was told, was not a feast, just an ordinary meal. The court lived very differently. And while the meal was overlong by Nell's standards, there were music and jugglers, and so many people to observe that she watched it all with fascination.

And being watched, she soon realized. Several of the men who sat with Lachlan made comments to each other behind their hands. Some, like the tall man with the copper-colored hair, simply watched, seeming to note everything Margaret and Rignor did. The red-haired man's gaze shifted to Nell now. He gave her a smile, fleeting, but warm, with the slightest of nods, accompanied by a rise of his eyebrows, as though they were already well acquainted. She stared, trying to remember if she'd been introduced to him earlier; she did not think so. He turned away then, responding to something Lachlan said, and Nell leaned closer, hoping to hear his voice, but the noise in the hall drowned it out.

* * *

Margaret tried to control her yawns, but they would not be denied, and at last she stood, a very sleepy Nell at her side, and gave her farewells to Uncle William, who nodded and returned to his serious conversation with the man next to him. A Stewart, she thought she'd been told, but in truth could not be sure. She'd met so many people that their names all ran together, and their stories, which she'd been meant to learn as well, were long forgotten. She said good night to Rignor and Lachlan and his men; Rignor, too far in his cups to care, simply gave a weak wave of his hand, but Lachlan insisted on accompanying them to their room, saying that they might get lost.

"The castle is not that large," Margaret said. "Someone would direct us."

"Directing ye is my task," Lachlan said to his men, with a wide smile. "And a large one it is. I fear I shall be occupied with it all my life." He joined their laughter.

Margaret kept her silence as they left the hall and went down the long corridor to their apartments, hoping the evening breeze let in by the arched windows would cool her temper. Norman arches, she thought, with a wave of resentment at all things not Scottish. French spoken by people whose families had lived here since the beginning of time. Chansons instead of songs. The Normans, the French influence, had permeated Scottish life. When had Scots lost control over their own lands? She glanced at Lachlan, whose thin nose and dark coloring betrayed his Norman blood. Their children might look like him, all dark angles, might act like him, arrogant and self-assured, traits which she had to admit were as much Scottish as Norman.

"A fine meal," Lachlan said, bringing her out of her reverie.

"Aye," she answered.

"Did ye not think it a fine meal, Nell?" he asked.

Nell, her eyes large, nodded.

"Nothing has changed, Lachlan," Margaret said, stopping in the dimly lit corridor. "I still dinna want to marry ye. Ye still betrayed me with Fiona. And all the pretending otherwise willna change either."

Lachlan's face was lit by the torchlight; hers, she knew, was in shadow—as she'd chosen. His struggle for control was obvious, but win he did. After a moment his expression was as smooth as his voice. "I still wish to marry ye."

"Why?" Margaret heard the curiosity in her voice. "Why me, Lachlan? Ye have money enough. Why not find another woman, who will look the other way?"

For a moment she thought he might actually tell her what was in his mind, for several emotions flew across his face. Ambition, hardly surprising. Stubbornness, again, predictable. A longing that startled her—surely not for her? And something else that she could not read. Possessiveness? Could that be the sum of it—that she'd been promised to him and, like a child who cannot eat another bite but who will not relinquish a sweet, he would not let her go?

"We are betrothed, Margaret."

"Is that enough for a life together? I will ne'er forget what ye did."

Lachlan's smile was brief and cold. "Here ye are," he said, gesturing to the doorway. He left them then without a backward glance.

"He could at least have answered ye," Nell said.

"Perhaps," Margaret said slowly. "Perhaps he doesna ken himself."

The night was uncomfortable, spent on pallets of straw in a crowded antechamber full of strangers. To be sure, the Comyn women were both welcoming and inquisitive, but Margaret hardly felt at ease among them. They watched her as though it was likely she might grow a second head, and she realized how very thoroughly she had been discussed.

She lay awake, thinking how foolish she'd been to think that she could come to court, survey the men, and choose one who would be suitable to her and her parents. This evening, set so far from the king and queen, surrounded by strangers who intimidated her, had made her face the situation. How could she choose amongst strangers? How would she be able to trust that any man she met here would be better than Lachlan? How could she think to see into the heart of a man she'd just met? Lachlan or the veil, unless she could convince the king otherwise. But would the king even grant her an audience? Much of the talk this evening had been of the situation in England and whether Scotland would be drawn into the conflict. Her own problems would be insignificant to King Alexander, and she'd have, at best, only a moment of his time. She turned over yet again.

"Are you awake, Margaret MacDonald?"

The whisper came from her left, the voice that of one of the younger Comyns, a sweet-faced girl who'd been friendly earlier.

"I am," Margaret whispered back.

"Is it true that you're here to try to end your betrothal?"

Margaret sighed to herself. Why deny it? All of court seemed to know her story. "My father sent me here, but aye."

"Tonight I met the man I'm to wed."

"And?"

"He seems kind enough. Older than I'd hoped, but . . ." The girl's weight shifted, as though she'd raised herself on one elbow. "We've been betrothed since my birth. But I'm thinking . . . if you are successful, perhaps I can end my betrothal as well. There's a lad at home. My parents do not approve, but . . ."

"It's time," said an older but not unkind voice, "to stop thinking and simply do yer duty, the both of ye. Ye are each betrothed for the good of yer family—and the good of yer country. Stop thinking of yerself as someone who gets to make a choice in such things. We none of us do, lasses, so stop pining for what will ne'er be. Find some good in the man ye are to wed. In time yer children will bring ye consolation. And remember, ye're marrying into means. What more could a woman ask for than security and children? Love is for Norman troubadours, lasses, not for the likes of us. Now hush and let the rest of us sleep."

In the quiet that followed, Margaret eventually found sleep, and the next day nothing of the conversation was mentioned. She never discovered which of the ladies had spoken.

The next day was a blur of faces as Margaret was introduced to apparently everyone at the castle. Dukes and earls and hangers-on and stray cousins—their names were all a muddle to her. She and Nell smiled and curtsied and tried to give sensible answers, but by midafternoon she longed for silence, and when Nell, safely seated at Uncle William's side and listening attentively, smiled and waved her away, Margaret leapt at the chance for solitude. She found it, or something approaching it, in the kitchen gardens, where no one was working and Lachlan's attendants would not think to seek her. She walked for several moments, lost in the comfort of the sun's warmth and the silence of the garden, stopping with a heart suddenly pounding when she realized she was not alone.

Seated on a bench on the far side of the garden, half-hidden by a tree's shadow, sat an old woman, her hands folded on her lap. She looked across the space at Margaret, her face unreadable in the dim light, but her manner expectant, as though she waited for someone. Margaret gave her a timid smile, then continued walking. But now she felt uncomfortable, for she felt the weight of the woman's gaze with every step. At the far side of the garden she paused to look over the plain below, the marshland's wet surface catching the sun, then releasing it, the glare blinding for a moment.

"I promised you my story."

The woman's voice, just behind her now, made Margaret freeze. She turned, slowly, half-expecting the gravel path to be empty, but there she was, looking no different than she had all those years ago.

"It canna be," she whispered.

The old woman simply smiled.

FIVE

No."

Nell turned to see who was stopping her from entering the garden. At the far end Margaret talked with an old woman, their conversation far too quiet for Nell to hear a word. The hand on her arm belonged to the tall red-haired man she'd noticed last night. His dark eyes were locked with hers. He wore the dress of a Highlander today, a feileadh and long cloak fastened with a garnet brooch, not the Norman clothing he'd worn last evening. She moved her arm, wondering if he would simply release her, but he tightened his grip.

"Let them talk," he said softly.

Nell raised her arm and her eyebrows, thinking that an imperious manner would intimidate him, but saw only amusement in his eyes. She turned away from him to watch her sister and the old woman. "Who is she?"

"Yer sister."

Nell gave a huff of air and turned back to him, replying tartly when she saw his wide smile. "Really? She looks so much older than I'd remembered."

He laughed softly and she looked more closely at him. He was younger than she'd thought him last night, his cleanly shaven face still unmarked by time, his lean body fit and well-defined. His eyes were a golden green, his hair, in the bright sunlight, far more blond than she'd earlier thought. A handsome man. She thought of all of Margaret's warnings about talking to the men at court and wondered if she should be cautious. She frowned at him.

He loosened his grip but still kept his hand on her arm. "Aren't ye a one, Nell MacDonald?"

"Aye, I am that," she said. "And ye are?"

"A one as well," he said, laughing again. "Liam Crawford, lass."

"Ye have the name of a Lowlander and the accent of a Highlander, sir."

He nodded. "That I do. Strange, is it not? But dinna fear, I've Highland blood enough to give me leave to wear the plaid. My mother's a Stewart and I've Ross and MacDonald blood like ye."

She tried to pull her arm free. His expression sobered immediately.

"Stay, Nell, please. Yer sister needs to talk to her."

"Who is she?"

His mouth quirked but he answered her this time. "The king's seer. She sees things . . . and they come true."

"Why does Margaret need to talk to her?"

"They met long ago, and the seer gave yer sister a prediction. I'll warrant Margaret's a wee bit surprised to see her here."

"How d'ye ken that?"

"She told me. The seer."

"Ye, out of all the people here? She picked ye to tell that she needed to talk to my sister? And ye not kenning Margaret at all? That's passing strange, sir."

"Aye." He let his gaze drift from her eyes to her hair, then down her body. "Ye're a child yet, Nell, but she tells me ye and I . . . we'll meet again another time. And we'll ken each other verra well."

Nell stared at him, openmouthed, not sure whether to be angry or to believe him. Or both. "I am not a child, sir."

"Liam. And ye are. But that's fine. I'm in no hurry. For a lass with such promise, I'll wait as long as it takes."

She snapped her mouth shut, ignoring her flushed cheeks. "Let me go, please, sir."

"Liam."

"Liam. Please."

"Will ye stay here and let them talk?"

She looked into his eyes. He did not look like a madman, although she was not sure what a madman would look like, but was quite sure a madman's gaze would not be so steady as it met hers, or his touch so confident, as if he did indeed know what he'd said to be the truth.

"Will ye let them talk, Nell?"

"Aye," she said softly.

He released her arm, but stood close enough to grab her, which she was certain he would if she moved. She looked across the garden, to where Margaret and the old woman now walked down a path, their heads leaning together. She wished she could see Margaret's expression, but her sister seemed unafraid. She turned back to Liam Crawford, who had followed her gaze and now met her eyes.

She meant her voice to be stronger, but it was barely a whisper. "What did she tell ye of me? The seer, what did she say?"

He was silent for a long moment, his expression distant, then gave her a rueful smile. "She told me that both of us would see much before we met again, and that . . ." The slightest hint of color stained his cheeks. "And that we would be . . . verra well acquainted. She told me yer Christian name, but not yer family name. I've met several Nells and wondered each time, but when I saw ye last night . . . I kent it was ye."

"How?"

"By yer eyes. I looked into them, and I saw ye."

She stared at him, searching for a hint of amusement now, or mockery, but saw neither. For a moment they stared at each other until, her cheeks scarlet, she turned away. "And if it's not true?"

His voice was hushed. "Then I would be sorry that it wasna."

She looked into his eyes for a moment longer, then away yet again, her mind tumbling. They were silent then, side by side, watching Margaret and the old woman, while the wind freshened and clouds scudded across the sky. He moved suddenly, leaning to put his mouth next to her ear.

"I will await ye, lass," he whispered.

She was not sure what to say, but he was already walking quickly away. She watched him leave, watched the swing of his shoulders and his long strides, the confident way in which he moved. He was several years older than she, young, but still a man. Hadn't her father been talking to the Stewarts? That was it, she decided. He was one of the candidates her father was considering. All the rest of it, the prophecy by the seer, that he would wait for her—that was nonsense. No doubt he was laughing at her now.

He looked over his shoulder just before he turned a corner, and raised a hand to wave, his movements reluctant. She felt a chill of premonition, then chided herself. He had to be one of her father's candidates. Otherwise . . . she wrapped her arms around herself and watched Margaret and the old woman.

Margaret had heard stories like this one before, but never from someone who professed to have lived such a life. It was difficult, looking at the small, wizened woman before her, to imagine her as a young girl. But still, there it was, the sparkle in her brown eyes, the lift of her chin. She had been a beauty once, before age had bent her back and curled her hands.

The old woman told her of her childhood in a desert land, surrounded by her family and her parents' families, in a small village near a wide river, not one person of the village of any importance to the world. And the men who had ridden in one day, a brilliant spring day, the old woman said, her wrinkled face wrapped in memory. The riders killed all the men of the village and most of the boys. Her father and brothers were among the first murdered. The fate of the women was simple; the young ones were rounded up and tied together in a long line. The older ones . . . did not live. None were left untouched.

She'd been taken to Greece, sold to a merchant who in turn sold her to a man from Rome, who had treated her well, had tried to convert her to his religion, had even professed his love for her before his death. After he was gone, his wife had turned her out of the lodgings he'd rented for her, and the wandering years began. She'd lived in Madrid. In Lisbon. In London. In York. In Edinburgh. And now wherever King Alexander and Queen Margaret lived. She was, she told Margaret with a wry smile, as important to the court as any jester or musician. There were, she said, few choices for women then, fewer still for a woman who had never been a wife, who had no family and not even a religion here to shelter her.

She'd been very young when she realized her gift for "seeing." She'd seen her village's destruction in a vision years before it had happened, had known that she would never have her own home, that one day she would be here, at the edge of the world.

"And I knew I would meet you again. Do you remember me telling you?"

Margaret nodded, still astonished that the woman was here and had not aged in the years since she'd been at Somerstrath. That she'd remembered Margaret. "I remember every word ye told me."

The woman smiled serenely. "As I do. Ye have grown well, Margaret of Somerstrath. Strong. You'll have need of that strength."

"Oh, aye. Dragons," Margaret said.

The woman smiled again but said nothing.

"What can ye tell me now of the future?"

"That it is almost here."

Margaret stared at the woman, trying to suppress the sharp rejoinder that had come to mind. "Aye," she said. "And?"

"That yer life will change in ways ye cannot imagine. That you and I will meet once again before I die. And that Judith at Brenmargon does not do well to mock me. I do not mock her faith."

Margaret stared at her. Nell, she decided. Somehow Nell had talked to her.

"It was not Nell," the woman said now. "Nor your brother."

"Then how . . . ?"

"You might as well ask me how I feel the wind, child. I cannot tell you, only that I know what I know. Judith fears what she does not understand. There is great comfort in a life without questions. She is told what to believe, and she helps others to believe the same. Still, her faith is real, and I will not mock it."

Margaret began a heated reply, then swallowed it. How could this woman know Judith? Had Uncle William talked with her?

"Still a skeptic, I see." The woman smiled. "I will tell you this, Margaret, and it will have to do. We will meet at a court that is not a court, and you will be with a man who is not yours, but who is only yours. Yours will be a life unlike others', but like so many others through the ages, women who are born at a turning point in time. May you be wise enough to see the path."

"Can I change it?"

The old woman laughed softly, her eyes merry now. "Of course. But then, the change will have been predetermined, will it not?"

"By . . . ?"

"Call it God. Or the Fates. Or Destiny. Or whatever you choose. If God is all-powerful, then He has planned this, has He not? And if the Fates determine your fate, then are the Fates not truly God by another name? Does it matter what the force is that moves our lives forward?"

"Yes."

"No, it does not. Know this, child. You must choose in the dark. And may God protect you."

"How can you believe in God?"

"How can I not when the evidence of Him is all around us?"

The old woman began to move away. Margaret hurried after her, catching sight of Nell waiting by the gate to the garden. "Please," she said. "Please tell me. Will I marry Lachlan?"

The woman looked into the distance, then at Margaret. "Yes. And no."

"That makes no sense."

"You scoff, child. The next time we meet you will understand."

"But how can the answer be yes and no? Will the king help me?"

"He will listen."

"But will he help?"

"The decision is yours alone. But every choice has a price."

Margaret shook her head in frustration. Every answer was a riddle. "And what of the golden man?"

"He waits."

"Is he Jesus? Is he here?"

"Choose wisely, child. See what is there, not what you wish to see."

"What about the dragons?"

"You will face them."

"Where? When?"

"As it is ordained."

The woman waved her hand in farewell and left Margaret staring after her. *He waits.* She stood for the longest time, her mind spinning, watching first the old woman disappear through the gate, then Nell slowly approach, her steps slow and her expression thoughtful. Behind Nell were two of the Comyn women, not the nicest two, who giggled behind their hands as they strolled through the garden. Margaret did not want to talk with them, to pretend that her mood was unruffled. She whirled around, to stare over the land far below, at the river winding through the marshland, a thin mist hanging over the water. That was her life, she thought, a course already determined but not visible. She forced back her tears. In the last fortnight she'd lost her betrothed and her dearest friend. Now she was apparently losing her mind as well. She let her head fall back and stared into the clouds. What was she to do? How would she know what was right? Did she have a choice in any of it, or was it, as the woman had said, already ordained and she only a pawn of the Fates? Were all people simply that?

"Margaret?" Nell's voice held a new note. "Are ye a'right?"

"No. I am not. And I dinna have the slightest idea how to change that."

"Nor am I," Nell said softly. "I have to tell ye what just happened."

Five days passed as one, the events of each melding together into an undifferentiable mix. Margaret talked to Uncle William about her dilemma, but found no help there.

"He has wealth and the ear of the king," her uncle said, his voice full of affection. "In time ye'll understand how important both are. Ye need to look past small concerns. Surely, Margaret, ye've realized that any children ye and Lachlan have will be cousins to the king and to his children."

When she told Rignor what William said, he nodded.

"What he says makes sense," her brother said. "Ye

may not like it, but we both should listen. When I am Somerstrath I'll need allies at court, Margaret."

"I see ye've decided for me then."

Rignor shook his head slowly. "I canna, nor would I. And I understand yer anger. But . . ." He shrugged. "We've been naive. No one here marries for anything but gain. Perhaps we should do the same. Look around."

Margaret did look around. She watched the men at court, studying them to see if a golden man were among them, but so many were richly dressed, so many wore as much gold as Lachlan, rings and brooches at their shoulders, that it was impossible to pick one. Some of the men paid outrageous attention to her, offering eternal love and asking for an hour alone, as though it were a game and she the prize. An hour, she knew, in which she would trade her body for flattering phrases. She laughed with them, flirted and pretended to consider their requests, then left them without another thought. There were other men, some older, some widowed with children about whom they spoke, their quest for a wife and mother obvious. She spoke kindly with them, seeing sometimes lust, sometimes simply loneliness, in their eyes. There was not one she would marry.

At night, when the court gathered in the hall, she joined the dancers, trying to learn the intricate steps of unfamiliar dances. She was a popular partner, not only for the dances, but for conversation, which she joined with alacrity, hoping to find someone in the crowds here. But none touched her, not her body, not her mind, and each night she went to her bed knowing she'd failed, that there were not two men here for her and Nell, that her great plan was in tatters. He waits, she thought; but apparently not here.

She pinned all her hopes on the audience with the

king that William had promised to try to attain. And on the sixth day, she was summoned.

When the page came for her, she stood frozen in a mixture of disbelief and fear. She'd spent so much time waiting and preparing her petition to the king, but now she stared at the boy with not an idea in her head of how to present her case. She followed him along the corridors, careful as they passed the stone walls being built and pulling her skirts back from the wooden walls full of mold and splinters that lined the passageway.

The worst of it was that Lachlan had been so very repentant and so charming these last few days at Stirling. How could she expect anyone to see him as she did? How to explain this to King Alexander and Queen Margaret, whose own arranged marriage was, by all accounts, a very happy one? Not at first, if the stories were true, but within a few years. And certainly now that they were parents. But try she must, if for no other reason than her own peace of mind. If she failed here, she'd have years to review it. How could she bear not having tried at all?

The room she was brought to was not large, but well lit, the afternoon sun pouring through the luxury of glassed windows, making the colors of the enormous rug that covered most of the floor vibrant, and lighting the hangings that closed off the corridors that led to the royal apartments, the golden threads in the silk shining in the diffused light. She'd hoped for a private audience, but the room was crowded with people, all watching her entrance.

King Alexander was seated in a large wooden chair, not really a throne, but tall and painted with the royal crest of Scotland, the scarlet lion rampant above his head. He was dressed simply, his robes beautifully cut, of fine material, but not ornate. Queen Margaret, looking even more regal than her husband, was seated on a smaller but far more ornate chair, which bent around her as if to protect her from the world. Her clothing was simple as well, but her overgown was trimmed with golden thread and the coif on her head banded with gemstones. Her waiting women, many of them Comyns, were gathered together like a well-dressed phalanx of guards, their expressions amused and expectant, as though they were about to be entertained. Very near them, dressed in his finest, was Lachlan, who bent low to her, his bow perfect, his eyes unreadable. Uncle William smiled at her warmly, but Rignor's expression betrayed his unease. When he would not meet her gaze, her heart pounded more heavily. Margaret's curtsy was awkward at best, but neither the king nor queen seemed to notice. Alexander gave Lachlan a glance, and Queen Margaret studied Margaret's person, her gaze lingering on Margaret's face, but missing no detail in its journey to her feet. At this distance Margaret was able to see how young both the king and queen were, just a few years older than she. Alexander smiled now, and the knot in her stomach loosened a bit.

"Yer Majesty," Margaret said, appalled at the croak her voice had become.

"I present my niece, Yer Majesties," William said, coming forward to join her. "My sister's child. Margaret of Somerstrath."

The king's smile widened. "Welcome, Margaret. Your father is a loyal man who keeps the west safe for Us. We are grateful for his efforts."

"Aye, Yer Majesty," Margaret said. "He does his best."

The titters of laughter around her made her cheeks

flush. With only a handful of words she'd shown her lack of sophistication.

"My father keeps the shoreline strong," she said, raising her chin.

"And does it well, from what I've heard," Alexander said, with another glance at Lachlan. "But that is not why you've come to visit Us, is it?"

"My niece asks for yer attention for just a few moments," William said.

The king nodded and gestured to Lachlan. "Our cousin has explained it to us. And apologized to you, I understand. Is that so, Margaret?"

She nodded. "It is, Yer Majesty."

Lachlan moved forward now, putting a hand on Margaret's elbow. He smiled at the king and bowed again. "By your leave, Cousin."

The king nodded, and Lachlan continued, smiling down at Margaret.

"I've offended her with my behavior. But I am determined to change that." He threw a glance over his shoulder at Queen Margaret's women. "As the Comyn women have told me, I must be a good husband to have one of their own. Her uncle, the Earl of Ross has done the same, as has Margaret's father. And I have listened well. I do remind them, and Margaret, that we are not yet wed. I have broken no vow."

"I ask . . ." Margaret began, quickly silenced by a gesture from William.

"By yer leave, Yer Majesty, " William said. "Margaret would like to speak."

At the king's nod, all eyes turned toward her. Margaret swallowed, then removed her elbow from Lachlan's grasp.

"I ask Yer Majesty to release me from the betrothal made so many years ago. We . . . are not well suited, and I ask that we not be forced to marry." She ignored the muffled laughter of the listeners. She knew how simple she sounded, but could not seem to remedy it. She felt a wave of cold wash over her, followed by another of violent heat, her cheeks no doubt scarlet.

"You are aware," the king said, "that your betrothal was determined years ago by those who had only your best interests in mind? This alliance will strengthen your father's family and my holdings in the west?"

"I am sure that is so, Yer Highness, but . . ."

Queen Margaret leaned forward, her tone kind. "You realize, of course, that my marriage to King Alexander was arranged?" She glanced at the king fondly. "It is possible to find happiness and comfort in such an arrangement."

The king smiled at his queen, and Margaret knew she was lost. Alexander waved his hand dismissively. "You are young, Margaret, and lovely. Surely Lachlan will attend you well."

Lachlan's smile was triumphant. "I will indeed, Yer Majesty."

Margaret threw her brother a look of appeal, but Rignor avoided her gaze, the flush on his cheeks the only sign that he knew she'd turned to him.

"But . . ." Margaret said, her words fading to silence as William whispered to her to curtsy, which she did.

The next few moments were a blur. Somehow she was bundled out of the hall, Lachlan and William at her side and Rignor nowhere in sight.

"Well, ye did it," Lachlan whispered. "Humiliated both of us. And for what?"

"Enough, Lachlan," William said coldly.

"That's it?" Margaret asked, her tears beginning to fall. "That's all the time I'm given with them? I dinna even get to talk. I dinna get to explain . . ."

"Ye said enough to shame the both of us," Lachlan said.

"That's enough!" William said.

Lachlan sneered at both of them. "I'm adult enough to live up to my obligations. Ye should do the same."

Margaret raised her chin but could not speak before Lachlan walked away.

He paused at the door. "I'll be sending for Fiona after we're wed. Ye'll be needing a companion." He left them staring after him.

They were silent for a moment, then William sighed heavily. "I've received word from home that I've visitors from Ireland awaiting me. I'll be leaving in the morning. I'll send men back for ye in a week, unless ye wish to spend the rest of the summer here. The Comyns have said they'll be happy to have ye stay."

Aye, for entertainment, Margaret thought, but did not say that to him. William was fond of his wife's family, and in truth, the Comyn women had been very kind. It was not their fault that she'd failed at her one chance with the king.

Nell was not pleased to leave before dawn, was not even sure why her uncle had hurried away, his face creased with worry. Problems in the north was all he'd said, but weren't there always problems somewhere? The past week had been most frustrating. She'd tried in vain to find Liam Crawford, or even anyone who had more than passing knowledge of him, but it was as though she'd conjured the man. She'd tried to find the old woman as well, but was thwarted there, too, told that the seer rarely left the royal apartments and no longer gave readings for the public.

Margaret had withdrawn from her since her audience with the king and queen, had said only that she'd failed, that instead of pleading her case with well-chosen words, she'd merely stood there like a ninny while Lachlan assured Alexander and Queen Margaret that he'd be the perfect husband. They didn't care whom Margaret married. Why would they? Nell thought Margaret's self-chastisement unnecessary; she did not believe that anything Margaret could have said would have made any difference.

Nell wished they weren't going home. What would happen now? Her sister would continue to defy her parents, and they would be furious. She'd asked Margaret several times what she meant to do, but her sister had little to say. Rignor was even less communicative. He rode with the Somerstrath men and avoided Margaret, who treated him coldly. Nell asked why, but neither would tell her anything.

The ride was easy, both the weather and ponies cooperating to make their journey west swift, as though God Himself were hurrying them home. Uncle William's men received messages from him twice, and they talked with Rignor in serious tones. She didn't need to be told that something had happened on Uncle's William's lands, nor that Margaret and Rignor had argued. Good thing she could see that for herself, because no one told her anything. She was treated like a child.

Except by Liam Crawford, who seemed to know that her body and mind were not the same age. She ignored

Margaret and Rignor then, losing herself in imagining how the two of them would become . . . what had he said? . . . well acquainted. Nell *Crawford*. She wished she could grow up more quickly.

Margaret took no comfort in their rapid progress west. She tried not to think, simply to be, to notice the heather's bright blooms on every hillside, how it crept up the sides of the mountains, lighting the darkest glens with its purples and bright hues. To see the trees filling more every day with pale green leaves, to hear the wind sighing through the pines, always a favorite sound, and the sights of summer in full flower. To feel the temperature drop as they followed the path into the shadowed Pass of Brenmargon, knowing she'd sleep that night at Brenmargon Abbey and that William's men would leave them to make the rest of their way home alone.

Rignor would not tell her what William's troubles were, and she'd been too proud to beg him for the news. She had better become accustomed to being ignored if she was about to become a wife. She sighed, thinking of how inadequate she'd been in her interview with the king. After all those speeches in her head, she'd failed. She should have heeded the raven that had screeched its warning as they'd left Somerstrath. This trip had been ill-starred from the beginning.

Judith's welcome that night at Brenmargon Abbey was as warm as ever, her hospitality frugal but adequate. After the others had found their beds, Judith gave her a long lecture about using the abbey as a place to hide from the world. Margaret kept her answers civil, but when at last she found her bed her heart was sore. Everyone, it seemed, had an opinion about her life and felt compelled to share it. And tomorrow, at home, her parents would tell her theirs.

William's men left them the next day to make the rest of their way home alone. Margaret, Nell, and Rignor lingered at the shielings, enjoying the warm sunlight and telling the Somerstrath people there all the news of court. Most of it. Margaret kept her disappointment with her visit to court, and herself, to herself.

Her pony smelled it before she did, and shied to the side of the track, causing Margaret to grip its mane with both hands. She could see no reason for its unease, but around her the other ponies were raising their heads and sniffing the air, and soon she, too, caught a whiff. Smoke. And something more, something foul and frightening. What was it?

She met Rignor's gaze over Nell's head. He raised his eyebrows and shrugged. She took a deep breath and coughed. The smell grew worse as they headed into the trees that clogged the glen east of the village, and the ponies' agitation increased.

Rignor, his brows drawn together now, took the lead. At the top of the rise that led down to Somerstrath, Rignor suddenly thrust out his arm, preventing anyone from moving forward. He stared down at the village, then turned to Margaret, his eyes wild. He pointed, his mouth working but no sound issuing from it. The smell was stronger now, the stench unlike anything she'd ever smelled before, of wood and something she could not identify. With a pounding heart she nudged her pony forward.

"It's all gone," Rignor whispered. "Gone."

SIX

The keep still stood, but its roof was now a smoldering mass. The walls of the village near the harbor had been breached, the gates battered open. Sections of it lay on the ground, barely visible under the bodies that littered it. The villagers' houses lining the pathway to the harbor had been burned, or lay open like broken eggshells.

The harbor was empty; her father's ships, drawn up on the shingle, were charred humps, not recognizable except by their long shapes. There were people everywhere, lying in pools of blood in the broken houses and in knots on the shore. Nothing moved in the wreckage below. The guards moved up to see, their harsh cries and strangled gasps loud in the sudden silence.

Margaret put a hand to her throat. "Oh dear God."

Nell screamed when she saw what lay below. "The head on the beach."

Margaret forced herself to be calm and look again. *Think.* Perhaps some of the people had escaped. Perhaps not all those lying below were dead; perhaps some needed tending. Perhaps her mother and father and their brothers were alive, waiting to be found, needing her help. She looked into Rignor's eyes, saw his fear, and felt her own fear swell.

"We have to go down there." Her voice shook. "Mother and Father . . . what if they're waiting for us, hoping we'll come?"

"Aye," Rignor said, then turned to the guards. "Stay here with Nell."

"My father is down there, sir," one said. "I'll no' stay here and wonder."

"I'm not staying here alone," Nell said.

Margaret and Rignor exchanged a glance.

"Then stay behind me," Margaret told Nell. "Be ready to run if I tell ye."

Nell nodded, her eyes huge. Rignor drew his sword from its sheath; Margaret did the same. It was little defense against the horror that lay ahead, but she'd been trained to use it, and if any of the beasts that had done this remained, she'd be ready to take them on. Behind her she heard Nell draw her dagger, and the guards grabbed their swords.

They moved slowly down the hill, through the inland gates, hanging open but intact. The outermost houses still stood, but even here, far from the harbor, there were none without damage. They paused, listening.

Overhead the wind blew, harder now, bringing clouds and the promise of rain. Somewhere, out of sight, a door banged open, then shut. There was no other sound. No laughter coming from the houses, no children's songs, no scolding or arguing, no quiet conversation. No dogs barked. Nothing.

She'd been wrong. The head on the beach had indeed been an omen, a portent of evil on the way. She took a deep breath and immediately regretted it as her lungs filled with smoke-filled air, and that dreadful, sickening smell she had not been able to identify earlier. She now knew what it was—the stench of burned human flesh, of roasted wool and timbers. The smell of the immolation of her home and everything she loved.

Rignor slid from his pony and stepped away from it, his sword held high. The guards did the same. As did Margaret, facing the closest house with a mixture of fear and dread and shameful hope that there would be nothing horrible to see, that when they entered people would be there, cowering, perhaps, but safe. Rignor pushed the door open with his fingertips, ready to spring back if necessary. His caution was not needed; there was no one to leap out, no one waiting to attack. He stood in the doorway for a moment, then backed away and vomited into the dirt.

One of the guards looked in and stared, turning to Margaret at last, his face unnaturally pale. "My father . . . I have to find . . ." he stammered, then ran down the hill.

The others seemed to melt away after him. Margaret did not have the heart to call them back. She knew each wife, each child, each parent they sought and feared she knew what they would find.

"What is it?" Nell asked at Margaret's elbow.

Margaret shook her head. Rignor wiped his mouth and stared at the house.

"Stay back," she said to Nell, then pushed the door open. There were two women here, three children. All were dead. The women had been brutally raped, their bodies bearing mute testimony of what had been done to them. An infant had died in its cradle. The two small children huddled together in a corner, their hands still gripping each other.

She heard her own groan, an incoherent sound of horror, and stumbled out of the house, her hand over her mouth. Rignor stood in the doorway of the next house, and turned now to face her, his expression ravaged.

"What is it?" Nell's voice was terrified. "Margaret . . . ?"

"Dinna look!" Margaret said, grabbing Nell's arm as her sister moved toward the doorway. "Dinna look in there!"

"Are they dead?" Nell whispered.

"Aye. God help us all, aye."

House after house was the same. Men had died in the streets, their weapons still in their hands. Some had died running away, others fighting at the doorway of their homes. No one had been spared—women and children had died by the score, some in their beds, some cut down wherever they stood. Margaret stumbled down the hill behind Rignor. They checked every house. They found no one alive.

Don't think, don't think, don't think.

They stopped before what had once been the gate-house, staring at the still-smoldering roof of the keep. *Don't think, don't think, don't think.* The chant ran through her mind, but thought was already very difficult. There was a roaring in her ears, almost like the sea. She no longer even saw the bodies of the men who had died here, simply stepped over the fallen who lay strewn across the stone courtyard and in the storeroom that had been the ground floor. Rignor waited at the foot of the stairs, dark and silent, that led to the private apartments. No one challenged them; there was no pounding of boots down the stairs to see who had entered.

Nell was shaking and clutched Margaret's arm convulsively, bringing her back to the present. Margaret already knew what they would find upstairs, and Nell must not see any of it. She opened the door to the tiny storeroom that held the guards' weapons, sending a prayer of thanks for its emptiness. She thrust her sister into the small space.

"Stay here," she said, pushing Nell to the back of the room.

"No!" Nell clutched at her. "Dinna leave me here! Dinna leave me alone!"

"You must stay here. I will come back for ye, I swear it. Dinna make a sound. If anyone comes, be silent. Do ye understand? Ye must be quiet."

Nell nodded mutely.

Margaret nodded in return, then joined Rignor. In the stairwell she clutched the walls as she climbed, taking stairs two or three at a time to avoid stepping on someone. There were dead on every step. Some she could no longer recognize, but others were men—and boys—with whom she'd spoken every day of her life, their faces all too familiar even in death.

Don't think, don't think, don't think.

They found their father's body at last, on the stairs that led to the family's quarters, killed along with his men. Margaret knelt beside him, taking his lifeless hand in her own, willing his heart to beat, his staring eyes to find her gaze. She wanted his mouth, clenched in a grimace, to move, to tell her it was all a sham. That none of this was real, that it was all a dream from which she'd wake. That such evil had not been done in the course of one summer's day.

"Is he . . . ?" Rignor's sword clanked against the wall, his face the same color as the stone. "Is he . . . ?"

Margaret nodded, and Rignor crumbled for a moment. Then they climbed the last few steps to their parents' chamber together, hoping against hope, but there was no hope this day. They were all here. Their mother lay on the floor on her back, her skirts bundled at her waist. She, like all the other women, had been raped, her legs askew. Rignor gasped and staggered backward into a corner with an animal-like moan, but Margaret, the roaring in her ears growing louder, leaned to pull her mother's clothing over her still-swollen belly, to smooth the hair, sticky with blood, from her mother's forehead.

Inghinn, her father's mistress, who had also been brutalized, lay in a corner, her baby's body not far away. They had died together, these rivals for her father's affections, tied now in death as they had been in life.

Don't think, don't think, don't think.

She turned slowly to see the rest. Her brothers had died together as well, Ewan in the forefront, his small sword still in his clenched hand. Cawley was on the bed, little Fergus tucked into the farthermost corner, his eyes closed and his mouth open in a silent scream.

She sank to the ground, closing her eyes against the sights before her.

Don't think, don't think, don't think.

Nell was so afraid. How could Margaret have left her alone? She shivered and hugged her arms around herself. It was so quiet. She'd been waiting a very long time, huddled here in this tiny room, watching the dead men in the courtyard. She was afraid to open the door wider, but even more frightened of being alone in the dark with the images she'd seen on her way through the village.

Where was her father? Nell asked herself for the hundredth time, and for the hundredth time stopped herself. She could think of no reason her father would not be with his men—and his men were all dead. And if her father were dead—what then had happened to her mother and brothers? Where were Margaret and Rignor? Had they forgotten her? She shivered in the dark, afraid to stay, afraid to go.

A movement at the far side of the courtyard made her shrink back into the shadows. Was one of the dead men rising? But no, the man who bent low and scurried across the stones with a sword in his hand was very much alive. She released her breath as she recognized one of the guards who had accompanied them. He paused, looking over his shoulder, then moved forward again, his expression intent. When he came into the guardroom, Nell stepped forward, calling his name.

"Jesu!" The guard lowered his sword and blew out a huff of air, then glanced over his shoulder again. "Where is yer brother?"

Nell pointed to the stairwell. "Up there. With Margaret."

"They've come back, miss. We have to get out of here."

Nell stared at him, unable to speak.

"Go and get Rignor, will ye, lassie? I'll make sure they dinna get past me."

She nodded and moved to the stairwell, but paused with her foot on the first step. "What about yer father?"

"Dead, lassie. Now go get yer brother and sister. We dinna ha' much time."

The first few steps were clear, but as she came around the first curve, she found the men of her father's personal guard. She gasped, willing herself to keep climbing, stepping over the bodies, concentrating on finding a path through the arms and legs and blood that blocked her way.

Her father lay on his back, surrounded by his most trusted men. Nell stared at him for several moments, her mind frozen, before she was able to move past. She was sobbing when she reached her mother's room.

Margaret lay huddled on the floor, her back to the door. For a horrible moment Nell thought Margaret was dead, too, but as she crept closer, she could see that her sister was crying, her cheek pressed against the wood. Rignor was near the window, and turned to her now, his face streaked with tears. And then she saw her mother and brothers. She screamed, then screamed again. And again.

Nell's screams roused Margaret from the oblivion she'd sought. She rose to her feet with a hoarse cry and drew her sister into her arms, rocking Nell until she calmed. Over Nell's head, Margaret stared at her brothers. Ewan, brave little Ewan, who had tried to hold back death with a ten-inch blade. And Cawley. And Fergus, who broke her heart. She caught her breath, then looked again.

"Davey," she said.

Rignor turned to her with a puzzled frown.

She pointed. "Davey's not there."

They all stared at the bed.

"Margaret!" Rignor cried. "He's not here!"

"Look under the bed," Margaret said, spinning to look where else in the room an eight-year-old could be hiding. The draperies had been torn from the window, the bedhangings from the bedframe. The clothes chests gaped open and empty. There was nowhere else to look. Rignor looked under the bed, then sat back on his heels and shook his head.

"Rignor," said a male voice. "Sir."

Margaret stared at the guard in the doorway. She'd forgotten about him. He glanced around the room, his face paling as he took it all in.

"We have to go. Now. They've come back. They're coming through the village now."

They rushed down the stairs, hoping to leave the keep and run inland, but when the guard peeked out the arrow slit, he said the men were closer.

Rignor looked. "We willna get out before they're here. We'll have to hide."

"In the storeroom," Margaret said. "Where Nell was."

On the ground floor they hurried into the storeroom, huddling together in the small space. Margaret prayed silently that the darkness would protect them. The storeroom door would not close without noise, so they left it partially open, affording her a view of the entrance. And then they waited.

It was not a moment too soon. She'd just tightened her grip on Nell and caught her breath when a man paused in the doorway.

He filled the opening. His shoulders were wide, his waist trim; the top of his head was well above the doorjamb. In his right hand was a long sword, its steel gleaming; in his belt was a battle-axe. A leather shield was slung over his shoulder, its leather band across his chest. Around his strong neck a golden torque gleamed against tanned skin. His clothing was simple: a long linen tunic over trousers, a cloak pinned by a golden brooch, leather boots. The tunic was bound by a leather belt that pulled the cloth against his lean torso. His trousers were tapered at the ankle and tightly fitted against his thighs. His hair was pulled back from his brow, cascading over his shoulders, long and blond. His eyes were dark and stared into the guardroom.

He moved his head as though listening, and she caught her breath as the light hit his face, highlighting strong cheekbones and jawline, the hollows of his cheeks. He was fearsome. Breathtaking. A Norseman. A Viking. A murderer.

Only the barbaric Norse would have done this. The head on the beach had been a warning that none of them had heeded, its blond hair a sign of those who would come with death as their purpose. No one had understood the danger it had heralded. And now one of the murderers stood here, drawn no doubt by Nell's screams. Rignor took a shaky breath, and behind him the guard shifted his weight.

Be silent. Don't breathe. Don't move. Don't think.

The Viking lifted his sword and stepped inside, glancing around before turning his gaze to the storeroom. He stared at it for what seemed an eternity, then at last looked toward the stairs. If he went up them, Margaret thought, perhaps they could sneak out into the courtyard . . . but her hopes of escape were dashed when yet another Viking appeared in the doorway, others visible behind him. The first man said something too low for her to hear, and the second nodded, relaying the message to the others. Four men entered the ground floor, and others moved outside.

Is this how we are to die?

The second Viking looked up the stairwell, then spoke quietly. The first man nodded, turning his gaze to the storeroom door once again. He raised his sword. And moved out of sight. Margaret's heart leapt in terror. There was nothing on that side of the guardroom to hold his interest, but from there he could come closer to their hiding place. The second man disappeared behind the storeroom door.

Dear God, dear God, protect us . . .

There was silence then, a long moment when no one moved. Margaret was sure the Vikings could hear her heart pounding. Nell sucked in her breath, the tiniest inhalation of air that seemed to reverberate off the walls. Margaret heard the scrape of leather on stone as one of the Vikings shifted his weight, then silence yet again.

A hand came from the side of the doorway, a long arm clothed in linen, a band of gold around his wrist, carved with Norse runes. Long fingers gripped Nell's clothing and yanked her, screaming, out of the storeroom. Nell screamed again as the Viking clasped her to him. He frowned fiercely as she struggled in his arms, kicking and raining ineffectual blows on his head. The door was pulled open wide, and the second Viking stood there, almost as tall and blond as the first.

There was no time to think, no time to talk to her brother, to form a plan. Margaret leapt from the storeroom to help Nell, her short sword raised high, her cries wordless. Behind her Rignor and the guard were shouting curses and taking on the others, but Margaret could see only this one man, huge and angry, Nell caught in his grip. He shifted her sister to his left side and faced

Margaret, his sword scything through the air with a whistling sound, not touching her, but holding her where she was.

She saw his surprise when he looked at her. She swung her sword through the air, hoping to use his surprise to her advantage, but he leaned back, out of her reach. And waited. Nell, clutched in his left arm, struggled and screamed, the sound piercing in the small space. Margaret swiped at him again. He slashed out to block her blow, his long sword meeting hers with a shivering clang that she felt up her entire arm. He did not seem to feel it.

There were no more sounds of battle from behind her, but Margaret dared not turn to see if Rignor still lived. Someone breathed heavily, and she prayed that it was her brother. Two of the Vikings moved closer to the one before her, and he thrust Nell toward them. They grabbed her, holding her between them, but the Viking did not watch. He kept his gaze on Margaret.

And then, with no warning, swept his blade through the air to land at her throat. His arm was longer, his sword longer than hers; she could not reach him without risking being impaled, and she saw that knowledge in his eyes.

"Let her go!" Margaret cried. "Release her, ye filthy murderer!"

He leaned forward, and Nell screamed.

SEVEN

"Oh, please, sir, dinna hurt Margaret!" Nell cried, sobbing now. The Viking looked into Margaret's eyes. "Give me yer sword," he said slowly in Gaelic, as if he thought she would not understand him. He had an accent, but with so few words she could not tell more than that.

His voice and tone surprised her. Did Vikings sound like this, like ordinary men? Did they speak her language?

"We mean ye no harm. Give me yer sword."

"Dinna trust him, Margaret!" Rignor shouted. "No harm, Norseman? Ye hold a sword to my sister's throat while the rest of ye hold us back. If this is no harm, I'll have none of it."

"Ye have no choice," the Viking growled.

Rignor lunged forward with a roar, struggling with the other Vikings. His attempts were short-lived; he was easily subdued again. The Viking before her had not watched, keeping his attention instead on her. He reached for Margaret's sword again with his left arm, this wrist banded in gold as well. "Give me the sword."

She could not move. She took a shallow breath, wondering if it would be her last. He could have killed her already if he'd chosen to, this giant who stood before her, his long, lean fingers wrapped around the sword at her throat. His arm did not waver, nor did his intent gaze, except for the flash of anger there, quickly subdued. She had no doubt that he could dispatch her in a moment if he chose. Was this how her mother and brothers had felt at the end? Had they looked into their murderer's eyes and known what would come next? Could death come in this guise, with a face like this, a form that was so pleasing? A man who looked like an avenging angel?

"Prove that ye mean us no harm," Rignor shouted. "Take yer sword from her throat, Norseman."

The blond man spoke without moving his gaze from Margaret's. "I'm no Norseman. I am of Ireland." His voice was melodic, lilting. His gaze searched her face, studying it. His tone softened. "Give me the sword, lass. Please. By all the saints, I swear I willna harm ye."

His accent was Irish. She stared at him, at his Irish clothing. His brooch was decorated in the Celtic manner, with enameled carvings of fanciful animals. His tone was mild; his hair, illuminated by the light from the door, was a halo around his head. His eyes were a deep blue and held no hint of trickery. But there was an axe at his waist and the hilt of his sword was decorated with Norse runes. He wore Norse wristbands. The torque and his clothing might have been looted from the Irish.

Her voice was a whisper. "Ye look like a Norseman."

"Aye, I ken I do. But I'm not. I will not harm ye." He stepped closer. "I give ye my word on that, Margaret of Somerstrath."

He'd remembered her name. She looked away, unnerved even more, then back into those blue, blue eyes. "Who are ye, and why are ye here?"

"My name is Gannon MacMagnus." He wrapped his hand around hers, pushing her sword to the side, his touch gentle. "We mean ye no harm. I give ye my word."

"And will ye give me yer word that ye willna harm my sister and brother, nor any of our people, nor will ye let yer men harm them?"

His sudden smile was mocking. "Ye're hardly in a position to bargain . . ."

He stopped talking as a large man paused in the doorway, then stepped into the room. The man's beard was gray under his helmet. He was tall and heavy, his leather padding tight over his round stomach. He wore a golden torque, much like Gannon's, and golden rings on his fingers. He pulled off his helmet with a weary gesture and ran his hand through his graying chestnut hair. "Did ye find Somerstrath?"

Margaret let out the breath she'd not even realized she'd been holding. *Rory O'Neill. Praise God.* O'Neill had been her father's ally for decades, her grandfather's ally before that. When she was a girl, he'd visited Somerstrath several times. Then he'd been the emissary from an important family in Ireland. Now he was powerful in his own right, despite the Norman earls, as the overlord and chief of Ulster, in the north of Ireland. Why was he here? And was it possible, as dreadful as it was to imagine, that his men had done this? But why would he? It made no sense. He wiped his eyes, and the knot in her chest began to loosen. The Rory O'Neill she had known would not murder and weep at the same time.

"How many have ye found?" he asked Gannon, then

threw a glance at Margaret, taking in Gannon's blade at her throat. "Is she dangerous?"

Gannon stepped back from her, sheathing his sword, his color suddenly heightened. "Only these."

O'Neill's gaze turned to Margaret again, his expression changing from weary to relieved. "Ah, I dinna see who it was. Thank God ye're alive. Where's yer da?"

"My father is dead," Rignor said. "Our whole family is dead, save my sisters and me. I am Rignor MacDonald, and these are my sisters Margaret and Nell."

"I ken who ye are," O'Neill said. "Ye've grown, the three of ye, but we've met before. I'm Rory O'Neill . . ."

"We ken who ye are. An ally, or so we believed. Why do ye attack us?"

O'Neill raised an eyebrow. "We dinna, lad. We've only just arrived."

"Our home was attacked, and ye are here. If ye dinna do this, then why do ye have Norsemen with ye?"

O'Neill followed Rignor's gaze to Gannon. "I don't. That's Gannon MacMagnus." He gestured to the second Viking. "That's his brother Tiernan. They're cousins of mine."

Margaret could see the resemblance between the brothers now. Both were tall, lean, with the same cheekbones and very blue eyes. And both were displeased.

"Why should we believe ye?" Rignor demanded, "I'll say it again: We were attacked. Ye are here. Tell me why I shouldna accuse ye of it?"

O'Neill drew himself up, his choler obvious. "I'll warn ye not to say that again."

"Ye have only to look at us," Gannon said tersely. "We have two hundred men with us. Ye'll find no signs of battle on any of them, no dead or wounded. Ye couldn't have this much fighting without both sides having losses."

Rignor thrust his chin out belligerently. "We found no dead but our own. How d'ye account for that?"

"I'm thinking they took their dead."

"Why would they?"

"Perhaps it's to keep ye from kenning who did it."

O'Neill made a sharp gesture. "We didn't attack ye, for God's sake, Rignor."

"Then why are ye here?"

"There were attacks on the coast in Ireland, in Antrim. I came to ask yer uncle William's help in discovering what he kent of them and found he'd had two attacks on his own land and was about to send word to me. He asked us to come here on our way home and tell yer da of it all. We found Somerstrath burning and dead men on the beach and came to see if anyone still lived. It's as simple as that."

There was a silence then, while Rignor and O'Neill stared at each other. When Rignor looked away, O'Neill nodded to himself. "Who was screaming?"

"Nell," Rignor said, his bravado gone. "She . . . saw my mother. Upstairs."

O'Neill glanced at the stairwell. "Ah."

Gannon watched Margaret, his blue eyes solemn and his face without expression. She looked away, still feeling his gaze on her.

"How many of yer people are left?" O'Neill asked.

"We've found no one," Rignor said. "We've just come from inland ourselves. We found all as ye see it, but we've not been down to the harbor or the lower village."

"There is no one alive down there," Gannon said.

Margaret raised a hand to her throat. It was impossible to believe that no one had survived. "Did ye look through all the houses?"

O'Neill nodded. "Aye, lass. There's no one left alive. They came from the sea, as they did in Antrim, and on yer uncle's lands."

"Norsemen," Rignor said, looking at Gannon.

Gannon crossed his arms over his chest. A wide chest, Margaret noted, and strong arms. A formidable man, his expression displeased. Rignor, she thought, would be wise not to antagonize him. She threw her brother a glance of caution, and he nodded almost imperceptibly. She turned back, to find Gannon watching her, and felt her cheeks color.

"Wait outside," O'Neill said to Rignor in a tone that brooked no arguments. He waved some of his men forward, then nodded at Gannon and Tiernan to follow him, cautiously leading the way up the stairs.

Rignor stalked outside into the courtyard, past O'Neill's men. Margaret and Nell followed. The courtyard was filled with Irishmen who stood in small groups, some blocking the gate, their manner making it plain that no one would leave. Margaret wrapped an arm around Nell and waited, trying not to visualize what O'Neill and the others would find.

"D'ye think we can trust them?" Nell whispered.

"Father did," Margaret whispered back, looking up at the keep, at the gray stones that had become a tomb. At the window of the room she shared with Nell, where now a tall blond man stood, looking down at her, his expression grim. She tore her gaze away. "I dinna ken, Nell. But what choice do we have?"

The sky darkened in the few moments it took them to

look through the keep, the wind cooling as it came off the sea. Night, such as it was, was coming. She looked away from the building as she heard the Irishmen pound down the stairs. They paused on the ground floor, their conversation hushed. She could hear O'Neill's gruff voice, but not the words, and Gannon's answer, terse and angry. Angry, she thought, feeling her own temper rise. What need had he of anger? It was not his family who lay dead, not his people decimated, not his home defiled. Why would Gannon MacMagnus be angry? But he was, for when he came through the doorway his expression was harsh, his mouth set in a firm frown, his eyes cold.

"I am sorry for all those ye've lost this day," O'Neill said, coming to her. "We've some daylight left. We'll take ye to yer uncle. Ross will need to ken what's happened here."

"We canna leave! We must stay!" Margaret cried. "Our brother Davey—he's only eight years old—we canna find him. He may be hiding; he may be waiting until ye all leave to come out. We canna leave until we find him! And we must bury our family, and all the others. How can ye think we could leave?" She took a deep breath to calm herself. "We thank ye for yer offer of help, Lord O'Neill, but we must stay."

"Ye canna stay here," O'Neill began.

She cut across his words. "We must! When ye go, would ye please return to Uncle William and ask him to send us help?"

O'Neill ran a hand through his hair, glanced at Gannon, who nodded. "Fine. We'll stay and help ye find the boy."

Her eyes filled; she blinked back her tears and fought

the urge to scream at him. "The only place we've not looked is the lower village. Please ask yer men to stand aside so I can go there now."

O'Neill's expression softened. "Have ye not seen enough death for one day? Stay here, lassie. We'll do it."

"One of us has to go, sir. Ye wouldna ken Davey from another lad."

O'Neill and Gannon exchanged another look. After a moment O'Neill nodded.

Gannon met her gaze. "I'll go with ye."

Gannon followed Margaret, Rignor, and Nell MacDonald along the pathway, but he watched Margaret. She was a tall woman, a very beautiful woman. Dark waves floated around her face, softening its angles. Her even features were lovely despite the fear apparent there, her cheeks rounded but pale, her jawline firm below clenched teeth. At another time, in another place, he would have enjoyed looking at her. He thought of her trying to battle with him, how ridiculous that had been, even for a moment. Amazon, he thought. Or Boadicea back from the grave.

Rignor went into the first house, but Gannon prevented Margaret from entering the second. "I'll go," he said, moving to block her passage.

She glared at him, her dark eyes angry. "Ye wouldna ken him."

"Stay here, lass," he said, more gruffly than he'd intended.

Her eyes flashed. "I've no need to do yer bidding. Step aside, sir."

"If I find a lad his age, Margaret, I'll fetch ye. Stay here."

"Is this yer home, sir, or mine? Are those yer clanspeople lying dead in there, or mine? Step aside, if ye would."

"I'm trying to spare ye, lass. Ye're not accustomed to this."

"And ye are? Ye've seen the like of this before?"

Memories swirled around him, of broken bodies and lives ended far too soon, of children's sightless eyes and the horror of knowing what had been done. Of four bodies laid out on an Irish beach.

"Aye," he said. "I have."

Nell's sniff drew his gaze; she was wiping tears from her cheek, looking so very small, so very young, that he had to look away, willing his memories to fade. He'd been her age. He turned back to Margaret, looked into her defiant eyes, saw the anger she was nursing. Good, he thought, for when the grief replaced the anger, it would be overwhelming.

"Margaret," he said softly, "no one becomes accustomed to seeing those they kent dead. But I've done it, as ye have. Believe me, ye dinna need to see more."

She pressed her lips together for a moment, then nodded. "Aye. Thank ye." She moved to stand with Nell and Tiernan.

Gannon went into the nearest house. There were three people in it, none alive, none an eight-year-old boy. He and Rignor repeated their tasks, moving slowly down the pathway toward the harbor. After each house Rignor shook his head. Nell was sobbing now; Margaret's expression was ravaged. She looked almost ethereal, like a tall fairy woman, dark hair blowing around her pale face. She looked like she could be made of marble—except for her eyes, dark and troubled, eyes that followed his every movement, but which she turned from him if he looked into them. She held herself stiffly, as though by controlling her body she could control her emotions, but her long fingers, threading through her hair, or clasping and unclasping her hands, betrayed her. Her wide mouth was drawn in a straight line. The women in Antrim had stood the same way, had held themselves together at first, but eventually each of them had broken, huge tumults of emotion pouring from them that nothing could repress. He'd not been able to watch them, but he could not look away from Margaret MacDonald.

He'd paid little attention on their way here to what Rory had told him about the Somerstrath children. Margaret was the eldest, he remembered that much, and was betrothed to some petty Ross lord who was cousin to Scotland's King Alexander, one of those betrothals negotiated at birth. Rignor was the eldest son; it was he who would inherit Somerstrath. Already had, Gannon reminded himself. And Nell and four brothers? Or was it five? It did not matter now. All were gone, poor souls. He tried not to think of his own father and his brothers.

When he found a child, he told Rignor, who went to look. He waited with the others, Margaret wrapped her arm around Nell. Tiernan gestured Gannon away from the sisters.

"D'ye think they took the boy?" Tiernan asked. "Any nephew of the Earl of Ross would be worth much in ransom, four would be worth four times. Why not take them all?"

Gannon watched Margaret push her hair back from her face, saw her turn and see him and shift her gaze. He shrugged. "The youngest would be a hindrance, and perhaps the older fought them. An eight-year-old is easily managed."

He thought of the stories he'd heard, of women and children abducted and taken to the Orkney Islands as slaves, some taken to Norway and Kiev, to Constantinople and even farther east, where Scottish and Irish women and children brought high prices. And beauty, whether male or female, was always salable. If Davey looked like his sisters, he would be valuable.

Rignor returned, shaking his head, then going into the next house.

If the sisters had been home during the attack, the best they could have hoped for would have been to be taken as well. And if they had been taken, where would they have landed? In Orkney, serving in a household? Or in a far different place and capacity? Beautiful and virgin, or por trayed as such—the combination would command a high price. He looked at the curves of Margaret's waist and hips and thrust aside the images that came to him. She turned to find him watching her again and looked away.

"Perhaps they took no one," Tiernan said. "Perhaps he went for help. Perhaps they dinna kill everyone. Perhaps some of the people escaped, and they'll be coming back."

"They killed everyone they could reach in Antrim and did the same on Ross's land," Gannon said grimly. "I'm not thinking we'll find many who escaped. And," he added, as a new thought came to him, "if they took the boy to ransom, they'll have questioned him. They'll now ken that his sisters were left behind. If ransom is part of their plan, they'll come back for them."

"We have to take them away from here."

"Aye."

* * *

Somerstrath's village had never seemed so large. The search took forever. Each moment that Margaret waited for Rignor seemed an eternity of fear and horror. And each time he reappeared, shaking his head, she fought the wave of relief that Davey had not been in that house, then the subsequent dread that he might be in the next. The search went on, no one speaking; there was nothing to be said. Gannon and Tiernan were entering the houses as well again now, and Margaret moved away blindly. Or not so blindly, for she found herself standing before Fiona's doorway. She put a hand on the doorjamb and pushed the sagging door inward.

Nell clutched her arm. "Dinna go in, Margaret. He won't be here."

The roaring in her ears drowned Nell's voice. She shook off her sister's hand. She had to know. *Ye'll die here in Somerstrath. Don't think. Don't feel. Don't remember two young girls, laughing and dreaming of the future. Don't remember standing here just days ago and seeing her with him . . . Ye'll die here in Somerstrath, Fiona.*

She stepped inside, ignoring Nell's cry of distress.

Fiona lay on her bed in the corner, her clenched hands and staring eyes mute testimony to the agony of her last moments. Hers had not been an easy death; the signs of her struggle were obvious, not just on her person, but on her home. The loom was shattered, the fine wool her father had woven for their wedding gift was gone. The table was in pieces, the clothes that Fiona had kept neatly hung on their pegs gone as well. Fiona's father's bed had been smashed apart, only splinters left where it had stood. Even the cooking pots were broken.

Did I do this? By wishing her ill . . . did I do this?

She moved across the floor, now strewn with ashes instead of the fragrant rushes Fiona had used, to stand beside her friend. Fiona stared at the bones of the charred roof, her jaw clenched. One hand gripped the side of the bed, the other the wall. Her neck, Margaret realized, was at an odd angle.

Why? She heard a keening sound, a wordless moaning, high and frightening. The room swam before her, and she swayed. Strong hands clasped her arms, a face leaned close to hers.

"Margaret, lass! Here, let me help ye. Come away, come away."

It was Gannon's voice, his hands holding her upright. He pulled her against his chest, wrapping his arms around her, but it was not her in his embrace. Someone else was weeping wildly, her breaths rasping through her tears. Someone else was gripping his arms, feeling the golden bands there and the hard muscles under the linen. Someone else was pressed tight against him when her knees began to buckle. Someone else was staring at the torque around his neck, at the carved ends that were now visible.

Dragons. Beautifully carved, in fine detail. Dragons. She felt an urge to laugh wildly, to throw her head back and scream until she had no voice. You'll face dragons, the old woman had said, and here they were.

None of this was happening. It was a dream, a nightmare, from which she'd waken, trembling. She caught sight of Fiona, and her laughter faded, replaced by deepening sobs. He held her while she wept, turning her slowly so she faced the door, where Nell stood waiting, her eyes huge.

"Shhhh," he whispered. "Ye're a'right now, lass. Ye're safe now."

He stroked her hair. She took a deep breath, then another. His tunic was soft beneath her cheek, the rhythm of his heart fast but even; he smelled like clean linen, like soap, like the sea. When he turned, his hair fell over his shoulder, golden against her dark. Safe. Her head began to clear further, and she leaned away from him. He loosened his arms, but kept her in his embrace, looking over her shoulder at Fiona.

"Who is she?"

She pushed away then, and he released her, letting his hands fall to his sides.

"Who is she, Margaret?"

"My friend. My enemy."

She stared at Gannon, his pale hair in stark contrast to the burnt wood behind it, his eyes brilliant blue. At the dragons at his throat. She looked at the sword at his side, Norse runes on its hilt. At the axe he wore. The men who had done this would have looked like him. The blade that had killed her mother and her brothers and Fiona would have been wielded by a tall blond man like this one. He was alive, and those she loved were dead.

"What kind of men kill a helpless woman?" she snarled. "Or a woman large with child? Or wee lads who are terrified? Norsemen did this. Yer people did this!"

He took a step back. "I'm Irish, Margaret. My father was born in Ireland."

"And his father?"

He paused, then answered coldly. "Norway."

"Norway. Of course." She nodded. "Where else do the wolves of death come from?" She turned away from the anger she saw in his eyes.

* * *

They did not find Davey in the lower village, nor at the harbor. Gannon had said that they'd found no one alive, but what he'd not told them was how many had died, and how dreadfully. Somerstrath was known for its deep and sheltered bay, for the rocky headlands that stretched into the water from the north and south like arms around a child, protecting the harbor and the people who depended on it, who had prospered because of it. But Margaret saw none of that, only a beach littered with the dead. There were no wounded to tend to, no people coming out of hiding to greet her and tell her of their terror. Margaret's hopes, that many had escaped, were gone. She stood at the top of the shingle watching Rignor and Nell turn over bodies and say the dead men's names to each other. Her father's ships and every one of the fishermen's boats had been burned to their bones. The destruction had been complete.

The Irishmen who had accompanied O'Neill stood on the shore—her father's shore—or on their ships, pulled high onto her father's beach as though they had a right to do so. One of them laughed at something, and she wanted to grab him and force his gaze over her dead, to scream at him that this was sacred ground, a tomb made of stone and sand and sky, and it was not to be desecrated. She tried to be reasonable. He'd meant no harm, the stranger who had laughed. She turned her head away. And found herself looking into Gannon's eyes.

She jumped, startled; she'd not heard him approach. His sword was sheathed, his shield pushed behind him, but he still was intimidating. He was motionless, but tension and emotion radiated from him. Was it the way he stood, straight and vigilant? Or the way his eyes missed nothing around him? He was a warrior, bred from generations of warriors.

He looked away from her, across the beach, where Tiernan stood talking with men near the Irishmen's ships. She followed his gaze and willed her emotions to quiet. It was all that had happened this day that unsettled her, not this man, not his size, nor his face, almost beautiful, with his strong features and long-lashed eyes. He was very male, handsome in a way that would be attractive to most women, even to her in normal times. But she was not most women, and these were not normal times. And his heritage made him one of them. Still . . . he had been kind this day. And she had not.

He held her gaze for a moment, then lowered it to pull something out of the bag at his waist and held out his hand. A small knife lay across his palm, the handle tooled in fine leather. "Do ye ken this?"

She took the knife from him and held it up, turning the hilt to read the inscription engraved there in Norse. She could only read one word of it: Skye. Skye, one of the largest and most important islands off the western coast of Scotland, not far from where they stood. It was ruled by Leod, the son of Olaf the Black, king of the Isle of Man, and of Christina, the daughter of a former Earl of Ross. Leod had held Skye for years, had increased his holdings when he'd married a Norsewoman. But deep as his ties with the Norse were, Leod also had agreements with King Alexander of Scotland.

She handed the knife back, looking from his hand into his very blue eyes. "Where did ye find it?"

"In the room with yer mother and brothers. Did it belong to one of them?"

"I've never seen it before."

"What was yer father's relationship with Leod?"

"Civil," she said. "We had few dealings with him, but Leod and my father respected each other. He's been a fair man to deal with."

"Aren't ye related to him somehow?"

"Aye, through my mother, through the Rosses. I canna believe Leod would attack us without provocation. Or Antrim either. Don't O'Neill and Leod have an agreement?"

"They do. As Leod does with my uncle Erik at Haraldsholm in Antrim. The lands attacked in Ireland were his. Banners from Orkney were on the ships, but one of the men wore the colors of Skye."

"Skye, which means Leod," she said.

"Or someone on the island. Perhaps he's simply looking the other way."

"But why attack my uncle's lands in Ross, or your uncle's in Antrim? It makes no sense. Why would Leod start a war?"

"We dinna ken that he did, only that we found a knife with 'Skye' on it."

They were silent then, while the waves stroked the sand and the men on the Irish ships went about their tasks. At each end of the shingle Irishmen stood, their weapons at the ready. Guards. She'd not seen them before, but now she realized that they'd been at the periphery of her vision all along. She wondered if they were guarding Somerstrath—or the man next to her. She stole a glance at him, at his stern profile and lips pressed together, at the fineness of the weave of his clothing and the gleam of the leather of his boots. At the golden torque he wore around his neck. He held himself like a man accustomed to command.

"Are they all O'Neill's ships?" she asked.

"One is mine."

"Which?"

"That one," he said, his voice full of pride.

He pointed to the closest one, a long, lean ship, its railings decorated with carvings painted with gold. Its hull was broad, beamy, and shallow, its prow and stern each curved from the hull to rise high above the railings to end in—what else?—a dragonhead. Its sail, furled now, was barley-colored and sagged heavily from the single mast. It looked well tended, the vessel of a wealthy man.

She looked again at the dragons on his torque. "A dragonship. Of course."

"It's not a dragonship."

"It has a dragon at the prow. And the same shape as a Viking ship. Norsemen built their ships to be adaptable to any sea condition and deadly in all."

"My ship was built for speed on the open water and maneuverability in shallow. Ye'll find ships of the same shape all over Scotland."

"Not with dragonheads at the prow."

His tone was cold now. "I'll not apologize for my Norse blood, Margaret MacDonald, any more than I ask ye to apologize for yer Danish blood."

"I do not have Danish blood. I am Scottish."

"Whatever that means." He lifted a lock of her hair. "Yer hair is black, yer eyes are blue, like the Danes, like some Normans. Yer brother's name is Danish, yer sister's Norman. Ye have Scottish blood, aye, but the Scots originally came from Ireland. And most likely ye have Pictish blood; the Picts were Celts as well as the Scots, ye know. Ye also have the blood of the men who invaded these lands hundreds of years ago. Ye look at my battle-axe with contempt, and at the inscriptions on my sword hilt, but look around ye. There are runes written on the stones on yer keep, and many of yer men's weapons are the same as the Vikings'. We're none of us pure, lassie. What ye choose to do with yer heritage is yer decision. I'll decide how to live with mine."

She pulled her head back; he let her hair slide from his fingers.

"My people are dead," she said.

"Aye, and I'm sorry for it." He stared across the water as though his mind was very far away, then suddenly turned his blue gaze to hers. "Ye want to lash out, to find someone to blame, to hate, for all the pain you're feeling. And ye've half decided that I will be that person, not because of anything I've done, but because of the color of my hair and my eyes. Ye ken nothing of me, Margaret. I am not responsible for what happened here, and I will not accept yer anger. Place it where it belongs."

She pressed her lips together in a vain attempt to stem the flow of tears that had sprung to her eyes. They streamed down her cheeks. She turned her face away so he would not see them. He was right, she knew. Her rage should not be directed at him, but at those who caused the horror around her. He watched her, raised a hand as though to touch her, then apparently thought better of it and looked out to sea until she calmed herself.

"I'm sorry," she said at last, wiping her eyes. "Ye are right."

He said nothing, but some of the stiffness left his stance. After a moment he turned to her again. "There's no comfort in it, lass. I am sorry as well."

She nodded. The wind was the only sound then, a soft keening for the dead. Her father had prided himself on his ability to keep this part of Scotland safe from harm. He'd been wrong, and he'd paid for his mistake with his life. As had his men and the people of Somerstrath, but, no, she would not think on them more. "How bad were the raids on my uncle's lands?"

"In Ross? Bad, but nothing like this. They attacked two tiny hamlets. Killed everaone, but there were few to kill. It was almost like the attacks there and in Antrim were practices for this one."

"How did they defeat us so easily?"

"They had a lot of men." He pointed to the edge of the water. "When we arrived, ye could still see the grooves on the sand where their ships came ashore, at least five of their big ships; each can hold a hundred men. They probably overwhelmed the men here at the harbor easily. No one expected a raid like this. We've not seen the like in Ireland in . . ." He paused. "In years."

"Have the old days come again, when the Vikings raided as they would?"

"If it is the Norse . . . King Haakon of Norway has treaties with us and with ye. I've not heard of them being broken. This would certainly be a breach."

Margaret gestured to the dead men on the beach. "Perhaps this is our notice."

He turned the knife in his hand.

The waves crashed, suddenly much larger, bringing to mind the stories she'd always considered absurd, of monsters coming from the water, of demons and ungodly creatures that tormented humans. Ungodly, she thought, looking up at the headland to the north, where the chapel door hung open, swinging aimlessly in the wind, mute testimony to the priest's death. And God's absence. She tried to pray, but she found no words, and she wasn't sure anyone was listening. What kind of men did this? What kind of god allowed it?

The evening breeze blew off the sea, lifting the hair from her shoulders and tossing it over her face as though to shield her. She told herself that there was only one thing to think about. If Davey was not here among the dead, then he was among the living. Small comfort, but comfort it was.

"Sir! My lord Magnusson!"

The man was running down from the north, waving his arm. Nell and Rignor ran toward her. Gannon slipped the knife back into the bag.

"My lord Magnusson! We found a Norseman!"

Gannon whirled around. "Alive?"

"Aye! Barely, but alive. They're bringing him to ye." He pointed to the group of men behind him, their arms laced into a sling, carrying a large man between them.

Gannon followed his gaze. "Are there others?"

"No, sir, he's the only one. He was dragging himself along the beach." At Gannon's raised eyebrow he continued. "He'll not last long."

"We willna need him long," Gannon said grimly.

EIGHT

The Viking, his hands bound before him, his face gray, was placed ungently on the ground. He watched the men gathered around him with wary eyes. The front of his tunic was stained with fresh blood. Gannon's men backed away as Gannon and Tiernan approached, Margaret and Rignor and Nell a step behind. One of the raider's legs was badly broken. His hair was dark blond, his beard long and trailing past his collar. He had no weapon save the small knife stuck in his belt. Around his neck was a torque like Gannon's, with fanciful birds in place of the dragons.

Nell gasped. "He looks like the head!"

"Look what he's wearing, sir," one of the Irishmen said to Gannon.

Gannon leaned over the man, wrapped a finger around the torque, his expression savage. "Where did ye get this?" He repeated his question in Norse, then raised his voice. "Where did ye get this?" When there was no answer, he looked at Tiernan. "It's from Haraldsholm." He gestured to Nell and Margaret and spoke to one of his men. "Get them back to the keep. They'll not need to see this."

The man nodded and gestured for Margaret and Nell to follow him. Nell took a step, but Margaret stayed where she was, unable to stop staring at the Viking before her, and Nell stopped. The Norseman glared back at Margaret, then let his gaze fall to her breasts. He licked his lips.

Rignor lunged forward. "Ye murdering swine!" He kicked the Norseman's broken leg.

The man moaned, glared up at Rignor, then spit at him, saying something low and guttural. Rignor leapt forward, drawing his sword. Tiernan grabbed Rignor's arm, but Rignor twisted away. Gannon shouted, pushing Margaret back as he started forward. With a savage roar, Rignor thrust his sword through the man's neck. Sickened, Margaret stepped quickly back. Gannon struck Rignor across the chest, knocking him to the ground, but it was too late. Rignor's sword, still in the man's throat, bounced in the air. With a shivering groan, the Viking slumped over it. Tiernan pulled his head up, staring into the man's eyes before releasing him.

"He's dead," he told Gannon, and wiped his hand on his thigh.

Gannon yanked Rignor to his feet and shook him. "Ye stupid fool!"

"He deserved it!"

"He could have told us something!"

Rignor tore himself from Gannon's grasp. "What? That he's a Norseman? That he was here? That he's a filthy murderer?"

Gannon loomed over him, and Margaret thought for a moment that he would strike Rignor again. But he didn't, stepping back instead, his hands clenched at his sides. "He could have told us where he is from, where else they are going, why they're raiding again, and who's leading them! Is this one man's work, or is all of Norway about to descend on us? Ye stupid fool, ye just killed the one man who could ha' told us if these are isolated raids or the beginning of a war! Can ye not, for one bloody moment, hold yer temper long enough to think?" Gannon swore, then swore again. He glared at Rignor, made a disgusted sound, and whirled away, gesturing to the dead man. "Take the torque. I'll be damned if he'll rot in Haraldsholm gold."

"Aye, sir. Shall we bury him here, sir?"

Gannon gestured to the dead Somerstrath men on the beach. "The Norsemen dinna bury them. Leave him for the birds to eat. Get the lasses back to the keep at once. And take their brother with them." He spun on his heel and walked across the beach to his ship.

Some of O'Neill's men guarded the perimeter of the village, others guarded the keep. They nodded but did not speak as Gannon's men led Margaret, Nell, and Rignor into the courtyard. O'Neill had been busy in their absence. The courtyard had been cleared of her father's men; there were neatly wrapped rows of the dead in the ground-floor room. The stairs had been cleared as well, and the hall, where they found O'Neill, overseeing his men scrubbing stains off the wooden floor.

He frowned fiercely when told of Rignor killing the Norseman, glaring at Rignor for a moment, before turning to Margaret, his expression still severe. "I take it ye dinna find yer brother."

"No."

"We'll spend the night, lass. Tomorrow we'll bury yer family; but then we'll have to go. We've got to spread the alarm."

"Aye," she said, too weary to argue. The Irish were welcome to leave any time they wished. She knew O'Neill would try to get them to leave as well, which they would not, but that discussion could wait.

"My men brought yer family down. They're ready for burial in the morning."

She nodded.

"We found some food left in the kitchens, and I've got my men preparing it. Sit yerself down, lass, and take wee Nell with ye. Ye look done in."

She did not reply, but sank to a bench, leaning her head against the wall. What did it matter what she looked like? She watched the sunlight slowly fade from the walls, heard the low murmurs of the men and the sound of bristles on wood as O'Neill's men worked. Her mother would be pleased; she liked the hall kept neat. Margaret closed her eyes. She would not cry. She would not think.

Their meal was sparse, but adequate. The Irish had ale and whisky, gifts to them from her uncle that they had been bringing home. Surprisingly, the attackers had not emptied all the food barrels; there was dried fish and venison left. Apples, tasting of their long months in the dark. Oatcakes and bread, prepared in the dawn hours by Somerstrath people, baked in the afternoon by the Irishmen. Margaret had not gone to the kitchens— O'Neill told her it was wiser. There would be enough for a morning meal, but after that Somerstrath's larder would be bare. There were not enough platters to go around; all the silver had been taken, even some of the simple wooden platters were missing. She'd almost cried at that, as though it mattered, with all else the Norsemen had taken from her.

Margaret sat between Rignor and Nell and picked at her food while Rignor argued with almost everything that was said, a sure sign he had had too much to drink. She blamed her brother neither for seeking oblivion nor for his anger, though her own had faded, leaving her so weary that she could hardly keep from resting her head on the table. O'Neill sat at the end of the table, Gannon and Tiernan across from her. None of them had said much. O'Neill watched Rignor with open distaste. Tiernan kept his head down.

Gannon had watched her all through the meal, but she'd tried not to look at him, tried not to see the light glint off his hair, the line of his cheek when he turned, the strong bones of his face. And not the contempt in his eyes when he looked at Rignor. She thought of his barely repressed rage on the beach, of his earlier anger. He was a stranger, vouched for by Rory O'Neill, but still an unknown, and obviously a man of strong emotion. One of his men had brought him the torque the Norseman had worn, and Gannon held it now, turning the golden collar in his hands, stroking a thumb along its fanciful carvings of birds.

"Is it from Antrim?" Nell asked.

Tiernan looked up and into his brother's eyes.

Gannon nodded. "Aye, from Haraldsholm, my uncle's fortress there."

"Did ye ken the man whose it was?"

Gannon's gaze was glacial. "Aye."

"He called ye Magnusson," Margaret said to him. "Yer man, when he came to tell ye of the Viking they'd found. He called ye Magnusson."

"Aye. What of it?"

She looked at O'Neill. "Ye said his name was Mac-Magnus. Son of Magnus."

"Which is," Gannon said harshly, drawing her attention back to him, "the same as Magnusson. When I am with the Irish I'm called MacMagnus."

"And when ye're with the Norse, Magnusson?" Margaret asked.

"Aye," he said.

"Which means yer men are Norse."

"Some of them."

"How are we to trust them then?"

"Because I tell ye to."

There was a long moment in which Margaret and Gannon stared at each other. His gaze was implacable and defiant. If she'd had a weapon, she would have struck him. And maybe he was feeling the same, for he stared at her with an intensity that was unnerving.

He spoke slowly. Coldly. "There is not a man among them who is not trustworthy. They are good men."

She looked away, reminding herself that he'd been kind, that they'd helped look for Davey. And that she'd spoken far too harshly, that killing every blond man on Earth would not bring her family back. Her anger left her as quickly as it had come, and when she looked at Gannon again he was not the symbol of everything evil in the world, but just one man—who had done nothing to merit her contempt.

"I'm sure they are," she said.

Gannon raised an eyebrow but did not answer.

"Tomorrow," O'Neill said, his tone brooking no argument, "we'll leave as soon as the burials are completed. We'll take ye to yer uncle's."

Rignor slammed the cup down and glared at O'Neill. "I will say when we leave, or even if we leave! I am Somerstrath now! Tell them, Margaret!"

She blinked in surprise. "I guess ye are, Rignor; I'd not thought of that."

"How could ye not? I thought of it as soon as I saw Father."

Gannon's tone was dry. "That was yer first thought, when ye found yer father dead, that ye'd inherited his title?"

Rignor reddened. "Eventually I thought of it. Eventually. And as Somerstrath, it's I who will say if we leave, and I say we dinna leave. We dinna need yer help anymore. We'll rebuild without ye. Ye can be on yer way in the morning. Or now. There's naught for ye here; Norsemen took it all."

Tiernan and Gannon exchanged a glance.

O'Neill sighed tiredly. "Ye're right that there's nothing here," he said. "No men to work the fields, no fishermen to bring food home to ye, no defenses. Ye'll be vulnerable to the human ravens who will descend on ye and take the very land. Ye'll need a lot of men and assistance to rebuild."

Ravens, thought Margaret.

Rignor waved a hand at the door. "I dinna need help from ye. My uncle William will help. Lachlan will help. Ye can go now." He struggled to his feet. "No one tells

Somerstrath what to do." He staggered out of the hall while they all watched.

Margaret sighed, her weariness returning tenfold. "I am sorry that Rignor has insulted ye. We've had much to deal with this day. He's obviously not himself. I'm hoping he'll remember none of this in the morning. I ask ye to do the same."

"Tomorrow," O'Neill said, "we'll do the burials, then we leave."

"I thank ye for yer help, sir. Please give my uncle the news."

"Ye can do it yerself. Ye'll be coming with us, lass."

"My lord, we canna leave until we find Davey."

"Margaret," O'Neill said, "listen to me. Yer brother's gone."

"He could still be hiding. He could have gone for help. And he's not the only one missing. There are at least a score or so. Women and children. They must have escaped."

"It's possible." O'Neill's tone belied his words. "It's more likely that they've been taken."

"Taken?" She heard the horror in her voice, heard Nell's gasp. "For ransom?"

"It's one possibility."

"Are there others?"

O'Neill answered reluctantly. "The raiders might be taking slaves, like in the old days."

"Who would buy slaves in Scotland?"

"It wouldna have to be in Scotland."

She sat back against the wall. "But why? Why?"

"Money. Power. Revenge," O'Neill said. "Someone wanted to annihilate Somerstrath, Margaret. This was not a siege, nor an invasion; they did not come to take yer father's land, but to destroy it. Ye need to tell us everything ye can think of that might lead us to who did this. Everything, even things that mightna seem significant. Did yer father have a falling out with anyone?"

She shook her head. "Not that I ken. It's possible, of course, but I'm sure he would ha' talked of it, if not to me, then at least to the other men. Rignor would have kent, and he would have told me. My father wouldna have let us go to the court if he were worried about an attack, or he would have sent word with us to Uncle William or the king."

"There was the head on the beach," Nell said. "We found a head."

"What head?" O'Neill asked sharply.

Margaret explained what they'd found. "My father heard of no unrest elsewhere . . ."

"If we'd been able to question the Norseman we found today," Gannon said, gesturing to the torque, "we'd have learned much more."

Margaret rose to her feet before she could scream at him. Nell rose as well. Margaret kept her tone quiet. "Forgive me, gentlemen. I'm too weary to talk more on it now. I thank ye all; we're grateful for yer help. I'm sure Rignor will tell ye the same tomorrow."

The men stood, but she looked at none of them.

"We'll talk in the morning," O'Neill said. "Get some rest."

She nodded to him in reply and left with Nell, knowing they watched her. They were barely through the door when she heard O'Neill's words.

"Now that Somerstrath is gone the western coast will

be vulnerable," he said. "Which means that we need to get to Ross as soon as we can."

"Surely Ross kens how weak Rignor is," Gannon answered. "Rignor canna hold this place. Even if he had men to lead, he wouldna ken how to do it."

"Aye," O'Neill said. "Ross might replace him with someone stronger."

"Rignor's his nephew," Tiernan said. "Perhaps he doesna see it."

"Then I'll explain it to him," O'Neill said. "It will take a strong leader to rebuild Somerstrath and keep this stretch of coast secure, decades to bring this clan back to where it was. Rignor has neither the coin or wits to do it correctly."

"And the lasses," Gannon asked. "What of them?"

"Margaret's betrothed to a cousin of the king, Lachlan Ross; the marriage was but a fortnight away. Perhaps he could hold Somerstrath in Rignor's stead."

Margaret, fighting the urge to return to the hall and argue with them, gestured for Nell to follow her up the stairs, her anger growing with every step. Who were these men to discuss Somerstrath's fate, to discuss her betrothal, to talk about Rignor like that? He was not the weak man they thought him. He had the blood of Scotland's most eminent families in his veins. Tomorrow Rignor would apologize. She'd see to it. Surely Uncle William would help them rebuild; surely he would not replace Rignor. Her brother just needed time, then he would grow into the man Somerstrath needed to lead them.

Wouldn't he?

* * *

Before they found their beds, Gannon and Tiernan checked on the guards posted around the village and at the ships. The men had seen nothing, but reported hearing noises, as though people walked through the village. They talked of other Vikings who might still be lurking, of the bodies all around them. Gannon reminded them that they'd searched the entire glen and coastline and only found one man, and that they would give the Somerstrath people a decent funeral on the morrow. His calm manner seemed to reassure them, but their reports unsettled him. And Tiernan, apparently, for his brother looked over his shoulder more than once as they walked through the village. They returned to the hall to find many of their men settling on the floor. Rignor was already asleep near the door, snoring noisily. They gave him a wide berth and joined Rory at the table.

The older man poured each of them a cup of ale. "All's well?"

"Aye," Gannon said, "but they're hearing things."

"Their imaginations' working. To be expected after what they saw today," Rory answered, rubbing his forehead. "Jesus, Mary, and Joseph. Death at home, death with Ross, death here. Has the world gone mad?"

"I dinna have a better explanation," Gannon said.

"What d'ye think? Same men as in Antrim, or do we have more than one group of raiders?"

Gannon took a long swallow. "They've used the same tactics. It could well be one group of raiders. Or one leader."

"Ye found that knife," Tiernan said, looking from one to the other.

"Aye," Gannon said, "but why would Leod do it?"

"D'ye think it's the Norse, that perhaps Haakon of Norway is still angry that King Alexander tried to buy his islands?" Tiernan asked.

Rory nodded. "Could be."

"So he sent men to raid the coastlines of both Ireland and Scotland?" Gannon asked. "Kenning that would start a war?"

"Maybe that's what he wants," Tiernan said. "Alexander's only been ruling in his own right for two years, and he's already tried to buy the islands. Maybe Haakon wants a war. Maybe he thinks he can bully Alexander into releasing more land to him to prevent a war. He's done that before."

"Listen to ye, spouting history," Gannon said. "Where'd ye learn all this?"

Tiernan grinned. "I do listen, ye ken, and God kens ye all talk on it a lot."

"Ye could be right," Rory said. "It could be that Haakon's testing Alexander, to see his strength. If he's found wanting, Haakon will grab what he can. Maybe Haakon's sending these raiders; maybe he's just looking the other way. It doesna matter much which. They have to be stopped. And it doesna explain the attacks in Ireland."

"Don't we need to get home?" Tiernan said. "What if they go there again?"

"I sent over five hundred men to Haraldsholm to help yer uncle Erik defend the coast," Rory said. "He'll be fine. And if there is a war, we'll need allies, so it's good we came here."

Tiernan snorted. "From what I've seen so far, it's the Scots who'll need us."

"Dinna underestimate them," Gannon said with a grin. "Originally they were Irish. The blood canna be that diluted."

The others laughed.

"So who d'ye think it is?" Tiernan asked. "Leod?"

"He's capable of it," Rory answered. "But why, that's the thing? Unless Haakon's bent on starting a war. When's the last time ye saw Leod?"

"At Da's funeral," Gannon said.

"Fourteen years, then," Rory said, "Even if Leod and Somerstrath had a falling out, would Leod risk bringing the wrath of the Earl of Ross—and perhaps the king of Scotland—down on himself? I doubt it. Leod's many things, but not a fool. Yer uncle Erik would have told me if he and Leod had had a falling out."

"Which leads us back to whether this is a new invasion from Norway," Gannon said. "And if it is, they'll strike again."

Rory nodded.

"We'll fight them off in Ireland," Gannon said. "Look what Erik did last time."

"Yer uncle was fearsome, aye," Rory said somberly, "but he was against a few hundred. If they invade, it'll be thousands, then thousands more as the word spreads through the Norse lands. The Danes will join in, perhaps the Swedes."

"Which means we have to repel them immediately before it grows," Gannon said. "Someone wants us to think it is Leod. Twice now they've left weapons that can be easily traced to Skye, in Antrim and here. And they left nothing else behind, except for the one man. If Erik's men had not been at sea and seen the ships leaving, they wouldna have seen the Orkney banners, and we all would have thought Skyemen were responsible. The Orkney Islands belong to Norway. Do ye suppose that now Skye does as well? Which means Leod does? But why?"

Rory nodded again. "That's what we need to find out. Leod plays a cagey game, is friendly with all who might be of aid, a true friend to none. I canna believe he has put himself under Haakon's yoke. Leod always did like his independence."

Gannon put the knife he'd found on the table.

Rory picked it up, looking at it closely. "Could it have belonged to one of Somerstrath's sons?"

"Margaret said she'd never seen it before," Gannon said. He thought of her standing next to him on the beach, small but defiant, her dark hair blowing back from her face, her cheeks soft and pale under those blue eyes. And thought of how often he found her watching him, how often he found himself watching her.

"Did ye ask Rignor about it?"

Gannon's mouth curled with distaste. "No. Nor will I."

Rory pushed the knife across the table. "Perhaps the raiders hit Skye on their way here. We'll throw it all in William Ross's lap and let him sort it out."

Gannon nodded. He'd gained some sense of the man when they'd met; Ross, even weary from the long ride from court and confronting the destruction of two of his coastal villages, had been reasonable. He seemed a moderate man, not prone to rash decisions. His only immediate action had been to have his wife and two young sons head inland for his wife's family's lands. And then he'd toured the villages devastated by the raids and listened to their stories of the same in Antrim.

"Ross is shrewd and dependable," Rory said. "That's why we're allies."

"What about Somerstrath? What was he like?"

Rory poured more ale. "I met the man many times and thought him reasonable, but it's possible that he was more like his son than I kent. He might have made enemies and not been able to control what came next."

"But that doesna explain the raids on Antrim and Ross."

Rory took another sip. "No."

"What are the other local chieftains like?"

"There are no chieftains near. Rufus at Inverstrath, the next bay over, was Somerstrath's underling. He's a loyal and decent man but not strong enough to replace Somerstrath. His daughter Dagmar might, though. Watch yerself with her. She's been widowed twice, and I hear she's looking for a third husband. Ye might just suit her, but don't let her suit ye."

Gannon snorted. "She'd not even look my way. I'm not a rich man."

Rory gave him a long look of appraisal. "Ye have a ship."

"Oh, aye, one ship that I've owned for a month. And it was a gift."

"It was no gift. It was yer da's money that funded it. Ye do ken that Erik wants ye to go back and stay with him?"

"Aye."

"Waste of yer talents, but I ken what Erik's thinking, that if anything happens to him, he'll need someone he can trust to step forward and help his sons rule. That's why he called for the two of ye after the raids, to see what the two of ye had become. Neither Erik nor I wanted ye to stay in Fermanagh, fond as we are of yer stepfather.

Patrick has sons of his own, and there'll be no place for ye there when he's gone. Ye cannot deny it."

"I don't," Gannon said. "Erik's summons came at a good time."

"It did not just happen. Erik and I planned it."

Gannon raised an eyebrow. "Did ye now?"

"We did, long before the raids. Those we dinna plan. Erik wanted ye home." Rory paused. "None of us who lead men have the luxury of only thinking of ourselves. Death is always only a heartbeat away. What will happen to our people after we're gone must be settled long before we expect to go. Erik and I have talked about what will happen when he dies. He wanted ye back in case he doesna live to see his sons grown. And that was before the raids. He's told me he's pleased with the both of ye and wants ye to stay. He's even picked a bride for ye."

Gannon shook his head. "I'll pick my own woman. It's the one luxury a poor man has."

"Ye're not poor anymore."

"I own no land."

"Easily solved." Rory leaned back. "Ye are descended from kings on both sides, the two of ye. Did ye think ye would not be asked to serve yer people? Ye must have kent when I became chief last year that I would call upon ye. I let ye have a few months to mourn yer mother, but now I need ye. Antrim must be kept strong, or we're vulnerable on that coast, and if anything happens to Erik, we're vulnerable at Haraldsholm. Half of ye is Irish; I want the leadership in Antrim to be held by someone whose loyalties will be aligned with mine."

"So how is it we're here in Scotland if yer plan is to keep Antrim strong?"

"Originally I'd planned only to get Ross's help in finding whoever committed the Antrim raids—someday it may be important that ye and William have met. But hearing of the raids on his lands and finding Somerstrath like this . . . it changes everything. Now I think I'll need ye here in Scotland for a bit."

"Why?"

"With Somerstrath gone, Ross will need to have this part of the coast secured. Rufus is not strong enough to gather the other clans to him; and after meeting Rignor, I'm quite sure they'll not follow him either. Which means William might well put someone else in here, and I want whoever it is to be friendly with us. So I think ye'll be staying."

"And if we don't agree?" Gannon asked.

Rory's grin was wolfish. "I'm yer overlord. What is there to say? Ye'll stay here while I need ye here. And if ye need more convincing, well, laddie, ye've kent me a long time. What d'ye think I'd do?"

Gannon laughed. "Make our lives difficult."

"Ye can count on it."

NINE

"Margaret! Wake up!"

She opened her eyes with a surprised gasp.

"Ye were asleep, Margaret," Fergus said. "In the day."

Margaret laughed and sat up, pulling the boy into her arms. "So I was." She hugged him, enjoying the little body curling against her, the smell of sunshine and earth in his hair.

"I get tired, too," Fergus said, dropping his head to her shoulder.

"Of course ye do," she told him. "We all do."

"Mother should take a nap. Like ye did."

"She should indeed."

"Let's go and tell her, Margaret. Let's go! Hurry. Hurry!"

Margaret heard the rain as she dragged herself from her warm bed, pulling her cloak tighter around her when the cool wind sought her skin. She had to tell Mother something. But why was she sleeping in her cloak? And why was the mattress on the floor instead of the bedstead? She was too sleepy to think why, and climbed over some obstruction to get to the door. *Mother will be furious at Nell for leaving such a mess. In the morning I'll tell her to clean it all up.*

She brushed her hair back from her face, surprised that she'd not braided it before she slept, and pulled the door open. But the door was already open, or part of it, was, hanging down in splintery pieces. She put a hand on the doorjamb as her mind cleared.

Dear God. It was a dream. But so real, as though Fergus . . . She tightened her grip as her body swayed. *They're all gone. The mattress is on the floor because the bedstead was chopped like firewood, and I'm sleeping in my cloak because I was too weary—and too afraid—to change into nightclothes because the keep is full of strangers and we have no real door on this room—and part of me is terrified that the Norsemen will return. The wind is pouring in because the window covering is gone, too, as though the raiders had been frenzied, taking things that could do them no good, or simply destroying for the sake of destruction. It was a wonder they'd left the bedcoverings.*

On the mattress behind her, Nell slept on, one hand under her cheek, the other tucked under her chin. She looked like a child. She was a child. Or had been, for what they saw yesterday had aged them all. Margaret backed from the doorway, hit her ankle on the debris on the floor, and stood, frozen, while her mind tumbled. It had seemed so real, so important . . . Or was this the dream? Would she awaken from the nightmare to stare into the gloom of near morning, wondering what monster had sent such visions? She felt a wave of hysteria, a wildness, threaten to overcome her. She fought it so that she wouldn't tear her hair and throw herself on the ground writhing, wouldn't rage at God and demand an explanation, wouldn't insist that He return Davey unharmed, wouldn't remember that she'd refused to do the last thing her parents had asked of her. How simple a request it seemed now, to carry out the promises made at her birth. But she'd parted from them, and from Fiona, in anger. She took deep breaths, willing her heart to stop pounding and her hands to stop trembling, and closed her mouth tightly so she wouldn't scream. And eventually the wildness withdrew.

The hallway was empty, the silver sheen of rain lit from behind as she passed the thin window slit on the stairs. It must be closer to morning than she'd thought. Her room faced west, and it had been dim there, but here, twelve steps up the stairway, outside her parents' room, the light was better. It was here that the sun usually announced its presence each day, one of the reasons her mother had kept this window uncovered in the summer, refusing to let the oiled leather be lowered until the winds of autumn arrived. But no sun greeted her this day. She pushed open the door of her parents' room.

She did not know how long she cried, or how long she lay there afterward, staring into space, shorn of all emotion. Eventually she slept. When she woke, stiff and weary, she rose, and without a backward glance, left the room, closing the door with a finality that seemed to ring through the keep. She climbed the stairs, past the room that had been her brothers', past the smaller room that Rignor had shared with no one.

But there she stopped, for the roof was gone and the stairs crumbled with ashes. And in the space where there had once been a door leading to the parapet, a man stood, silhouetted against the rain.

Gannon turned at her cry, a shuddering, horror-filled noise that was little more than a gasp. Margaret stood there, her hands clasped over her perfect breasts, her eyes wide, her face gray in the dim light. She put a hand against the stone wall as though to steady herself.

"Margaret. Dinna fear, lass. It's only me, Gannon." When she did not move, he climbed down the few steps that separated them. "It's just me."

Her voice was a harsh whisper. "Why are ye up here?"

"I'm looking at the rain is all. I couldna sleep."

"Nor I . . . I keep wondering where Davey is this night."

"Ah, lass, ye need to face it. The boy's gone."

"Ye're so certain! All of ye, so certain that he's dead! Or taken by them. But what if ye're wrong? What if he's out there, in the rain? What if he's huddled under a tree, wondering when all of ye will leave? Did ye ever think of that? Did ye ever . . . ?" She paused, as though a sudden thought had struck her, then continued, her voice calmer. "He could still be here."

"All right. Let's say he could be. There are a score or so missing, right?"

"Aye."

"If ye'd been here and escaped . . . where would ye run?"

"To Inverstrath. The next village. Rufus would take us in . . ."

"Then we'll go there and look."

She studied him, wondering how one moment he was a foe, then suddenly an ally. And how much she wanted to let her fear and antagonism go. "Ye would do that for us?"

"I would do that for ye, Margaret."

His words shook her, but she tried not to let it show. "Thank ye. Rignor will be himself in the morning; he'll thank ye as well."

"I'd prefer he dinna."

Anger flashed in her eyes. "He's no' the idiot ye make him out to be. Anyone would do as he did. It's naught but a bit too much to drink."

"He wasna drunk when he killed the Viking. And not everyone would do as he did. Ye dinna."

"He was overcome with grief."

Gannon raised an eyebrow. "And ye're not?"

"Grief takes people different ways."

"I heard ye crying when I passed yer mother's room." He watched her realization that he had seen her huddled on the floor, sobbing. "Ye fair broke my heart, Margaret. That's what grief sounds like. I've seen Nell's tears as well, and the way she seems so lost. That's what grief feels like. I've seen nothing like that from him."

"He is grieving!"

"The first thing he thought of when he saw yer father's body was that he had inherited the title. That's grief?"

"He was drinking when he said that."

"So which am I to believe, then? His unguarded words with a head full of liquor, or his guarded words when he's sober? Which will tell me he's grieving?"

"Perhaps ye dinna ken what grief feels like."

"I . . ." He stepped back from her, his emotions far too close to the surface. He waited until he could speak evenly. "When they raided Antrim they attacked two villages, both on my uncle's lands. I kent everyone who died. I helped to bury them. I was five when both of my grandfathers died on the same day, ten when my grandmother died. Years ago I buried my father and my brothers, and last winter I buried my mother. I do ken what grief feels like. And I ken what's before ye, the years of wondering 'what if,' of wondering why ye were the one to live and they the ones to die. The times ye'll start to tell them something, only to realize ye'll never tell them anything again. The times when a song, or a color, or a torque on a Norseman, will bring back memories ye'd thought ye'd forgotten and make ye long for times that will never come again . . ."

He stopped, furious with himself. All these years, all the people he'd talked to about his father and brothers . . . he'd never let his emotions rule him like that. Margaret was staring at him, her mouth partly open. Why her? Why now?

"I'm sorry," he said, feeling like a fool.

"No," she said. "No. Dinna be."

She reached to stroke his cheek, her touch soft, then gone. How long had it been since a woman touched him in simple tenderness? He had a sudden urge to clasp her to him, to feel that soft body against his. To stroke his hand over her curves and to touch that skin. To let her comfort him. Instead, he simply looked at her.

"It is I who am sorry," she said. "I had no idea of yer losses. I've only been thinking of ours. I should have kent ye'd lost people in the Antrim raids. I'm sorry."

He nodded, afraid to say anything more. Behind them the rain slowed, then became mere drops falling on the stones. He could see her better now, could see where streaks of tears had crossed her cheeks. They had both faced death. He had done it before, but he suspected this was her first brush with it.

When she spoke her tone was calmer. "Were the Antrim raids like this?"

"They were much smaller."

"Were ye there?"

"No. I was away. Inland. If I'd been in Antrim . . ."

"D'ye think ye could have made a difference? Ye're just two men."

"We might have made a difference."

"Ye canna know that."

"No," he said. "I will never ken that."

She did not try to sleep when she returned to her room. The conversation with Gannon kept repeating itself in her head. Who was this man, who could be cold one moment, flaming with emotion the next? Who talked of death easily, yet, as he'd done in the village, averted his eyes from the body of a woman or child, his eyes haunted? Who watched her every movement with hunger in his eyes? And was kind to Nell, yet made no attempt to hide his contempt for Rignor?

Her brother was suffering, of that she was sure. And yet . . . he'd not cried, had not talked of the horror of what they'd seen. His first thought had been that he'd inherited Somerstrath. She shook her head, sure she was being far too harsh on him, concentrating instead on what she'd remembered while she'd talked with Gannon, that there was one place at Somerstrath that Davey might yet be, one place he might run to seek shelter.

She should go now, while most slept, before anyone else was about. She touched Nell's shoulder. "I'm going to look for Davey. I willna be long."

Nell's eyes flew open. "Don't leave, me, Margaret!"

"I'll be back. I promise ye, I'll be back. And God willing, with Davey."

"I'll come with ye."

"No, I'll need ye here, to tell them I'm still asleep, or in the garderobe . . . whatever ye need to tell them. Just dinna let them come after me."

Nell nodded then, and Margaret slipped out of the room, pulling the remains of the battered door closed as though it could protect her sister. She paused, listening; all was quiet in the keep. No one stopped her as she descended, no one saw her pause outside the hall. Rignor was here, near the door, his snores letting her know she could expect no help there. Downstairs, on the ground floor, the men on guard merely nodded to her; no one moved to block her passage. She did not pause for more than an instant, did not look at them or at the bodies of her family. But she had seen the pity in their eyes. She looked only straight ahead as she walked through the village, not down when she needed to step over an obstacle, telling herself it was not a person she'd known all her life but an obstacle.

In the upper village, hidden from view from the keep, she called Davey's name as quietly as she could, then stood listening, her skin prickling with the sensation of being watched. Last night she had been disdainful, would not even listen when O'Neill had talked of human ravens, scavengers who would come and pick the bones of Somerstrath clean. But this morning, in the half-light of dawn, she thought of the Viking they'd found. She'd been a fool to think, even for a moment, that she and Nell and Rignor could stay here.

She headed southeast, quiet now, not calling for her brother, but hurrying, knowing it would not be long before she was missed. She turned from the wider path onto a much smaller one that wound through the trees and up a gentle slope, not slowing her pace at all. Nor did she pause when she parted the branches of a huge fir tree and scurried beneath it.

The glade was just the same as Margaret had remembered it, even after years of absence. There was the pool, water spilling into it from the burn above, and there the opening of the cave. She stood for a moment at the edge of the small space, inhaling the fecund mixture of rich soil and luxuriant growth, while images flowed over her, of being a child here, playing with Fiona, making dolls of sticks, with clothing of leaves. The houses they'd made from branches, and wreaths of flowers for their hair. Of Davey's excitement, his whispered delight, when he'd told her of the secret cave he and Ewan had found. She'd never told him that she already knew the spot, that probably countless generations of Somerstrath children each thought they were the first to discover it.

She called Davey's name, then waited, hearing only the murmur of the water, the wind sliding through the pine branches above her head, and through the ferns that grew as tall as her waist. She pushed them aside and peered into the shallow cave. "Davey," she whispered.

There was no answer. The cave was empty, its stone floor covered with moss. No footprints had disturbed that surface to give her hope, no small voice answered hers. Grief overwhelmed her, and she retreated to stand by the pool, trembling, then sank to the ground. Some part of her had believed that he would be here, that she would find him safe. She lowered her face into her hands, but before she could let her tears claim her, she froze with fear at the unmistakable sound of a sword being unsheathed.

"Dinna move, ye filthy Viking!" a rough voice shouted angrily.

* * *

Nell turned from the window; Margaret had been gone a long time. At first she'd dozed, then woke fully as she'd heard the sounds of men moving in the courtyard. Perhaps Margaret had already returned, was even now busy below. Nell dressed quickly and peered through the window slit another time. She could not see Margaret, or Rignor, only Irishmen moving about in the courtyard, but that was to be expected since her view was so limited. She would go down and find out.

The first thing she saw when she opened the remains of the door was Tiernan. He leaned against the opposite wall and smiled at her, as though waiting outside her door was an everyday occurrence.

"Good morning," he said cheerfully.

She threw him a doubtful look as she stepped into the hallway. "Good morning. Have ye seen Margaret?"

"Not today."

She thanked him and started for the stairs. He followed. She stopped and he stopped. She frowned at him, not bothering to hide her suspicion. "Are ye following me?"

He nodded. "I am guarding ye."

"Why?"

"Well . . . Rory O'Neill told me to."

"And ye always do what he says?"

"I do. Rory is the chief of all Ulster. He's like yer uncle William. If William told ye to do something, ye'd do it, aye?"

Nell nodded slowly. "Aye."

"And before Rory told me to guard ye, my brother had done the same."

"And ye always do what Gannon says as well?"

"Not always. But he's a fair bit older than me, so usually I do what he says or pay the price for it."

"Does he beat you?"

The corner of Tiernan's mouth curved upward. "Oh, aye, something fierce."

Nell gave him a look of disdain. "He does not."

Tiernan laughed. "No, he doesna beat me. I'm a bit old for that, aye?"

"Then what does he do to ye?"

"Makes me feel bad about not doing what he asked."

Nell sighed. "Margaret does the same."

"And so ye do what she says, aye?"

"Usually. Do yer parents make ye obey him?"

Tiernan's expression sobered. "My father was killed years ago. My mother died last winter. Neither of us has married, so it's only me and Gannon left."

"Oh. I'm sorry."

"So, ye see, we ken, Gannon and me, some of what ye're feeling."

Her eyes widened. "Aye."

"It's frightening, isn't it, to have yer world change so quickly?"

"Aye."

"Rory will see that ye get to yer uncle's safely."

"Rignor says we should stay here."

"Aye, well, yer brother says a lot of things when he's drinking."

"Margaret wants to wait to see if Davey or the others come back."

"We canna stay, and ye're not safe here without us, Nell."

"But we canna leave until we find Davey!"

He said nothing, but she could see his pity, his obvious belief that they would not find her brother. She stared at him for a moment, her mind in a whirl, then started down the stairs. "I have to find Margaret."

He followed her silently.

The hall was almost empty, but Rignor and Rory O'Neill were there, leaning over the table, looking at a map spread before them. Rignor pointed at something, then looked up as Nell and Tiernan approached.

"Where's Margaret?" Rignor demanded.

"She went looking for Davey. A long time ago," Nell said.

"She'll be fine," O'Neill said. "She's being guarded."

Rignor spun around. "Why was I not told?"

"Because ye were sleeping," the older man said briskly, rising to his feet. "This map helped. Now, show me where ye buried the head ye found."

Rignor was sullen, but he did as O'Neill asked, leading the Irishman, and Nell and Tiernan, from the keep to the graveyard where O'Neill's men were busy digging long shallow graves. O'Neill did not need Rignor to point anything out; his men called him over to an open shallow hole.

O'Neill reached into the ground and pulled the head out by its hair, holding it high for all to see. Nell, her stomach roiling, turned away. If the head had been hideous then, it was a thousand times worse now.

"Norseman." O'Neill spit the words.

"What does it mean?" Tiernan asked. "How did he get here?"

Nell heard a thud, and O'Neill walked past her, wiping his empty hands on his thighs. His men shoveled dirt back into the hole.

"That man did not die in his bed; he died in battle, and not too long ago. I think that they took their dead from Antrim out to sea and dumped them there." O'Neill moved away, giving orders as he left.

Rignor moved to Nell's side. "Dinna be fooled by him, Nell, nor by Gannon. Somehow they plan to gain from this."

"What would they gain?"

"My land. Who wouldna want Somerstrath? Ye're young, little sister. I think they lie with every breath." Rignor stalked toward the gate.

Tiernan's voice behind her was quiet but firm. "Gannon doesna lie. Rory doesna lie. And none of us want Somerstrath."

Nell whirled around, realizing that he'd heard their conversation. His gaze held hers for a moment, then she looked away.

Margaret spun around. Just outside the glade, in the shadow of the pines that towered over the pathway, stood Rufus of Inverstrath, a circle of his men, weapons drawn, around Gannon. She'd had no idea anyone was following her.

"We caught the bastard," Rufus said. "He was following ye, Lady Margaret, the Viking swine. God only kens what he meant to do."

Gannon's gaze met hers, his eyes a deep blue. If she said the word, Rufus's men would kill him, or try to. She could see his knowledge of that in his eyes—and, of all things, impatience. But not fear. How could he be so calm? Who was this man, who did not cringe with a blade at his throat, who watched her with such intensity?

She moved closer to him, to be sure Rufus's men did not harm him.

"Put up yer weapons, Rufus," she said, more calmly than she felt.

"Have ye gone daft, Margaret MacDonald? Somerstrath has been attacked and this Viking was following ye and ye want us to put up our weapons?"

"He's not a Viking," she said. "He's Irish."

Rufus gave Gannon a skeptical appraisal. "What's an Irishman who looks like this doing here just the now? If he's Irish, I'm an elephant. I dinna believe it."

"He's here with Rory O'Neill. Put yer weapons down, Rufus."

Rufus ignored her, turning to Gannon. "Why were ye following her?"

Gannon's tone was calm. "I followed her to protect her."

Rufus snorted. "It's ye who needs protection, Norseman. Ye might notice that it's ye at the wrong end of the sword. And who are ye protecting her from?"

"The likes of ye. How d'we ken it wasna ye who attacked Somerstrath?"

Rufus's men exchanged looks. Several moved closer to Gannon.

"That's absurd, Gannon," Margaret said. "This is Rufus MacDonald, from Inverstrath; he's my father's tacksman. Rufus, how is it that ye're here?"

"Some of yer people came to us in the night, telling tales of Norsemen."

"Was Davey among them? How many came to ye?"

"Twelve is all, lass. And no, he wasna."

"Twelve." The word hung in the air between them. Only twelve people had escaped to Inverstrath? "Who?"

As Rufus said the names, Margaret did the tally in her head. There were the twelve at Inverstrath. Those at the shielings. And the Somerstrath dead. All were accounted for—except five small boys.

"Did they tell ye aught of Davey?" she asked.

"Aye." Rufus's mouth twisted but he met her gaze. "The Norsemen took him with them. Some of yer people saw them. They took him and a few others and put them in the dragonships."

"Dragonships."

She looked at Gannon. Rufus's man leaned closer to him now, the tip of his sword against Gannon's neck. Gannon's stance shifted, and his fingers tightened on the hilt of his sword. He turned his gaze from Margaret to Rufus for a long moment, then, without warning, whirled on the man behind him. Margaret gasped and stifled a scream. One twist, one swift kick and the man was on the ground, his sword in the dirt. Gannon put a foot on the man's chest and held his sword at the man's throat, staring at the others, his blue eyes cold, his gaze calculating, his body ready.

She'd known that Gannon was a strong man and assumed that he could defend himself quite ably; but she'd been unprepared for the swiftness of his attack, for the murderous look that had come into his eyes, for how easily he'd subdued Rufus's man, who lay on the ground, his eyes bulging as he looked up at Gannon. There was a nervous muttering among Rufus's men, but none moved.

"Get back," Gannon said. "Margaret, get yerself behind me."

She shook her head. "I ken these men. They willna harm me."

Rufus was unshaken. "Irish, ye say. Interesting time for a visit."

"There were raids in Antrim," Gannon answered, "smaller than here, but still brutal. We came to tell Ross and discovered he'd had raids of his own."

"On Ross land?" Rufus asked.

"Aye."

Rufus nodded to himself, as though verifying something. "I'd heard as much. Let my man up."

"Tell the rest of yer men to back away."

"Not until that one is safe. Ye canna escape all of us."

"I'm no' trying to escape."

"Let him go, Gannon," Margaret said. When he ignored her, she turned to Rufus. "His name is Gannon MacMagnus. Between them he and O'Neill have over two hundred men at Somerstrath and three ships on the beach. Ye must have come overland or ye would have seen them."

Rufus heard her warning. "Aye, we did."

"Let him up, Gannon," she said.

Gannon gestured to Rufus's men, who still held their swords at the ready.

"Rufus," she said.

There was a long moment in which Rufus and Gannon stared at each other, then Rufus gestured for his men to lower their weapons; they did so with obvious displeasure and distrust of him. Gannon watched them for a moment, then sheathed his sword, the blade sliding into place with an icy sound that made her shiver. The man on the ground scrambled to his feet, his face gray.

Rufus put out his hand to Gannon. "No harm done, aye?"

"No harm done," Gannon said as he took Rufus's hand.

Rufus turned to Margaret then. "Come, lass, let's find yer Rory O'Neill." He led the way toward the village, his men at his heels, moving quickly away from Gannon, but with glances over their shoulders at him.

Margaret stared at Gannon for a moment, thinking of the man who had wrapped his arms protectively around her in Fiona's house. Who had followed her this morning. Who could kill as easily as he could walk.

Rufus cleared his throat. "Come, lass," he called.

She did, leaving Gannon where he was. She had not intended to turn to see if he followed; but of course she did. And of course he was there, his gait sure, his gaze on her.

The Irishmen's horns sounded hollow in the sudden mist that swept over the village, closing the graveyard from the sky and muting the sounds of shovels digging into soil. Margaret stood with Nell and Rignor, her hand in her sister's, unmindful of the moisture collecting on her clothing, watching through a tunnel of regret as the bodies of her parents and brothers were carried by strangers, her heart matching the slow beats of the drums. The horns sounded again, and the bodies were carefully placed on the ground.

They would be buried in the same grave. Her father was first, the thane of Somerstrath no more, just a broken man who had died violently and in vain, his sacrifice not enough to protect his family nor keep his people safe. The Irishmen lay him in the middle of the hollow, handing his sword to Rignor, the simple motion conveying the title of Somerstrath and all that meant. Her mother was next, her swollen body still discernible beneath the coverings.

A brother or a sister I'll never ken. And there's Ewan, brave lad, still a boy, but dying with a sword in his hand. And Cawley, just learning about the world. And Fergus, only four years on this earth, a bairn still, who died in terror, cringing in a corner while the world went mad. She looked up at the sun, hiding behind the mist as though it could not face this task either. *And somewhere out there, God kens where, is Davey.*

The drum beat again, slowly, the sound curling through her body and up the side of the ruined keep, to soar, finally, into the heavens, taking with it, she prayed, the souls of her family, to reside at last at the right hand of God. Rignor stood stiffly at her side, and Nell sobbed loudly, but Margaret felt nothing, just a numbness that made it all feel like a dream, as though she watched this happening to someone else. It was not real. It could not be real, for if it were, she did not know what next to do.

She tried to listen as Rory O'Neill said a few prayers, but her mind wandered, remembering small moments. Fergus handing her a flower before she left. Father, holding Nell as an infant, her tiny finger wrapped around his, telling Margaret that she'd looked just the same when she was a bairn. Fiona's face, twisted with anger when they parted. The day Ewan had been born and she'd first tasted whisky, her father so delighted with his second son that he'd stood on the parapet and sung to the moon. Cawley dancing in the waves, his head thrown back and arms wide with delight. Her mother, large with child, leaning into the light to finish the hem on one of the gowns Margaret would bring to her new life. The hall, full of music and laughter while the rain pounded on the roof and no one heard. Was that all that life was, a series of images, threaded together by a common cord, whether of blood tie or love?

She did not hear the drumbeats end, but suddenly realized that Rory O'Neill was watching her and Rignor and Nell, waiting for them to do something. Rignor stepped forward, lifted a handful of soil, and dropped it slowly onto the bodies, then took a shovel from an Irishman and began to fill the grave. As Margaret bent to lift another shovel, Gannon stepped forward, taking it from her without a word. She met his gaze briefly before he looked down into the grave. She stepped back. The wind rose, from the sea this time, bringing the smell of the water, clean, untainted by death, the sun just behind it, warming the air quickly, steam rising from the ground and their clothing.

She could not bear to watch her family disappear from her forever. She looked at the trees that lined the graveyard instead, at the mountains visible between the boughs. At Gannon's bright hair, spilling across his shoulders as he lifted the dark soil in rhythmic strokes that matched Rignor's. She would remember this all her life, she knew, the sound of the scrape of the shovel through soil, the soft tumbling of the dirt, Nell's anguished sobs, and her own tears running unchecked down her cheeks. She would remember Rignor's face, harsh with grief. Tiernan's shaky breathing, Rory O'Neill wiping his eyes. And Gannon's hair catching the sunlight.

He will be golden. She shook, as though she'd been touched. The old woman's voice had sounded so clear, so near. She looked around, sure that others had heard it, but no one seemed to have. Except for Gannon, who paused to look at her as though he, too, had heard the words. She looked away, but the echoes lingered.

He will bring life after death.

They buried Inghinn and her babe next, her father's bastard tiny in the ground. The prayers were fewer this time, and again Gannon helped fill the grave. She watched him again, unable to tear her gaze away from his golden hair, from the golden wristbands he wore, to the woven armbands revealed when he'd shed his shirt, bands that tightened on the muscles of his arms as he worked. *He will be golden.*

Hours later, when they'd buried all the Somerstrath dead, Margaret walked numbly through the village toward the harbor. They would sail with the tide to Inverstrath, where Rufus had vowed to provide them with a decent meal and a safe bed. She tried not to look at the empty houses they were passing, not to name those who had lived behind each door, not to remember running though these streets as a girl, when death had only been a word talked about in low tones by adults. At Fiona's door Nell paused, her face ashen, but Margaret kept walking.

She let one of O'Neill's men carry her from the shingle and hand her to the waiting hands that brought her aboard O'Neill's ship, while behind her another carried Nell. Some of Rufus's men would travel overland to Inverstrath with the ponies, but the rest climbed into O'Neill's second ship, Gannon and Tiernan into their own. *Gannon's Lady,* his ship was named. She could not look at the Norse runes that decorated his ship's railings, tried not to see the mixture of Celtic and Norse symbols carved into the wood.

She stood in the stern of O'Neill's ship with Rignor and Nell while O'Neill's men pushed the ship deeper into the water. She shivered as a cool wind came suddenly from the west, pushing clouds forward to cover the sun and drain the very color from Somerstrath, leaving it gray and silent, as though the wind that raced through the homes and into the mountains had come simply to take with it the last traces of life. *How can we leave?* She glanced at Rignor, whose expression was ravaged.

"We'll be back," she assured him. "We'll rebuild it all." Her words sounded thin and false. He did not respond.

O'Neill's men rowed the ship away from shore. The sail was being raised now, the canvas fluttering, then filling as the wind lifted it, but Margaret looked only at her home, not even turning when at last the tide caught the ship, gliding it through the arms of the harbor and to the open sea. The men rested on their oars, staring with her at the remains of Somerstrath. First the trees at the foot of the glen faded from view, then the houses, one by one melding into a gray mass. Only the keep and the burnt bones of her father's ships on the beach were visible now, the ribs of their hulls dark and naked, as though they'd died on the strand like beached whales.

You'll be torn from your home . . .

The girl who had scoffed uneasily at an old woman's words was gone. This was what the woman had meant, this time, these deeds. *You'll face dragons.*

Margaret looked across the water to Gannon's ship. A dragonship. A man with golden dragons around his neck. As though she'd called him, Gannon turned to meet her gaze. The sun caught his hair again, lighting it and the gold of the brooch at his shoulder.

You'll face dragons. You need to prepare yourself.

Margaret crossed herself. This was only the beginning.

TEN

The Norseman sailed home with his ships full of plunder and his mood triumphant. Six raids, the one on Somerstrath the most successful of all. As he entered the harbor he raised his hand and made an obscene gesture to the sky. Then beached his ships and strode ashore.

His men bragged that they'd left no one alive in Somerstrath. Which was true, except for the five small captives they'd taken. He was pleased. A few more raids and all of Ireland and Scotland would know of him. The Scots and Irish would have one summer of terror, then a winter of worry. And next spring, when he sent his men to demand gold in lieu of a visit from his dragonships, they would all scramble to pay.

The scheme was not new. It was as ancient as men; he was simply one more in a grand line of warriors, stretching back to the dawn of time, who took what they desired from those too weak to prevent them. Men would flock to join him and soon, when the gold came to him with no effort but transport, he'd be powerful and noteworthy. The leaders of these islands, the thane of Orkney, even the kings of Ireland and Scotland and Norway, would know he was a force to be reckoned with.

His bloodline of Vikings and warriors would be carried forward by the children he would father, mixing with those of the women he chose to receive his seed. His name and his blood would live forever. Who could ask for more? His success was sweeter than he'd expected, not the least for the discomfort it brought his brother. Ander had watched his homecoming with a sour expression.

That night the Norseman had slept in his father's house, and no one as much as commented, let alone tried to stop him. He slept well, enjoying the comforts of his father's bed as much as the symbolism of his presence there. He was joined by one of his favorite women, the wife of a man who had accompanied him on the raids, and none gainsayed him there either. She told him that sharing his bed was now a goal for many of the women; he gave her a necklace for it.

The next evening he hosted a great feast that most on the island attended, some delighted to be included, some fearful of declining the invitation. Throughout the evening, he dispensed gifts to show these people he could be as generous as he was ruthless. His nephew Drason received a woolen cloak lined with fur that had been taken from Somerstrath. But before his nephew could do more than unfold it, his brother ripped it from Drason's hands and threw it across the room, shouting that neither he nor his family would accept gifts from a murderer.

"Calm yourself, Ander," the Norseman said, his tone disdainful. He smiled to hide his anger. "I have simply done what you were unwilling to do—brought your son the finery he deserves. When he's old enough to grow a beard he'll get his own. Until then he must rely on me, for you're too timid to do it."

"Finery!" Ander shouted, holding the cloak high. "This was stolen from a man who never did you harm, whose only sin was to live close to the shore."

"Those foolish enough not to protect themselves lose what they have."

"Including their lives?"

"Including their lives. I do not set the laws of nature, Ander. I merely observe them and act accordingly. Some of us are brave enough to face the world; others risk nothing and wait at home in safety. Which are you, brother?"

"You twist words! What you have done is not brave, it is barbaric."

"Someone must feed our people. I don't see you doing that."

"We are not starving."

"We are one bad harvest from it. One needs to plan for the future, Ander, not simply let it come. Unlike you, I am thinking of more than my own household. Someone must keep our people well fed and safe. And if, in doing that, we also bring our own people some small luxuries, who are you to oppose it?"

Ander made a disgusted sound and stormed out of the building. His son, with a glance over his shoulder, followed. The Norseman called for music and more wine, his tone untroubled, as though he were not seething inside at his brother's opposition.

But Ander was not the only one openly to oppose him that night. When the island's priest arrived, fresh from seeing a soul into the afterlife, the Norseman offered him Somerstrath's golden chalices and the priest's vestments embroidered with golden thread found with them.

"I will accept none of these things." The priest glowered at those who had taken part in the raids. "What you have done is wrong; you must repent and return these whence you have stolen them, then ask God to forgive you."

The Norseman pretended not to hear the murmurs of his guests. "Does God not give us each tools with which to live our lives, Father?"

"He does."

"So, if God has given me the mind and the will to take these things from a priest who did not keep them protected, are my actions not God's will? How do you know He did not wish me to do exactly as I have done, to bring them to you to treasure and protect? If God had not wanted me to raid Antrim and Scotland, He would have stopped me, Father. He did not; I cannot think that He wants me to do other than what I have done."

The priest's face grew scarlet. "What you have done is not God's will."

"How do you know? Perhaps God has provided them for you, through me. God did not smite me down, Father, nor did Christ protect the former owner of these. You may have misunderstood God's intent. Perhaps He meant for me to do exactly as I did, and perhaps you are very wrong in not accepting these as His gifts through me."

"You risk the fires of Hell."

"I am doing God's will."

"Blasphemy! Heresy!" the priest cried, drawing himself taller. "You will be punished for your sins. You will all be punished. I beg you, in God's name, to stop the killing. I demand it! God demands it!"

An uneasy murmur ran through the people.

The Norseman laughed. "If God wants me to stop raiding, He will stop me. Until then, I will do as I wish."

"Perhaps God will be more merciful with you than you have been with those poor souls you have murdered. I cannot stay to see any more of this." The priest rushed from the building.

The Norseman clapped his hands. "More wine! We have much to celebrate!" He ignored the looks the people exchanged among themselves. Fools! The course was set; this was no time for hesitation. He felt no remorse, only a sense that he was fulfilling the destiny set out for him. In time, they would see how correct he was; they'd praise him for his forethought and wisdom; his name would be listed among the great leaders of his people.

In the morning the priest was gone.

The next few days were calmer, as the men of the island returned to their usual tasks. Life returned to normal. Almost. Ander's glowing anger did not diminish with time but burned brighter. The Norseman knew his brother talked behind his back, and that, as the glow of triumph from the raids faded, his words would have more impact. He needed another successful raid. And he had to silence Ander.

Those who had accompanied him on the raids swaggered through the village and talked of future trips. Those who had stayed behind were divided into two camps—those who wished they'd gone and those who were horrified by what had been done. Arguments were becoming commonplace. The Norseman ignored them. Let them argue, he told himself. And fight each other if they would. The strongest and most ruthless would win and they were the ones he wanted with him. These voyages were not for the faint of heart. Which was why neither of his brothers was here with him now.

To those who muttered comments criticizing him, those who were brave enough to make their distaste public, he showed contempt and his men followed his example. Some left, abandoning homes and farms, and he gave their holdings to others. He told himself he was a man of vision. He wore fine linen, new bands of gold on each arm and a thick Irish torque around his neck. His home was decorated with the rugs and chairs they'd taken on the raids. He feasted on olives from Sicily and oranges from Spain, courtesy of the laird of Somerstrath. At night his bed was shared and his body well served. These rewards were rightly his.

Men came from other islands to talk, some to join him, some bringing with them stories of others now planning similar attacks. His fame had spread, and his followers increased threefold, and he pointed this out to his brother with a self-satisfied tone. Ander glowered, and the brothers argued again, loudly and publicly, their shouts ringing through the hall. It could not go on, this public opposition.

And it did not. He killed Ander. He'd had no choice.

It had been so very simple. Late one afternoon he called his brother to him, greeting Ander warmly and offering him wine, saying that they needed peace between them. Ander would have none of it at first, telling the Norseman that he must stop the raids, send the men from the other islands home, and call back the priest. The Norseman had agreed to all, pretending that he regretted what he had done, telling Ander that he now understood that he had offended God with his actions, that the priest had been right in damning him. And begging Ander's help in setting it all right. Ander had believed him. And paid with his life.

His brother should have been wary—his accusations of murder had been correct, after all—and yet Ander had been so easy to fool. The Norseman, on the pretense of going to talk to the priest, had lured Ander on to his small boat. On the way out to sea Ander had said that the priest would not be easily found. The Norseman amused himself by agreeing—the priest, his body weighted and probably already eaten by sea creatures—would be very difficult to find.

Ander never saw the blow that struck his head. He died without a sound. It had been so simple then, to tie the ropes around the notched stones he'd thought to bring, then around Ander's body, to push him, heavy and awkward in death, over the railing and into the water. He sank quickly, silently, only the slightest disturbance of the water to mark his passing, a circle of ripples that were soon caught by the current and torn apart.

The Norseman watched the water until the surface was calm, then raised his fist to the sky. "Take that, old man," he roared. "And you as well, brothers." He smiled at the thought that his father and Thorfinn might know what he'd just done. His father might have understood. The old man had mellowed in his last years, faltered, but he'd once been a formidable warrior; he might have embraced his plan and seen in it the future of his people, the reclamation of his own legacy. But his brothers? The Norseman spit into the water. Good riddance.

No one ever spoke of seeing them leave the village

together. The hue began at nightfall, when Ander's wife Eldrid came to him, asking for Ander, saying the last time she saw her husband he was coming to the Norseman's home. He spread his hands wide and shrugged, saying that he and Ander had argued and Ander had left a short time later. None of his guards said otherwise, though they exchanged glances with each other. He'd chosen his men well.

One day passed with no trace of Ander, and while Eldrid wept and shouted that he'd killed his brother, the Norseman stayed calm. The next day he called her to him, sending his men away. When she began her foul accusations, he slapped her, once, then again across her mouth. She gasped and held her hands before her. He slapped them away, then shoved her against the wall and leaned heavily against her, keeping his voice very quiet.

"Listen to me carefully," he said. "If you accuse me again of killing Ander, by word or deed, or even by so much as a look, Eldrid, I will kill Drason."

Her eyes grew wider and her mouth fell open. "You wouldn't. He's your nephew."

"It's your choice."

"I'll tell the world."

"Then you will mourn your son as you now mourn your husband."

She opened her mouth to protest, but he covered it with his, and slowly, with great care to detail, ripped her clothing from her. She fought him, but he was stronger and when he took his knife and ran it along her shoulder, she stopped moving. He watched the thin line of blood, vivid against her pale skin, roll from her collarbone to her breast. He dipped his finger in the blood and stroked it along her lips, looking into her eyes.

"A token, Eldrid, of what's to come if you talk."

She whimpered and fell limp against him. He took her there, brutally but quickly, leaving her in a crumpled heap on the floor when he was finished.

She did not accuse him again.

Gannon shaded his eyes against the glare off the water, scanning the horizon for sails. Nothing. He'd not expected to see any sign of a dragonship, but he looked anyway, enjoying the empty sea. He let his gaze drift along the shoreline; they were almost to Inverstrath. The journey had been short and uneventful; Somerstrath's children had sailed with Rory, and Rufus and his men on Rory's second ship. He'd tried not to look at Margaret as the ships pulled back from the shore, but he'd not been able to resist watching her. It had been a long time since a woman had kept his attention for more than a few hours, but Margaret of Somerstrath did. She was so lovely. She would, he decided now, still be beautiful despite the passage of time, like his grandmother had been. Like his mother, had she lived long enough, might have been. Like few women were. Something in the way she moved, in the way her hand would rest at her throat, such a feminine gesture. In the way her gaze found his as often as his found hers.

But nothing would come of it. She was promised elsewhere. And he had better things to do than stay in Scotland longer than Rory needed him here. He and Tiernan would go home to Haraldsholm, to become part of their uncle's retinue, or to join Rory O'Neill elsewhere.

And soon he'd forget her dark eyes and darker hair, the way she looked at him. Let the Scots take care of their own. He was sure they could. Margaret MacDonald would wed her Lachlan Ross, and they'd never meet again.

And yet . . . *Will he keep her safe?*

It was not his concern. The raids were extensive, sure to garner the attention of King Alexander and Scotland's powerful lairds. The Scots would soon be guarding their coastline, as Erik would be at home. Margaret Mac-Donald's uncle was a powerful man; she would be protected.

Rory's ship drew abreast of his, and Gannon sought her out without thinking, her soft body in sharp contrast to the men around her and the sea beyond. He willed her to look at him, and as though she'd heard his thoughts, Margaret turned and met his gaze. The sounds of the sail overhead and the water slapping the bow faded from his notice. He smiled. She lifted a hand in a small wave, then brought it to her throat as though displeased by her own gesture and turned away. He fought the emotions that swept over him. She was a lovely woman. Of course he noticed her. He lowered his hand and checked the lines, concentrating on sailing, on the changing coastline, and, as they passed what proved to be the final headland, on his first sight of Inverstrath.

Rufus's home was very different from Somerstrath, although both were protected by jutting headlands north and south, and both had very serviceable harbors. But where Somerstrath was built on land that sloped from the deep harbor to the foot of the glen, Inverstrath's fortress sat behind a deep flat plain that rose only slightly from the water. Instead of Somerstrath's tall stone keep, surrounded by fortified walls and a prosperous village enclosed by yet another wall, Rufus's fortress was a long string of two-story wooden buildings that looked like they had once been separate buildings, joined at a later date. The rambling structure was surrounded by wooden fortifications, yes, but the walls looked easy to breech, the gates insubstantial, although well manned. And the fortress had been built in a dip between two headlands that jutted out to sea, lower than the hills behind it. It could easily flood in a wet year; in a dry year the wind could help fire roar through its halls. And at any time, an enemy could station himself on one of the headlands and attack the fortress from above, or set up a siege on the unprotected plain before the gates.

He would have done it very differently. He would have built atop one of the headlands, and built of stone, as the Normans did, rather than burnable wood. Someday, when he at last came to it, his home would be built with security as the primary concern; within its walls his family would be safe. He'd study the winds and water patterns and learn from them. He'd build in harmony with the land, using the mountains as a defense, the headlands as foundations, and the water as an ally, recognizing it for the highway it was. And when that day came, if that day came, his men would be trained and vigilant, his woman and children protected. He turned to look at Margaret one last time, then they arrived.

The Inverstrath men were armed and wary, relaxing their guard only when Rufus jumped from Rory's ship and waded ashore, calling for them to welcome their visitors. The men who had traveled with him jumped from the ship, then Rory and his men followed with Margaret and

Nell and their brother. Gannon and Tiernan and their men were last, walking past the villagers who came forward to welcome Rufus home. Gannon ignored the whispered comments of Rufus's people that he looked like a Norseman, ignored the fear in their eyes as he passed, ignored the way the people moved back from him as though he might murder someone at any moment.

Margaret turned to throw a glance at him over her shoulder, then told the villagers, her voice clear and carrying, "No, he's Irish. He's protecting us."

The last woman to defend him had been his mother, and that a very long time ago. He smiled to himself as she turned yet again and saw him watching her.

Rory stepped aside and waited for Gannon to join him. "We'll have to have ye dressing like the Scots soon to reassure them."

"No' likely," Gannon answered. "I'll wear no skirts."

"Dinna tell the Scotsmen ye think they're wearing skirts, laddie. Some of the fiercest men I've ever kent have worn the feileadh. It's what's underneath that counts, and ye have those."

Gannon laughed with him then, watching Margaret's body move as they approached the gates, watching her hair sway with her steps, her hips move, her skirts lifting with her steps, revealing slim ankles that tapered up . . .

"Dinna stare at her," Rory said quietly. "They might forgive ye for looking like a Norseman, but they'll not forgive ye for acting like one."

"How did I survive all those years without yer help?"

Rory gave a grunt of laughter. "Not well, I can tell ye that. Ye've much to learn still, lad." He paused, then continued, his tone thoughtful. "On the other hand . . . if we

can find ye a Scottish heiress . . . not this one, she's land-
less and promised. But it's a thought worth pursuing. Try
and look harmless, aye?"

Gannon swallowed his smile and followed Rory
through the gates, past the curious crowds gathered
there, and into Rufus's fortress. The hall was large, and
dimly lit, its rough-hewn walls undecorated, benches
polished by use, not oils, and a handful of tables, their
surfaces scarred and pitted. Rufus, it seemed, was a man
who wasted neither coin nor effort on comfort. Gannon
and Tiernan were ushered forward, to stand with Rory
and be introduced to Rufus's subordinates, and then to a
pretty woman who came to stand at his side, her stance
assured, breasts outthrust, her gaze direct.

"My daughter, Dagmar," Rufus said.

This, then, was the woman Rory had warned him
about. She was tall, her dark blond hair pulled back to
show even features, winged eyebrows above brown eyes.
She wore deep red, the same color on her lips, and she
smiled with unmistakable welcome. Her open appraisal of
both brothers amused Gannon, but Tiernan stared as
though transfixed, which amused Gannon even more. A
serving girl placed a tray of ale on the table and Dagmar
leaned low for two cups, her bodice falling forward, revealing her ample breasts; she pretended not to notice, but gave
herself away with her sidelong glance. She gave Rignor a
cup of ale and a long, slow smile that made him take a half
step forward toward her. So that's the way of it, Gannon
thought, as she handed cups to him and Tiernan. She took
one for herself and sipped, looking at Gannon over the rim.

"Welcome to Inverstrath, my lords," she said, her
voice warm and deep and full of invitation.

Tiernan mumbled something incoherent. Gannon thanked her, then watched his brother stare at Dagmar. She was giving Rignor her attention now, leaning forward, her mouth slightly open, one hand at her throat, as he told of what had happened at Somerstrath. Gannon drank deeply of the ale; it was almost as good as William Ross's. Rufus might not know how to build a strong fortress, but he knew how to brew. And his daughter knew how to captivate men.

Interesting mix, Gannon thought, then turned to see how Margaret was faring. She and Nell had been enveloped by a group of people as they'd entered the hall, almost all of them talking at once. Margaret was weeping as she listened.

"Those are the ones who made it here from Somerstrath," Rufus said, following his gaze. "The women and children were in the upper pastures. The men were hunting. They saw some of the fighting, and they're the ones who saw Davey and the others taken."

"We'll have to talk to them," Gannon said.

Rufus raised an eyebrow. "Ye'll be the last one they'll talk to."

"Then let Rignor talk to them. We need to find out everything we can about how the Norse attacked, how they got into and around the village so quickly."

Rory nodded. "Whether they saw anything that could lead us to who did it."

"Are ye going after them, then?" Rufus asked.

Rory and Gannon exchanged a glance.

"We'll wait for William Ross," Rory said.

Margaret wept as she embraced the handful of Somerstrath villagers who had escaped and come to

Inverstrath. Twelve in all, six women, four children, and two men. None had seen the Norsemen arrive, but they had heard the screams and the clash of weapons. Margaret listened quietly while they told of their terror, of the dreadful things they'd seen, of their headlong rush to Inverstrath for their safety, and their guilt for surviving.

"Did ye see them take Davey?" Margaret asked.

One woman nodded. "He was kicking and screaming when they took him. They hauled the boys like sacks of meal, all five of them."

Margaret closed her eyes, then opened them immediately as visions of Davey's abduction filled her mind. He's alive, she told herself. If the Norsemen had meant to kill him, they would have saved themselves the bother of taking him along. Which meant he was still alive, and that was what she would remember.

"Lass." Rory O'Neill put a hand on her arm, his voice gentle as he nodded to the Somerstrath people. "Come, if ye would, all of ye, and tell us what ye saw."

Margaret sat woodenly, trying not to visualize their words as the survivors told their tales, her thoughts tumbling. She watched Rignor, suddenly realizing that he'd not joined her and Nell to greet the Somerstrath people. He'd waited for them to come to him. And even now, as they poured out their hearts, he hardly listened, watching Dagmar instead. Scowling as Dagmar, returning with a pitcher of ale, settled herself between the MacMagnus brothers rather than next to him. Dagmar's expressions of dismay were well timed, her gaze flashing often to Gannon. When he ignored her, she turned her charms on Tiernan, and found more success there.

Margaret let her gaze drift to the distance, wondering what she would have done if she'd been at Somerstrath when the Norsemen came, or if they'd arrived home to find the attack under way. Would she have run into the thick of the fighting, only to be killed herself? Or would she have hidden, as these survivors had done, and lived to tell the tale? What was courage, what prudence, or honor or foolishness? She no longer knew.

The topic turned from what had happened to what they should do about it. Rory O'Neill said he'd stay until Uncle William or his men arrived to be sure Inverstrath was secure. Rufus thanked him, but his ambivalence was obvious. When he wondered aloud how he was to feed and house two hundred additional men, Rory O'Neill bristled.

"Surely ye dinna begrudge us food while we stay and protect ye?"

"Of course I'm grateful, my lord," Rufus protested.

Rory, mollified, nodded. "My men will help hunt and fish," he said.

Rufus thanked him, and the men continued talking. But Margaret, meeting Gannon's gaze, did not hear another word. Something had ignited in his blue eyes, something flashed between the two of them now. She pushed her hair off her suddenly warm neck and watched him watch her. She looked away from his smoldering gaze. Rignor's gaze was heated as well, but her brother's emotion was easy to understand. He scowled as Dagmar edged closer to Tiernan, their heads together and their voices hushed. Nell nudged Margaret and gestured at them. Across the table, Gannon leaned his chin on his hand and watched his brother.

After Rignor had made a speech of vengeance and Rufus and his men had loudly proclaimed their assistance, after the men had exhausted all topics of discussion, after the Somerstrath survivors had been distributed among the houses of the village, and the Irishmen started stretching out to sleep on the floor of the hall, Margaret turned to find Dagmar at her elbow.

"I'll show ye where ye'll sleep," Dagmar said.

None of the men, leaning over a crude sea chart, seemed to notice when she and Nell rose to follow Dagmar. They went up the narrow stairs at the end of the hall, around a corner, and down an even narrower and very dim hallway. Margaret tried not to compare Inverstrath's spartan comforts with the luxuries of Somerstrath. Her father would have widened the stairs. Mother would have painted those beams, would have had tapestries to soften the harsh lines of the hall below, soft rugs underfoot, torches to light the way to bed. *Don't think.*

Dagmar flung open a door. "Ye'll use my room. Ye'll share the bed."

"With ye?" Nell asked, her tone suspicious.

"I'll find somewhere else."

Somewhere else, Margaret thought, and no doubt someone else. She ignored Nell's disapproving huff. She thanked Dagmar, then waited until the door had closed behind her before turning to face Nell's outrage. She put a finger to her lips.

"Ye ken where she'll sleep!" Nell whispered indignantly. "With Rignor! Or if not with Rignor, then with Gannon or Tiernan. D'ye not think Tiernan's far too young for her?"

Margaret pulled the bedcoverings back and searched for bedbugs. "Rignor's too young for her; Rory O'Neill is too young for her. Calm yerself, Nell, Tiernan's probably safe from her predations. Dagmar wants a wealthy husband."

Nell nodded, seemingly mollified. "And Tiernan has nothing. Even Gannon has no land, only the one ship." She untied her laces and kicked off her shoes.

"And how is it ye ken all this?"

"Tiernan told me. Both their parents are dead; their father died years ago, their mother only last winter. They were living with their stepfather until she died, then they went to Haraldsholm, on the Irish shore, where their uncle lives."

"Tiernan told ye this?"

"Not all. Some of it I overheard. And I asked some of the Irishmen. And Rory O'Neill told me more. They're neither of them married."

"That's hardly surprising. As ye've said, Tiernan's young."

"But Gannon isna."

No, Margaret thought, remembering his arms around her, his body against hers, his gaze locked on to her own. Nell gave a small scream, batting a spider away from the bedcoverings. She stamped on it, then looked up.

"I hate it here! I hate Inverstrath! It's dark and crowded and we've got spiders in our bed and did ye see how dirty the hall was, and the filth on the tables, and the platters! Ye could scrape yer nail in the muck! And look at this room! Her father's the laird, and her room is this tiny hole. Look at the bed, Margaret!" Her voice was almost a wail now. "How long will we have to stay here?"

Margaret sighed and gingerly moved a pillow, half-expecting more spiders to leap out. "Until Uncle William arrives; it's safe, and that's what's important now."

"Why did this happen to us? Why are they all dead?" Nell burst into tears.

Margaret sighed, close to tears herself. She had no answers. They'd had this talk a thousand times already and she'd asked herself the same things a thousand thousand times. She waited until Nell's tears slowed, then gestured to the room. "Ye're right. Ye wouldna even ken a woman lives here, would ye?"

"And one clothes chest is all," Nell said with a sniff. "And if ye tell me that we've always had more than Dagmar, and I should be charitable, I shall scream."

"And excuse her behavior because of that? Nay. This room looks like she's visiting, not living here, like she's not planning to be here for long."

"Why dinna she stay at her second husband's home?"

"D'ye not ken the story?" When Nell shook her head, Margaret continued. "Mother probably dinna tell ye, thinking ye were too young, but ye would have heard it soon enough. Dagmar's first husband—he was that ancient man who lived near Lachlan, remember?—left her some jewelry, but little else. Her second husband sent her home to Rufus in shame. When he died, he left her nothing; his lands and home went to the daughters of his first wife. I suspect he'd seen her for what she was. She's lovely, Nell. And ambitious. But not bright."

"I dinna even think she's lovely. But Rignor does."

"Rignor's not looking past her breasts and her willingness. I'm thinking she doesna intend to stay a widow long. She's looking for a wealthy man who can give her children. One son and she's secure. While Father and Mother lived there was little chance of Rignor marrying her. And perhaps even less now. Our wealth is gone. Rignor now has nothing."

"He still has the title. And the land. And if William helps us rebuild, perhaps she'll still want to marry him. What will happen to us then?"

"I dinna ken. We can only hope he sees her for what she is."

"Not likely."

"Then we need to hope she finds someone else to pursue," Margaret said. "But enough of Dagmar. We're safe now, and we have to think on that."

"I'm trying to, but . . . It just doesna seem real. None of it seems real."

"Nor to me. Nor to me."

It was the noises in the corridor that woke her. Margaret sat up, trying to get her bearings, then remembered she was in Dagmar's bed. Dagmar's, of all the people in the world. Nell slept on, but fitfully, her mouth forming whispered words that made no sense, her head slowly shaking as though even in her dreams she denied what had happened. Margaret slipped from the bed and tiptoed across the room, listening at the door. When she heard Dagmar's voice, she opened the door a crack. Dagmar stood in the middle of the corridor, her back to Margaret, facing Gannon MacMagnus. Dagmar was laughing, the laugh of seduction, not of mirth.

Gannon had ignored Dagmar's obvious invitations all evening, was not surprised to see the beautiful woman here now, stepping out of the darkness of the hallway to greet him as he stepped away from the stairs. She smiled and walked slowly forward, the floorboards creaking under her feet. She'd chosen her time well. Rory was still below in the hall with Rufus; Rignor slept where he'd fallen on the rushes beneath the table where they'd talked, drunk again.

"Gannon," she said, her voice low and breathy with promise.

"Dagmar," he whispered. "Yer da showed us our room a'ready."

"Aye," she said. "I ken. Ye're sleeping with O'Neill and Rignor and yer brother. I thought . . ." She bent forward, shrugging her breasts from her low neckline and thrusting them forward for his touch. "I thought to offer ye a softer resting place."

He took a step back. She gave a low laugh and came closer.

"Are ye afraid of me, Irishman? Fearful that I'll bite?"

She was beautiful, and so were her breasts. He was tempted to reach for them, to feel her lushness in his hands, her warm body against him, her lovely mouth on him. To take the hand she extended to him and let her lead him away. He was sure it would be both memorable and satisfying.

"Terrified, Dagmar," he said with a smile.

She smiled widely, putting her hands on her waist and leaning forward, letting the moonlight coming through the window touch just the tips of her nipples. "I promise not to hurt ye."

She rose up and put her mouth on his cheek, then brushed it across his lips, her breasts crushed for that moment against him. His body reacted instantly. Behind her he heard a noise, but could see nothing in the darkness of the hallway. He laughed low in his throat and stepped back, knowing he was about to make an enemy of her. He yawned widely. "Thank ye, but no."

She jerked back out of the light, her hands covering her breasts. "What does that mean?"

"Think on it. It'll come to ye." He laughed and walked away, hearing her curse him and knowing she would retaliate.

Weary as he was, he did not seek his bed, but went back downstairs, so later, when Dagmar's whereabouts were discussed, none could say he'd been with her. It shouldn't matter what anyone might say. He was his own man, with no wife to answer to, no mistress to accuse him of unfaithfulness. He crossed the hall to the table where Rufus and Rory still sat, sharing the last of a stone bottle of whisky that Rufus had produced after the others had gone to sleep. Rory gave him a tired smile, and Rufus poured another cup for him as he sat on the bench.

"Got lost, did ye?" Rory asked. His tone was mild, but Gannon had no doubt that Rory had a good idea of what had just happened.

"Aye," Gannon said, and took a deep drink of the whisky, trying not to remember the tips of Dagmar's breasts in the moonlight. Perhaps he was a fool.

ELEVEN

Gannon was awake before dawn. He stood on the narrow porch that overlooked the courtyard while rain pelted the fortress, ignoring the sidelong glances he still drew from Rufus's people. Short of shearing his hair and stooping, he could think of no way to change what he looked like. But perhaps Rory was right, perhaps it was time to dress like a Scot, to don their clothing and hope they could see the man, not the Norseman. He watched the people as they worked, thinking of the little things that could be done to make their tasks easier. He was still studying them when Rufus came to stand at his side, crossing his arms over his chest as he looked out at the rain.

"Ye're up early," Rufus said.

"Aye, as ye are."

"There's always work to be done, and more when ye're housing an extra two hundred men."

Gannon gave him a sharp glance. "Would ye have us leave, then?"

Rufus shook his head, as though considering it. "No. O'Neill says he'll send some of his men hunting today."

"Aye. And mine as well. We'll help ye feed us, while we're protecting ye."

"Good." Rufus paused. "I met yer da when he came once with O'Neill."

"I dinna ken that."

"Aye. A good man. Ye have no wife in Ireland?'

"No."

"Nor land?"

"None."

Rufus nodded as though pleased. "Ye'll be staying when O'Neill goes home?"

"Until William Ross collects his family and secures the coast."

"Could be a while, then."

"Could be."

"Have ye given any thought to staying beyond that? We can always use good men, more so now than ever with Somerstrath gone."

"Rignor's now Somerstrath."

Rufus snorted. "He'll never be the man his father was. He'll never rebuild Somerstrath alone, and is unlikely to do so even with help. And Ross kens that. I'm not sure he'll replace his own nephew, but I am sure he'd be glad to ken a strong man is nearby, and I'm sure he'll continue to be a generous overlord."

"Ye're here."

"For now, but no one lives forever. My lass is getting older, too, and I've no grandchildren yet. What will happen to Inverstrath if Dagmar doesna marry a man strong enough to follow me?"

"I'm not looking for a wife."

"What man is? Think on it, lad. There's opportunity here now."

"My uncle is expecting me back in Ireland."

"There's land to be had here." Rufus laughed. "Think on it, MacMagnus. In the meantime, in exchange for my hospitality, I'll expect ye to teach my men to defend themselves against a Norseman's axe. Ye can do that, aye?"

"I can."

"Good. Start today," Rufus said, and slapped Gannon's shoulder as he left.

When the rain stopped, Gannon checked on his men at the ships, finding them safe but restless. Several were playing dice and invited him to join them. He smiled and declined, then looked north, toward the beach that was on the other side of the headland. Beyond that, if one walked far enough, was Somerstrath. To the south the arm of land that enclosed Inverstrath's harbor continued, rising steeply, its rocky crest shielding whatever lay beyond from his view. He walked toward it, southward along Inverstrath's beach, then up the headland, clambering over huge boulders and around the occasional clump of green that grew on its inhospitable slope, until at last he reached the top.

The view was worth his effort; on his right the headland continued even farther, its sides barren where it leaned out into the sea; barren on the opposite shore as well, where the ground fell from a narrow crest to disappear into the cobalt water below. The sea loch was narrow at its entrance, the two guardian headlands gray and unwelcoming even now at the height of summer. At the end of the one on which he now stood were the remnants of a tiny fort, perhaps a broch, the cylindrical towers that one found all over Ireland and Scotland. This one, unlike the others, looked not to be a safe haven, but a lookout, a protected place from which to view all who entered the loch or passed by on the sea. Its roof was gone, but the walls still stood, and from here the view was magnificent.

Just below him the loch widened, its waters still the rich blue of deep water. Navigable, he thought. The opposite shore grew even taller, a slab of gray. There was no sign of habitation, except for the path to his left that wandered along the crest of this ridge. He followed it for some fifty feet, then saw that what he'd supposed to be a shadow on the far shore was actually the mouth of a cave, gaping open, revealing a watery floor studded with boulders, like teeth in its maw. He stared at the cave, thinking of stories he'd heard as a boy, of caves where dragons lived. Or where dragonships could rest. The cave was too small to shelter one of the Norse ships, but the loch, which continued to the east, might not be.

The path stayed atop the ridge for a while, then dipped steeply to the shore. It was here that he stopped, feeling his heart's slow thud and the hairs on the back of his neck rise as the wind sighed through the trees behind him.

Welcome home.

He'd seen this view before, seen this valley, had stood at this very spot before. He'd stood on the other side of the loch, across the wide expanse of quiet water that could safely shelter two score ships, and knew, without turning, that behind him the meadow melded into the trees, the mountains towering above them. And across the water, rising from the valley floor, the ruins of an ancient wooden fortress. He did not need to travel around the end of the loch to know that he would find the fortress built as he would have built it—perhaps had built it. He did not need the whispers to tell him he'd been here before. Had loved here, for part of the memory was of a woman who stood at his side and slipped her hand in his.

Imaginings, he told himself. Dreams. He'd dreamed this place, or it looked like a spot in Ireland, which he was half-remembering.

Home. The whispers mocked him for doubting. He ignored them, concentrating on the fortress across the water. Most of the wooden walls no longer stood, but were moldering into dust. There was an outer wall halfway up that slope, its gate sideways to the water, the path to it steep and winding so attackers would have to scramble rather than march to the opening.

Below him the water lapped softly on the shore as the tide waxed to full. Then overhead to the east, the harsh cry of an eagle drew his attention to the mountain that stood sentinel over this valley. He took a deep breath, inhaling the scents of pine and salt water and heather, of sunlight on rock, and somehow, of roses, not the protected beauties of enclosed gardens, but wild roses. He thought of Rufus's offer, of Dagmar's lush body. His own land. He took one last look at the glen, wondering why no one lived there, why Rufus's people were clinging to a flat beachhead that was difficult to defend when this magnificent valley was here.

He was still pondering the question—and Rufus's offer—when he reached Inverstrath's beach. Was still mulling it over, when he saw her.

It had rained overnight and the air still smelled of it, the freshness welcome after the stifling warmth and closeness of the fortress. Margaret slipped from her bed at the first sound outside her door, grateful that the long night was over. She'd slept little and when she did, she'd had nightmares.

The field outside the walls was empty, the beach beyond it the same, but she could see men moving on and near the Irish ships. She walked slowly closer to the water, telling herself she was not searching among the Irish for one blond head that was familiar. For him. When she realized he was not among those who guarded the ships, she walked southward instead, letting the steady rise and fall of the waves comfort her. The tide was coming in and with it the wind, bringing the clean smell of the open water.

She turned away from the sea then and went into the village. Dagmar's neglect had not reached here. The homes were small, clustered together, built of stone or daub and wattle, their roofs thatched. Many had fireplaces and chimneys, as had the Somerstrath villagers, which made life in the tiny houses so much more livable than in the old days. Doors were opening as she walked, people spilling out to begin the morning's work. Children peered from behind their mothers' skirts, giving her shy smiles. She knew them all, could name each family that lived here, each family that had lost loved ones in the attack on Somerstrath or had taken in the survivors. These were all that were left of her father's people. They were her responsibility now, or more properly, Rignor's.

She was surrounded at once by the villagers. She asked about their well-being and heard all the latest happenings, even some wonderful news about an expected baby. And then, unsettling, the people told her their doubts about Rignor's capabilities to lead them. She listened, thanked them for their time, then took her leave. But heard the same worries from others as she left the village. Many others. One man stopped her to remind her that in the old days the clans would elect the next leader.

"It wasna always the old chief's son . . ." the man said, his face reddening.

Margaret nodded, trying to sound cheerful. "We'll be facing that soon enough. The first thing we need to do is make sure everyone's safe, aye? My uncle will be here soon."

"And the Irish will leave?"

"Rory O'Neill will stay until my uncle arrives."

"We've heard he'll be leaving some men behind for a bit."

"I've heard that too. Does that concern ye?"

"Did ye hear Gannon MacMagnus came through the village last night?"

"No."

"He said he wanted everyone to ken who he was and that he was no Norsemen. Looks like one, though."

Margaret nodded. "He does."

"He told us his men were no' to be feared either, and if there were any problems with them, to come to him. That set well with most of us. So, if it's Gannon that's staying behind, we won't be complaining."

"Ah," she said cautiously. "I'm sure we'll ken more soon."

She left quickly then, walking briskly before anyone else could tell her anything. She could not bear to hear any more complaints about her brother. She returned to the beach, knowing that when Uncle William arrived she'd have to tell him what she'd heard. And wondering what it meant for the future of her home and what was left of her family. It would kill Rignor, she knew, if he was displaced as her father's heir. But surely it would not come to that. Surely the people would follow Rignor, and surely her brother would become the leader they needed. Wouldn't he? She stared out over the water, trying to sort it out.

She didn't know how long she stood there, nor what made her turn, but she did, as if he'd called her name, although no one had spoken. But there he was, Gannon, moving swiftly along the strand toward her, his hair lifted by the breeze, his cloak swaying from his shoulders, his chin lifting when he saw her. He moved even faster now, his smile wide. For a moment she felt the rightness of this, of her waiting for this man to come to her, as though they'd done this a hundred times before. She swallowed, straightening her back, fighting the urge to run to him. He would open his arms, of that she was certain.

And then what?

"Margaret." His voice was hushed, meant for her alone. "Good morrow, lass. Ye're up early this morning."

She nodded, momentarily speechless. He'd not shaved; the golden bristles of his beard caught the light and drew her eye to his jawline. His tunic was not laced closed; through the opening she could see his chest, tanned skin and lower still . . . She met his gaze instead, surprised by the excitement in his eyes, the smile that transformed his face from fearsome warrior to handsome man with a secret to share.

He did not wait for her answer. "Have ye ever been south of here?"

"Aye, but not for years. There's nothing there."

He extended his hand. "Nothing, ye say? Come, let me show ye."

She did not question him, nor what she should do. Without thought, nor any look behind her, she put her hand in his and let him lead her southward, along the last of Inverstrath's beach and up the steep headland. He helped her over the larger rocks, his touch gentle but firm, his larger hand wrapping around hers, warm and strong. At the crest he released her hand and walked along the ridge, showing her the ruined fortress she'd forgotten about, as she'd forgotten how splendid the view was from here. He talked of why this sea loch was so perfect for defense,

"It's not wide enough for two ships here," he said, pointing. "Any attackers would be vulnerable from above. And there, where the loch turns, ye could have a ship waiting to meet anyone arriving. Ye could watch from the other side and have plenty of warning of anyone who approached. Come along here."

He showed her all the reasons why this valley was different from the rest of the coastline, the meadows that could be tilled, the freshwater burn that tumbled from the mountain and joined the sea loch at its most inland point, the mountains that surrounded and protected the valley, the perfect rise of rock on which to put a home, a fortress, he said, which had already been built once. She only half listened, caught more by the emotion behind his words than the words themselves, by the glow in his eyes, as though he'd triumphed in discovering this spot. By the pleasure he seemed to take in showing her.

He pointed at the ruined fortress, showing her how well it had been considered, the placement perfect for defense. And beautiful as well; the view from there would be lovely. She'd been here before, but had never noticed how blue the water, how green the trees, how majestic this valley was.

"Ye could live well here," he said. "Ye could make a home worth the effort."

"Is it a home ye're looking for, then?"

His expression closed at once, and his eyes, warm blue a moment before, turned glacial. Be careful, she told herself; a moment or two of closeness did not mean she should lower her guard. She would do well to remember that he was a stranger and not be captivated by his confident manner, his pleasing form and face. His touch, his smile. He pushed his hair back from his face with long fingers that had held hers just a few moments ago. A strong hand that had held a sword to her throat and clasped her against him in Fiona's house. That had caressed her cheek and struck Rufus's man down with equal ease. A man of changeable moods who had won over Rufus's villagers in one night and did not bother to hide his contempt for her brother. They knew so little of each other, she and Gannon MacMagnus, and perhaps that was just as well.

His voice was polite, nothing more. "We have a home in Antrim."

"Ye have land there?" she asked, remembering what Nell had told her.

"I have no land of my own."

"Where do ye live?"

"After my father died, my mother married Patrick Maguire. Tiernan and I went with her when she left Haraldsholm to go inland, to Fermanagh, where Patrick's lands are. We stayed there until Rory O'Neill came to tell us about the raids on my uncle Erik's lands. We'll live at Haraldsholm again now."

"What is it ye'll do there?"

He shrugged. "Whatever Erik needs."

"Does he need ye here in Scotland?"

His eyes flashed, and he opened his mouth, then closed it, looking from her to the view, then back. "I'm admiring the land, lass, not coveting it."

"Are ye admiring it for yer uncle or for Rory O'Neill?"

"It never hurts to ken yer allies."

"I've heard that O'Neill wants ye to stay in Scotland to watch us and report back to him."

She felt rather than saw his displeasure. "Who told ye that?"

"It doesna matter."

"It does. Where did ye hear that, Margaret?"

"When ye were talking in the hall at Somerstrath, not everyone was asleep. So does O'Neill want ye to stay in Scotland?"

"Aye."

"Ye'll be staying to protect his interests?"

"And to help. We're not so hard-hearted that we don't see that ye need us."

"Nor so hard-hearted that ye'd tell us ye'll help search for Davey."

He went very still. "Lass, ye need to face that the chances of finding him, or any of those that were taken, are small. And if he's already been sold as a slave, ye may never find him."

"That's cruel of ye to say."

"I dinna mean to be cruel. It's the truth."

"No one in Scotland would buy a slave these days."

"Ye dinna ken that. And he might not still be in Scotland. He could be in Ireland, or on one of the islands, or even in Norway perhaps. There are unscrupulous men in every land."

"Ye found the knife . . ."

"Aye, and I'm thinking that although we're supposed to be thinking Leod carried out the raids, or Skyemen at least, there is only one place under Haakon's control where Norsemen live within easy reach of both Ireland and Scotland, yet out of the reach of the leaders of either. The Orkneys."

The Orkneys, a collection of islands just off Scotland's northern coast, were run as independent fiefs, but all were under the rule of the thane of Orkney, and Haakon, the king of Norway. It would be a short voyage to sail from any of the Orkney Islands to Ireland and the west of Scotland.

"The problem is," Gannon was saying, "to discover which island, which leader, was doing the raids, without antagonizing all of them and starting a war. Relations are delicate enough now between yer Alexander and Haakon. It wouldna take more than a spark, and to accuse them might just do it."

"Ye make it seem impossible to find Davey."

"It might be. It might also be dangerous. There's more here at stake than a handful of children."

"What could be more important?" she demanded.

"If it were my brother, I'd be saying the same things. But what if these raids are being directed by Haakon himself, or by the thane of Orkney with Haakon's blessing? What if starting a war is their goal?"

"I dinna see how that affects my searching for Davey."

"Ye search for him?" He shook his head. "Why would ye be the one to do it?"

She bristled at his manner. "And why not, sir? He's my brother. How better? Or is it simply because I am a woman?"

"No. It is simply because ye dinna have a ship, nor many men, nor are ye thinking of what could happen to ye if ye went smashing into Orkney."

"Ye're . . ."

He cut across her words. "What if we're wrong? What if I just think it's Orkneymen because of . . ." He paused suddenly, then continued in a much quieter tone. "What if it is Leod? Or a group of Scots—or Irish—who think to use the old Viking ways themselves?"

"Why would Leod raid Scotland and Ireland both?"

"Why would he raid at all?" Gannon shrugged. "I dinna ken. But it's possible that he is behind this."

"Then we go to Leod and find out. That's simple enough. I can do that."

"Dinna even think on it. Leod's not a man to be swayed by a woman, even a beautiful one with a sad story. It would not go as ye think if ye visited him."

"What am I to do, then, simply forget Davey and go on with my life? Because I willna, no matter what . . ."

"Margaret, I dinna say that, nor do I mean that. I'm just trying to get ye to see how difficult it may be."

"I will spend my life looking for him."

His smile was rueful. "I ken ye will."

"Do not mock me, please."

"I'm not; I'm recognizing myself in ye. Were I ye, I would do the same."

"I ken he's alive. I dinna ken how I ken it, but I do"—

she gestured to the glen below them—"just as ye kent this place. And that means I have to find him."

When he didn't answer, she continued.

"Would ye not look for yer brother? If Tiernan were missing, would ye not search to the ends of the Earth for him?"

"Aye, of course."

"I canna bring my parents and my other brothers back, but I can look for Davey. As ye would. And I'll start on Skye."

He sighed. "I have no doubt that, were ye a man, ye'd do just that. But ye're not a man, and ye dinna ken what could be involved . . ."

"I need a reason to get up each day. Caring for Nell and looking for Davey gives me that."

"Yer brother should be saying this, not ye, lass."

"He has enough on his mind."

Gannon snorted. "What? He's not the one who's been caring for Nell. He's not the one who comforted the Somerstrath people; he dinna talk with them for more than a moment. He was not the one to be sure they all had beds in the village and food in their stomachs and a promise that they'd be safe. That was ye, Margaret. It's ye who acts like a leader, but it's Rignor who has the title. Let Rignor go to Skye. Let him go roaming across Scotland looking for yer brother."

"Ye dinna understand. Rignor . . ."

"What was he like, yer father?"

The question surprised her and she paused. "Cautious," she said at last. "Careful of his position."

"Not like yer brother then. Was it yer father who instilled the feeling of duty in ye, or yer mother?"

She thought of Father, with his endless lectures of responsibility, of Mother, who lived her duty, not cheerfully perhaps, but thoroughly. "Both."

He was quiet for a moment, then touched her shoulder, quickly withdrawing his hand, as though afraid to let his fingers linger. "It's hard, what ye're going through, Margaret, the mourning. And now ye're wondering why they all died, and ye lived, aye?"

She nodded. "And why anyone would do this to innocent people."

"That, lassie, I dinna ken, except for the greed and evil of men." He looked over her head, his gaze distant. "I've asked myself the same thing a thousand times, why I lived, and they died."

She watched him, waiting for him to go on. What was it about this man that made her want to be with him, to know his thoughts? She waited another moment.

"Gannon," she asked quietly. "Who died?"

He came back to her slowly. "My da and my three brothers. Fourteen years ago. I was the only one to live. And I've always wondered why."

"What happened?"

"There's little to tell. We were fishing, my da, and my brothers and me—I was the eldest—and not paying attention to anything but the fish. We were laughing when we first saw the ships coming for us. Then we saw that they were dragonships. Three of them. My da told us to row, but they were too close, and we too far out for anyone ashore to get to us in time. The last thing my da asked me to do was to take care of my brothers, then he was cut down. They killed him and shoved his body off the boat. And then they came for me."

He paused, then continued in that same hushed tone. "I backed away from them. When they swung at me I leaned back even farther. When they struck me I fell off the boat." He touched his chest, near his shoulder. "And then they killed my brothers and threw them in the sea with me. The last thing my da asked me to do I couldna do. I failed, Margaret, and even though my mind tells me it's absurd to think I could have done otherwise, my heart tells me I should have found a way to save them. It's that I'm trying to save ye from, the feeling that ye could have changed anything. Life is harsh. If the gods had not been with me, I would have died that day, too. And if ye'd been at home . . . so would ye have. But we're both alive, lass, and all I ken is that it's for a reason."

"I'm sorry," she said.

"It was a long time ago." His eyes were surprisingly calm.

"Ye were so young. Ye couldna have changed anything."

He nodded. "I ken that. It's little comfort in the wee hours of the night, though, is it? Would it have been better if ye and I had died with the others? Would it have served any purpose?"

"No," she whispered.

"Aye. And so we go on."

"Did they attack again?"

"At the time everyone thought it was the first of a series of raids they'd planned. We dinna ken why they never came back, whether it was my uncle Erik's response that was so strong, or whether it was just a group of men who found sport in killing one man and some boys and taking a small ship. Whatever the reason, there were no further raids. Until now. Erik will do his best to keep Antrim safe again, as he did then. But now there have been raids here as well, and with the fall of Somerstrath this part of yer shoreline is unprotected. And that, lass, is why Rory wants me here. If there are more raids—and I'll be surprised if there are not—if Scotland's western shore falls, they could set up colonies here. And then they could easily raid the rest of Scotland. And our shores as well. Does that make sense to ye?"

"Aye."

"And it's more than that." He took a deep breath, his chest rising with it, his cheeks coloring slightly. "Men who can do such things are evil. It's that simple. They're people of the darkness, and we have to stop them or perish. What does it matter if I'm Norse or Irish or ye Scots? We're none of us safe now, and we have to band together to stop them."

She stared at him, surprised at the intensity of his words, at their calmness when she could see the rage in his eyes. The old woman's words echoed suddenly in her mind. *Go home, child. The darkness is coming.* This is what she'd meant. All those years ago, the woman had known. She let her gaze fall to the dragon torque around his neck.

"People of the darkness," she said slowly. "Aye. That's what they are. But how do we stop them?"

"We go after them. We smoke them out of their nests. What else do ye do with snakes? By letting them and their ilk ken that such things canna be done here, not to us, without reprisals. If they win here, no one will be safe. If they are allowed to do what they did at Somerstrath without retaliation, what will they try next? This is about more than yer village or those in Antrim. It's about stopping evil and making life safe again. We have no choice; I have no choice. I'm thinking ye and I, we are bound to the same . . ."

He stopped suddenly, clamping his mouth shut, looking into her eyes, then immediately away, leaving her shaken by what she'd seen. Rage, of the same intensity that she felt herself. Determination. And something more—a yearning, a deep loneliness—that shocked her. She felt her body respond as though he'd touched her. She raised her hand toward his cheek, then stopped herself when something flashed in his eyes. She let her hand fall, saw him note that. He looked away. She watched his profile. The breeze flowed over them, lifting his hair again, and hers as well, billowing her skirts from her ankles and streaming his cloak away from him, pushing the linen of his trousers against strong legs, and her cloak between them, as though mere wool could separate them now. She watched him press his lips together, then lift his chin, as though he'd made a decision.

"Who lived here before?" he asked.

"No one. Well, someone did, obviously, but no one's lived here for as long as I can remember."

"Why?" He shook his head. "I canna understand it. Whose land is it?"

"My father's . . . Rignor's now."

He frowned as he looked from the fortress to the heights behind it, then to the end of the loch. "Ye should have been living here, Margaret. Yer people would have had warning that the Norsemen were coming."

"Or they would have been trapped."

"No, they could have escaped. Look," he said, pointing, "there, where the trees start, see them, where they're so thick? There's a path there that leads into the glen, then east. If ye needed to, ye could escape there." At her raised eyebrows, his arm lowered. "At least I think there is."

"Have ye been here before?"

"No." He gave her a rueful smile. "But I feel as though I have."

"Ye have the Sight, then."

"No." He shrugged. "Perhaps a bit of it. My grandmother did."

"Yer mother's mother, the Irish grandmother?"

"Aye."

"She kent things before they happened?"

"She had dreams."

"And ye do as well?"

When he did not answer, she smiled. "Ye do, don't ye?"

"Sometimes." He waved his hand to indicate the valley before them. "Sometimes it's verra clear, like here. Sometimes it's a bit hazy."

"And people? D'ye ever feel ye ken people?" At his silence she almost laughed. "I'll tell no one, Gannon MacMagnus, ye dinna have to fear that."

His smile lit his eyes. "I'm no' afraid of ye telling people, lassie. I dinna care what they think of me."

"Truly?"

His smile faded and his gaze fell from her eyes to her mouth. "Truly. It's only yer opinion that matters."

Her heart gave a small jump. She ignored it, just as she ignored that he was leaning closer. "So do ye, Gannon? Do ye feel ye ken people?"

He looked into her eyes as his hand rose, his smile

slower this time, revealing lines at the side of his mouth. "Aye," he said softly.

"Who?" she asked, though she knew what he would say. And what he was about to do.

"Ye, Margaret. Ye."

His hand slid along her jaw, lifting her face to his. His kiss was firm, hungry. Possessive. His lips were surprisingly soft, his fingers gentle on her skin. He touched her only with his fingers and lips, but desire radiated from him. He leaned closer, still not touching her, but so near that she could feel his heat, could sense the rising of his chest as he breathed, see the pulse at his throat and the long, lean line of his jaw as he claimed her mouth again, this time lingering. She'd been kissed before, even caressed before, at court, but no touch of skin on skin, no lips that met hers, had ever felt like this.

His mouth fit hers perfectly; his hand moved on her as though he'd done this a thousand times, as though he'd caressed her cheek before, had let his fingers slide down her throat to her collarbone, tracing along her skin and setting her body on fire. No one had ever kissed her like this, had ever made her body lean toward his warmth, had left her yearning for more.

And he knew it. He lifted his head, let her see the triumph in his eyes, and took a half step back. He was not unshaken; his cheeks were flushed, his eyes overbright. She put her hand to her mouth, feeling her own wave of victory.

"We have met before, Margaret."

And kissed before. And more . . .

He did not say it, but the words reverberated between them as though he had. His smile was exultant and she felt a wave of wonder at him, at herself, at the comfort she found in the thought that they had somehow, sometime, known each other. *Madness. But . . . have we?* She thought of that moment at Somerstrath when she knew that he would not harm her, that no matter how fearsome he appeared, she was safe from his wrath. She'd been right then. And it was right now to trust him, to be in this place with him, to let him kiss her.

He did not touch her again, just held her gaze, then turned and took a deep breath, surveying the glen one last time, as though bidding farewell to a much-loved place. "I ken ye're bound to another, lass, and I will respect that. But I dinna have to like it."

His words, and the thought of Lachlan, were like a breath of icy air. She stepped backward.

"I can see ye dinna wish to speak of it," he said.

"No."

The light went out of his eyes. "I'd best get ye back," he said, and led the way.

TWELVE

Nell frowned as she saw Gannon help Margaret down
the rocks of the southern headland. She turned to
let the wind blow her hair from her face, then turned again
as she saw Rignor watching them as well, his expression
stormy. Her spirits, already low, tumbled further. Something had happened between Margaret and Gannon, that
much was obvious in the way he looked at her. In the way
Margaret avoided his gaze, then turned to meet it again, as
though she could not look anywhere but at him. Nell
sighed and cast a glance at Rufus, who watched Gannon
and Margaret with a sardonic gaze. And Rignor, crossing
his arms and glowering. At Tiernan, standing with Rory
O'Neill, his smile widening at something O'Neill said,
but his gaze following his brother.

Something had happened between Margaret and
Gannon that prevented them from seeing all those
around them. His touches were short, but each time he
looked into her eyes, and each time Margaret would give
him a half smile, then look away. Then back. It was
Gannon who first noticed them watching. He slowed his
pace, and said something to Margaret that made her look
up. Her expression, already guarded, grew warier.

"Gannon!" Rufus's voice, behind Nell, was untroubled. "Ye promised to teach my men about axe fighting. Are ye visiting the next clan instead?"

Gannon laughed. "There's plenty of daylight left, Rufus. I was just making sure we dinna have any surprises coming from the south."

"The only surprise is the two of ye," Rignor said loud enough to draw many stares but not loud enough for Gannon or Margaret to hear.

"How could ye be surprised?" O'Neill asked, walking forward to meet Gannon, talking loudly about the sail on one of his ships.

Gannon answered and altered his course, leaving Margaret without a backward glance to join O'Neill. Margaret did not look after him but walked toward the fortress.

Nell lifted her skirts and ran to join her, thinking to head Rignor off, but he was quicker. As Margaret neared him, he grabbed her arm, wrenching her sideways and leaning his face close to hers. Whatever he said made her rear backward as though slapped. She replied, apparently angering Rignor even more, then pulled her arm from his grasp.

"I am not!" Margaret said heatedly as Nell neared them.

Rignor sneered. "Ye . . ."

"They're all watching," Nell whispered loudly. "Look behind me. They're all watching the two of ye."

Rignor's gaze flickered from Margaret to Nell, then over her shoulder. He spun on his heel and walked into the fortress, his color high. Margaret rubbed her arm and glared after him.

"What happened?" Nell asked.

"He's angry because I was walking with Gannon."

"Aye, I saw that. What happened with ye and Gannon?"

Margaret's gaze met hers, then dropped. "Nothing."

"Nothing?"

"Nothing," Margaret said fiercely, then followed Rignor inside, leaving Nell staring after both of them.

She followed Margaret up to their room, closing the door quietly behind her while Margaret paced across the room.

"What did he say to ye?" Nell asked.

Margaret's expression softened. "He wanted me to see the next glen. He thinks it would be a bonnie place to build a fortress. He says . . ." She looked at Nell and stopped talking.

"I meant Rignor," Nell said.

Margaret nodded quickly. "That I was not to behave like a whore. That I am to remember I am about to be married. All because I talked with another man. That's all I did, Nell! But Dagmar, who has never been faithful, can do no wrong, who slept with a stranger last night . . ." She stopped, wide-eyed.

"I ken! I saw Dagmar and Tiernan this morning. I heard them in the night. She's the whore, not ye!"

"But," Margaret said slowly, "perhaps this is good. Perhaps Rignor will see her for what she is and be cured of her."

"He says he's going to marry her."

"That's nothing new."

"And he says he needs ye to marry Lachlan, that if ye dinna he would lose Uncle William's backing for certain, and perhaps the king's. He asked me to talk to ye and get ye to see that ye have to abide by the troth."

"When did he say that?"

"Today. When ye were with Gannon. He saw ye leave the beach with him. A lot of people saw ye leave with him." She paused, unwilling to continue.

"What else did he say?"

"That Gannon was being attentive to ye only because he hopes to get Somerstrath, that Rory O'Neill is planning to marry Gannon to a Scottish woman with land and family and that ye're conveniently here."

"That's Dagmar talking. She's afraid she'll be supplanted. What else?"

"That Gannon was asking why ye dinna inherit the land since ye're the eldest. And that . . . Gannon has a woman waiting for him in Ireland."

"I thought Tiernan told ye neither of them is married."

"He did. Rignor says Gannon has a woman, not that he's married. What will ye do?"

Margaret's gaze was sharp. "I'll ask him."

Nell hated Dagmar. She hated everything about her: the smug way she carried herself, the coy looks she threw at the men, especially Rignor and Tiernan and Gannon— and even Rory O'Neill, as advanced in age as he was. The way Dagmar tossed her hair over her shoulder and followed it with a glance at whichever man she was stalking, making sure his attention was on her as she walked away, as if it would be anywhere else. All the men watched Dagmar; she could have her pick of them, and still it wasn't enough. Nell hated that Margaret did nothing about it, just watched Dagmar with a guarded expression, while Rignor and Tiernan watched her every move with open lust.

As long as she could remember, Dagmar had been leading Rignor on and he'd been trailing after her. Dagmar did not care for him. Why was it that Rignor could not see it, when it was so obvious? And why was Tiernan doing the same thing, as though Dagmar were astonishingly desirable and there was not another female around? Her anger rose again as she thought of seeing them down the hallway this morning, of the way his hand had lingered along Dagmar's shoulder, drawing her back against his naked chest for yet another kiss. He'd not seen Nell there, hoping the floor would open and take her away. Not that he would have noticed even if she'd been standing in front of him. He'd probably already forgotten that Nell MacDonald was alive.

Alive. A wave of shame washed over her. She was so selfish. She was alive, blessedly so, and to think of such stupid things as Dagmar and how much time Rignor and Tiernan spent with her was wrong. She should be praying for the souls of her parents and brothers, and all the people of Somerstrath, for Davey, wherever he was, asking God to keep him safe. She should be thinking of how fortunate she was to be living still, to be here and safe. She should not be staring at Dagmar and wishing her anywhere but here.

Nell was not the only one to watch Dagmar with displeasure. Gannon watched her, too, saw her calculating how to play her part, watched her pitting Rignor and Tiernan against each other, all the while throwing glances at him that were meant to entice but which only had the opposite effect. He'd not smiled in return, nor followed her when she left. He'd openly watched Margaret, and Dagmar had watched him, her irritation visible. Her annoyance amused him; her actions did not. She was poison. Rignor and Tiernan could hardly be civil; each watched the other with growing enmity, which worried him. The enemy was without, but neither Rignor nor Tiernan seemed to remember that. Gannon tried not to notice that Rufus watched him as he watched Rufus's daughter, occasionally winking as though to remind him of their conversation. How did one tell a man that his daughter was the last woman on Earth he'd bed?

He spent the morning training men and avoiding women. He and Tiernan had argued—his fault for being foolish enough to think he could warn his brother about Dagmar. He'd repeated what Rory had told him, that she was looking for a husband, and cautioned Tiernan that she should not be trusted. But he'd injured his brother's pride, and Tiernan had angrily told Gannon that, strange as it might seem, a woman as fine as Dagmar might actually prefer Tiernan to him, then stalked away. Gannon watched Tiernan with a heavy heart, but he was damned if he'd break their silence.

He was glad of the company when Rory found him at his ship, gesturing Gannon away from his men with a nod.

"I canna stay any longer, laddie," Rory said, walking briskly across the field toward the clustered houses of the village.

Gannon nodded; he'd expected as much. Rory's responsibility was to Ireland, not to Scotland.

"But ye'll be staying, as we've said."

"Aye," Gannon answered. They were almost at the first house. "Where are we going, Rory?"

The older man gave him a wide grin. "Ye're about to become a Scot."

"Not likely."

"Aye, well, ye'll look like one anyway. Rufus and I agree that if ye're to stay, ye'd best not strike fear in the hearts of all those who look upon ye. I've found ye a feileadh to wear. A kilt, laddie. Dinna look at me so askance. It's been cleaned. I wouldn't want ye wondering what was crawling on ye under yer skirt."

"Rory . . ."

O'Neill held up a hand. "Dinna argue. And aye, Tiernan will be wearing one, too. I heard the two of ye had words."

"Does everyone talk?"

"What else is there to do here? The woman's dangerous. Ye'd best watch him. Rignor thinks she's his. I thought of taking Tiernan with me." He continued before Gannon could protest. "But I ken ye wouldna like that. And even if the two of ye have argued, Tiernan will still guard yer back. So he'll stay."

"Good," Gannon said, relieved. He'd patch it up with his brother. He'd much rather have Tiernan with him than across the sea just now.

Rory stopped before an open doorway. "It's in here, laddie. Just let them show ye how to wear it. Ye can wear yer own shirt."

"God love ye," Gannon said as he stepped through the doorway with a grin.

"He does," Rory said, and strode away laughing.

* * *

The men who fitted the feileadh to him laughed at his ineptitude, and he joined them; it was more difficult than he'd thought. It was nothing more than a long piece of cloth, folded on itself, then wrapped around his waist, the end of it thrown over his shoulder. He fixed it with the simple hammered brooch that his grandfather had given him. It took several tries before he could dress himself in the feileadh. He tolerated the snickers of the men, determined to learn how to wear the damn thing, imagining Margaret's expression when she saw him.

It was sooner than he thought. He was lying on the floor, wrapping his belt around his waist and the mass of wool when he heard her voice.

"Lord O'Neill told me ye wanted me?" she said.

"Just to see this, Lady Margaret," one of the men answered, moving so Gannon was visible.

Gannon scrambled to his feet, clutching the feileadh to him. Margaret's eyes widened as she saw him, and he grinned at her.

"We're teaching the Irishman to dress properly," one of the men said. "He's a bit slow about it."

Margaret's gaze touched the length of him, and he felt his body react, glad now of the bulk of material between him and discovery.

"Ye look grand, Gannon," she said softly.

He grinned again. "Like I've worn it before, d'ye think?"

She flushed, but gave him a smile. "It should be under the belt, sir, not just near it," she said, and disappeared from the doorway.

Gannon looked down to find the kilt dangling on one side. He swore cheerfully. One of the Scots pulled the wool away, leaving him only in his thin linen shirt, his erection tenting the cloth.

"He's proud," one of the men said, and the others laughed.

Gannon laughed with them. "Aye, well, if God had favored ye as He has me, ye'd be enjoying yerself, too."

Margaret heard the laughter behind her as she hurried away. He'd been right; he had looked like he'd worn it before. But that was not what had affected her. It had been his laughter, his smile, his easy camaraderie with the Inverstrath men that had shaken her. Just for a moment she got a glimpse of what it might have been like if she'd met him under other circumstances, of the man he might be during peaceful times. She'd seen his light-heartedness and humor, and she'd been undone in an instant. Good God, how could she want a stranger so much with her family barely in their graves? Was she as wanton as Dagmar? Or was it simply nothing more than a yearning for the light Gannon brought with him?

He will bring life after death.

She stopped walking. Was that it, then? Was it not just her body that yearned for him, but her soul? Or was that all ancient nonsense, half-remembered words told to a young impressionable girl, now recalled in a time of sorrow and grief and altered to fit her needs? Margaret hurried back to the fortress. She would not think of Gannon. Nor of Davey, nor Lachlan, nor of the future. She would, she decided, keep herself so busy that she would not be able to think at all. There was much to be done, candles to be made, clothing and bed linens to be washed, and the garden needed tending. She had much that could keep her occupied until Uncle William arrived. Work would be her solace. She'd keep her body busy and hope her mind followed.

Look away. Her mother's words echoed in her mind. Was that what women were supposed to do—to look away from what they should not see, from what hurt them, from what they desired? Look away from anything but duty? Lie beneath a man someone else chose, bear his children, and manage his home? Was that all life was meant to be, to bring another generation into the world to repeat the pattern yet again? If so, she prayed she would have only sons, for she feared she could never tell her daughter to look away. Nor was she sure she could.

Tiernan found Nell at midday, coming to stand at her side in the kitchens where she was scrubbing platters after the meal. Around her Rufus's staff hurried about, their complaints about all the extra work brought on by the Irishmen's arrival stopping when he entered.

"Rufus doesna have anyone else to do tasks like this?" Tiernan said with a smile, gesturing to the tub of wooden trays before her.

"I volunteered." At his raised eyebrow, she went quickly on. "It's better than everyone dying of some horrible disease from eating on these things. I dinna think they've been washed since before I was born. This is the dirtiest place I've ever been."

"It's good of ye to do it."

She stared into the tub, scrubbing at the same platter again, but loath to look up at him.

"Nell?" His tone was coaxing. "Are ye no' speaking to me?"

She felt her cheeks redden. "I ken where ye were last night."

"Do ye?" he asked, but his tone had changed, letting her know he knew what she meant.

She stole a look at him and regretted it immediately. How could anyone's eyes be that blue? How could anyone smile like that? How was she to think when he stood so close to her? He brushed her hair over her shoulder, and she pulled herself away, beyond his reach.

"Nell. Lassie, when ye're older . . ."

She lifted her chin and stared at him, outraged. "Oooh! Dinna say that to me. Ye think I ken nothing? That I dinna ken what happens between a man and a woman? I saw ye leaving her this morning. Ye kissed her, Tiernan!" He glanced around the kitchens. Let the world hear, she thought, but she lowered her voice anyway. "Ye're not even old enough to be with her."

His laugh was low. "But I am, lassie. And I please her well."

"Ye think she likes ye," she cried, her tears blinding her, "but she likes all men. She tells Rignor she'll marry him, and she spends her nights with him when she's not with ye. But it's Gannon she really wanted; Margaret saw them in the hallway. She pulled her bodice down and offered herself to him, and he laughed. He laughed, Tiernan. And then she spent the night with ye. How can ye think ye were her first choice?"

His cheeks colored. "It's not true."

She nodded as quickly as she could. "It is true. And dinna tell me I'm not old enough to ken these things. My mother was my age when she married my father and only two years older when she had Margaret. Ye may be older than me, Tiernan MacMagnus, but of the two of us, ye are the child if ye think Dagmar cares a whit for ye. She's using ye! She's deciding which of ye can offer her the most. And trust me, it willna be ye! Ye have no wealth and no land. Ye're a fool, Tiernan!"

She tossed the platter into the tub and ran from him, past the others who had watched them, through the door, and into the kitchen garden, where she threw herself against the wooden wall and sobbed until she was out of tears.

If her mother were here, she'd run her hand over Nell's hair and tell her to ignore it, that you cannot change what you cannot change, and then she'd tell a long story of what life was like when she was girl, and Nell would be comforted. But her mother wasn't here, nor would she ever be again, and more than anything, Nell hated that.

No one came after her. No one came to comfort her, or even seemed to notice that she was missing, and eventually she made her way back through the kitchens and into the hall. The people were gathered near the door.

"It's some of yer Somerstrath people come," one of the women said.

Gannon was entirely wrong, Margaret thought later through her tears. He'd called her a leader, but she was certainly not one. A leader would have remembered that some of Somerstrath's people were still at the shielings, that they might hear of the attack and come home to find their loved ones already in the ground and their village destroyed. Which is exactly what happened.

The Somerstrath people arrived at Rufus's fortress at midday, pale, shaken by what they'd seen, their fears of having been abandoned visible. Rignor greeted them calmly, telling them he'd been too busy to send for them, but she knew the truth of it, that neither he nor she had even thought of the people still in the mountains. She talked to them, apologized to them, overwhelmed with guilt when they brushed her words away, saying she'd had great losses and that they understood. She listened to their stories of stopping, as she and Rignor and Nell had, on the bluff, and seeing the village below, of finding the long line of graves marked only by crude wooden crosses, of stumbling through what had once been their homes and finding nothing and no one.

A leader would have foreseen this, would have prevented it, but she was no leader. Nor was Rignor, she realized anew, watching her brother's gaze shift from a weeping Somerstrath man to Dagmar, who threw her hair over her shoulder and gave Rignor a long smile full of promise. The Inverstrath people crowded close, eager to talk to the newcomers, and Margaret turned blindly away, seeking solitude. She walked along the beach as quickly as she could, then stopped on the headland, letting the air and the waves calm her as they always did. She should have remembered the people at the shielings. Next time, she vowed, she'd do better.

The wind grew stronger, bringing the scent of the sea and the lace of the foam to brush her cheek. In the surf two seals played, sliding through the water with grace and speed. Their joy in the water and in each other lifted her heart; there was healing in these waters. And in her people, she realized; they had already begun to face the future. Now it was her turn to do the same. Her dark thoughts were simply a reflection of what she'd lost. She needed to remind herself that she was not alone, nor was the future entirely bleak. Frightening, and perhaps dangerous, but where there was life, there was hope. She had her duty to her people, and perhaps that would be enough. She turned her back on the water and the wind and walked back to the fortress. To the future. She would find the strength to face it, whatever it held.

Rignor was waiting for her when she returned to the fortress, leaning against the outer wall, his arms crossed and his face unreadable. She kept her expression sanguine as she approached him, but when he lifted himself from the wall with an agitated movement, her mood sank.

"Margaret."

"Rignor."

"Where have ye been?"

"Walking."

"Alone?"

"Aye."

"Ye should not go out alone."

She crossed her arms over her chest. "Nor with someone apparently. What is it that ye want?"

He gave her a rueful smile. "To apologize. For speaking so vilely to ye earlier. I am sorry. I couldna understand how ye could do something so damaging to yerself."

"I did nothing damaging to myself."

He shook his head quickly. "That came out wrong, too, did it not? I'm sorry, Margaret. I lost my temper when I saw ye with the Norseman."

"He's half-Irish."

"As if that's any better. Margaret, ye need to be careful. People talk."

People talk. She thought of the comments last night about Rignor falling asleep in filthy clothing and stinking of ale from his drinking.

"I'm trying to protect ye, Margaret," he said, his tone now soothing. "I'm sorry for my words this morning. My head was hurting something awful. I had no right to talk to ye like that."

"No."

"It willna happen again."

"It had better not."

"We're all we have left, ye and Nell and me and a handful of our people. I was wrong, and I beg yer forgiveness."

She nodded, feeling herself thaw. "We should have thought of the people at the shielings."

"Aye," he said, and sighed heavily. "I'll have to learn this, to lead, will I not? But ye'll help, Margaret. Tell me ye'll stand by me and help."

"Aye, I'll help, but ye must promise two things."

A shadow crossed his eyes, quickly gone. "Aye?"

"Never to speak to me like that again."

"Aye. I willna. Never again. And the second?"

"That we will look for Davey."

"We will. We will. With Uncle William's backing and the favor of the king, I'm sure we'll find him. Lachlan has enough wealth to equip an army."

"Which he willna offer if I dinna marry him, Rignor."

"But ye must!" His face suffused with color. "The king said ye must! I need this alliance, now more than ever. Ye'll live by the contract."

She shook her head. "How can ye ask this of me? Ye ken what he did!"

"That was before the attack, when we might have found another wealthy husband for ye. Look at ye, Margaret! Ye're hardly a prize now, and even less of one without a dowry. If Lachlan will still marry ye, ye'd best jump at the chance. Ye ken what it could mean to me, to our people. Ye need to think of more than yer own desires." He turned on his heel and marched away.

"Rignor."

He turned at her voice, his expectation obvious. She kept her tone cold.

"Find out where Dagmar slept last night and then talk to me."

"What does that mean?"

"She was not with Nell and me, Rignor. Discover where she was, then tell me again what to do."

Rignor flushed deeply, then whirled away, his head high and shoulders back. She watched him leave, then turned to see whose gaze it was she'd felt upon her. Rory O'Neill, standing not ten feet away from her, raised an eyebrow.

"The cat has claws after all."

She turned her face away, embarrassed to have had her cruelty overheard.

"I'm glad he apologized, lassie. And gladder still ye stood up to him." O'Neill moved to stand before her, lowering his voice. "Gannon told me ye asked if he was going to stay after I leave. He is, and I'll tell ye why. His mother was my cousin; his father was my friend, and a good man. He died fourteen years ago this summer with three of his sons, all killed by Norsemen."

"Gannon told me."

O'Neill's surprise was obvious. "Did he now? I've never

heard of him telling anyone." He cleared his throat. "He kens what ye're going through, ye see. He still bears the scar of their axe on his chest."

She thought of the boy he had been, so young to face death. "Was it Orkneymen?" she asked.

"Many thought so. It's sure they were Norse. If they'd kill those who share their bloodline, what pity d'ye expect them to show to those who dinna? It shows ye that no one is safe, aye?" He paused. "Ye can trust Gannon, lass; I do. That's why I'm leaving him here."

"And to see to yer own interests as well."

"What kind of a leader would I be if I did not make sure our allies continued to be our allies? I have no designs on Scotland, Margaret MacDonald. But who rules the western coast here affects me and mine, and I'd just as soon it were not the men who raided yer home."

"Ye think they'll come back?"

"I do. I think they hit Somerstrath first to destroy yer father and weaken this part of the coast, then they'll hit again to settle and raid from here. I'm leaving Gannon behind to protect this coast, but he'll only stay until Scotland's secure. Then he'll go home. We'll not be staying to claim land here, which is another reason to trust him. There's nothing here he wants." He paused, looking into her eyes. "I should say that differently. There's nothing here I'll allow him to take. I'll leave him for a while with ye, but he has no future here, and no one should be thinking otherwise." He strode away, leaving her looking after him.

Gannon spent another day on the field before the fortress, teaching Rufus's men how to fight against the

battle-axe, how to lunge and attack the opponent's legs,
how to watch for the moment just before the swing of
the axe, when the wielder's arms were raised and the rest
of him vulnerable. Rufus's men learned well, and the
hours passed quickly. He'd not had a moment to think,
and perhaps that had been for the best. The sunlight
was slowly fading into the soft gloaming of summer's
evening. In the hall the evening meal would soon be
served.

News had come this afternoon that there had been
more raids, in Ayreshire to the south, and more in Ross,
which probably explained why William Ross had not
yet come. Rory said he'd leave with the morning tide,
and Gannon wondered how long he and Tiernan would
remain. His men were growing steadily restless. He'd
sensed something more, too, watched his men watching
the women of Inverstrath. He'd warned them that no
misbehavior would be tolerated and reminded himself
of the same, banishing his own wandering thoughts.

He shifted his weight, feeling the wool of the feileadh
brush against him. It still felt strange; it would take
more time to accustom himself to the drafts the skirt
allowed. He'd already entertained half of Rufus's people
by forgetting to sit so he wasn't presenting his wares, and
the other half when he bent too far to pet a dog, but it
had stopped the fearful looks thrown his way and set
them all laughing, which was far better than them fearing him. And that, he suspected, was just what Rory had
planned. Tiernan was wearing the kilt as well. Things
were much better between them now, since Tiernan had
at last come to talk with Gannon, a bit defensive at first.
He'd relaxed when Gannon made no mention of their

earlier disagreement, and soon the awkwardness passed.

As everything did, he reminded himself. The sun was setting earlier each evening, and more southward, its movement measurable against the islands offshore, a reminder that the summer days would not last forever.

"Gannon." Margaret's voice was soft.

He turned toward her with a smile. "Lass. Fine evening, is it not?"

"It is. And it would be finer still if we were searching for my brother."

He felt a wave of disappointment, then chided himself. What had he expected her to say? She might not have fought his kiss, but they both knew any further attentions from him would put her in an untenable position. They'd hardly spoken in the last few days, but he'd not been able to stop watching her whenever she was near, could not stop his mind from its own meanderings, which went much further than a chaste kiss.

When he did not answer, she tilted her head and gave him a tight smile. "I ken, ye think it a fool's task. But I would still rather have it under way."

"Of course."

"Dressed like that ye look like a Scotsman."

"Supposedly I'm less likely to frighten children."

She smiled softly. "It's not fright ye inspire."

He threw her a glance, but her expression told him nothing.

"Ye've been training Rufus's men hard."

"Aye, but not enough yet. They need to make it part of them."

"Kenning how to fight with a battle-axe?"

"Kenning how to survive a fight. They're fishermen,

Margaret, and cattlemen and farmers. None of them thought they'd need these skills. Most men don't."

"Ye had them already. How is that?"

"In Ireland it was my responsibility to keep my stepfather's lands safe."

"In Fermanagh?"

He shot her a glance. Had he talked that much of himself? He didn't remember. Like now, he was paying more attention to the curves that drew his gaze and set his body afire. To the swell of her breasts above her bodice that made him want to touch her. To the feminine way she moved, the way she brushed her hair from her cheek, how her mouth had softened when he kissed her, the fine bright eyes that saw too much. She was waiting for his answer.

"Aye," he said.

"Will ye go back there, to Fermanagh?"

"I'll be going home to Haraldsholm, to Antrim."

"I'm told," she said in a quiet voice, "that Rory O'Neill has plans for ye to wed a Scottish woman."

"If he does, I've not heard of it," he said, wondering how much Rory had told her about him.

"And I'm told that ye have a woman waiting for ye in Ireland."

He laughed briefly at that. "That much is true. I've yet to meet her, but I'm told my Uncle Erik has chosen her for me."

"Will ye marry her?"

"Probably not. Unlike ye, I've no father to promise me where I dinna wish to be." He paused. He could not look away from her.

"A sail, a sail!" The cry came from the headland, and

everyone turned to look at the man who waved his arms and called to them. "The Earl of Ross is arriving!"

"I must tell Nell," Margaret said.

He grasped her arm before she could leave. "Margaret, this marriage—do ye wish it?"

"No. And I dinna ken how to change it."

He did not tell her that in Celtic Ireland, if not Norman Ireland, women could pick their husbands and nullify betrothals. Nor did he tell her that in earlier centuries Scottish women could have done the same, but not since the Normans brought their laws and customs, which all here now obeyed. A marriage contract, signed by her father, desired by the groom, and validated by the king, would be near impossible to void. She would not be the first bride, nor probably the last, to be brought unwilling to her nuptials. Nor he the only man to regret the fact.

"I canna see what choice ye have," he said.

For a moment they stared into each other's eyes.

"Rory O'Neill," she said in a hushed tone, "tells me ye have no future here, that ye'll stay awhile, then go home to Ireland."

He thought of all he might say, of how much he'd wanted to kiss her again, of how sorely tempted he was to lean now and claim her mouth. Of Rory talking about a Scottish heiress. Of the glen south of here, where a man might build a life and a home to be proud of.

"Aye," he said, watching her eyes fill with tears. "I will go home to Ireland."

Margaret twisted from his grip and hurried away.

THIRTEEN

William, the third Earl of Ross, arrived with two ships full of men and little fanfare. It had been the same when Gannon had met Ross at his home. The man had had little patience with ceremony then, less now. He was among the first to leap from his ship, striding up from the beach, his expression grim. Even if Gannon had not met him before, he would have guessed that Ross was kin to Margaret and Nell. His resemblance to them was uncanny; the bloodline he'd shared with their mother, his sister, had given all of them their height and long bones. Their beauty. Rignor, he thought, must look like his father.

Ross nodded to Gannon as he passed. "God's blood, lad, ye look just like Magnus. I ken I told ye that before, but it takes me back years. It might come in handy, that Norse blood of yers. We're going after them. Enough of waiting for them to come to us." He ignored the cheers of the men around him. "Where's O'Neill? And Rufus?"

"In the hall, sir," one of Rufus's men said, and led the way.

Ross gestured for Gannon and Tiernan to follow him to the fortress. The gates and the doors to the hall had been thrown wide open and Ross strode through, calling for his nieces. The staff was hurrying to the kitchens to prepare food and drink for the newcomers, but everyone else watched Ross greet Margaret and Nell, including Gannon, who stepped back from Ross's side when Nell ran forward to throw herself in his arms.

Ross wrapped her in his embrace, then reached for Margaret. "Praise God," he said, not hiding his emotion. "I thought I'd lost ye as well, that ye'd arrived home just in time to be murdered with the others. I went to Somerstrath; I saw what they did."

"They took Davey, Uncle William!" Nell cried.

"Took Davey?" He leaned back from her. "The Norsemen took Davey?"

"And four others," Rignor said. "All boys."

Ross met Rignor's gaze. "But not yer other brothers?"

"No," Rignor said. "We buried them."

"Are ye sure the lads are not just hiding or have gone to safety?"

"They were seen being taken," Margaret said. "Ye will go after them?"

Ross's eyes narrowed. "I swear to ye that we'll find the men who did this." He looked over Margaret's shoulder. "O'Neill. Thank ye for staying until I could come. Now, tell me what happened."

William Ross wanted to hear everything. He listened, grim-faced, to Margaret and Rignor, then Rufus and Rory, tell their stories. Nell was silent, her tears glistening in her eyes while the others spoke, making Gannon, sitting quietly with Tiernan on the edge of the group, think more of revenge than strategy. Gannon crossed his arms over his chest and listened; Tiernan watched Dagmar organizing a hastily prepared meal.

When at last Ross had no more questions, he sighed heavily. "There have been more raids in the north and tales of longships going south. This is only the beginning."

"We've heard of raids in the south, in Ayreshire," Gannon said.

"Sounds like the start of a war," Rory said. "Hardly surprising. Haakon of Norway and yer King Alexander have been arguing about the islands for years, decades if ye go back to Alexander's father. It's been building. I just dinna think it would come to this."

"Nor I," Ross said. "And everyone at court was worried about England's turmoil and possible war with France."

"What about yer King Alexander?" Rory asked. "Or is he too busy with what's happening with his wife's family in England?"

Ross nodded. "They're paying close attention to it. Henry of England is hiding in the Tower while Prince Edward fights de Montfort. King Alexander's trying not to be drawn into it, but his queen is Henry's daughter. If de Montfort wins . . ." He straightened his shoulders. "We're on our own. Rignor, ye'll need to find out if there are more of yer people still alive, then start the rebuilding at once. Winter's not far off. Ye need to repair the walls and start on some new ships. As soon as I can, I'll send men trained in that, but if they're needed elsewhere more, ye'll have to wait. I'll leave some men with ye, but ye'll need more. Rufus, can ye help with that?"

Rufus nodded quickly. "Of course, my lord. As many as he needs."

"Ye're not to stretch yer own men too thin. O'Neill, I am beholden to ye for staying now until I could come."

Rory waved his words away. "Who would have done

differently?" He looked at the men in turn. "I'll be leaving ye now. Stopping by Skye on my way. I'll leave Gannon and his men here for a while until yer men arrive."

Ross nodded. "Again I thank ye. But there's no need to go to Skye. We're going after the raiders ourselves. We'll start with Leod, give the man a visit and see what he'll tell us, then we'll visit the other islands and see what the news there is. And then we'll go north. We've talked of a meeting in a fortnight, at Thurso in Caithness, with all the northern clans and the Irish leaders. Will ye come?"

"I'll be there," Rory said, "or send someone."

Ross nodded, shifting his gaze to Rufus and Rignor. "Ye dinna have much time to secure yerselves. Ye'll need to use yer time wisely. I promise ye two things, that I will find my nephew and that I will avenge my sister. Margaret, Nell, ye can be part of neither, and I'll not have ye placed in danger. I've sent for Lachlan to come at once for ye. He'll be here soon. Ye'll wed at once, then ye and Nell will go to his home and be far from this threat."

Margaret paled. "I canna marry Lachlan now, Uncle William! We have to find Davey! And Rignor will need my help."

"Rignor will be fine," Ross said.

"But Uncle William," Nell cried. "Lachlan was unfaithful with Margaret's friend Fiona. Everyone kent."

Margaret's gaze flickered to Gannon, then away. "I dinna wish to marry him."

"I ken all that," Ross said. "Ye'll forgive Lachlan in time. He's young, and young men dinna always think things through. I'll talk with him, Margaret. He'll make ye a good husband, or I'll ken the reason why. Ye'll not be shamed again."

"Please, Uncle William!" Margaret's voice was tearful.

Ross leaned across the table and clasped her hand in his for a moment. "It's for the best, lassie. The whole world's in turmoil, and ye expect me to allow ye to walk away from a marriage that would keep ye safe. No, I willna be swayed, and dinna ask me again. No more now."

Margaret stood, tears streaming down her face, then fled without a word.

Ross watched her, then turned an impassive face to them. "Now, to Leod. I'm thinking ye'll want to come with me, aye, O'Neill?"

Rory nodded. "Aye."

"My lords," Gannon said, "if Leod has led these raids, he's not likely to let past alliances stop him. Each of ye alone would be a prize; together ye'd be worth a king's ransom. Think of what the loss of ye would mean to Ireland or Scotland. We need yer leadership, not yer heads flying from pikes as trophies."

"Thank ye for that image," Ross said dryly.

"Laddie," Rory said, "if it's too dangerous for us, why is it safe for ye?"

"I'm not important enough to kill." He held his hands up to stop their protests. "It's the truth. I own no lands; I have no title. I have no wife, nor children. If I die, there will not be a war to avenge me."

"There ye're wrong," Rory said. "I'd start it."

Gannon gave them a rueful smile. "A'right, then. If Leod kills me, there's the two of ye to help lead a war to avenge me. And dinna forget, Leod is half-Norse and half-Scot. I'm half-Norse and half-Irish. I'm betting the Irish will prevail."

"Ah, well, there's that," Rory agreed.

Rufus snorted.

* * *

Gannon would go to Skye. William and O'Neill would wait at Inverstrath for two days; if Gannon had not returned, they would assume the worst and gather their forces. Tiernan insisted on accompanying his brother and would brook no argument to the contrary. Nell was horrified. She'd heard the stories of Leod's ferociousness. She'd not wanted William to go to Skye, but neither did she want Tiernan and Gannon to go. She'd hoped that someone else would volunteer, but no one had. Rignor had sat back farther and farther in his seat. She'd met his gaze across the table and realized with a shock that her brother was afraid. But Gannon was not, and that was both brave and foolish. She told herself that Gannon would know the right thing to say to Leod and would return safely. But why did Tiernan have to go too?

When at last the talking was over, she followed Tiernan until he stopped. "Are ye really going to Skye?" she asked. "Can Gannon not go alone?"

Tiernan's smile was crooked. "Are ye worried about me, Nell?"

She looked into his eyes. "Aye. Ye could die!"

"And I could return with glorious news of yer brother."

She nodded, miserable. She wanted Davey home safely, but . . .

He put a hand to her cheek, then removed it. "Sweet Nell, I will not stay behind while my brother walks into the lion's den. We'll go together, as we do everything. If anything happens to him, it'll happen to me." He started away, then looked over his shoulder. "I'm glad ye're speaking to me again."

* * *

The Norseman was pleased. He'd lost only a score or so men on his raids, and brought home more gold and silver and riches than any of them had ever dreamed of. And this was just the beginning. Men from the other islands were pouring in to join them, swelling their numbers even more. Of course, many of the island families were leaving just as quickly. His village was now overcrowded with men and far too few women to service them. He had to solve that. And what better way than more raids? This time he'd not kill the women but bring them back for his men.

He hosted a feast that night, letting his men drink heavily, then spend their energy as they chose, ignoring the outraged protests from the husbands and fathers whose women had been appropriated. The women would live, and perhaps they'd produce sturdier stock from these couplings. The villagers' complaints did not worry him; the arguments between his men did. He needed each one of them to be fit and happy, so he let them do what they wished.

Where to go next? His spies reported that the Antrim coast of Ireland was well manned by Erik Haraldsson, who was not likely to relax his guard for some time. The western shore of Scotland had been hit twice, one raid wonderfully successful. But the raid on Somerstrath was sure to have raised the ire of the Earl of Ross. Strike again on the western shore, before they organized? Or find a new target? He looked around the hall again, at his men, at last sated, then rose when he saw Eldrid and Drason rising to their feet. He strode quickly to the back of the hall and met them as they approached the door. The boy had grown, and looked, the Norseman realized now with a start, more like himself than his brother. Had he had Eldrid all those years ago and not remembered it afterward?

"Eldrid," he said. "Drason has been approved."

Eldrid glanced at her son. "Approved?"

"He will travel with me on our next voyage."

"No!" She put her hands on his chest. "Please! Leave him alone!"

He let his tone grow very cold. "You are displeased?"

He watched her consider, saw the frightened glance she gave to her son. "I was thinking," the Norseman said slowly, "of our last time together."

Her face paled.

"I've missed our . . . conversations. Shall we have one now?"

She shook her head and put a hand to her throat.

"Good." He looked at Drason over Eldrid's head. "Be ready to leave in two days."

Drason shook his head. "I want no part of it, uncle."

"Two days," the Norseman said, and left them staring after him.

He'd know by morning whether she'd told the boy or not. If she had, Drason would come in a rage, and he'd have to deal with that. If not, she'd convince the boy to join him. Either way, Drason and his mother would not oppose him.

But two days was too long. He'd underestimated the problems several hundreds of warriors could cause within their own ranks, the arguments fueled by wine and ale and boredom. He spent most of his time overseeing the men rather than quietly planning, and that made him uneasy. He hurried them to finish their preparations, noting with satisfaction that Drason was now among them.

They were ready at last, then delayed by a summer storm that came without warning, lashing rain and hail on them, followed by a savage wind from the wrong quarter. He paced his hall, too full of idle men, and refused to hear the murmurs that he and his raids were cursed, that the ghosts of his brothers had been seen in the few hours of summer darkness, had sent the storm to block his progress. He needed a successful raid, a spectacular success—or possibly a series of them—and the doubters would be silenced. He stared out at the dark sky and thought.

The evening before Gannon and his brother were to set out for Skye, William Ross talked at length about what they could expect from Leod, what the brothers should and should not do and say. Gannon, weary from the endless instruction, finally escaped for a moment to stand outside in the cool evening air. Their course was set. He did not believe Leod would harm them. He could be wrong about that, in which case he'd die a fool, but at least it wouldn't be Rory and Ross dying. Small comfort, that.

The gloaming was fading into the deep blue of a summer's night when the gates swung open and a company of men, thirty or so, entered, bringing dust and the smell of hard-run horses with them. Their leader was of middle height, lean, his nose and tone sharp, his face very ordinary. A forgettable man, except for his manner. He tossed his reins to the ground as he dismounted, letting Rufus's men run forward to grab them, then strode forward, giving the Inverstrath people only cursory greetings. Gannon disliked him on sight.

"Ye'd think he was important," one of Rufus's men said.

"I heard he might be a bastard of the late king," a second man said. "There's some connection."

The first man snorted. "It's nothing that grand. His mother is some kin to King Alexander is all. Look at him. Does he look like the king?"

"Who is he?" Gannon asked.

"Lachlan Ross."

So this was the man who would marry Margaret MacDonald. Gannon looked more closely. He was more finely dressed than anyone at Inverstrath, including William; his belt was of gold, his sword hilt jeweled, his cloak lined with fine wool. His boots were polished and his linen shirt freshly pressed. He looked like a wealthy man's son, accustomed to being well fed and pampered, which was probably what he was. Interesting, Gannon thought, that a liegeman should dress more richly than his earl, and behave as though he were royalty, instead of what he was— a petty laird in a small country.

Lachlan threw a comment over his shoulder, and Rufus's men ran forward again to disrobe him, unpinning his cloak as though Lachlan Ross were unable to do it for himself. Gannon turned on his heel and walked into the hall.

Margaret and Nell had retired, but he heard Ross give instructions that Margaret was to be told Lachlan had arrived. An eager bride would have hurried down to greet him, but the stairs, Gannon noted with satisfaction, remained empty.

In the dark of the night, Rignor came to their room, scratching at the door like a cat. Margaret, now awake, listened in confusion until he spoke.

"Margaret. Open the door."

She did, barely able to make out his shape in the dim hallway; he was lit from the back by the pale moonlight coming through the window near the top of the stairs. He leaned forward, his breath stinking of ale.

"Lachlan's here," Rignor said.

"I heard."

"Ye dinna go down and greet him."

"I have nothing to say to him, Rignor."

"William says ye asked to be married by a priest."

"Aye," she said. It had been a delaying tactic; the priest who served both Somerstrath and Inverstrath had died in the raid. The closest one was days away.

"He's sent for a priest and says ye'll be married as soon as he arrives. I tried, Margaret. I told him that it was unseemly with our parents so newly in their graves, but William was firm. I swear to ye I tried to stop it. Or delay it. I tried."

She rested her head against the doorjamb, knowing he was lying.

"I need this, Margaret. I really need ye to marry Lachlan." He hurried through the rest of it, all the same reasons he'd used before. "If we anger William, or Lachlan, I'll pay the price for yer willfulness. Surely ye'd not do that to me? Ye kent yer whole life that ye'd marry him. Why refuse now? Surely ye see that this is about much more than just us. I dinna ask this for me, Margaret. I ask for all those who would be affected if we fail. We canna think only of ourselves."

"Just a moment ago ye said ye'd pay the price for my willfulness. That sounds like ye're thinking of yerself, Rignor."

"I meant that it would not go well for the people of

Somerstrath. There's only a few left, Margaret. Surely ye want the best for them now."

"How is it ye despised Lachlan before all this happened, Rignor, and now ye canna find a fault in him? It was ye who told me he was vain and selfish. And ye who was willing to kill him at Somerstrath when I found him with Fiona."

"That was in the heat of the moment. Margaret, ye've made too much of it all. Ye were not wed yet. What harm was done but to yer pride?" He sighed. "Do as ye will, Margaret, but ken that there are a lot of people whose future rests on ye. I ken ye'll do what's best for all and no' just yerself." He walked away, his shoulders slumped as though defeated.

Margaret had not even gotten back into the bed when he scratched again. She reluctantly opened the door again. "What is it, Rignor?"

"Let me talk to Dagmar."

She stood, frozen, for a long moment. There was no reason that she should protect Dagmar. "She's not here."

"Aye, she is. Let me talk to her."

Margaret opened the door. "Look for yerself. She's not here."

He did, shuffling toward the bed, bending low, squinting his eyes at Nell. He straightened, then gave Margaret a look she would never forget. And left without a word. She closed the door behind him with a heavy heart and leaned her head against it. Rignor, she thought, how could you not have known?

She dreamt of her family, of running up the stairs of the keep and finding them alive, smiling at her. Of Davey with them, laughing that she'd worried about him. She woke in the dark to find her face wet with tears and her heart heavy. What was duty? What was loyalty? And where, in all this, did the yearnings of her own heart fit? She was still lying awake when she heard the shouts and the thumps, then the sounds of men moving on the stairs. Doors flew open, and men called out in alarm.

Margaret rose, Nell with her, roused by the noise, grabbed her cloak and opened the door, half-expecting to be told that the Norsemen were at the door. But the hallway was quiet; the shouts were below now, and she flung her cloak over her shoulders, running down the stairs with Nell at her heels. The hall was dark, lit only by the remains of the fire in the huge fireplace, but even as she strained to see, men brought torches, placing them in the torch holders where they smoked toward the black ceiling.

"Bastard!" Rignor shouted from the center of a group of men. "Rutting bastard! I'll have yer head!"

"Which one, laddie?" It was Tiernan's voice, taut and excited.

Tiernan, she realized, had been drinking as well. Margaret tried to move through the crowd toward her brother, but quickly realized that was futile. She leapt atop a table and could at last see. Rignor and Tiernan were in the middle of a circle of men, Rignor drunk and waving his sword, shouting vengeance, Tiernan defiant, bleeding from a wound on his arm. A wild-eyed Rufus tried to calm Rignor, but was pushed angrily away. Margaret watched in horror; this was her doing. She'd been willing for him to know Dagmar was not with her, but she'd never envisioned this. Nell climbed atop the table and gasped.

"Bastard!" Rignor shouted again, lunging forward.

Tiernan laughed, lithely jumping out of Rignor's reach. One of the Irishmen tossed him a sword, and Tiernan laughed again. "Come for me, then, Rignor. Ye'll find it a bit more difficult now that I'm armed, but come on, laddie, have at me." The men called encouragement to each of the combatants, the Scots and Irish each choosing their own. Rignor lunged forward again, his sword swinging through the air to meet nothing. Tiernan thrust his weapon forward so quickly it was hard to see, and Rignor's cheek sprouted scarlet.

"Did no one ever tell ye not to pick a fight when ye're drunk?" Tiernan taunted. "Makes ye slow, Rignor." He sliced her brother's other cheek, then stepped back and laughed. "Of course, aren't ye always drunk?"

"Tiernan!" Nell cried. "Stop! Ye'll kill him!"

Tiernan held his sword high but kept his gaze on Rignor. "I'll let him live just for ye, sweet Nell."

"Enough!" William's roar was loud as he pushed through the men. "Enough!"

"Tiernan!" Rory O'Neill shouted, in William's wake. "Jesus, Mary, and Joseph! Have ye gone mad?"

"It's him that's gone mad," Tiernan said. "He came after me, not I him."

"Rutting bastard!" Rignor shouted.

William motioned for his men to capture Rignor, which was quickly done. Her brother, his arms held behind him and sword removed from his grip, glared across the circle at Tiernan.

"Put the sword down, Tiernan," Gannon said, appearing from out of the crowd. He was barefoot, his hair tousled and wild, his expression thunderous. He wore only his kilt, his chest and legs bare. "Put it down," he said again, coming forward into the light.

Tiernan paused, looking from Gannon to O'Neill, then, smiling crookedly, handed his brother the sword. "He came at me."

"Rutting bastard!" Rignor shouted. "Ye fucking Irishman, coming here and trying to take our women!"

"I took nothing that wasna offered," Tiernan shouted back. "She's not yer woman, Rignor. Ye fool yerself. She makes herself available to anyone."

Rufus leapt forward with a roar of protest, but William grabbed his arm and held him back.

"Enough!" William shouted again. "Go back to yer beds. There'll be no more to see." When the men hesitated, he roared at them. "Go!" They moved reluctantly away.

Gannon held his sword before him, warily watching the crowd. He pulled Tiernan back toward him. Rory O'Neill came to stand with them, and several of the Irish moved closer to Gannon, guarding his back. Gannon spoke quietly to his brother, and Tiernan's mood sobered. He nodded slowly, his defiance fading.

Margaret and Nell stayed where they were until the men dispersed, ignoring the glances thrown their way; then they climbed down from the table and started toward Rignor. Lachlan, who had been at the far side of the crowd, stepped forward now into the light, meeting Margaret's gaze across the room. Rufus had disappeared, and, Dagmar, Margaret suddenly realized, had never appeared at all. William threw her and Nell a fierce glance.

"Go back to bed, lasses." He nodded at the stairs. "Get ye gone."

"I need to tend to Rignor," Margaret said.

William's lips curled. "No. That's part of the problem. Go to bed."

With a quiet word to William, Lachlan left the others, coming to stand before Margaret for a moment, then gesturing toward the stairs. "Come, Margaret, I'll see ye safely upstairs."

Margaret threw Rignor a look, but her brother turned sullenly away.

"Margaret, Nell, go!" William said fiercely.

The sisters followed Lachlan as he grabbed a smoking torch, then led the way up the steps. He did not speak when they'd reached their door, waiting until they'd passed into the room and turned to face him.

"Latch the door." He paused. "I am sorry for yer loss. Yer losses."

"Thank ye." She summoned her courage and looked into his eyes. "Lachlan, will ye release me from this sham of a marriage? We neither of us want this. Let's not feign otherwise."

He shook his head. "I have agreed to marry ye, and I will do it." When she did not reply, he continued. "I have no choice, nor do ye; William has made that plain. It is not a love match, but we can at least be civil."

"There's no benefit to ye to marrying me now. Why do it?"

"Yer uncle is one of the most powerful men in Scotland, Margaret. The king expects our families to be united with this marriage, and so they will be."

"Lachlan . . ."

"What is it ye want, Margaret?" he asked, his tone angry now.

Her own anger flared to meet his. "What is it I want? I want my family alive, I want Davey home and my village intact and no one dead. I want the monsters that destroyed Somerstrath to be struck down and destroyed. I want my trust in ye and Fiona restored. And I can have none of that, can I?"

He stared at her for several moments, then shook his head. "No, ye can have none of it. But we can at least begin afresh from this moment. The priest should be here tomorrow, and we'll be wed. Let us at least not start our marriage as enemies."

She stared at him in surprise.

"Margaret, we will never be lovers, but we need not be enemies."

"No," she said softly, "we need not be enemies."

She could not fall sleep again. It was time to face that she had no choice but to marry Lachlan. There would be no last-minute reprieve, no sudden renouncement of pledge, no gallant knight riding in to save her, and it was time to face that. She'd put the actual details of her marriage out of her mind, but now, lying awake in the dark, she thought of the ceremony and what would come afterward. The wedding itself would be simple, held in the hall, with all of Inverstrath's inhabitants and guests as witnesses. The priest would bless their union, and there would be a feast of sorts afterward. Rufus had promised them a room alone, a luxury in the crowded fortress, but there would be little privacy beyond that. How could she bear it?

She slipped carefully from the bed. Nell slept on, not stirring when Margaret pulled her cloak on over her chemise. She'd walk through the hallways until weariness overtook her. She longed for the night air, but only a fool would attempt to walk through the throngs of sleeping men belowstairs.

The hallway was empty and cool; she walked from her dark doorway to the square of moonlight coming through the high open window above the stairway, a beam of silver in the dimness of the hall, the breeze shifting to send a whiff of night air to her, then pull it away, taunting her with what she could not have. As she paced between the stairway and her door she thought of Lachlan, naked and straining above Fiona. She shook her head to clear the vision. Could she run away? For a wild moment she considered living in the forest, foraging for herself, growing old in a hut she'd made of twigs and fern branches. Absurd; impossible. She'd not last the winter. It was not the act of union that frightened her; it was the imprisonment of a marriage she did not want. Whatever secrets the marriage bed held would be revealed soon enough. She did not fear them, but she regretted learning them with Lachlan.

The breeze stirred again, drawing her gaze to the window and the moon beyond, the symbol of all that was feminine. She stared at the pale orb, trying to draw strength from it, from all the women who had gone before her into the unknown, to find some peace with the course of her life, simply one more in so many courses of womanhood. I want love, she told the moon. And peace. Can you bring them to me? There was, of course, no answer, and she smiled at her foolishness. She should have resigned herself to this years ago. And someday perhaps, surrounded by the children who would be her compensation for marriage to a man who didn't want her—would she think of this night and laugh at her trepidation?

She heard the latch click and shrank back into the shadows, expecting a sleepy person in need of the garderobe farther down the hallway, or, worst case, her brother leaving Dagmar. What she'd not imagined was a naked Gannon MacMagnus stepping from the room he shared. He shifted something from one hand to another and turned to close the door quietly, his long, pale hair skimming across his back.

He paused, as though listening, then leaned against the wall, the left side of his body lit by the moonlight, the rest in shadow. His sigh was audible. After a moment, long arms shook out the trousers he had held and lean legs stepped into them. He tied the drawstring all too soon at his waist.

She should not be watching him from the shadows, but she could not tear her gaze away. He was magnificent. And now he was heading right toward her, where she stood at the top of the stairs. If she moved, he'd see her at once. If she did not move, he'd see her a moment later. She took a deep breath and stepped into the brilliant square of moonlight that was before her.

He stopped and stared at her. Only half of his face was illuminated, the rest in darkness, but she could see his surprise. His cheeks were dark hollows; his eyelashes cast long shadows; his wide mouth was softly lit from the side, the strong lines of his lips drawing her gaze. His collarbone was at her eye level; his shoulder, where it caught the light, wide and well muscled. His chest, with its pale dusting of hair, rising and falling with his breath, was not two feet in front of her. And across it, running from his neck to his ribs, a long, pale, ugly scar, the one he must have received when the Norsemen killed his father and brothers. She fought the urge to touch it, to touch him. Her heart began pounding.

FOURTEEN

Gannon thought he was dreaming. It took a moment for him to realize that this was no apparition, but Margaret herself who stood before him, her face, framed by her hair and the shadows, ghostly. She wore her cloak over a loose gown that was open at her throat. He could see the top of one milky breast as it rose with her breathing, saw her pulse beat at her neck and her hands clutch at her cloak. Her eyes were dark, her cheeks sculpted by the light that fell softly on her. He stared at her, at her breasts, at her lips, wondering what she'd taste like, what she would feel like under him. Around him. Had there ever been a lovelier woman? Or one he'd wanted more? She'd been here, he realized, when he'd stepped naked into the corridor. He glanced down the hall; there was enough light for her easily to have seen him.

"Margaret," he whispered, "what are ye doing here, lass?"

"I couldna sleep."

"Nor I," he said.

"I just wanted . . ."

Her gaze fell to his mouth, and he felt his body stir.

". . . some air," she said.

"D'ye want to go outside? I'll take ye there." He extended his hand. She took it, wrapping her smaller fingers around his.

"I canna go down there, with all those men."

"No." He lifted their joined hands into the light, looking from them to her, then leaned to wrap his other arm around her waist. "Just one kiss, Margaret, before we part forever. Just one. To remember me by."

She put her hand on his shoulder, let it glide down his chest, smiling softly. "I'll ne'er forget ye, Gannon."

He lowered his mouth to hers, gently at first, then madly when she responded, pulling her tighter, feeling her breasts against him, her soft hands on his chest, on his shoulders, wrapping around his neck, threading through his hair. He kissed her mouth, her lips and cheeks, the sweet hollow of her neck, then her mouth again, claiming it, exploring it, pushing her against the wall, dizzy with desire. And when her tongue probed into his mouth, he slipped the cloak off her shoulder and put his hand to her breast.

She heard them first, the noises behind them. He lifted his head from hers and turned to see Lachlan watching them with a grave expression. Behind him someone moved, and Rory's face appeared from the shadows. Margaret buried her head against his shoulder with a soft moan.

"Ye bastard!" Lachlan cried. "Get ye hands off my woman."

Gannon kept his arms around her. "She's no' yer woman yet."

"She's promised to me."

"Promised, not yet wed," Gannon said.

"Get yer hands off her."

"That's for Margaret to decide."

Rory stepped forward, holding up his hands for them to stop. Margaret leaned away from Gannon.

"It was only a kiss," Rory said calmly. "Nothing more. Get yerself off now, lassie, before these two start a war over ye. Lads, we're all tense. Let's not make this more than it is."

Margaret nodded and moved past Rory. Lachlan grabbed her arm.

"It was one kiss, Lachlan," she said.

"What is the difference," Lachlan asked, "between this and what happened between Fiona and me?"

"There is a world of difference," she said. "Ours was only a kiss, yers much more. But ye're right; both times the lass was willing."

Margaret faded into the shadows. A moment later they heard the soft latch of her door. Lachlan threw Gannon a look full of hatred, then spun on his heel and stalked back to the cramped room.

"For God's sake, lad," Rory said. "Have we not enough on our plates with ye adding this?"

"It was one kiss, Rory."

"It was much more than that, and ye ken it. Find another lass, Gannon." Rory was still shaking his head as he left.

Gannon pounded down the stairs, through the maze of sleeping men and into the courtyard, where he stood in the night air, willing his body and emotions to subside. She'd marry Lachlan tomorrow. He should not be tempted by her lovely form, her dark eyes, should not remember the feel of her breasts against his chest, the feel of her fingers on his skin, the softness of her lips and the warmth of her response. Lachlan's woman, he told himself, and best forgotten. He swore, then again. Why her? Why now, when the world had gone mad?

They left shortly after dawn, his men yawning and complaining about the hour. Tiernan, slightly green from the aftereffects of his drinking last night, was silent. They wore Irish clothing, and Gannon was glad of it; he was ready to leave Scotland behind. He'd never be a Scot. Why pretend? Rory came to see them off, as did Rufus. And Lachlan, who stood, arms crossed over his chest, on the berm above the beach, his stance stiff, his face expressionless.

"I dinna have to tell ye to be careful," Rory said now, standing with Gannon on the shingle while the last of his men climbed aboard *Gannon's Lady*.

"No," Gannon said.

"Nor to tell ye that if ye think ye're in danger, get out."

"No."

"Nor to tell ye how fortunate ye were last night that it was me with Lachlan and not William. After Tiernan and Rignor's brawl . . ." He let his words trail off. "It's not to be, laddie. There are other women." When Gannon did not answer, he continued. "I'm serious, lad. There are other women. We'll get ye home to Ireland, and ye can have yer pick."

"What about the Scottish heiress?"

"I'm thinking it's not such a good idea now. We'll get ye home."

"To do what, Rory? Be Erik's lackey? I want land of my own someday."

"Aye, and Rufus offered ye Dagmar and Inverstrath when he's gone. I ken; he told me. And if ye took it, ye'd be laird here. But ye'd be Rignor's liegeman and yer wife would be in his bed constantly. Can ye do that?"

Gannon stared into the distance. "I dinna think so."

"Aye." Rory gave him an appraising look. "If ye want land of yer own, we'll find it, aye? Ye always have a place with me, laddie."

"I thank ye for that."

"Aye, well, ye might not later. Ye'll carn yer land. Ye're starting with this trip to Skye. Leod is wily. Remember that."

"Aye."

"Ye're young. In time both ye and the lass will forget, though ye dinna think that possible now. Get ye gone, lad. Safe journey and God speed ye home." He gave Gannon a quick embrace, then slapped his shoulder and strode away.

Gannon watched him for a moment, looked at Lachlan, still watching on the ground above, and turned to his ship, giving orders quietly. Rory was wrong. He'd never forget.

The Isle of Skye. Gannon stood in the stern of *Gannon's Lady* with Tiernan as they slid by the tall cliffs that guarded the entrance to Leod's fortress. They'd traveled without incident from Inverstrath to the most northwestern part of the island. He searched for signs of the watchers he knew would be there, men who would report their arrival; and soon he saw them, each signaling to the next man, holding banners or flags, of various colors.

Leod took no chances on being surprised, and he'd

chosen his site well, but that was hardly surprising; he was a wily and thorough leader. Most likely someone had already reported that they were gliding across the cobalt waters toward Leod's fortress, past Dunvegan Head and into Loch Dunvegan, where they passed the fishermen's boats and the many small craft that filled the loch. The entrance to the large loch was wide and open to the sea; it embraced several islands within its waters and was large enough to hold many ships. Dunvegan was at the southernmost point of the loch and of course *Gannon's Lady* had been seen. The flat land near the shore held clusters of small and ancient houses, most whitewashed and thatched, the people near them stopping to stare as they passed.

He'd approached Skye carefully, remembering the stories of the ships that had been run aground in her treacherous waters, or lured into a seemingly safe harbor only to find fierce men waiting for them. Skyemen were known to be a breed apart, a ferocious bunch; they'd been bred to it, tested by the mettle of invasion after invasion. It was difficult to find a Skyeman who did not carry Danish and Irish and Pictish and Scottish—and now Norse—blood. Cuchulain, Ireland's greatest warrior, had come to train here, and it was said that his blood still ran through the people. The island had little arable land; its inhabitants had always been hardy. The south of the island, in the shadow of the Cuillins, Skye's unforgettable mountains, was the most fertile. Their blue and gray peaks dominated the sky, inhospitable and alluring, thrusting into the air and daring those who looked upon them to approach. Few did; fewer returned from them, and those who had returned brought back tales of strange happenings and even stranger creatures that dwelled there.

He'd been here before, as a young boy, had sailed here with his father and uncle, and sat with them, listening while the men talked of war. He couldn't remember if Leod had been there, or what had been decided, but he did remember his father telling him on the way home to do more listening than talking in discussions like that. "Ye already know what's in yer own mind," Magnus had said. "Learn what's in his." Which is what he hoped to do now. He knew much of Leod's history, that he was the son of Olaf the Black, the king of the Isle of Man.

Tiernan spoke now, as though reading his thoughts. "He has agreements with King Alexander of Scotland and with Haakon of Norway, aye?"

Gannon nodded, noting those on the shore who had stopped working and were watching their approach. "That way he canna lose, can he?"

"Erik said he was a fair man."

"Aye, Erik always said so. We'll find out soon enough, won't we? Or not. Like as much he'll tell us nothing. Ye understand what we're up against, d'ye not? It won't take much to set all of Ireland and Scotland at war with Leod and half the Norsemen in the world. If it's Leod doing the raids, and I'm quite sure it's not, which is why we're here, he's likely to throw us in chains or lop off our heads and it's only by us not returning that the others will ken that it's him. If it's not Leod, God only kens what the ones who are doing the raids are like. All we ken is that they're ruthless and dangerous. And if it's not Leod, he'll probably play both sides. Which means he'll send word to the raiders that we're looking for them."

"Won't they have figured that much out already? Surely no one can think to do what they've done and not be hunted."

"Aye. But what if that's exactly what they're hoping we'll do—come looking?" He shook his head. "All I need from Leod is a name."

"All we need is to get out of here alive."

"Rory will retaliate if we don't."

"Which will be the least of our worries," Tiernan said. "I've not done enough good deeds to be assured where I'm going."

Gannon laughed. "Nor I. Remind me to remedy that sometime, aye?"

He shaded his eyes as they neared the shore. Overhead the sun was still bright, and the glare off the water made it hard to see, but the runners going up the hill to the fortress were visible enough. He waved for his men to trim the sail and ready their oars. He wasn't sure of their reception; it might be wise to be ready to flee, although how they'd get through the outer lochs and to the safety of the sea he wasn't sure.

Someday, when he had his own home, his own land, he would do what Leod did to protect his own. But he would not think on that now, would not remember that this day Margaret would become Lachlan Ross's wife, and this night Lachlan's lover. He would think only that for whatever reason, Leod was allowing them to land unmolested. He raised a hand in response to the greetings they received, and watched his men throw lines to the men who waited ashore to pull *Gannon's Lady* to the dock. It was time to see what Leod was made of. And perhaps himself.

* * *

The gods favored them. The seas were calm, the winds strong and steady. His ships made good time, and the Norseman was pleased. He had twelve ships with him now, lightly loaded with men, which left plenty of room for plunder and slaves. His men were eager and rested. His spies had returned with some pleasant news. And some not as pleasant.

His plan would stay the same. His ships would break into two groups; one would raid in the north of Scotland, visiting the Sinclairs, then the Munros. The second group, the one he led, would venture farther, to a place whose leader was not shrewd enough to see its weaknesses. He'd strike, then visit an old friend on the way home to hear all the latest news. He'd be welcomed, he was sure, despite the entanglements his visit might represent. His nephew was with him, the boy's unhappiness palpable. The Norseman smiled to himself; by the end of the voyage he'd have Drason's measure. Either the boy would rally and find his blood ran high during an attack, or he'd prove himself a coward. Either way, the dilemma Drason presented would be solved.

And when these raids were done, when his enemies at home were afraid to talk of him and his enemies abroad could talk of nothing else, then he'd start the second phase of his plan. His power would grow, and soon the kings of Ireland and Scotland and Norway would recognize him as an equal.

He poured the last of Somerstrath's wine into the water. A libation for the gods, he thought, watching the drops disappear into the waves. And to ask for a small favor. The unwelcome news his spies had brought was that one of the boys he'd stolen was Somerstrath's son.

Who could have known that? The boy had not been in the keep with the others, nor had he been richly dressed. He'd looked like just one more village child. Now rescuing the boy would become a quest. Ross, his spies said, was already sending messengers out across Scotland with the news of the raid on Somerstrath. Soon the Norseman would lose the element of surprise he'd had earlier; the Scots would be prepared, waiting for his ships.

He narrowed his eyes against the sudden glare off the water as the sun came from behind the clouds. It was bad enough that others were emulating him, some said even to have the backing of King Haakon of Norway. The good part of that was that he no longer feared royal censure. He might have to share some of his plunder with the king, but no one would stop him.

He smiled as the wind freshened. *Let it come, whatever lies ahead, let it come.* He glanced behind him, to find his nephew watching. He tossed the gold cup in his hand into the water, laughing at Drason's shocked expression.

"There's more where that came from! Stay with me, boy, and see things you've never imagined. Gold, silver, jewels. Women. Whatever you dream of will be yours. All you need is the courage to take them."

He turned his back on Drason then, letting the wind sweep his hair over his shoulders. Overhead the sail snapped as the wind shifted and strengthened. *A sign. We're being sped to our goal. Even God wants us to succeed.*

Lachlan had nothing to say to Margaret when they met at the morning meal. He nodded when she and Nell appeared, and watched her while he ate oatcakes and cheese and drank ale, but said nothing to her. Nor to anyone. Rory O'Neill told William that Gannon and Tiernan had left at dawn for Skye, that they should be with Leod shortly. William had little to say, only that the priest had not yet arrived. Rignor, like Lachlan, spoke to no one; Rufus talked enough for them all, his tone cheerful. But Margaret heard the undertone of worry in his voice, saw him note how many oatcakes were eaten at breakfast and count the cups of ale consumed and the worried glances he threw at his daughter, who did not look up once.

The priest had not arrived by midday, nor by the evening, so there was no wedding. There was a brief flurry of excitement when a hooded figure was seen approaching, but it turned out to be a monk, not the priest. He came, dusty and barefoot, explaining that he was on a pilgrimage. The others were gone; it was Margaret, Nell, and Rory O'Neill who joined Rufus in welcoming him. They settled at the table as Rufus plied the monk with food and ale, asking for his news.

"Ye should see everyone along the coast," the monk said, his mouth full of food, "building walls and training men. Everyone thinks that these are just the first raids, that the Vikings are going to invade, that these are tests of the new king."

"New king?" Nell asked Margaret. "He's been king since he was eight."

Margaret shook her head. "Officially. But he's only just begun to rule in his own right in the last year."

"Aye, that's right, lassies," the monk said, his gaze sweeping from Margaret to Nell. "Any sign of the Vikings here?"

"None," Rufus said, "but Somerstrath is verra close. It could have been us."

The monk took a deep drink of the ale. "Ye were blessed to be ignored. I assume ye've been watching out, aye? Keeping yer men on their toes? Of course, how does one prepare for a Viking raid?"

"I dinna ken. Do our best to escape their notice."

"Ye've seen naught of them since? No strange ships passing?"

"The only strange ships we've seen are yers, aye, Lord O'Neill?"

Rory O'Neill looked from the monk to Rufus with a slow nod. "Aye."

The monk looked at O'Neill with interest. "O'Neill? Irish?"

"Ye're talking to the overlaird of Ulster, sir," Rufus said proudly.

The monk's eyebrows raised. "Am I now? What brings ye here?"

"There were raids in Ireland," Rufus continued. "They came to tell Ross of them and found Somerstrath."

"And they're staying here?"

O'Neill stood abruptly. "A word with ye, Rufus." He strode quickly away, leading Rufus halfway across the hall, talking in a low and intense manner.

The monk watched them, then turned to Margaret. "Frightening times, eh?" He turned his attention to his food then. The evening passed quietly, and in the morning the monk left, walking south, clutching the pack of food Rufus had sent with him.

The hours passed slowly for Margaret; the day felt three days long. Rignor disappeared. Dagmar was silent, speaking to no one. Rufus took Lachlan, William, and Rory O'Neill hunting and on a tour of his lands, including the glen to the south, the one Gannon had showed her, the one she now thought of as Gannon's glen. Lachlan's men played dice in the courtyard, underfoot when Rufus's staff tried to work. William's men had retreated to the shingle, where they talked with the Irish or among themselves. All of Inverstrath waited for one man to arrive. Margaret felt deadened, her limbs heavy. She worked through the afternoon in the village with the Somerstrath women, repairing and washing clothing, coming back to the hall only when the men had returned with their prizes. She found her uncle and asked for a moment alone, which he granted with a wary expression.

"Ye canna change my mind, Margaret."

"I have accepted that. But I have a question." At his arched eyebrow she went on. "If I refused to marry Lachlan, would ye withdraw help from Rignor? He said you would."

"Yer brother's an idiot, Margaret. And yer parents were fools for allowing his behavior to go unchecked, but I'll not speak ill of the dead. No, I would not withdraw support from him. And no, he dinna mention the marriage to me at all. We talked about his behavior and the argument with the Irish lad and the damage it did to the peace ye had here. And by the bye, whatever it was that happened between ye and Gannon is over, lass."

"Nothing happened."

"Ye are still . . . ?"

She raised her chin. "I am still . . . intact, William."

He colored. "Of course ye are, of course ye are. Forgive me."

"Is there nothing I can say to dissuade ye from this wedding?"

"Nothing, Margaret."

Her eyes filled with tears and she left him quickly before she began to beg.

At sunset she walked on the beach with Nell, letting the wind surround them. In the evening she sat with the others and pushed her food around, but could eat little. And when at last it grew dark, she stood in the courtyard alone, looking up at the darkening sky and wondering how Gannon MacMagnus was, how soon he would return. Whether he would return. And if the priest would ever come.

Leod's ale was delicious. His whisky was even better. The older man poured Gannon another cup of the amber liquid, then himself the same. Gannon swirled the whisky in the cup, wishing he could just toss it back and enjoy it, but he was drinking sparingly. He'd given his greetings and his name to Leod's men at the dock, waiting while the message was delivered up the hill. A short while later he'd been invited to join Leod and had left Tiernan with the ship.

"If I dinna return or send word by dusk, leave. Never mind the tide, nor what ye think is happening with me. Get out and tell Rory what happened."

Tiernan's jaw had thrust forward. "I'll no' leave without ye."

"Aye, ye will. I'm counting on ye to go and get the others and get me out of here. Like as not, none of this will be needed."

Tiernan's reluctance was obvious, but he'd nodded.

Gannon had been shown up the hill and within the

first set of walls. The gates were guarded even here, the gatehouse full of armed men who silently watched them pass. Leod was a cautious man, and his men wary. Inside the fortress he was shown not to a spot in the spacious hall but up the stairs and down a hallway, then through a wooden doorway. The room was large, richly decorated with tapestries, a faded rug on the floor, and pillared iron candelabras flanking the tall fireplace. Two windows, uncovered now, let in the light breeze and the view of the loch below. Leod's fortress, high on the cliffs, looked out from its perch like a sea eagle. And like that bird, Leod saw everything that happened in his territory—and probably much beyond. Their approach would certainly have been noted by anyone watching from this room.

The large man who sat at a desk in the middle of the room looked up from the sea charts before him, then leaned back in his chair, a Norman design but decorated with Celtic and Norse artwork. He folded the vellum partially onto itself and rose to his feet. Leod was an imposing man, tall, with wide shoulders and the manner of a man accustomed to being obeyed. It had been fourteen years since Gannon had seen him, and the years had taken their toll. His hair, once blond, was gray now, silver actually, pulled back from a strong face that showed both the signs of age and weathering. His hands were scarred across the top, sure signs of a man who had been in his share of battles. He stretched out one of those hands now, clasping Gannon's in a firm grip and gesturing to a chair in front of the desk.

"Welcome, Gannon Magnusson. It's been a very long time. You were not quite up to my knee the last time I saw you."

"That would have been my brother. I was up to yer elbow at least."

Leod laughed. "I've not thought of Magnus in years, not since his funeral. You have the look of him."

"I've been told that."

"I'm sure you have. The women loved him, wouldn't leave him alone, even after he married your mother. Do you have the same problem?"

"No."

Leod chuckled. "How is your mother?"

"She died last winter."

"Another one gone. So what brings Magnus's son to me? Have you come to claim the land I offered him all those years ago?"

"No."

"You look surprised. You didn't know about that, did you?"

Gannon shook his head.

"Years ago, when your grandfather ruled Haraldsholm, I tried to get your father to come to Skye. I know a valuable man when I see one."

"Obviously he didn't come."

"Obviously," Leod said dryly. "Of course, if he had, he'd be alive now."

"Aye." Gannon watched the older man and took a sip of the whisky, turning the stone cup to see the striations of the rock. It was carved from one piece, with spiral designs from the stem to the lip, the possession of a man who appreciated fine things. As his home showed. If Leod took sides, he might risk this home and all the fine things it held.

"So why are you here?"

"I've come to get ye to tell me things without ye kenning that that's what I'm doing."

Leod stared at him for a moment, then roared with laughter. "Is that so? Is that so? And what is it you want to know, Gannon Magnusson?"

"There have been raids in Antrim, near Haraldsholm. And in Scotland, at Somerstrath and Torridon. Orkneymen were seen in Antrim; the men who raided Somerstrath were Vikings."

"And?"

"And Rory O'Neill and William Ross want to ken what ye ken about that."

"Ah, Rory O'Neill, who smiles and makes jokes but misses little. A lion of a man. And William, the Earl of Ross, who covets my island as much as King Alexander." He leaned back. "I heard of the attacks."

"Do ye ken who did them?"

"I've heard it was Vikings, perhaps Orkneymen."

"Aye, I just told ye that. Who else has?"

"The seas are busy, Gannon. Men stop here from many places."

"And the seas are wide, Leod. Where do these men come from?"

Leod grinned.

Gannon put the cup down and leaned forward. "They attacked three of my uncle's villages, killing everyone who was there and stealing from the churches. In Scotland they killed Somerstrath and most of his family. They took his son, along with four others, all boys. Everyone else was killed. They nailed heads to doors, men, women, children. Almost every woman was raped. They spitted babies and cut dogs in two. The village was torched, and Somerstrath's ships were burnt to cinders. Now we've heard that there's been a raid up at Torridon."

The older man's expression did not change, but his tone was thoughtful. "I'd not heard that any captives were taken. Are you sure they're not hostages?"

"No ransom demands have been received."

"Who does your uncle think did the raids there?"

"Orkneymen were seen."

"Or those masking as Orkneymen."

"Aye."

"And in Scotland?"

"Some of the Scots are calling for revenge on Norsemen. All Norsemen." He did not have to tell Leod that that included not only men from Norway and the Orkneys, but also the Hebrides and the Isle of Man. And of Skye. "Which is understandable. Somerstrath's wife was the Earl of Ross's sister. His daughter is married to a kinsman of King Alexander. If they'd not wanted retaliation, they should have chosen another target."

Leod looked thoughtful. "And Ross says?"

"Ross is verra angry."

"Which is why you're here."

Gannon took another sip of the whisky, then put the cup down on the table before him. It would be easy to relax and forget how important this conversation was. And how powerful silence could be. Leod was watching him; appraising him, he knew. Gannon kept his gaze on the older man's face. Leod steepled his fingers and bounced them. The guards by the door exchanged a glance. Leod's dog, stretched out at his feet, scratched his ear, then chewed on a paw. Gannon did not move. He knew he had to be disciplined, to be wily, in order to be successful. Leod knew something of the raids; he could see it in the man's face, in his manner. Which side would he choose? Or would he try for a middle course?

Rory's words echoed in his mind. *Find out what Leod kens, and whether he'll harbor these raiders. If this becomes a war between the Norse and the Celts, a contest between the kings of Norway and Scotland, it will be long and bloody. If it's simply civilized men against a group of renegades, it will be quickly handled.*

Gannon waited. The chart on the desk between them was of the Minch, the waters around the island. On the shelf behind Leod was a model of a dragonship, the kind shipbuilders used to sell their wares. Was Leod building a new ship? Or had someone visited, leaving the model behind as a gift, or a reminder of how powerful a war weapon a dragonship was? If Leod joined the raiders, his base on Skye would provide shelter and easy access to much of Scotland's coastline, a dangerous situation for the Scots. And far too close to Antrim for the Irish to feel safe. If Leod was one of the raiders, Gannon had already told him too much.

Leod bounced his fingers. "Orkneymen, you say?"

"Aye."

"Have you gone to Kirkwall?"

Kirkwall, the capital of the Orkneys. That would be his next destination, Gannon thought, to talk with Orkney's leaders. "We thought we'd talk to ye first, as an ally of both Ireland and Scotland."

"I'm sure the thane will look into it."

"I'm sure he'll tell us that he will, then do nothing."

Leod arched an eyebrow. "Ye have a poor opinion of the man."

"No one in the Orkneys did anything when my father was killed."

"Ah," Leod said, nodding. "The wound must still be fresh."

Gannon bit back a sharp reply. "Where would ye look?"

"For Somerstrath's son?"

"Aye."

"In the Orkneys, ye mean?"

"Aye, or anywhere. Where would ye go?"

Leod's expression grew thoughtful. "Most of the islands are alike. No trees, lots of rock. Some have standing stones. I'm not sure which of them would be the best to see."

"I'm looking for men who go Viking, not a spot for a holiday."

"What about Norway?"

"Ye think the raiders are from Norway?"

"It's happened before."

"Long way to go home between raids. They'd have had to stay somewhere closer to do all these raids so quickly."

"So you're thinking they're in the Orkneys?"

"Or on another island."

Leod leaned forward abruptly. "They're not here."

"Have they been here?"

"No one came here and told me of his intention to raid Ireland or Scotland."

"But ye've had visitors."

Leod leaned back. "Of course I have."

"And if those who did the raids come here? Will ye welcome them?"

"I will offer them whisky and listen."

"Do ye buy slaves?"

"No."

"Do ye shelter men who do?"

Leod smiled slowly but did not answer.

"Will ye join them in these raids?"

"I will offer them whisky."

"And if the men who have done these raids are found and destroyed . . . ?"

"I would listen to the story of how it happened."

"Would ye join in revenge for them?"

"I'd listen first."

"But ye'd no' rule it out?"

"Depends on what happened. I'm not overfond of William Ross."

"Yer mother was a Ross."

"Your mother was Irish and your father was Norse. Surely you, more than most, can understand my position."

"Do ye ken who it is?"

Leod smiled again. "I hear a lot of things."

Gannon stood. "I thank ye for yer time and for the whisky, sir."

"You'll stay the night," Leod said, rising to his feet. He came around the desk and gestured to the window. "It's already late. I'll send for your brother to join us."

When Gannon hesitated, Leod laughed.

"I give you my word I will not harm a hair on your head. You and your brother and your men will be safe. You can leave in the morning and go back to tell O'Neill and Ross that I was at least hospitable."

"But not talkative," Gannon said.

Leod laughed again and slapped Gannon's shoulder. "Your father should have come to Skye. I could have used him and his sons. Send for your brother."

"I'll go and get him."

"What did you do, leave him with orders to sail if you didn't return?"

Gannon smiled. "He'll be glad to hear my hair will be safe here."

Tiernan's relief was obvious when Gannon came back down the hill, but he frowned when Gannon said they'd been invited to spend the night.

"Think we should?" Tiernan asked.

"We dinna have much choice. If we leave now, we'll insult him, and we dinna want to do that." Gannon shrugged. "Maybe we'll learn more."

Tiernan glanced up the hill. "I've heard about his fortress."

"He's a wealthy man, and his whisky is very fine. We'll be verra comfortable, I'm sure. Wait until ye see how careful he is. We can learn from him."

"If we live."

"He gave his word."

Tiernan grunted, but he followed Gannon back up the hill.

The evening meal was lavish, the whisky and ale free-flowing, and Leod at his most charming and talkative, but Gannon learned nothing more of value. When Leod began to yawn, Gannon excused himself, saying he needed to check on his men and ship.

"Listen and see what ye can learn," he whispered to Tiernan as he left.

Outside the fog was thick, swirling in spirals around his head as he moved. Swallowing the walls he knew surrounded him and leaving him in a gray cocoon. The men at the gatehouse were shadows, then suddenly loomed from the mist, greeting him politely. He told them he'd soon be back and they nodded, not surprised. He wondered if his every movement had already been reported to all of Leod's men. The sea was not visible outside the walls, but he could hear the waves lapping on the shore somewhere to his right, the clink of shackles from the dock ahead. All was well on *Gannon's Lady*. His men were wrapped in their cloaks against the dampness, but said the meal Leod had sent down to them had been generous, his ale delicious. He left them in good spirits and headed back up the hill, stopping halfway up when he heard his name.

"Gannon Magnusson."

FIFTEEN

He looked carefully around him, his flesh rising. The whispers. His name, his Norse name, was spoken softly from the fog, then again, this time closer. Not the whispers then, but still unnerving.

"I am here," he said.

The woman walked slowly toward him. He did not move as he watched her body take form, her clothing come into view. She was tall, wraith-like, her hair as gray as her cloak, as pale as her face. She was no longer young, yet not so old that he couldn't see the traces of the beauty she had once had. She came closer and stared up at him, as though she already knew him. He had never seen her before. She moved closer and raised a hand. He thought she'd touch his face, but she pulled her hand away.

"You are so like him. I would know you anywhere as his son."

"Did ye ken my father?"

She laughed, the sound as brittle as she appeared. "Aye. In another time." Her manner grew brisker. "The man you seek, Gannon Magnusson, the man who has been raiding Ireland and Scotland. The man you came to ask Leod about, Magnus's son. His name is Nor Thorkelson, the son of Thorkel. Fathers and sons. Some so alike. Some so different. I heard that your father was killed by Orkneymen."

He stared into her eyes. "Aye."

"The patterns of life continue." She circled him, her eyes brighter now. He did not move, and at last she stopped before him. "Leod cannot tell you about him without breaking his word. He has agreements with King Haakon of Norway."

"And with the laird of Ulster and the king of Scotland."

"Aye. And with the thane of Orkney. You see his difficulty."

"No. Who is this Nor Thorkelson?"

"An Orkneyman. From Ketelsay."

"You're sure he's the one?"

"So I've been told."

"Why do ye tell me?"

"I am no friend of Nor Thorkelson's."

"Why?"

"He took something from me that cannot be replaced."

Gannon waited for her to explain, but instead she took a step backward. He clutched her arm, surprised at how firm it was. "Wait! Tell me more. Why does he raid? What does he want? Why do ye tell me?"

She paused, a strong emotion fleeting across her face. "I knew your father; I was fond of him. He was a good man. I am hoping his son is as well. Why am I telling you this? I want you to stop Nor."

She looked at his hand on her arm, then at him. He released her.

"He took my daughter, used her, and threw her away when he was finished."

"Ye are from Ketelsay?"

"No. He came here. He's been to Skye many times, Gannon Magnusson. He has had men here too, sometimes staying for weeks."

"Where?"

"South of here. South of Bracadale, but not as far as Sleat. His men come here for women."

"And Leod kens this?"

"I don't know what Leod knows. I only know what I needed to tell you." She took another step back. "Find him."

"Does Nor raid for Leod?"

The woman shrugged.

"For King Haakon?"

"I do not think so."

"Why does he raid?"

"I cannot tell you why Nor raids. The priest would tell you about good and evil."

"And what would you tell me?"

"About what is. Nor is. Death is. Gold is."

"He does this for gold?"

"I cannot answer that. Perhaps for gold. Perhaps for power. His father died not long ago. His older brother, who should have led the men of Ketelsay, has disappeared, as has his younger brother. There are whispers that he disposed of them."

"And Leod kens all this?"

"Leod has been told many things."

"Did Leod tell ye to tell me this?"

She smiled, stepping back into the mist. And was gone, leaving him staring, his flesh crawling at her sudden disappearance. Like a spirit, he thought, staring into the fog, unable to see any trace of her. But no, she'd been real, a woman as alive as he was, who used the mist like an actor used the stage. Nothing more. He looked up the hill. He had some new questions for his host.

But Leod was as wily as ever, and despite his best efforts, Gannon went to his bed with no new information. Every question he'd asked had been parried with a ready answer that gave nothing away. He'd even asked who Nor Thorkelson was—and had been met with a blank stare and a change of subject. But a flicker of Leod's eyes let him know he'd been right.

He'd had only a few moments to tell Tiernan of his encounter with the woman, of the name and information she'd given him, and then his brother rejoined Leod's captains, loudly playing dice and drinking heavily. Gannon retreated to the comfortable room he and Tiernan were to share for the night, stretching out on the large bed, grateful that at least Leod's household understood the needs of a tall man, but worried that his brother, full of Leod's ale, might give too much away. He stared at the bedhangings, then closed his eyes. But he did not sleep, for his mind was too full of images, of Leod, of the woman in the mist. Of Margaret, who was probably Lachlan's wife now. And this her wedding night.

Tiernan came in at last, his movements lax. He closed the door behind him and leaned against it. "Good ale, but I had far too much of it."

"What did ye hear?"

Tiernan crossed the room, peeling his outer clothing from him. He threw himself on the bed with a sigh, sitting against the headboard and waiting while Gannon pulled the one chair in the room to the side of the bed and sat astride it.

"They ken who he is," Tiernan said quietly. "He is an Orkneyman, just as she said. He's been here several times in the last few months. Leod's men dinna trust him, say he cheats at dice—I lost, by the way. Ye need to pay me back for that—and he likes to fight. He cheats at that, too. He thinks he's brilliant. He's very vain."

"They all talked of him?"

Tiernan shook his head. "No, just one, young and not too drunk to be a bit cautious at least; he waited until everyone else was gone or asleep. He says that many of Leod's men and the Skyelanders are angry about Nor. They think he's likely to drag them into a war they dinna want. He says many of them think Leod should cut his ties with Norway and Orkney, that the Scottish kings have wanted the Hebrides for decades and that they'll either buy them or find another way to rule them. D'ye think they're playing us for fools, telling us that Nor is doing the raids and having us go running off to Orkney? Perhaps it's not Nor, and they're in league with whoever it actually is."

"And sending us off to insult an innocent man in Orkney and irritate the jarl there?" Gannon nodded. "Perhaps. But we dinna have to play it like fools. Or perhaps it is Nor, and everyone wants us to rid the world of him. Who kens what the truth of it is? All we ken is that one woman told me a name and a story to go with it."

"And a man confirmed much of it."

"A trip to Orkney will tell us and I'm thinking that's exactly what we'll do."

Gannon woke from a nightmare to stare into the dim morning light, then take deep breaths, telling himself he was on Skye, that Tiernan slept nearby, that all was well, that it was the whisky he'd had that had brought the dream, or the talks with Leod. Nothing more. It meant nothing. He sat up, his body tense and stiff, then climbed from the bed. He would not seek slumber again. He held his hands before him, seeing them tremble, and clenched them, forcing them to steady and his heart to slow. A dream. He leaned his forehead on the sill of the window and breathed the cool morning air, then straightened as he realized the cliffs in his dream had been much like those just outside this opening. It was, he told himself, nothing more than the pieces of the recent past, nothing more than a mix of his experiences. Nothing more than his acknowledgment of the responsibility of this visit, of the importance of discovering who the raiders were. The dream was only a symbol of the tension he felt. And his fears. In the dreams he always failed.

It had been Margaret's shrill, frightened voice, her screams, which he'd heard, that still echoed in his mind. Calling his name. Not a memory this time, unless there was some way to have lived this all before. And dear God let it not be a foreshadowing. He could not bear to hear her terror. He'd not been alone, nor she. There had been others, too, screaming, but he'd paid them little mind, hearing only her voice, knowing death was at hand.

He rubbed his hand across his forehead, then pulled on his clothing with shaky movements that annoyed him; he slowed his body until it once again moved as it should, and, dressed now, he opened the door. He might never drink whisky again, just in case.

Hours later Gannon bid farewell to Leod at the dock, then turned his attention to the task of wending their way back through the loch to the open sea. Leod had grinned as they left, and Gannon had the uncomfortable feeling that his amusement was at their expense. He looked away from the older man, looked over the water, thinking of what he'd learned. He'd been right all along; it was Orkneymen who had done the raiding. And he had a name of the man who might be their leader. Before they returned to Inverstrath he'd search Skye for dragonships in hopes that he might find a man to accompany the name.

Morning brought rain to Inverstrath, but still no priest. He could not be found, they were told, although that was strange, for he was a man of regular habits. No matter, William said, when she brought the news. He sent for the monk who had been there the day before.

"He's not a priest," Margaret said.

"He will do," William said briskly.

The monk arrived that afternoon, dusty from travel and bearing news of more raids in the north. William listened with a grim expression, then told Margaret to prepare for the wedding.

"I'll be leaving shortly thereafter," he said. "Let's get this done."

Nell brushed Margaret's hair until it gleamed, then helped her dress in the light blue silk bodice and matching overskirt that she'd worn to her audience with the king. Nell thought the color perfect and the styling quite lovely—even if the clothing had brought her no luck last time. The sisters had said little while they readied Margaret for the wedding, but Nell had expected that. She brushed Margaret's dark hair one more time, then spread it over her shoulders, pleased with her work.

"Ye look beautiful, Margaret."

Margaret gave her a wan smile. "Thank ye."

"Are ye afraid?"

"I'm sad."

"About marrying Lachlan?"

"Aye, that and . . . it doesna matter."

Nell put her hand on her sister's cheek, and Margaret's eyes filled with tears. "And what?" Nell said quietly.

Margaret sighed. "I keep thinking of how Mother would be scolding us, and the boys would be running around under foot. Sometimes it doesna seem real, that they're all gone. I forget, and think 'I'll tell Mother that' or 'Rignor best not say that in front of Father.'" She smiled tearfully. "I'm so sorry, Nell. It's none of it like we thought, is it?"

"Maybe the worst is over. Maybe Lachlan will be a good husband to ye and ye'll fall in love with him and he ye."

"Aye."

"Maybe we'll find Davey soon."

"Would that not be bonnie?"

"What do slaves do?"

At Margaret's puzzled expression, Nell continued. "D'ye think Davey's working in a field? Or sweeping floors? What would they have him do? He's only small; he couldna do much. He might be able to watch cattle."

"I hadna thought on it."

They were quiet as Margaret laced on her shoes and smoothed her skirts, the silk soft under her hands. She pushed her hair over her shoulders and bent to let Nell place the wreath of flowers on her head. She'd delayed as long as she could. It was time. William had sent a man to say that all was ready. Rignor waited in the hallway to escort her downstairs. She said a prayer, then lifted her skirts. Her brother smiled and stepped forward when she opened the door, offering his arm. Nell slipped into place behind them.

"I canna thank ye enough, Margaret," he said.

He spoke as though they were discussing a small favor, not the matter of the rest of her life. It was just as well, she told herself, that he had no idea of what was in her heart.

"I'll make it up to ye."

"How could ye possibly, Rignor?"

"Once I get Somerstrath strong again, I'll be a wealthy man. I'll send ye jewels. Ye'll see; it'll all be worth it. We'll both be wealthy."

She stared at him. How could he know her so little? "Jewels."

"Aye. As soon as I get Somerstrath rebuilt, we'll change things; we'll be wealthier than ever. And I'll remember what ye did here today. I promise ye that."

"Rignor, I dinna want jewels."

They did not speak again as they walked down the narrow stairway, nor when Rignor took her arm again and led her across the hall, filled with men who shuffled their feet and looked away from her, clearly uncomfortable, or smiled, blithely unaware of the tension in the room.

Lachlan, standing stiffly next to the monk, was finely dressed in soft wool and saffron-dyed linen, the gold of his brooch and rings catching the light as he smoothed his shirt and kilt below. The groom, she noted, was nervous. And better dressed than his bride.

Don't think.

Uncle William stood between Rory O'Neill and

Rufus, his expression somber. She met his gaze, saw his discomfort, and looked only at Lachlan then, not allowing her gaze to sweep across the assembled men in search of one tall blond man. Surely if Gannon had returned, someone would have told her. Or perhaps not. It would undo her, she knew, if he gave her even the slightest hint that she should not do this. Nor did she turn to look at Nell, who had followed them without a word, her silence more telling than anything she could have said.

Father, Mother, I do this for you, for your honor, as I promised.

The monk stepped forward. He smiled at her. She looked away. The rays of afternoon sunlight streamed through the open doors, turning the shadows of the hammered ceiling black and calling dust motes to dance in the light. Her skirt swished against the floor. Behind her Nell moved restlessly, her gaze darting from left to right as though expecting someone to interrupt them.

But of course no one did. No one stepped forward to argue that the ceremony could not go forward, no one raised his voice in protest.

"Kneel, child," the monk said, and she did.

She answered all the prompts that he gave her. The ceremony seemed strange to her, but she'd only seen a few marriages and had hardly listened to the words. Perhaps everything would seem strange just now. She repeated what the monk said, then heard Lachlan do the same, his tone smug and carrying across the room. The monk finished his prayer, made the sign of the cross on her forehead, then on Lachlan's, then pressed their hands together and folded his hands over them, saying words in Latin that she hardly listened to, his voice fading into the background. She concentrated on the small things, the monk's frayed sleeves, Lachlan's golden cuff resting on his wrist, the scuffle of dogs under a table somewhere behind her, Nell's sniff that let her know her sister was crying. The shadows that crossed the rays of light and let her know someone was now standing near the door. She thought of Somerstrath as she'd last seen it, destroyed, desecrated, of all she owed to the memory of her family.

"It is done," the monk told her. "Ye are married now. Greet yer husband."

She stood slowly, lifting her gaze from the floor to Lachlan's. He gave her a tight smile, then placed a perfunctory kiss on her cheek, holding her hand in his, raising them together as he turned to face the others. She let herself be turned, heard them announced as husband and wife, heard the polite cheering.

Some of the women were crying, some smiling, some wore worried expressions. Uncle William watched with a stern expression next to a frowning Rory O'Neill and a somber Dagmar. Rufus nodded when she met his gaze, as did Rignor, his satisfaction obvious. She could not look at Nell, could not search the crowd for the one face that would undo her. He was gone, and that was for the best.

He was too late.

He'd expected to return to find Margaret's marriage a day old, and she and her husband perhaps even already gone. He'd not expected to have to walk in just as the ceremony was ending, just as their vows were sanctified, just as he lost her forever. The watchers gave a tepid cheer and sat down, ready for their meal.

He cursed himself for a fool for wanting her so much, for

not having spoken to her of his feelings earlier, for not having known their intensity until now, when he knew her pledged to another. Why had he not thought of stealing her away to Ireland with him? But how could he? There had been no admission of anything between him and Margaret; he had no claim on her, nor she on him. They were strangers, the bond between them temporary and formed by the shared experience of death. And desire. Nothing more. Still, if she'd given him one sign that that was what she wanted, he would do it, even now. But she did not look up, did not see him standing there like a stone, his throat tight.

Her head had been bent as she repeated the last words the monk intoned, her voice quiet. Her dark hair had caught the light, flashing blue and black and a deep red in the sunbeams. Her lashes had been lowered, casting shadows on her cheeks, her hands pressed together. She looked calm and beautiful. She must want this. And how could she not? Lachlan Ross was a wealthy man; her life would be secure, and how could she not want that now more than ever?

Rignor watched with a contented smile; Nell bit her knuckle, her distress obvious. The monk blessed their union, asking Margaret and Lachlan to kneel and ask God's blessing as well. The sense of loss, of despair, he felt was absurd, unreasonable. He told himself that it meant only that he was lonely for a woman, which was easily solved. He'd return to Haraldsholm and see whom Erik had chosen for him. If she pleased him, he'd marry her; if not, he'd find his own woman. And think of Margaret MacDonald for the rest of his life.

He was greeted then by the Inverstrath men and brought to a table for the meal. The bride, who look dazed, spoke only to those in front of her, accepting their congratulations with a tight smile. She did not look across the room, did not see him where he and his brother sat with their men in the shadows. Which was as well, for he would need time to school his emotions and be sure they did not show on his face.

The meal was interminable, the feast adequate but not festive. When men were rising and stretching and obviously ready to leave, Lachlan stood, raising his cup for a toast. The ribald jokes, begun long ago, surfaced again. Lachlan waited for them to subside with a stiff smile, then raised his cup higher.

"To my bride."

There were murmurs of approval and a repeat of the toast. Lachlan waited for silence, then continued.

"To my bride, who will sleep alone this night. And every night for six months until I can be sure she does not carry another man's child."

Margaret stared at him, hardly hearing the outraged protests and exclamations around her. Rignor shouted something, but it was lost in the din.

William rose to his feet, his face scarlet. "What do you mean by this?"

"What I mean, my lord," Lachlan said, "is that two nights ago my bride-to-be was found in the hallway with Gannon MacMagnus. He was half-naked. She was kissing him. I cannot share her bed until I ken whether she carries his seed."

Rignor turned to Margaret, his eyes blazing. "What have ye done?"

"I have done nothing," she said.

"I'll kill him!" Rignor shouted. "I'll kill him!"

"Then do it!" Gannon's voice came from the back of the hall, and all turned, craning to see, as he strode forward. "Here I am, Rignor!"

Lachlan watched Gannon's progress with visible surprise, then turned to Margaret, speaking loudly so that all could hear. "I care not whether ye are a virgin, Margaret, nor whether ye've had one man or ten. But I'll not share yer bed and have a child come of this night—or two nights past—and wonder with everyone else who its sire is. Ye'll sleep alone tonight, and for six months. If ye dinna have a child on the way by then, I'll accept ye into my bed."

Margaret rose to her feet as Gannon came to a stop before their table, his chest heaving and his expression murderous. She met his gaze and smiled; he quieted, his puzzlement obvious. She picked up her cup and held it high, waiting until the murmurs subsided. She did not look at Lachlan as she spoke, only at the tall blond man before her. She met his gaze and smiled again.

"To my husband," she said, and saw Gannon's eyes flicker. "To my husband in name only, who has now publicly shamed me twice. Who, after the first time, promised to be faithful, yet broke his word again the same day. Who holds me to a standard he himself will not meet." She turned to Lachlan now. "I will not share yer bed this night, nor any other, Lachlan Ross. This marriage will never be consummated. It will be annulled."

Dagmar's laughter broke the silence that followed.

"No." Rignor's hoarse whisper was horrified. "Ye dinna mean it."

"But I do, Rignor."

"Ye promised," he hissed.

Lachlan grabbed her arm. "Ye dinna deny that ye were with Gannon MacMagnus two nights ago, do ye?"

"Let go of her," Gannon cried, moving forward, his hand hovering above the hilt of his sword. Behind him the Irishmen came to their feet.

Margaret was calm. "It's a'right, Gannon." She turned to Lachlan. "I kissed him in the hallway. Nothing more happened."

"I kissed her," Gannon cried. "One kiss. There was nothing more than that. There will be no child. Margaret, I apologize again."

"There is no need," she told him. "I was not forced."

"Enough!" William roared. "We will talk of this in private! Rufus, surely ye have a room to which we can withdraw."

Rufus, obviously distressed, nodded. "Of course, my lord. Come." He led them to a small room near the door to the kitchen courtyard.

They closed Nell out, not even answering her when she asked why she could not stay with her sister. Rignor scowled at her; Margaret, already in the middle of the circle of men, must not have heard. When the door closed, Nell hit it twice with her fist, then stormed back to the hall, throwing herself on the first bench she found, her arms crossed over her chest. Behind her the people were buzzing with talk of it, Lachlan's men defending him, the Somerstrath people and Rufus's men defending Margaret. The Irishmen were wise enough to stay quiet. Nell, miserable, stared at the wall and fought her tears.

"May I join ye?"

She looked up at Tiernan and nodded.

"They wouldna let ye in?" He sat next to her, leaning forward, dangling his hands between his knees.

"No! They even let Rory O'Neill in, but not me!"

"Nor me."

She watched him look across the hall, then back at her, and her anger faded. "What will happen now?"

He shrugged. "We'll find out together."

"I hate Lachlan."

"I'm not so fond of him myself."

"He planned this. He meant to shame her."

"Aye. And he did. But she did well."

"She's scared," Nell said.

"She's angry. That will see her through."

"Gannon shouldna have kissed her."

"She should have stayed in her room."

"Rignor's furious."

"Aye, well, yer brother is always angry about something, isn't he? He'll get over it. They're still married."

She stared at him. "But they're not. Margaret said she'd get it annulled."

"That's for the bishop to say, not her. She'll have to apply to the bishop; if he agrees, the marriage is annulled. If not . . ."

"Surely no one can expect her to live with Lachlan now!"

"I dinna ken what they'll expect of her. Or of Gannon."

"What d'ye mean?"

"They could annul her marriage to Lachlan and yer uncle William demand that Gannon marry her."

"Would that be so bad?"

Tiernan grinned at her. "Aren't ye the fiery one, Nell? I'm not saying it's good; I'm not saying it's bad. That's for my brother and yer sister to say, isn't it?"

SIXTEEN

argaret took a deep breath to calm herself. Rignor glared at her. Rufus watched her as though she'd grown a tail. Rory O'Neill was amused at something, but blessedly silent. Lachlan's color was high, his fingers rubbing his chin and betraying his agitation. The monk held his hands pressed together before his mouth, as though to keep from speaking. Gannon, at her side, still looked murderous, but had not spoken.

William stood before her, holding both hands up to quiet the mood. "We'll go through it again," he said calmly.

Margaret hardly listened. She should have known how foolish it was to talk with Gannon that night, should have stayed in her bed, or run back to her room when she saw him. But she did not regret a moment of it. And if this—not consummating her marriage, perhaps nullifying it—was her punishment, she was delighted. She fought the wave of laughter that kept bubbling up within her. Had she known that it would be so easy to end this sham with Lachlan, she would have done so sooner. And more publicly.

Gannon was defending her ardently, telling William

again that he had acted without her permission. When she tried to comment, William had waved her words away. And each time she'd started to say that the kiss had been mutual, she'd felt the pressure of Gannon's elbow on her arm. At last she said only that yes, he had kissed her, then she'd returned to her room, that both Lachlan and Rory O'Neill had been there.

William ran a hand through his hair. "I can see no harm here."

"No harm!" Lachlan cried. "She went walking with him to the next glen, alone! We can none of us be sure what they did there. Or whether there were other times that I've not even been told of. She's tainted goods!"

"Tainted goods?" William's tone was glacial. "Ye'll not speak of my niece that way again. Margaret, ye'll come home with me while we await the bishop's answer."

Rignor looked at William in disbelief. "Ye dinna mean to apply for annulment? Tell me ye're not. We can wait the six months . . ."

William's eyes narrowed. "Why is it me defending yer sister's honor, Rignor, and not ye?"

Rignor reddened. "She promised . . ."

"Aye," William said. "And she fulfilled that promise. Ye canna ask more of her. Ye willna ask more of her. Go on home to Somerstrath and start the rebuilding. Lachlan, we'll talk later, ye and me. Gannon, ye'll not bother my niece again, aye? I will no' have ye near her."

Gannon stiffened. "Ye have no authority over me."

"Swear to me," Lachlan shouted at Gannon, "that ye'll not touch her again! Ye owe it to me!"

"I owe ye nothing," Gannon told him.

"Ye owe me the civility of not taking my woman."

"I dinna 'take' her, Ross. I . . ."

"Men have been killed for less," Lachlan growled.

"If ye stayed out of other women's beds . . ." Gannon said.

O'Neill spread his hands wide. "Let's be calm. We've no need for this now."

"I find it interesting," Margaret said, "that ye're all telling me what ye think and what I should do now, but none of ye have asked me what I think."

Gannon threw her a glance, his eyebrows raised. She turned away from him to look first at her uncle, then Lachlan and Rignor.

"I kept my promise. I married Lachlan. I never promised to be a virgin, though I am. I never promised my heart, which I have not given to Lachlan, nor will I. I never promised not to kiss another man before marriage, nor do I regret that I did. I was willing to be a good wife, willing to spend my life with ye, Lachlan, but ye could not accept that gift graciously. I have now withdrawn it. I will write to the bishop immediately and ask for this travesty to be annulled. Dinna fear, Rignor—William has told me he would not withdraw his support from ye even if I were not to marry Lachlan. Uncle William, I'm holding ye to that."

"Ye have my word," William said.

"Thank ye," she said. "All my life I have done as I have been told, by my father, my mother. Now my family is dead, and my dutiful days are over. There is nothing any of ye can do to convince me to be Lachlan's wife. What we need to be discussing is how to get Davey back and whether we'll be attacked again, whether we're on the edge of war, whether the very future of Scotland is in jeopardy, not whether one vain man has had his pride wounded."

They all stared at her. She looked at each man in turn. Rufus nodded. Rory O'Neill grinned at her. Rignor looked away when their gazes met. Lachlan flushed and clenched his jaw. William watched her with a thoughtful look. And Gannon held her gaze, his smile slowly widening, his eyes bright.

"Good for ye, lass," he whispered. "Good for ye."

"Do ye think," Margaret said to the monk, "that the bishop will grant the annulment?"

"I will recommend that he does." He looked at Lachlan, then continued with that same strange smile. "I've never known the groom to be the one shrinking from the marriage bed. I'm sure the bishop will find that interesting."

Lachlan flushed, threw a heated look around the room, and stormed out.

"There doesna seem to be any more to say, does there?" William asked with a sigh. "We'll need to hear about yer trip to Skye, Gannon. What did Leod tell ye?"

"Leod told us verra little. We heard the same name from one of the Skye women and from Leod's men. Nor Thorkelson, an Orkneyman."

The monk stepped back, causing a tray full of cups to clatter to the floor.

"D'ye ken this Thorkelson?" William asked him.

The monk shook his head. "No, my lord. The name itself is frightening, is it not? A man with a name like that could be capable of anything."

William turned back to Gannon. "And?"

"He's said to visit Skye often," Gannon said, "but no one else would talk about him. We searched along the coast. There was no sign of them, but we did find an abandoned camp, not far from Leod, so I'm thinking he was there. And that we need to go to Orkney."

"Did ye hear aught of Davey?" Margaret asked.

Gannon shook his head. "No, but I'd wager that if we find Nor, we'll learn something of Davey."

"Go and tell the others," William said, gesturing at the door. "Ye've a hall full of people waiting for the news. Margaret, a word with ye."

He waited until they were alone, then closed the door with finality and leaned against it, his expression stern. "Ye shouldna have been with Gannon. Ye shouldna have kissed him."

"No. I'm sorry."

"Aye, so am I. God help us, what a mess! Why isn't yer Aunt Jean here? She'd ken what to do." He smiled ruefully and shook his head. "I canna tell ye how glad I am that I have sons and not daughters."

"Thank ye for believing me that nothing happened."

"But it did, did it not?"

"I am still a virgin, Uncle William."

"I never once thought ye werena. But dinna tell me nothing happened between ye. Something did, and we all ken it."

"One kiss. If we were at court, no one would even have commented on it."

"Not true, lass. The married women do what they like, but the unmarried ones are held to a different standard. And ye ken that."

She nodded. William sighed again.

"Och, dinna fret, Margaret. It's done and might be for the best after all. There are other men in the world. Let's remember that we have bigger problems than yer marriage just the now. But dinna tell me ye're no' pleased."

She smiled. "I won't."

"Lassie, if I dinna ken ye better, I'd wonder if ye planned it."

"I dinna. But I am pleased."

He laughed and left her alone then.

But Rignor didn't. He was waiting outside the room, stepping out of the shadows to stand before her.

"Ye promised, Margaret. All ye had to do was wait."

"For Lachlan to determine whether I'd been with another man? Why is my word not enough? He shamed me twice. There willna be a third."

"Why not wait? There's no harm to it."

"Because I willna be Mother! I willna be married to a man who hurts me and expects me to endure it simply because I must. I'm sorry, Rignor, truly I am."

"Ye had no intention on ever seeing it through, did ye? Bravo, sister. Yer plan worked."

She stepped back. "I dinna plan this."

"I think ye did. I think ye waited for Gannon. Or would any man have done?"

"Rignor, how can ye think this of me?"

"Did he help plan it all?"

"Why would he?"

"He has no land, Margaret. No wealth of his own."

"Neither do I, Rignor. I bring nothing to a marriage but myself."

"Ye have a brother who's a thane, and land that can be reclaimed. Was that yer plan, the two of ye, to wrest Somerstrath from me?"

"No! Why would I? Why would we?"

"It was ye who talked of rebuilding! Ye who told me ye'd be there. I just dinna understand what ye intended. Ye mean to take it from me, d'ye not?"

Something ugly flickered in his eyes, and she realized that Rignor was serious, that more than simply anger powered him, something so distasteful that she had to look away. She took a deep breath and tried to calm herself. "I dinna want Somerstrath, Rignor. It's yers. But I would like my brother back. Where have ye gone that ye should think such things of me? We ken each other too well to do this. Please!" She spread her hands wide in supplication. "I dinna plot to take it from ye. If it had been my plan to stop the wedding by being with Gannon, it would have been I who talked of it. I would have shouted it from the rooftop. And I wouldna have stopped at a kiss."

"Ah, the slut reveals herself."

She slapped him across the face, then stepped back quickly as he raised his hand to strike her back.

"Ye'll no' be doing that," Gannon said, his hand clasped around Rignor's wrist. "If ye hit her, I'll hit ye tenfold. Understand?"

For a long moment the two men stared at each other, then Gannon released Rignor, who glared at him as he rubbed his wrist.

"I dinna want yer Somerstrath," Gannon said, his voice low and menacing. "We neither of us planned this. If we had, we've have done a better job of it, and she wouldna have wed him. Ken this: if ye touch her, ye'll pay. D'ye understand?"

Rignor stalked away.

Gannon looked after him, then turned to Margaret, his expression still thunderous. "Can the man not simply walk away for once? Must he always stalk away as though he'd murder the world?" He shook his head. "Are ye a'right, lass?"

"Aye. I will not stay married to him, Gannon."

"Are ye still that angry? Maybe ye care more for him than ye think . . ."

She made a scoffing sound. "It's not just Fiona, not just that he lied to me. He's a weak, vain man who thinks only of himself. He has lands, but he doesna manage them. He spends all his time at court, preening and flirting and decorating himself. I told myself I dinna see the things he was, that Rignor was wrong when he told me about them. Now they are all that I can see. Lachlan will never be content anywhere but at court. I've been there. It's not the life I want, playing games for power. We're only on this Earth for a short while—some shorter than others—but it should mean something, should it not? Life at court with Lachlan would be a kind of death to me."

He laughed softly. "A woman without opinions, I can see."

She flushed, but he put his hand on her cheek and leaned closer.

"Gannon." Rory O'Neill stood silhouetted at the end of the corridor.

Gannon pressed his eyes closed, then opened them as though praying for patience. "Rory, will ye give us a moment?"

"Laddie," O'Neill said quietly, "the two of ye need to come out into the light."

"We're fine where we are," Gannon said.

"No, ye're not. Get her free of Lachlan, then do as ye wish. With my blessing."

"I thank ye for that," Margaret said.

"And if the annulment is not granted?" Gannon asked.

"After hundreds of people here witnessed what happened?" O'Neill laughed. "Ye saw the people out there. They're all yer people tonight, lassie; not one of them is siding with Lachlan. Dinna give them a reason to change that. Lachlan left, by the way, took his men and rode off with nary a word."

"Lachlan's gone?" she asked, surprised.

"Did ye really expect him to stay?"

They did as O'Neill asked, but they did it separately, she sitting with O'Neill, Rufus, Nell, and Rignor. And Dagmar, whose neckline seemed to have slipped even lower. Gannon sat with his brother and his men, playing dice, their laughter comforting. She memorized the fall of his hair against his cheek, the shadow his long lashes made, his intent expression as he watched. She took a deep breath. Her brother might be missing, there might be madmen beyond the breaking waves, but somehow Gannon made her think that all would be well eventually. She talked with Nell and O'Neill, ignored Rignor's anger, and faced the close appraisal of Rufus and William Ross. The musicians that Rufus had had brought in for the wedding feast played, and the mood gradually lightened.

Tiernan danced with Nell, laughing as he learned the Scottish dances and laughing again as he taught her his own. Nell glowed with happiness, but Margaret saw the looks Tiernan threw at Dagmar over Nell's head. And remembered, with a start, that this was her wedding feast. She was a married woman, wed in a very strange ceremony, but wed nonetheless. She stole a glance at the monk, who was drinking heavily and watching the dancing avidly. Perhaps, she thought with a laugh, that was why the man had had to go on a pilgrimage.

The Somerstrath people made their sympathy for her visible; they passed the table where she sat with the men and smiled at her, or nodded, or even stopped for a word, their attentions not unnoticed by Rignor, who spent his time, jaw grimly set, staring at Margaret as though his thoughts were of her. And not happy thoughts. She refused to acknowledge him, but watched him drink steadily, more heavily with every passing hour. How could she have been blind enough to ever think he could be the leader her father had been?

"What of me?" Rignor asked now. "I should come with ye as well, William."

"I need ye to start the rebuilding at Somerstrath," William said.

"And what of Gannon?" Rignor demanded. "Is he not to be punished?"

"Punished for kissing yer sister?" O'Neill asked. "In Ireland we encourage our lads to kiss lassies. No, Gannon willna be punished. He'll come home with me."

William raised an eyebrow. "Then who's to guard Inverstrath? Rufus doesna have enough men, Rory."

Rory O'Neill glanced at Margaret, then nodded. "We'll talk on it, William."

No one heard Rignor's protest, for one of Rufus's men threw the door open, shouting, and everyone took notice.

"A sail, sir! Coming from the north, flying the Ross banner."

The ship, sent by William's men, brought frightening news. Haakon was in the Orkneys with a huge fleet of ships said to be heading south, but whether for Irish or Scottish waters was not known. King Alexander had ordered all those along the northern and western coasts to prepare their defenses, was sending men to reinforce the strongholds, and was said to be heading west himself.

"So it's true," William said. "These raids were but preludes. I'll leave at first light. Rufus, get yer people readied. Rignor, ye'll stay here with him."

"What about Somerstrath?" Rignor cried. "Ye said . . ."

"Let's see what Haakon's about. Somerstrath is the least of our worries now. We're talking about Scotland surviving now, not one . . ."

"I am Somerstrath, William! I will decide if it's abandoned."

William gave Rignor a long look. "Then hold it. But ye need to assist Rufus."

"Somerstrath comes first."

"Yer people come first!"

Rignor colored. "Aye, of course. That's what I meant."

"Good," William said, turning to Margaret and Nell. "Ye'll go to Brenmargon Abbey in the morning. Unless ye want to go to Lachlan . . . ?"

"No," Margaret said.

William waved a hand, accepting her decision, then looked at O'Neill.

"Gannon can stay," O'Neill said, answering William's unspoken question. He glanced at Gannon. "Will ye?"

"We can care for our own!" Rignor cried.

"Ye dinna have enough men to hold Inverstrath," William said. "Gannon?"

"On one condition, sir," Gannon said. "That the letter to the bishop be written before ye leave."

William raised an eyebrow. "Ye understand what it is ye're asking? And what ye're saying to me?"

Gannon nodded. "Aye, sir, I do. On both counts."

Margaret's heart leapt, then quieted. He'd said nothing to her . . . but she'd known, hadn't she? The corner of O'Neill's mouth quirked. Rignor protested, but William, silencing him with a gesture, apparently as weary as Margaret was of how predictable her brother had become, watched Gannon.

"I need yer word that my niece will be safe with ye until she leaves."

"Ye have my word."

"And yer word that ye'll remember she's another man's wife."

"Aye, on that, too."

"Then it's done," William said, rising. "We have much to do."

The others all faded away, leaving Margaret and Gannon alone. But still he did not speak. She tried to keep the bubble of mirth down but failed.

"Gannon?"

He turned to her at once. "Aye?"

"Can ye believe it? All that happened?" She laughed aloud.

He joined her, slowly at first, then with a guffaw that amused him even more. "Did ye see his face when ye toasted him?" He laughed again, but a moment later his tone quieted. "I was so proud of yer courage, lass, standing up to him like that."

She smiled. "Thank ye for defending me with William."

"How could I not? It was I that kissed ye."

She shook her head. "No, Gannon. It was both of us. I wanted it more than ye'll ever ken."

They looked into each other's eyes for a long moment. He lifted a hand as though to touch her cheek, then glanced around at the people still watching them. He let his hand fall.

"Margaret, did ye mean what ye said, that ye'll ask for an annulment?"

"Aye. I meant every word. I promised to marry him, and I did. I dinna promise to stay married."

His smile was wide. "There has never been a lass as fine as ye."

She laughed softly. "And did ye mean what ye told William—or what ye led him to believe?"

"That I want this annulment? Aye." He took a deep breath. "I thought I'd lost ye, Margaret. I kept telling myself that it couldna be helped, that ye'd been promised to Lachlan long before I met ye and that especially now, with the world gone mad, I was a fool to think that anything else would happen but that ye'd marry him. Last night, when I was on Skye, I couldna sleep for thinking that ye'd married him. That it was yer wedding night and . . . and when I walked in and ye were taking yer vows . . . it was everything I could do to stop myself from thundering across the room and stealing ye away. When ye get the annulment—if ye get the annulment, I'll marry ye myself. If ye'll have me. I love ye, lass."

She could not speak. Her heart was too full, her mind spinning too fast to form words. She reached for him, ignoring those who might be watching, clasping him to her while her eyes filled with tears and she buried her face against his shoulder. She could hear his heart pounding, could hear his ragged breath. He put his arms around her, kissed her hair, then her cheek, then let her go.

"I told yer uncle . . ." he began, but she waved his words away.

"I ken, I ken. And I'll not ask ye to break that promise. But ken this, Gannon MacMagnus. I love ye. I love ye with everything in me, and I'll wait to be yers for as long as it takes."

His smile was radiant. He took her hands in his and leaned to kiss her mouth, but did not pull her into his arms. The kiss was sweet and far too short. He released her hands and smiled again. "Let's not make it verra long, Margaret. I want ye in my arms and in my bed. I want to kiss ye without wondering who's watching and to ken that no one can stop us from being together."

"And I want the same, Gannon," she said, letting her gaze drift from his face to his waist. And below, then back to his eyes. "But it's much more than a kiss that I'm wanting."

He laughed, and her heart soared.

O'Neill was the first to leave, his ships scraping off the shingle at dawn with the first movement of the ebbing tide. Gannon and Tiernan waved from the shore, Margaret, Nell, and William from the berm above. The Irish leader left with fanfare, his drummer beating time for the rowers, his horns sounding as the ships turned and faced the sea. When he was gone and the harbor once again quiet, William turned to Margaret and Nell.

"I wish I could take ye with me, but I canna. Ye'll be safe with Judith."

"We'll be fine here," Margaret said with more confidence than she felt. "Inverstrath is too small to attract attention."

"Ye will go to Brenmargon," William said sternly. "Aye?" Margaret smiled.

William, satisfied, continued. "I've told Rufus to keep runners out to the other clans for news. And Gannon will have men guarding from the sea. If aught happens while ye're still here . . . save yerselves. Promise me."

Nell nodded, her eyes fearful.

"We'll be careful," Margaret said. "Ye need to be as well."

"Aye." He paused, then put a sealed letter in her hand. "I'm told ye've written yer own already."

"Last night."

"The monk will take them. Ye ken that I have no control over the bishop. He might refuse to consider it."

"I understand."

"And perhaps little sway with the king. And there's something we've not talked on. Ye ken that thanes like yer father, like Rignor now, are direct subjects of the king, not of the earls, that Rignor is tied to me by blood, not law."

"Aye," Margaret said, confused.

"The marriage contract cannot be canceled except by the king. He may ignore my wishes. He may leave the decision to yer closest male relative."

"Rignor?"

"Aye. The king may decide to let him have the final say. Heal the friction between ye, Margaret."

"I would have tried to anyway."

"Aye, well, now ye have even more reason." He leaned to kiss her forehead. "God keep ye safe."

"What about Davey?" Margaret asked.

William's face clouded. "He's in God's hands now. I can spare neither the time nor the men to search for him. I'll keep him in my prayers. And all of ye."

"Ye'll be in ours," she answered.

The sky was clear, the wind strong and from the west and their ships slid across the sea like fingers on silk. Nor Thorkelson looked to his left, where the sails of his companion's ships were lifted high above their hulls, then to his right, where in the distance the outlines of the islands of Harris, Lewis, and Uist could be seen, gray against the indigo water. A short visit with a friend, a chance to hear the latest news and for his men to sate themselves with willing women for a change, and they'd be off again.

It would not last, he knew that. The Scots and the Irish would grow weary of his depredations, and would in time resist even his simple requests for payment instead of slaughter. They'd go to Ketelsay, complain to the thanc of Orkney, perhaps even to King Haakon. But there they'd reach a deaf ear, for Haakon, it was said, was weary himself of Scottish demands. Scotland's Alexander would find himself outmatched by Haakon's experience and ruthlessness and undone by the Scots themselves. They called themselves a nation now, but all who looked at them from without knew them for what they were: a fractious group of peoples united only by their fierceness and inability to change.

He was actually doing them a favor by mixing Norse blood with theirs. Or he would have been doing them a favor if he'd let the women live; in the future, perhaps he would. Perhaps it was time to change what the Scots were. It would take time, three generations at a minimum, but it would happen, at least along the western seaboard. He smiled as he pictured tall blond boys with his agility, his intelligence, then frowned, remembering what had happened in Ireland. Norsemen had taken Dublin, mixed with the Irish, and formed a race that then fought their own. Danes had fought Norsemen, forgetting that Denmark was once part of Norway. And Norsemen now called themselves Irish.

No, he'd been right in the beginning. Take what they had and leave nothing behind. He glanced at Drason. His nephew had refused to fight in the last raid and was now bound and huddled in the hull. It was time for an accident, a most unfortunate occurrence. His men wouldn't mind; the boy was a reminder of Ander and his objections, and that would not do. *Eldrid, Eldrid. You raised a weakling. And weaklings are intolerable.*

He should have married, should have sired a slew of boys who would have made him proud, instead of wondering how many bastards he'd fathered. At least he knew Drason was not one of them. Any lingering doubts he'd had about his nephew's parentage had fled during that last raid, when the boy had begged him to stop, saying they simply could rob the Scots, that they didn't have to kill everyone. How could Drason not understand? Terror was not terror if it was mediated. It must strike fear in their hearts, not simply in their purses. Nor shook his head, thinking of how exactly to rid himself of this irritation.

Then smiled as the solution came to him.

* * *

The equinox brought strong storms, as it often did, sheets of rain that soaked them to the skin in moments, and cold winds that crept through the tiny cracks and under the doors, bringing the first taste of winter. They stayed inside, in the dim hall, waiting for the weather to clear. The end of September already.

"Damn wind," Rufus muttered, pulling his shirt closer around his neck.

Snapping wind. The words came from nowhere. Margaret had not thought of that phrase since the day she'd left Somerstrath. Davey's phrase; she could almost hear him say it. At the far end of the hall Rufus's men played dice. Rufus himself sat near her, counting rents with one of his captains. Nell was doing needlework. Dagmar was nowhere to be seen, nor was Tiernan. Margaret sighed, knowing where the two of them were and what that would lead to. How Rignor could not know it was beyond her, but despite his ill temper, he seemed unaware of it. Others saw what she did, for Nell or Gannon would exchange a look with her that let her know Dagmar and Tiernan being together again had not escaped them. But no one spoke of it.

Runners arrived constantly with news of more raids, in the east, in the south. Rumors flew. Haakon had claimed all of southern Scotland; he'd murdered everyone in Edinburgh; he'd claimed the English throne. Alexander had pushed Haakon out of Scotland; he'd seized the Orkney Islands and the Hebrides; he'd claimed the English throne. There was more news from England, of even more turmoil. King Henry was still cowering in the Tower. Queen Eleanor had pawned her jewels to the Templars to pay the mercenaries in the royal army, but

Prince Edward, under the guise of inspecting her jewels, smashed the treasure chests and took not only his mother's jewels, but the Templars' gold and silver as well. All of London was in an uproar and now invited de Montfort to take the city and the throne. There would be no help from that quarter.

News came then that Haakon had gone to the southwest of Scotland, anchoring his fleet off Arran and Bute and that there were negotiations between him and King Alexander. And then more news, confirming that Haakon had landed, but instead of war, the two kings were in discussions. When the news was confirmed yet again by runners from William, Rufus broke out some of his best wine. That night they toasted Alexander of Scotland and said a prayer for the success of the negotiations and talked of peace. People ventured beyond the walls again; fishermen sailed without Gannon's ship in their sight, Rufus's men went hunting to replenish Rufus's larders, and life became peaceful.

For a few days.

SEVENTEEN

It was two days later, in the middle of a sunny afternoon, that Rignor found Margaret and Nell. His movements were abrupt and his face flushed, but whether from anger or drink she could not tell. He did not greet them. Margaret watched him warily. They'd not had words; she had no idea what had caused his mood.

"I'm going to Somerstrath," he said flatly.

Margaret blinked. "Now?"

"Now. And in a few days, Dagmar will join me. And I willna hear any complaints from ye about it."

"I have none. But should ye not stay . . . ?"

"Ye willna tell me what to do!" he roared.

Margaret took a step back and bit back her angry response. Perhaps Rignor going to Somerstrath for a bit was the best idea for them all.

"Rignor!" Nell cried. "What about Dagmar and Tiernan? How can ye . . . ?"

He glared at her. "Dinna say it, Nell! I'll not hear a word about her, and not from ye, who kens nothing. The filthy Irish bastard tricked her is all that happened. She shouldna have been so trusting, and she kens it. It willna happen again."

"But she . . ." Nell began.

He cut across her words. "Ye dinna understand, Nell. Dinna try to." He stalked away.

"He's an idiot," Nell said.

Margaret looked after her brother, wondering what he was planning.

Rignor left in the gloaming with a handful of men. Nell and Margaret went to the courtyard to see him off, but should not have bothered. Rignor did not even look at them, did not answer their waves of farewell, just leaned from his pony to give Dagmar a quick kiss and a few whispers, then was gone. Dagmar stood in the center of the courtyard as the gates closed behind him, then smiled smugly as Tiernan stepped from the shadows to join her. Nell felt part of her heart die. It was not enough that she was invisible to Tiernan; apparently she was meant to watch them together as well.

"I'll talk with him," Margaret said. "I'll go to Rignor and see if I can talk sense into him. He needs to see what Dagmar is before he does something rash. We have to heal this breach between us, Nell. We canna have this."

But there was no need for Margaret to go to him, for Rignor returned in the night, on the pretext of having forgotten something. And found Dagmar and Tiernan in bed together. He woke the entire holding, his roars all but taking the roof off. He was stopped from killing Tiernan by Rufus, who would not listen to Rignor's tirade against his daughter. Nor would he allow Rignor to shout curses at Gannon's brother, nor even to draw his sword. Rignor was escorted out through the hall and courtyard, passing Gannon as he went. Rignor spit at

Gannon, swearing vengeance on all Irish. Gannon neither spoke nor moved except to wipe the spittle off his cheek.

Margaret, watching with a pit of dread in her stomach, tried to talk with Rignor, but he shook her hand off his arm.

"Dinna touch me!" he growled at her. "Ye're just as bad. Ye betrayed me as much as them!"

"I never did!" she said, trying to keep her voice from trembling. "I never would!"

"Ye did, Margaret! I needed yer marriage, and ye wouldna even try." He threw a wild glare at the assembled people and was gone. "Ye all ken I was being betrayed, and none of ye stopped it. None of ye told me! Ye will regret yer actions! Ye will all regret what ye have done!"

The gates were locked behind him.

She could not sleep, worrying about what Rignor would do, what he was feeling and thinking. She would not put it past her brother to attack Gannon's ship or do something else quite mad. He must, despite all his earlier protestations, have known what Dagmar was. He'd planned his return, knowing what he might find. He was hurt, no doubt thoroughly shamed by Dagmar's betrayal. She turned over, staring into the darkness, knowing what she must do.

Morning came, full of the usual duties. She should, she knew, be pleased with the changes she'd made at Inverstrath, at the clean rooms and new routines that she'd taught Rufus's people, purposefully ignoring Dagmar's position as the woman of the household and knowing Dagmar could do nothing about it. She told herself it was simply so that Inverstrath would be run properly, but she took great satisfaction in knowing that she'd usurped Dagmar altogether. It was a petty revenge, and fairly ineffectual, since Dagmar did not even seem to notice, but it was a revenge nonetheless. Which brought her thoughts back to Rignor, for whom revenge was a passion rather than a petty occupation.

She would go to him as soon as she could. In the late morning, when everyone was busy, she slipped away from the others, not telling Nell what she was up to, nor Rufus, and especially not Gannon. She made her way to the kitchens to gather food for her brother. It was there, with all the kitchen staff, that Gannon found her. He entered the room slowly, ducking his head under the lintel and straightening, looking large and formidable, as he had the first time she'd seen him. And as then, he surveyed the room, his gaze narrowing when he saw her.

"Margaret," he said. "I would have a word with ye, lass, if ye would."

She knew by his tone and manner that he was angry, but still she followed him outside. The kitchen gardens were green, the last of the summer's vegetables and herbs about to be harvested. Shadows were short, with the sun almost directly overhead, and she shaded her eyes with her hand as she looked up at him.

"Are ye going somewhere, Margaret?" he asked.

"I'm going to take food to Rignor and talk with him."

"It's a fool's errand, lass."

She froze, thinking of all she might say. "Then I am a fool," she said at last.

"Did ye not hear what he said to ye? To all of us there?"

"And did ye not ken how hurt he was? How could Tiernan do such a thing?"

"Tiernan? He's the least of it. It's Dagmar who . . ."

"And Tiernan who joined her. If he hadna, she might have gone to Somerstrath with Rignor, and I might have had a chance to smooth things over between us. Now he thinks we've all betrayed him."

"No one betrayed him. He needs to think of more than himself."

"Which is exactly what he told me."

"Ye need to let him be a man, Margaret. He's no longer a wee lad. He's a man and should act like one."

"He is acting like one!" she cried. "The woman he cares for was with another. That's a man's pain, not a boy's. And it's yer brother who was with her, despite kenning how Rignor felt about her. What kind of man does that?"

"He's besotted, lass. He's not thinking straight."

"And that's forgivable? But Rignor's being angry about it isna? Strange way ye have of thinking, Gannon."

"Strange way ye have of thinking, Margaret. Ye've coddled him so much he thinks the world should obey his every wish. Dagmar lied to him, but that's nothing new, and if it hadna been Tiernan with her, it would ha' been another."

"Tiernan kent the pain he would cause, and he dinna care."

"Dagmar kent the pain she would cause, and she dinna care. It's none of yer concern anyway."

"None of my concern?"

"No. Ye canna be going to Somerstrath on yer own. I willna allow it."

"Ye willna allow it?" She kept her tone quiet, trying to

keep her anger in check. How had she, even for a moment, had dreams of a life with this man? He was no different than the rest of them. "Who are ye to allow me to do anything?"

"Lass," he started, but she shook her head and walked away.

"Ye have no say in what I do, Gannon MacMagnus," she said over her shoulder. "Ye're not my father, nor my kin, nor my husband."

"Margaret . . ."

She hurried into the hall, hoping he would not follow. But when he didn't, her mood only grew more foul.

She left early that afternoon, when Gannon was training Rufus's men on the strand, when Nell was in the village, and Rufus was busy overseeing the rethatching of the cottages before the winter rains. It took only a few moments to ask Rufus's groom to prepare a pony for her, only a moment longer to gather the food, only a moment to clear the walls of the fortress and head north along the inland trail. This task was hers alone. Rignor was her brother. She'd go to him alone and try to mend this rift. He needed comforting, and she would be there.

The fog was hovering overhead as the pony walked briskly through the trees. The inland path, they called it, but it wound through the clumps of trees, sometimes far from the water, sometimes at the very edge of the shingle. There were seven headlands between Inverstrath and Somerstrath, four streams that had to be crossed, and she counted each one rather than let herself think of what it would be like to return to Somerstrath. The breeze blew briskly off the sea, and although the sunlight was dimmed by the low-hanging fog, it was plentiful now. She took a deep breath of the clean air, closing her eyes as she raised her face to the sun and cleared her mind, hearing the waves and the calls of the seagulls.

On a day like this her mother would sigh and say the fog would lower and then the laundry would never dry. Then she'd tell the story about how her grandmother had strung lines across her husband's hall and laughed when he'd not even noticed the wet clothing overhead. She thought of all the times she'd hoped that Rignor's obsession with Dagmar would end. But she'd never envisioned it happening like this. And if he spurned her offers of peace? But she would not think of that now. She'd count the headlands and the streams and think of nothing more than the journey itself.

It was unnerving to approach her home and hear nothing. No voices of the people calling to each other, no barking of the dogs and shouts of the children as they came to meet her. She steeled herself, knowing that there would be no bustle of a busy village to see as she came over this last rise, no children playing on the strand, no fishermen mending nets or women at their looms. She would not stop for a visit with Fiona, would not talk with every person she passed.

Despite her preparations, she'd not steeled herself enough. Nor the pony. It shied away as they neared the village, and she could not blame it. The sight of the charred wood rising into the gray sky, the blackened shells of homes, assailed her. The bodies might be gone, but the stains of blood—and more—were still evident, and her mind supplied the missing details. Where there was only the outline of a doorway, she remembered the fallen body of a child; where a bench was stained a rusty color, she remembered the man who had died upon it.

And the smells. The odor of the burned homes still lingered, the stench of charred flesh and hair, the rank odor of food still in pots, mixed with ordure. Flies were everywhere, crawling on dark stains and through the occasional body of a dog that had not yet been buried. She clamped her hand over her mouth and forced her pony forward. She could not see the harbor from here, nor the keep, and she made her way through the ruins with care.

"Lady Margaret."

The man, one of Rufus's, stood before her, lowering his sword as he greeted her. She stared at him, then took a breath, reminding herself that she'd known Rignor had men with him. But it seemed strange to see a healthy man amidst all the destruction.

"Sorry, miss, I dinna mean to startle ye. We're guarding the village, ye ken."

"Is all well here?"

"Oh, aye. We've begun fixing the wall around the courtyard of the keep. It's going well."

"Rignor's here, I assume?"

The man's expression did not change, but he stiffened. "Aye."

"I've come to talk with him."

The man nodded and gestured to the path behind him. "Mind yer step."

She thanked him and moved forward, her heart pounding as she saw the keep and now heard the noise of men working. She stopped for a moment, gathering her courage, then slipped from the pony's back.

She saw Rignor the moment she walked through the

gates, standing over two men who were digging a trench. She took two steps, then stopped as he looked up at her without expression. She met his gaze across the space between them. He looked somehow diminished. There were lines around his mouth, and his hair was lank as it hung around his pale face. He looked worn and weary and yet somehow energized, his tension visible, as though excitement simmered under his stern manner.

There was a flash of affection, only a flash, in his eyes, and regret, quickly smothered, as though he were fighting an inner battle, not sure whether to rebuke or embrace her, as though there were two Rignors: the brother she'd been raised with, whom she loved, and the new Rignor, filled with hate and distrust and thoughts of revenge, who hated as fervently as he loved, who ignored actual slights and focused on imagined ones and had no room for anyone's needs but his own. The new Rignor, whom she feared. And feared for.

"Rignor," she said. "How are ye?"

He gestured around him. "How could I be, Margaret?"

She nodded, taking in the dusty courtyard and the men who watched her, some with welcome in their eyes, some with only curiosity. "I came to talk."

"Have ye brought more food? Or more men?"

"I brought some food. It's on the pony."

"Who brought ye?"

"I came myself."

He raised his eyebrows. "Who sent ye?"

"No one. I was worried about ye."

His laugh was bitter. "Aye, I've already seen how concerned ye are."

"Would ye like some water, Lady Margaret?" one of Rufus's men asked.

"Aye, I would," she said, and moved forward to take the cup from his outstretched hand. She drank deeply, aware of Rignor moving to her side, then handed the cup back to the man. "Thank ye."

"We can talk in here," Rignor said and walked into the keep without looking back to see if she was following.

They did not speak as they climbed the stairs, nor when they passed the spot where their father had died. The hall was empty, the tables and benches in disarray, as though men had pushed back from them and left. Which, she supposed, was exactly what had happened. A few stone cups had been left scattered on the tables, and bundles of blankets and packs were lined up against the walls. Rignor threw himself onto a bench and, from the floor, lifted a stone bottle that she'd not noticed. He poured himself a measure of the ale and drained it.

"Well?" he asked.

She did not answer at once, turning instead to look across the room, envisioning it full of her family and music, remembering far too much. She sank to a bench and leaned against the wall behind her. "Oh, Rignor."

He looked at her, then poured another measure in the stone cup, surprising her when he pushed it toward her. "Drink. It helps the memories fade."

She did, passing the cup back to him. "I don't think they will ever fade."

He poured himself another cup and drained it. "What is it ye want? Have ye come to tell me ye've reconsidered yer marriage?"

"No. I married him, Rignor."

"I ken that. I was there. I ken what happened. Ye married him, then announced ye'd have it annulled. Ye broke yer promise."

She nodded, noting the tension in his shoulders and the tight grip he had on the cup. "I was hurt. Humiliated."

"Despite yer promise to me ye willna reconsider?"

"I married him, Rignor. That's what I promised; that's what I did."

His smile was caustic. "Ye were always good with words, Margaret." At her silence he laughed again, an ugly sound. "What if the bishop refuses to annul yer marriage?"

"We'd not be the first to live apart." She took a deep breath, then plunged ahead. "And I'm sorry about Dagmar."

He shrugged, but she could see the anger in his eyes.

"Rignor," she cried. "Let us not do this! Come back to me. Be my brother again, not this stranger ye've become!"

There was a flash—of longing, of loneliness—in his eyes that made her heart leap. He looked away suddenly, as if realizing that. And the flash was so quickly gone, his face once again a mask of indifference, that she wondered if she'd imagined the moment. He held his cup high. "A toast," he said flatly.

"I have no cup."

"We'll share."

He tilted the bottle over the cup, then handed it to her. It held only the dregs. Appropriate, she thought, and raised it to her lips.

"To Somerstrath's survival," he said. "And to retribution."

She repeated his words, hearing them echo eerily from

the stones. Rignor laughed again, a hollow sound, and rose to his feet.

"Safe journey, sister. We have nothing more to say to each other."

"But, Rignor . . ." She stopped when she heard his boots on the stairs.

She took a moment to look through the keep one more time, memorizing it. She might never come here again, for, whatever happened in the future, their relationship had been altered for all time. The man who had looked at her had been as a stranger, as though someone had spirited Rignor away and left another mind in his body. She shivered, remembering all the stories she'd heard of such things as a child. She had never believed them; now she did.

He was gone when she reached the courtyard, but she did not ask after him, only bid farewell to the men working there and returned to her pony, to find that the packs of food had already been taken. She stared into the distance for a moment, then straightened and climbed atop the pony's back, lifting the reins.

"Lady Margaret." It was the man who had offered her water. "I'll see ye safely onto the trail."

She nodded, not trusting her voice, and let him lead her through the village. She would not try with Rignor again, would not attempt to cajole him from his anger. Those days were over. At the edge of the trees, far from the houses, Rufus's man stopped.

He leaned close, his voice low. "There is something ye need to ken."

"Aye?" she asked, although she wasn't sure she wanted to hear more.

"We had a visitor earlier. A man who said he was a runner coming from the Sinclairs. But we're thinking he wasna what he said."

"Why?"

"We're not sure even why we think that, but there was something about the man . . . he dinna look like the other runners. Dinna sound like them." He shrugged. "But it wasna so much what he did . . . as what Rignor did. He talked with yer brother for a long time, Lady Margaret, and when he left Rignor was much cheered, but it was a strange kind of cheer, if ye ken what I mean, like . . . well, like he'd just made a deal with the devil himself. We followed the man for a while, but he went north, and we stopped following him then. Did he stop at Inverstrath?"

"No."

"It's probably nothing." He glanced around them. "Being here . . . it makes the mind see things that may not exist." He straightened. "I'll see ye home, Lady Margaret."

"Thank ye, but there's no need. I canna get lost."

"The fog's coming in."

"Halfway, then," she said. "It's shorter if we walk on the shore."

He nodded, and she set off, suddenly glad of his company as she began her ride home. Home, she thought, which is now Inverstrath. How strange life was.

Margaret wrapped her arms around herself more tightly. It was not cold, but the damp was chilling her. Rufus's man walked in front of her with the pony, his steps sure and quiet. The fog hung above them, occasionally swirling down to engulf them, then dissipating as they walked on.

To her right the waves met the shore in muted rhythms. They had talked little on their journey, for which she was grateful. Her thoughts of Rignor and Gannon kept her busy, but she put them from her mind as they climbed the third headland. Four more to go before Inverstrath. She paused at the top. This was halfway to Inverstrath.

"Ye can leave me here," she said softly. "I'm safe enough now."

"I'll see ye safely home, Lady Margaret."

"My brother will miss ye. He'll not be pleased."

"Surely he'll not mind me keeping his sister safe, aye?"

Margaret smiled, no longer sure of the answer to that. "One more headland, then. Ye dinna need to come with me the whole way."

He looked weary, and she suspected he'd be glad to find his bed.

"One more headland then," he said.

She led the way, picking her path carefully, stepping onto the sand with relief, man and pony behind her. The fog swirled, then thinned, letting her see the waves to her right. The tide was receding, leaving her the packed sand on which to walk. She moved swiftly now, knowing the fog could thicken again any moment. Then stopped as a shape loomed above her in the mist.

A dragon's head.

She could not breathe, but stared up at the creature, trying not to scream. The head was black, its eyes gold, dull in the fog, and its tongue, hanging out from between its teeth, a vibrant red.

The dragon's head was not alone. Behind it she could see three more, their eyes staring inland and waiting, their mouths open and smiles cruel and shocking. They were attached to prows, of course, of long dark ships, pulled high on the sand. And ahead of her now, suddenly audible, were the sounds of men moving and talking quietly, the clink of metal on metal, an occasional laugh. She could even see the faintest of outlines of a fire around which they moved.

She stepped backward, moving as slowly as she could, not breathing, willing her heart to slow and not pound as it did now, and the fog to thicken and hide her. She took another step back, then another, then collided with a wide male chest. Arms reached to enclose her, a hand clapped over her mouth to stifle her gasp.

He did not believe she would defy him, but when Gannon looked for Margaret, she was nowhere to be found. He knew at once where she'd gone. He'd sought her out to apologize and offer to take her to Somerstrath, to explain that he'd only been worried about her safety. But she was already gone. She'd told no one, not even Nell, had simply taken a pony and left with the food she'd had prepared. The fog that had hovered all day was thicker now, the air damp and cloying. Damn the woman. One lass, armed only with her wits and that ridiculous short sword she thought was a weapon, out in a world that held men like Nor Thorkelson. What was she thinking?

He could not sail in this fog, but he left at once, taking one of the Highland ponies that the Scots all seemed to think were so fit. His legs all but dragged on the ground, but the pony seemed not to notice, setting off at a brisk pace. He knew Tiernan would be displeased that he'd not been told, but Gannon wanted no other company in this journey. He needed to talk with Margaret alone, wanted time alone with her to sort out their argument. He should not have acted the way he had. Nor should she, but that no longer mattered. Having her with him was all that mattered.

He did not know the inland path at all; it would be foolish to wander through the forest in the fog. But if he kept the water to his left he could not get lost, and so he walked the pony along the shore. The fog was lifting here, and he made good time across the first headland and along the bay beyond it, before it thickened again, muting some sounds and making others louder.

He was a fool. She was probably safely at Somerstrath, sitting in front of a fire with her brother. They'd probably healed the rift between them, and neither would welcome his interruption. He should leave her and Rignor alone, let them try to sort it out without him. He'd go to the second headland, then turn back.

But when he reached the second headland, he kept going.

EIGHTEEN

The man holding Margaret bent to whisper in her ear.

"It's me, Lady Margaret," Rufus's man said. "Dinna scream."

He pulled her slowly back with him, taking his hand from her mouth, then releasing her waist. With a hand over the pony's nose, he backed all three of them into the forest, slipping between the trees until their footfalls were muted by the pine needles underfoot. They ran along the pathway until they were out of breath.

"Did ye see them? The dragonships?" she asked. "Did ye see them?"

His eyes were wide with fear. "It's them, isn't it? They've come back again."

"Aye. We have to warn everyone. Ye need to go back and tell Rignor."

"And leave ye here? I canna do that, lassie."

"I'll go to Inverstrath. Ye have to warn Rignor. We dinna ken which way they're going."

"Why would they go to Somerstrath? They've taken everything."

"For the land itself. Perhaps they want it for settlement. Ye must warn Rignor. D'ye not see? We must both go—ye to warn my brother and I to Inverstrath! Every moment counts."

He shook his head vehemently. "I canna let ye go alone. Ye'll have to pass them, miss. Surely they'll have sentries out. I dinna ken how we got so close without seeing any, or the sentries seeing us, but ye can be assured they have them. Ye'll have to come back with me. It's closer."

"No, I have to get back to Inverstrath! We're halfway there. Please, please go and warn my brother!"

He stared at her, clearly wavering.

"We have to hurry! If the fog lifts . . . there's no telling when they'll leave."

"I canna leave ye to just walk past them."

"I willna go on the beach. I'll stay on the inland path. I've got the pony. It will find the way. Go, now, please!! Be careful. May God be with ye."

"And ye, miss."

She watched to be sure he did go back to Somerstrath, then hurried on herself. The trees were thicker here than she'd remembered, the path narrower, but she could see well enough and was glad with every step that she put between her and the dragonships. The path would turn soon toward the sea, and leave her on the headland that overlooked Inverstrath. She would be there soon, would soon be able to warn the others. Gannon would know what to do. She kicked the pony into a trot, glad of the carpet of pine needles muffling the sound of hooves on stone. *Dear God, let me be in time.* Surely they would not attack in the fog; surely she would have time to warn Nell and the others. There would be time for everyone to flee inland to safety.

But what if the Norsemen were going to Somerstrath instead? Rignor had only a handful of men. He could not hold off three ships full of Norsemen intent on taking the land. Could it happen again?

She burst from the trees, feeling rock beneath the pony's feet, and knew she was at the headland at last. *Almost there.* She slipped from the pony's back and led it across the stones, toward the sea, and toward the path that would take her to Inverstrath. She'd not gone ten feet when she saw him, a tall man on a Highland pony, walking away from her, toward the north. Toward the Norsemen. As she recognized him, she breathed a prayer of thanks.

"Gannon!" she cried, hurrying toward him. "Oh, thank God! Gannon!"

He stared at her for a moment, slipped off the pony, and rushed to her, clasping her in his arms. "Margaret, lass, are ye a'right?" His face clouded with anger. "What were ye thinking to go by yerself?"

"Listen!" she said breathlessly. "I was on my way back . . . they're here, Gannon! Norsemen! On the beach. They've come with dragonships, three ships at least! We must tell everyone!"

"Ye're sure, lass? It's Norsemen?"

"Aye! The ships have painted dragon's head prows, and thank God for the fog or they would have seen me as soon as we came over the headland. I could hear them, but I couldna see them and I dinna go any farther. There might have been more ships behind them that I couldna see." She clutched at his arm. "We've not a moment to lose! Come, we must warn everyone!"

He held her tight against him for an instant, then lifted her chin and kissed her, deeply, pressing her closer, his mouth searching hers as though he'd been a lost man. He released her at last and reached for the pony's reins. "Margaret, lassie, I couldna bear it if aught happened to ye. Thank God ye're safe, at least for now."

"For now. Dear God, Gannon, I canna believe it's real, that they're here."

He nodded grimly. "It's real a'right. Let's get ye away from here."

The smell of fear filled the hall when Rufus gathered his people. The night was half over, the fog still deep as they were summoned from their homes. They huddled together, casting terrified glances at each other, some of the women and children sobbing. Margaret sat with Nell, waiting for the people to join them. She knew what Rufus had decided, had heard him and Gannon discuss Gannon's plan. But would Rufus's people agree?

Rufus turned to Gannon while he waited for them to settle, his tone furious. "Could they attack when we had hundreds of men here? No. They waited until William Ross left and took all his men, and Rory O'Neill did the same, and I've sent thirty of my men off with Rignor. Look at them," Rufus said, gesturing to his people, "a handful of men strong enough to fight and women and children who will be easy targets!"

"My men are here as well," Gannon said.

"It'll take all of us," one of Rufus's men said.

"Ye can count on us," Gannon said.

Rufus gave Gannon a long look. "I'll not lie to ye. I wasna pleased with ye, choosing Margaret instead of my lass, even though I understood it, what with her and Tiernan and all. But I think I'll forgive ye now."

Gannon snorted. "God love ye."

Rufus grew serious. "Let's hope He does. It'll be a hell of a battle."

Rufus's captain stared. "Ye're not thinking of fighting, sir?"

"Ye think we should run?" Rufus asked him.

The captain's face reddened. "Ye think we should stay and fight three hundred men with what we have here? And there could be more than three hundred; she only saw three ships. We could have a thousand Vikings about to descend on us. A prudent man runs to fight another day, sir. Let the king come and rid us of these monsters."

Rufus watched him without expression. "Ye'll take the women and children with ye and go inland, then. I want only my bravest men here with me."

"Ye're not serious, sir? Ye're going to fight them?"

"I am. I'll not have it said I ran from them." He turned to the people, raising his arms for silence.

"Silence!" Rufus shouted, and the hall fell quiet. "We have not much time. Ye need to listen and listen well. We all ken the news, that Margaret's seen the dragonships between us and Somerstrath and that they might be coming here in the next few hours. We thought Haakon's fleet had bypassed us, but apparently not. I'm not running. I'm going to stay right here, in my home, and fight. We'll be ready when the fog lifts. Let's give the Norsemen a taste of Scottish hospitality."

The deep roar of approval that met his words surprised Margaret with its intensity. She and Nell exchanged a look.

Rufus grinned. "I thank ye for that. Those of ye who want to leave, may. Those of ye who are willing to stay are most welcome. But ken this. If any man leaves, thinking that he'll keep his land after we win, think again. If ye leave, ye forfeit yer land. If we win, I'll give it to another. If we lose, ye'll have lost it anyway."

The second roar of approval was quieter, but still strong.

"I've been talking with Gannon and he has a plan," Rufus said. "I think it's a good one, so listen. Ye'll all have tasks."

Gannon stepped forward. "We have surprise on our side. They'll not be expecting us to ken they're coming, nor that we ken what they'll do. They'll come into the harbor under sail, or rowing, depending on the wind. I'm going to move my ship out of the harbor, to the next bay."

"Just like an Irishman," one of Rufus's men shouted, but his tone was light.

"She has my name on her," Gannon said with a grin. "Ye don' think I'd risk a ship named *Gannon's Lady*? How many horses and ponies do we have? How many men can ride? How many archers are here?"

They listened closely while he outlined his plan, then asked a few questions, most of them about minor details of tasks. No one argued, no one disparaged his ideas. When he had finished, the people were nodding and saying it just might work, and asking for assignments, as though it were an everyday occurrence to face Norsemen at dawn.

Rufus stepped forward again. "It's time for the women and bairns to go. Take yerselves inland across the loch, to the mountains. I'll send men to row ye across the loch so ye dinna have so far to walk. As ye go, spread the word of what's happening to the crofters along the way. Send any man willing to fight to me; we'll need every one of 'em. And send runners east and south to find the king. God speed ye on yer way."

He waited while many of the women rose, bundling their children to them. Many more stayed where they were. A few of the men rose as well, their faces crimson.

"I'm just helping her as far as the forest," one said, his words met with relieved laughter. Others were silent and shamefaced as they left.

"Go with them," Margaret told Nell. "I'm staying."

Nell's expression was horrified. "I'm not leaving without ye!"

"I need to ken ye'll be safe," Margaret said. "And when it's over, go find Rignor and tell him what happened."

"I'll not leave without ye, Margaret." Nell folded her arms across her chest, but her eyes were fearful as she watched those saying their farewells.

"Ye must go, Nell. At least one of us has to live to find Davey."

"Rignor can find Davey. Or Uncle William. I'll stay with ye and help as well. Either we both go or we both stay."

"Nell." Margaret lowered her voice. "Ye saw what they did at Somerstrath."

Nell's eyes filled with tears. "Aye, and I'm afraid of that, but I'm more afraid of living if ye've all died. Dinna ask me to stay safe and watch from the hills. I willna do it. I'll stay. I couldna bear to live kenning I'd fled like a coward."

"Ye wouldna be a coward."

"I would. In my heart, I would always think myself a coward, and that's a form of death I'd rather not have. These are my people, too, Margaret, and I'll stay with them. If I die, it will be fighting and not hiding."

"Nell . . ."

"Ye canna protect me, Margaret. It's time to let me be an equal."

Margaret looked at her sister for a long moment, then nodded.

Margaret and Nell joined the women, melting all the tallow they could find, keeping it warm for later. Dagmar, who had also refused to leave, was organizing her staff, tearing sheets into strips and dipping them into the hot tallow. She gave orders without emotion, moving with an efficiency Margaret would not have thought possible. Rufus's men would use the arms he'd provided, ones not used in years, and were preparing themselves now, men strapping swords to youthful waists and leather breastplates around thickened chests. The inland crofters had arrived as well, leading their ponies, armed with pikes and arrows and whatever else they thought would help. Men were hurrying to man the walls. And down in the stable yard Gannon was explaining to his men what they needed to do.

He stopped talking in midsentence when he saw her, striding across the stones to tower over her, his expression fierce. "Margaret, ye shouldna be here. There's still time, lass. Go."

"Look around us, Gannon. Most of the women are staying. What would ye have me do, wait in the forest while ye battle them, not kenning what was happening to ye? These are my people. Ye are here. I'll stay."

"Please, lass . . ." He stopped.

"Gannon, look at ye, risking yer own life for me and mine. Can ye not understand that I need to do the same? How could I live with myself if anything happened to ye, and I was sitting in safety while ye fought my enemies?" She thought of her family's broken bodies. "No one has more claim on hatred than I. And, Gannon, I will be with ye. Whatever this day brings, we'll face it together. Dinna deny me this."

He was silent for a moment, then leaned to kiss her, heedless of who saw. "God help us all."

When everything that could be done was done, she stood with the others just outside the open gates of the fortress, looking out into the harbor. The fog was slowly lifting; already she could see the edge of the water. *Gannon's Lady* was gone, as were most of Rufus's ships and boats, a handful scattered on the beach to fool the Norsemen, sacrifices to the element of surprise. The harbor appeared quiet and unmanned, which had been their goal. Soon the sun would rise . . . and they would come.

"Margaret."

She turned with a slight smile when he came to her side; she'd known he would find her, or she him, before it all began. She could see the chain mail beneath his tunic, the golden bands on his arms tight around his muscles, his hair bound back and his expression calm.

"We'll be closing the gates soon," he said, his tone hushed. "It's not too late. Ye can still go, lass."

She shook her head.

"Please. I'll have no peace of mind if ye're in here."

"And I am to have peace of mind kenning that ye'll be outside these gates?"

"I'm trained to do this. Ye're not."

"No one is trained for this, Gannon."

"Ye're wrong. I've only just been realizing that the whole of my life has been leading up to this. I've been training for this every day that I drew breath."

"And I as well," she said softly. "I was born to face dragons."

He gave her a puzzled look, but she did not explain.

"Will ye leave, Margaret? Please, will ye go?"

"I canna leave, any more than ye can. Better that I die here, fighting, than to live with the knowledge that my efforts might have made the difference and I'd not offered them."

"Ye ken what will happen if we fail?"

"Aye, I do."

"Are ye not frightened?"

"Of course I am. What fool wouldna be? Are ye?"

He grinned then. "Aye, of course I am. What fool wouldna be?"

She laughed softly.

"Margaret, I love ye, lass. Whatever happens, ken that I love ye."

She stared at him. "And I ye, Gannon Magnusson. I've been waiting all my life for ye."

"What madness to find ye in the middle of all this," he said. "I kent, that first day I saw ye, the worst day of yer life, that ye were something special to me. But I dinna ken how special ye'd become. I need ye to breathe, Margaret."

She touched his cheek. "As I do ye. I love ye, Gannon. Whatever comes this day, I've had that."

"It's not enough. I love ye, Margaret. We'll grow old together."

She felt tears gather in her eyes. "I will hold ye to that, love."

He lifted her chin and kissed her again, his touch so quickly gone that she had no time to respond before he released her.

"God keep ye safe, Margaret my love. I'll see ye when all this is over."

"Come to me then," she said, but did not trust herself to say more.

He left her. She stayed where she was, wondering what this day would hold, was still there when Gannon walked through the gates with his men. He did not look back. Tiernan raised his hand to her in farewell, but leaned to place a hand on Nell's head and whisper something to her. Nell nodded, then stepped back with Margaret and Rufus into the courtyard as the gates were slowly closed and barred. She would, Margaret knew, remember that sound, of wood on wood, closing with finality, for the rest of her life. She was locked within the walls and the man she loved without, facing the enemy with only a handful of men and his determination.

As though hearing her thoughts, Rufus nodded. "It's in God's hands now. And Gannon's."

They waited then, for dawn, for the fog to lift, for death to come to them from the water, borne on the wind and carried by dragonships. The waiting was the hardest, for the mind had leisure to think and to fear.

And then the cry came, and the word spread. The men who had been lying on their stomachs all night on the beach, watching, had reported back.

The Norsemen were moving.

It was the sun that heralded their arrival, streaming through the fog as though holes had been poked in a gray blanket. And then the wind lifted the tattered mist from the land, leaving the earth steaming, and returning colors to the fortress and to the sea beyond.

Margaret, standing amid the handful of Rufus's men atop the fortress walls, shaded her eyes against the glare off the water and shifted her weight. These few men would be the only ones visible, pretending to be the normal contingent of guards that any prudent leader would have on duty. Crouched at their feet were many more men hidden from view, bows in hand, ready to rise and fight when the signal to show themselves was given. But far too few. Had they gone mad, thinking to repel the barbarians with only this many men?

The silence around her was unlike anything she remembered, alive with shivers of emotion and unsaid thoughts. She prayed, for Nell, for Rufus and his people, for Gannon and his brother and the volunteers with him outside the gates. They would be the first to face the Norsemen, the first to fall, the last to be rescued if it came to that. *May God be with him. And us all.*

The ships came through the glare one by one, huge, magnificent, malignant, their red and yellow sails vibrant, their prows and sterns rounded and topped with painted creatures. Their hulls were full of men whose shouts melded together into a deep roar. As they neared land, they lifted their shields from the railings, raising them high and roaring again. The wave of fear that passed through the men around her was almost tangible. Four ships, she counted, and swallowed. Each ship could hold a hundred men. How were they to stand against such a force?

"Dear God, protect us," the man on her left whispered.

"And those we love," she whispered in return.

"Go inside now, Lady Margaret. We'll ken soon enough what this day holds."

"I'll stay, sir. Look around ye. The women are all here,

including my sister. We'll stay with ye. We'll be wrapping the arrows."

"If they break through the gate, lass, we willna be able to protect ye."

She gestured at the wooden doors to the hall. "If they break through the gate, that willna stop them either. We'll be here with ye."

He nodded and turned to look at the shore. She followed his gaze. The Norsemen's ships did not slow as they approached the beach, but seemed almost to leap ashore as though alive, one by one, a line of dragons, their hulls scraping along the shingle in a tearing sound that shivered up to where she stood. Before she could even take another breath, the Norsemen were pouring from the ships, their axes glinting in the sunlight, their shields raised high. They were giants, these men who gathered now in lines and waited for orders, tall men with blond and silver and reddish hair, helmets of bronze and steel. They wore leather vests, like Gannon's, or breastplates of steel, or chain mail, or pelts of animals sewn together. They carried long swords and axes and round shields of wood, some studded with long spikes. They walked like men who expected to prevail.

They roared again as they spotted Rufus's men atop the fortress walls, and Margaret shrank against the timber next to her as though it could hide her. She'd not thought of what it would feel like to face Vikings with nothing but far too few yards of beach and slope between them. *Gannon.*

Rufus's men played their parts well, running now along the ramparts, waving their arms as though surprised and horrified. The Norsemen's answering roar was mixed with laughter this time.

"Bastards," said the man at her side. "Beg yer pardon, lass."

"Ye dinna need to. Ye're right. Bastards they are."

"We'll get them," he said. "Now get ye down so they dinna see ye."

She nodded, not trusting herself to speak, and scrambled to the ground, to join Nell and the other women. Some ran inside, the door to the hall banging shut behind them, closing the rest of them in the courtyard. She turned to look at the walls, where the men waited; they had once seemed so solid and secure, but now she knew they would not hold the enemy for long. If the Norsemen made it past Gannon, there would be no escape.

No one spoke as they waited. She hoped she did not shame herself when her time to die came, and she hoped God would forgive her for letting Nell stay. She thought of her parents, facing their own deaths, and of her brothers, but she could not imagine what small boys would have felt facing such men. Perhaps soon she would. From the beach there came another low roar, sounding less like men this time than a great beast. The roar came closer, and Margaret began to pray.

Gannon leaned forward, peering around the corner of the fortress, his hand stretched behind him to still his men. Four ships, but lightly loaded, carrying far fewer than the four hundred they could have brought. Still the odds were in their favor, not his, and these were Norsemen, dangerous and well skilled at war.

He glanced behind him at one of Rufus's men, who was having trouble keeping his horse still, his glare enough to make the man double his efforts. Tiernan was at the opposite corner of the fortress with his own band of men, Irish and Scots mixed together. *Wait.* He sent the thought to his brother again. *Wait.*

The Vikings were moving now, clambering up the hill in a mass of weapons and will. A tall fierce-looking man led them, his blond hair streaming behind him as he ran, his voice louder than the others. Gannon noted him, the leader; he'd find the man. *Cut off the head and the body will follow.* He gestured again to his men, waving his hand lower, and silence fell behind him. It was Rufus's turn first.

The Vikings were running toward the fortress, their voices raised together, weapons above their heads. Wait, he thought, this time aiming the command at Rufus. *Wait. Almost.*

Now.

The Norsemen ran directly into the hail of arrows that Rufus's men unleashed. Several fell, but far too few, and when the next volley came, the Vikings were already gathering together in their phalanx, their backs to each other and shields held before and above them. They moved toward the fortress again, slower now, but steadily.

The third volley of arrows was even less effective, and Gannon straightened and turned to give the signal. By the time the fourth volley of arrows was launched the Vikings would be at the gates. It was time.

Gannon raised his sword arm high, settled his shield on his arm, then spurred his horse forward, his own battle cry loud in his ear. They rounded the corner running, and smashed through the very middle of the Vikings, killing many who had been caught off guard. Men shouted with alarm, fell back, knocking others off their feet. Some were trampled by the horses, others leaving themselves open to the arrows that would come next. And then the horses were gone, rounding the corner, where Tiernan and his men waited to repeat the maneuver.

Gannon's men cheered each other and shouted encouragement to each other and to those on the walls above. And then it was their turn again.

They did it twice more, the slash-and-run attacks, forcing the Vikings to protect their rear and flanks. It worked. The Vikings' phalanx was disintegrating, and the arrows that rained from above were more effective. Gannon pulled his men back, his horse dancing beneath him, as Rufus's men poured burning pitch on the Norsemen at the gates. They fell, screaming, but were soon replaced by more. Gannon waited for the next phase.

This was the trickiest, for it took timing and daring from horses who were accustomed to pulling plows and many men who had never seen battle. Ten horses, pulling burning piles of cloth and rags and hay, ran through the disarrayed Vikings, forcing them farther apart and rendering them even more vulnerable to the blows Rufus's men were doling out.

Rufus shouted something from the ramparts and pointed to the fortress gates, which were bursting open, expelling men who attacked with surprising savagery. And he'd worried whether the Scots were up to this. Had there ever been men more valiant?

He left his men to do the next pass on their own and took the burning torch that was handed to him, waving the handful of men who would join him forward. They skirted the Vikings and raced for the shore, striking down the men who had been left to guard the ships and dumping their loads of tallow-soaked cloth and hay into the first three ships. Gannon waited until the sticky mass settled into the bottom of each ship, then leaned to set the pile aflame before moving to the next, but at the fourth ship he stopped. A man was tied to the mast, his head covered by a hood.

"Free him," he called to his men, then whirled to face the battle again.

Already the Vikings were scattering, many being run down by Tiernan's men, and he joined them to reinforce their strength, slashing through the enemy, looking for their leader, but could not see him in the maelstrom.

Behind him three of the ships caught fire, the flames stretching quickly to engulf the still-lowered sails. The Scots who had hauled the bound man off the ship now faced the Norsemen who had held him. Gannon spun his horse around and slashed through the Vikings, which allowed the Scots to get away.

He found himself at the edge of the fray and caught his breath, then laughed fiercely. Dozens of Norsemen were retreating now, running for the shore, more joining them as they saw their ranks thin. Gannon whirled his horse, looking once more for their leader, and, finding him at last, standing on the beach, waving his men toward the only ship not afire. He cursed himself for not seeing that one destroyed as well and spurred his horse toward the beach to do just that.

He did not get there. He was at the top of the rise, surrounded by frantic Vikings running for the ship, when one of them spun around and thrust his axe into the belly of Gannon's horse. The horse screamed in agony and went down heavily, rolling onto Gannon as it fell, pinning him to the ground beneath it.

The world seemed to spin, then settle as the Viking raised his axe again. Gannon, powerless to move, put his shield between himself and the axe. The Norseman's weapon thudded against the wood, splintering part of the shield but not going through. Gannon slashed beneath it with his sword, but sliced through only air. The axe was raised again. The second blow shattered the shield, and Gannon stared into the man's pale blue eyes. He lifted his sword and prepared himself.

NINETEEN

There were roars of victory from outside the gates and Margaret stood frozen. Were those shouts from the Scots or the Norsemen? Her question was soon answered as the gates swung open. Margaret and Nell ran through the gates and onto the battlefield with the others. Around her the women scattered to search among the fallen for their own, or to meet the embraces of the men who rushed to meet them. Many bent over a loved one who would not rise again, still more found their men among the wounded, of which there were many, especially among those who had ridden with Gannon through the throng of Vikings. But most of the dead were Norsemen. She paused on the rise to take it all in, amazed at how few of the defenders had been harmed. And to look for Gannon.

The victory was premature. Men were still fighting on and above the beach. The Norsemen's ships were aflame, all except one. And though that one was crowded, more Vikings tried to clamber aboard. Some were being beaten back to fall on the shingle, or meet their deaths at the hands of the Scots who waited for them. She saw a man on the ground, pinned under a horse . . . Her heart stopped.

* * *

Gannon's sword met the Viking's axe, the blade ringing against blade, the impact numbing his arm. He could not hold out much longer. He forced his arm up again to meet the next blow.

Nothing happened. Instead of striking him, the man held his gaze, his eyes wide and surprised, then jolted forward and crumpled to the ground. Tiernan pulled his sword from the Viking's neck with a satisfied expression.

"Close," Tiernan said.

Gannon, unable to speak, fell back onto the ground and stared at the sky.

Margaret screamed when she saw him fall and his sword arm thump to the earth beside him, screamed again when Tiernan kicked the Norseman away and called for help, pulling at the horse atop his brother. She ran forward, calling Gannon's name, heedless of those around her. She reached him as he was being pulled free of the horse and lifted to his feet. His leg buckled under him and she could see his wince of pain, but he was alive and whole. When she screamed his name again, he looked over his shoulder and grinned at her.

"Gannon!"

"I'm a'right, lass! We fought them off!"

"Ye did it! Ye fought them off, Gannon!" she cried, rushing into his arms, feeling him solid in her embrace, his heart beating, as hers was again now. "Look what ye've done! They're leaving!"

He wrapped an arm around her, kissed her, then turned her to look at the harbor. Three of the Viking ships were well ablaze, but the fourth, full of men, was afloat and being rowed out into the harbor. More Norsemen were running into the water and being pulled on board, but even more were stranded on the beach, turning with grim faces to meet the Scots and Irish that now rushed toward them.

"Dinna kill them!" Gannon shouted. "Dinna kill them yet. We'll question them first!"

The men on the beach slowed, surrounding the last of the Norsemen, who withdrew into a circle and watched warily.

"Look," Tiernan said, and pointed to the mouth of the harbor, where *Gannon's Lady* had just come into view, on a tack to block the dragonship's escape. The Vikings raised their sail and rowed even faster, trying to outrun her. At first it seemed *Gannon's Lady* would catch the Viking ship, but it was the dragonship's sail that caught the air first. It was all she needed. She glided into the open sea, where the wind was stronger, leaping forward as her sail filled, and the gap between the two ships widened. *Gannon's Lady* gave chase until it was obvious she'd not catch the Norsemen, then swung around and headed for the harbor.

It was over.

The Scots went wild with joy, shouting their victory to the sky, whooping with delight. They poured past Margaret, lifting Gannon onto their shoulders and parading him around the field, shouting his name. He laughed, raised his sword arm high, and laughed again when they at last deposited him before Margaret like an offering. When he smiled at her and pulled her against him the people cheered wildly as if it were a new victory. Gannon's kiss was deep, that of a victor, a man who knew nothing would be denied him now. He held their joined hands up between them and faced the people, who cheered anew. The sound seemed to echo off the mountains.

* * *

Nell felt stunned as she walked past the pile of dead Norsemen being buried in mass graves, past the heap of their armor and weapons and clothing, sickened when she had to hold her skirts high to keep them out of the blood and gore beneath her feet. On the beach three of the dragonships were burning. A group of Inverstrath men were leading the Norse captives, bound and well guarded, past their own dead; some of the prisoners were defiant, but most looked around them with faces filled with dread. Their fear was well-founded. The people of Inverstrath were vengeful, many spitting on the Norsemen, or calling out suggestions of what should be done to them. Most of the captives were men of middle years, but there was one much younger, a tall thin stripling with golden hair and intense blue eyes, who seemed out of place. He alone met her gaze when he passed; she could see fear in his eyes. And something more: a calm acceptance of his fate. She watched him being led within the fortress with the others and wondered at his manner.

Margaret and Gannon were surrounded by Somerstrath people who were now clapping Gannon on the shoulder and praising him. Gannon's arm was around Margaret as though he had a right to put it there. There was little doubt of their feelings for each other. Nell smiled to herself, then screamed as she was picked up and spun around.

"We drove them away, Nell!" Tiernan cried with a whoop of triumph. "Did ye see them run? We lost twenty men, only another forty or so wounded! They lost hundreds!"

He kissed her, leaving her gasping, then left her to join the Irishmen. She put her hand on her mouth, knowing she would never forget the moment.

Inside the fortress all was madness. The women were returning and families reuniting with cries of joy. Dogs were barking, children were running through the throngs of people. The wounded were being treated, the Scots and the Irish who had died were being taken to a village house to be prepared for burial. Ale was being handed out to anyone who did not already have a cup. On the sand the dragonships were burning to their bones, and the dead Norsemen were being placed in rows on the ground.

Rufus leapt atop a table, raising his hands for silence and at last his people obeyed. "First we need to thank God for this victory," he said and led them in a short prayer. "Then," he continued, his voice rising with triumph, "we need to thank Gannon for his plan and leadership!"

The people cheered again, the noise deafening as they stamped their feet and pounded on tables and shouted. Rufus gestured for Gannon to join him. When Gannon jumped up beside him, Rufus slapped him on the shoulder and raised his cup high. "To the Irishman who fought like a Scot!"

The cheers were louder. Gannon grinned and raised his cup again. "To the Scots who fought like Irishmen!" The cheers were filled with laughter this time. "I thank all of ye for yer courage and determination. I'm proud to have been here today with ye!

"Yer plan was brilliant, brother!" Tiernan shouted.

"It's ye who was brilliant, Tiernan," Gannon said. "If ye hadna killed the Norseman who had me pinned down, I wouldna be here. I thank ye for yer courage. And yer timing."

"As I do," Margaret said, drawing many smiles.

Gannon lifted his arm in a toast. "To ye!"

"To Gannon!" the people shouted back and cheered again when he bent Margaret over his arm and kissed her.

Gannon stood with Rufus before the prisoners. He could hear the music in the hall, exultant and loud, could hear the laughter and talking, and he longed to be there, celebrating with Margaret, rather than here with the prisoners. Thirty-seven captives, large, hostile men, stared at them with cold, sullen expressions, taking his measure when he spoke to them in the Norse language. They looked at his clothing and his hair and the torque around his neck and recognized him for what he was. Among the men was a boy whose eyes revealed more than they should. There was fear there—it was in all the men's eyes despite their pretense to the contrary—but there was also a fierce pleasure in the boy's eyes that confused and intrigued Gannon. Why would this boy be pleased at the Norsemen's defeat? He stopped before the boy.

"This is the one who was bound to the mast, sir," Rufus's men told him.

Gannon looked at the boy with even more interest. "Who are ye, lad?" he asked in Norse.

The boy met his gaze but did not answer. Gannon repeated the question, then turned as the door opened, revealing Margaret in the doorway. She was pale, but calm, and Nell was behind her.

"Margaret," Gannon said, "ye shouldna be here."

"Are these the same men who attacked Somerstrath?"

"I think so."

"Ask them if they ken where Davey is."

He did, but the captives simply glared at him, or

looked away sullenly. He asked a second time, but there was still no answer. He could see Margaret's anger as she stepped closer to the men.

"I want to see what men who can kill small boys and a woman large with child and destroy an entire village look like. Before ye kill them, I want to look into their eyes."

She didn't know what she'd expected, horns growing from their heads, or blood-red eyes. They looked like ordinary men. Large men, but still ordinary, one a mere boy. She wondered as she met his gaze how someone his age could have chosen this path. Some wore wedding rings, and the thought of them having wives and children of their own and still choosing to murder her family renewed her rage. She stood over them, feeling her chest constrict and her fingers itch to do them harm. And yet at the same time she felt nothing. Men who could do the things they had done would not be moved by words. There was no way to reach through their defenses and find minds that would feel remorse. And even if they did, what difference did that make now? No amount of sorrow would bring her family back, no penance, no forgiveness would change what had been done.

Nell, her arms wrapped around herself, looked from one to the next with wide eyes that brimmed with tears, and it was her sister's visible grief that moved Margaret to speak. She put an arm around Nell and looked at the men crowded together on the floor.

"May God have mercy on ye, for we will not. I ask no more than that ye be held accountable for yer deeds, for they are so foul as to have no defense possible for them. And when ye take yer last breath, ken that ye've been cursed for all time, for that is what I do to ye now. May every one of ye who murdered my family at Somerstrath live in eternal Hell. And should there be no such place, may ye live forever as ye are right now, trussed, defeated, and stinking of fear. I curse ye, and yer children, and yer children's children for a thousand generations. May the men ye've spawned be forced to watch the end of their kind. And may ye take every breath left to ye thinking of facing God and explaining what ye've done."

She watched the Norsemen's faces while Gannon translated. A few of them looked away, their faces uneasy, but most of them watched her with no change of expression. What had she expected, that men who could do such things would have souls to risk or consciences to be bruised? She spun on her heels and blindly made for the door.

"His name is Nor Thorkelson." It was the young boy who spoke in Gaelic, his manner calm and his words clear. "From Ketelsay in the Orkneys. It was he who attacked Somerstrath. Many of these men were with him."

Gannon leaned forward, his gaze intent. "Nor Thorkelson? Ye're sure?"

"I am. He is the man you seek. He is the man you must stop."

Margaret retraced her steps to stand before him. "What is yer name?"

"I am Drason Anderson, the son of Ander, whom Nor murdered."

The man next to the boy spit at him and spoke in Norse, his words bitter and harsh. Gannon raised his eyebrows. The boy pressed his lips together and looked away from the Viking.

"What did he say?" Rufus demanded.

"He said," Gannon said, looking from Rufus to Margaret, "that Nor Thorkelson is the boy's uncle."

"Wait," Rufus said. "He was the one tied to the mast. Why would Thorkelson do that?"

"We'll have to ask him why. Separate him from the others," Gannon said. "We'll need to talk to him before we go after his uncle. But not now." He gave the others a sudden grin. "Now it's time to celebrate our victory."

"Wait," Margaret said, looking into Drason's eyes. "Please. Do ye ken where my brother Davey is? He's one of the boys taken from Somerstrath. Can ye tell me anything of him?"

Drason swallowed visibly, but shook his head. "I can tell you nothing."

Margaret stepped back, her disappointment obvious. Drason's gaze shifted away from her, caught Nell's and shifted away again as his color rose. Margaret narrowed her eyes. This one merited more questioning.

"Come," Rufus said. "It is time to celebrate. We'll leave them until morning."

But it was not yet time, it seemed, for Gannon had no sooner left the room than he was called to the door of the hall by several men, their voices tight with excitement. He joined them, weary and wary, realizing that these were the men assigned to burying the Vikings. He could spare these men a kind word and a moment. Their task was unenviable.

"What is it?" he asked.

One pointed behind him and the others cleared a pathway. "Ye need to see it for yerself," the man said. "We none of us would have believed it."

He swallowed his annoyance and stepped forward. One of the Norse dead lay on his back on the stones of the outer porch. He was not a particularly large man, but Gannon could see little else in the dim light. He looked up at Rufus's men. "Aye?"

"Look closer, sir," one said.

Another handed him a torch. He held it over the man, seeing nothing unusual about him. Until he looked at the man's face. And stopped breathing.

"It's the monk," one man said. "The one who married Lady Margaret. He was fighting with the Vikings. We found him on the beach."

"It canna be . . . but it is." Gannon looked up. "Get Rufus. Get Tiernan."

"No need, we're here," Rufus said, coming forward. "Let me see him . . . Jesu! It is the monk! What the hell is he doing dressed like that?"

"Why would a monk dress like a Norseman?" Tiernan asked. "And die with them, fighting against us, unless he was one of them?"

"He wouldn't," Rufus said.

"Aye," Gannon said. "He wouldn't. Which means . . . Get Drason."

They waited while the boy was brought to them, Gannon's mind spinning. The monk who was not a monk, the Scotsman who was not a Scotsman. And all that that might mean. When Drason arrived Gannon held the torch over the body.

"D'ye ken this man?" Gannon asked him.

Drason nodded. "He was one of Nor's spies. He pretended to be a monk on pilgrimage so he could talk to everyone. He was very good and Nor paid him well."

They all looked from Drason to the man on the ground.

"Jesus, Mary, and Joseph!" Rufus exclaimed with a laugh. "That means the marriage wasna valid. He's no more a monk than I am. Lady Margaret isna married after all!"

Gannon stared at him, then turned to Drason. "Are ye sure?"

The boy nodded. "Yes. Ask the others. They'll tell you the same."

"We found this on him," Rufus's man said, holding out his hand.

Gannon took the wooden rosary, distinctive for its golden beads, and held it high. "It's the same one the monk wore, isn't it?"

"Aye," Rufus said and let out a bark of laughter. "All that fuss and she's still unwed! Wait until Lachlan Ross hears! Ha!"

Gannon's smile was wide. "It wasna valid. She's not married." He glanced at Rufus's man again. "Go get Lady Margaret, will ye? She needs to see this."

Margaret stared as he had when she saw the man on the ground, listened when Tiernan told her who the man was, and met Gannon's gaze when Rufus said her marriage was not valid. She stared again at the man, and she smiled. Then she laughed, and then she held her hand out to Gannon.

"It's time to celebrate, aye, sir?" she asked, and led the way back inside.

It was Rufus who announced the discovery, leading his people in cheers that Margaret was not a married woman. The hall, already alive with music, drums pounding the rhythm to which the dancers moved, whistles and bodhrans sounding above the talk, grew steadily louder. Listeners drummed hands on tables, women began moving sinuously to the music, beckoning men who moved now to put their hands on a waist, wrap their arms around a willing form, and soon, while no one watched, fade into the shadows near the walls, or leave the hall altogether.

Ale and whisky flowed freely, for what celebration could be more important than this one? But the people of Inverstrath did not need the effects of fermentation; the thrill of merely surviving the day was exhilarating enough. They had defeated the Norsemen; anything seemed possible. It was not only appropriate, but necessary to celebrate life and the Inverstrath people celebrated in the oldest way known to men and women.

Gannon danced for hours and drank and laughed with the Scotsmen. And through it all Margaret was at his side, her hand often in his. He watched her laugh, saw the sadness in her eyes that did not leave despite her jubilation, looked at the way she moved, at the curve of her waist and her breasts, at her hair catching the light, shining dark as night. At her long slender fingers threaded through his own, at how small she seemed, yet how perfect. He was lost. He'd never been more sure of himself.

He would make her his. And he would wait no longer. If the situation were different, he could offer marriage. Now he was supposed to be content to wait for a king and a bishop—and a fop named Lachlan—to decide whether he could ever offer it. The marriage might not be valid, but the betrothal still was. He drained another cup of whisky and took Margaret's hands.

"Will ye come with me, lass? For a bit of a walk?"

Margaret tilted her head. "Outside?"

"Aye."

"In the night?"

"Aye."

"Alone?"

He laughed. "Oh, aye, lassie, verra alone. Ye and me and the stars in the heavens."

Her smile was arousing. "Then take me, sir."

He laughed again, not trusting himself to answer in a prudent manner, reaching for her hand and leading her through the hall door, then the gates. He wrapped his cloak around her, glad that he had it with him—in case she'd agreed—and led her to the berm above the beach. The waves were soft tonight, the sky crowded with stars, the moon just making her appearance. He kissed her, lingering, tasting her lips and cheeks and neck, feeling his body's readiness.

He took both her hands in his and faced her. "I love ye, Margaret."

She smiled into his eyes. "And I ye."

"I want ye with me, lass. I want to share my days with ye, then my nights. Will ye?"

She held their joined hands up between them, leaned to kiss his fingers. Her voice was hushed. "I thought we would die today, Gannon. I thought they would plow through ye and yer men and burst open the gates to kill us all. I thought I was prepared to die." She took a shuddering breath and smiled. "May God be praised, I was wrong. What I learned today is how verra precious life is. And how much I want to live it, really live it." Her smile deepened. "Ye're already in my heart. I want ye in my bed. Would ye consider it?"

He stared at her for a moment, then he threw his head back, laughing. "Oh, lassie mine, I've been doing little else. I was going to get to that next." He waved a hand toward the hall behind them. "And we willna be alone. How many children will be born next spring as a result of this night? But are ye sure?"

"I've never been more certain."

He was undone. "Come, love. I ken just the place."

The moon was high enough, her light pale but adequate to show them the way along the beach, then up the path to the southern headland. At the top of the ridge Gannon took a deep breath of the night air. They needed no candle here—the moon and the stars provided enough light for him to see her face.

"What about Tiernan, what about Nell?"

"Tiernan will understand. And dinna fret about Nell. He'll guard her."

She nodded. She, too, had seen Tiernan dancing with Nell, had seen the careful way he touched her, but the way he still found Dagmar's gaze. It was time, she told herself, to let Nell take care of Nell. Gannon pulled her into his arms.

"I love ye, lass. We'll not do anything ye dinna wish to."

"I want ye, Gannon. What I wish is for ye to want me."

He laughed then and looked down at himself. "Oh, I do, lassie, as ye can see. But I dinna want ye to regret . . ."

"I don't. I won't."

"Then ken this." He took her hands in his and knelt before her. "I pledge myself to ye, Margaret MacDonald, for as long as we both shall live. I will guard ye and love ye and give ye the best of me for all my life."

She knelt to face him, never more sure of what she

was about to do than now. "And I pledge myself to ye, Gannon MacMagnus. I will guard ye and love ye and give ye the best of me for all our lives. For all eternity."

"Eternity. Aye, that's better," he said, his smile playing around his mouth. "For eternity then." He kissed her, and again, then pulled her to her feet.

"Here?" she asked.

He shook his head. "No, lass. Come."

He'd only moved a few feet when she knew where he was going, to the ruined fort at the edge of the world, where the view of the sea and the sky, if she ever looked away from him, would be amazing. They rounded the curved walls and stepped within, to the soft grass that grew here. Gannon spread his cloak on the ground and turned to face her.

"Are ye sure?"

"Never more, sir."

"Then wear this," he said, taking the golden torque from his neck and placing it on hers. "Wear it when we make love. And after, every day until we're wed. I have no ring to give ye, but this way everyone will ken ye're mine."

It hung loose around her neck, heavy, and still warm from his skin. She touched it with pride, then raised her mouth to meet his. "Make me yers, Gannon."

With a grin, he stepped back from her and unlaced his shirt. He'd shed his leather vest and chain mail earlier, and she'd watched him then, thinking of what those very male hands would feel like on her body. Now she watched again, blessing the moon for her light, feeling her body respond as he pulled his shirt out of his belt. He kicked his shoes aside impatiently, and with a quick yank of his wrist, unbuckled the belt around his waist. Leather and wool slid away. Then he pulled his shirt over his head and stood naked before her. His bones were long, she'd known that, his body lean and muscled, his form splendid. But what she'd not known, not even imagined, was what he would look like aroused and ready for her. She felt her face flush, and she moved toward him, reaching to touch his shoulders, tracing the long scar that seamed his skin, then sliding her hands down his side, stopping at his waist.

She met his gaze. "Teach me, love."

He did.

They did not speak for a very long time then, lost in each other. They sank slowly to the ground, oblivious to the rising wind outside, heedless of the stars above and the waves that roared ashore, heedless of everything but their joy in each other. He taught her how to savor each touch, how to use her hands and mouth, to tease and pleasure him. And he did the same to her, removing her clothing slowly, touching each newly revealed part of her as though it were sacred, tracing lines of kisses along her body that set her aflame, making her long for his touch, for more of him. All of him.

He stretched out next to her, then above her, and she sighed with wonder at the sensation of his skin against hers, the lines of his body so different and yet so familiar. And when he entered her at last, she arched to receive him, wondering how she had ever lived without this, how perfect the union of man and woman was, how satisfying this could be. He was patient, she was eager to learn, and the hours passed quickly. They took their fill of each other, stopping only when they were each sated and languid, lying entwined together. Margaret lay cradled in his arm, her head on his shoulder. His hand caressed her shoulder absently.

She sighed with contentment. "I never kent it could be like this."

"This, love, is but the beginning. There's so much more," he said, his hands already moving to cup her breasts.

He kissed the curve of her neck, then her shoulder, then dipped lower to capture her nipple. She stroked the back of his head, threading her fingers through his hair, then grasping his shoulders, wide and strong and so very male, feeling his lips on her, his chest against her stomach, his body responding to hers yet again. She laughed softly, and he raised his head.

"I canna imagine life without this, without ye," she said.

"Nor I. Nor will I. Ye are mine now, Margaret, and I'll not give ye up, not for any man, not for any law of church or king. Ye do realize that?"

"Aye. I feel the same."

His smile was both fierce and tender. "I dinna ken where we'll go from here, what the rest of the world will think or what they'll want us to do. Yer brother will no doubt disapprove, and perhaps yer uncle. And surely Lachlan, but I dinna give a damn what he wants, or anyone else. I'll not relinquish ye."

"Nor I ye, Gannon."

"Renegades, then, the two of us?"

She laughed. Margaret of Somerstrath as a renegade. She rather liked the idea. But what choice did she have? How could she spend her life without this man? Without the joy of love given willingly, not because of a contract but because of her heart? Without the mysteries of lovemaking being revealed by a man who was gentle and kind? How impossible it now seemed to spend her life with Lachlan.

"Ye are mine, Margaret."

"And ye mine, Gannon."

"I always have been. I always will be. It doesna matter what they think, lass. I pledged myself to ye, as men and women have since creation, and nothing will change that. If ye wish it, I will stay here and help yer brother rebuild Somerstrath. Or we can go to Ireland. I have no land, no riches, but I have a ship and a strong back. Ye willna go hungry, and when children come, they will be cared for. If ye will, lass. If ye'll have me for the rest of yer life."

She put a hand to his cheek. "Aye, love. And a thousand times aye."

He pulled her atop him. She received him eagerly, leaning back when he filled her, seeing the stars and the moon. I want love, she had told the moon, not realizing then that her plea had been heard. And granted. It was heaven being a woman, she thought, and thanked the moon again as Gannon moved within her. He was less patient, less gentle this time and her pleasure became intense. She arched, then bent forward when her body took command, clutching at his shoulders, lost in sensations she'd never dreamed of. She stretched out above him, her head on his chest, feeling his heartbeat under her cheek. And then he began to move again and she was lost.

Hours later they lay on their backs, looking at the stars overhead in the inky autumnal sky. She stretched, then curled against his warmth again, pointing to a faint cluster above the entrance to the loch. "What's that one?"

"That's Draco. The dragon."

She fingered the torque at her neck, golden, like this man. "A sign, then."

"Aye."

She pulled herself up on one elbow and looked into his eyes. "Never leave me, Gannon."

"No," he said.

"Swear it."

"I swear it."

She lay back, content once more. He slept then, his long limbs wrapped around hers, his warmth comforting as the night cooled. She sighed and looked up at the stars. Eternity, she thought, might not be enough.

He did leave her eventually, waking her in the twilight before dawn, dressing slowly, their bodies now familiar to each other. She watched him move, feeling as though she'd started the day with this man a thousand times before.

"Are ye ready, lass?" he asked, when they were both dressed. "Nervous?"

She touched the torque and gave him a wide smile. "Let them say what they will," she said, and kissed him.

But no one said anything, greeting them as though it was right that they'd been together. Tiernan nodded at her, his manner no different than any other day. Nell watched Margaret with wide eyes but no reproach. Rufus made no comment. Nor did anyone, and she realized that she and Gannon had not been the only ones to celebrate in the age-old manner. Dagmar restricted herself to a sly smile and swayed her hips in Tiernan's direction again. And life went on.

Margaret laughed at herself, both for her trepidation and from sheer joy. Gannon's woman, she told herself, looking down at her hands which had done things the night before she'd never known possible. Gannon's woman, she told herself, touching the torque at her neck.

TWENTY

Nor Thorkelson swore as he looked at the morning sky. The clouds were obscuring the sun, darkening in the west and racing toward them on a wind that increased with every moment. It fit his mood.

He'd gone to destroy more of William Ross's lands, hoping that perhaps Ross himself would be there. Or his nieces, who he'd heard were taking refuge at Inverstrath. Holding three members of Ross's family would no doubt have given him an advantage when they at last came to parley. But none of that was to be. He had failed. One ship, sixty-three men, was all he'd managed to save out of the four ships and three hundred men he'd had the day before. The rest had been killed or left on the beach. Including Drason. Some of the men left at Inverstrath would remain silent, no matter how they were provoked. Others would talk as soon prodded, and he was sure that the Scots would question his men forcibly.

And Drason. His nephew was supposed to be at the bottom of the sea, not telling the Scots all he knew. He thought of what Drason could tell them. His name, but he'd been about to reveal that anyway. His home, but let them come; he'd prepared for that. How many men he had, but that was changing with every success. Nothing of importance. He'd been wise to not trust Drason with his plans.

And perhaps he was worrying for no reason. No doubt the Scots would blame his raid on King Haakon's fleet, and think that Nor was simply following orders from his king. He told himself that he could not always succeed. A small setback was all it was.

They'd sailed all night, north, but not to Orkney. He'd previously arranged to meet the other half of his force so they could split the spoils before returning home. He congratulated himself now on his foresight. He needed to hear their account before he decided what was next.

The first thing he would do when they reached a safe harbor was to call his spies to him for their reports and immediately send them out again with a new task. He wanted the name of the man who had planned Inverstrath's defense.

It took eight days, but he got the name he desired. Gannon MacMagnus. Half-Irish, half-Norse, from the lands they'd raided in Antrim. MacMagnus had accompanied Rory O'Neill to Inverstrath, had stayed behind when O'Neill and Ross left. He had a brother. And a woman.

Gannon stretched his legs before him and considered the young man on the other side of the table. Drason Anderson met his gaze without flinching. Rufus leaned his chin on his hand and watched them both. The other prisoners were still being held in the small room at the back of the hall, but Drason had been sequestered, then brought to Gannon early this morning. So far the boy had said little, only that yes, his uncle was Nor Thorkelson and yes, he'd been tied to the mast. But nothing more.

"It's this simple, lad," Gannon said now, idly tracing his finger tip along the edge of the dirk that he'd set between them for just this purpose. "Ye can tell me the whole of it. Or I can turn ye over to the Inverstrath people, or worse, the Somerstrath people. Or I can return ye to yer companions and see what it is that they do to ye."

"You do not frighten me," the boy said, and indeed he did not look fearful.

Rufus leaned forward. "Or I could use this knife to cut a body part off ye for each hour ye keep silent."

Gannon saw the flicker in the boy's eyes.

"That is not frightening," Drason said with unconvincing bravado.

Gannon laughed. "Of course it is. But we'll not have to do any of it, will we? Ye spoke last night because ye hate yer uncle, and that is why ye'll tell me where to find him. Revenge is a powerful emotion, and I see lust for it in yer eyes. Why?"

The boy looked down, then off into the distance, for so long that Gannon thought his ploy had failed. Then Drason met Gannon's gaze and nodded.

"It is revenge that drives me. I will tell you where to find him. But I must have a promise from you first."

"Depends on what it is."

"When you capture Nor, I will be the one who determines how he dies."

It was Gannon's turn to look off into the distance as he weighed Drason's request. It seemed a small thing to offer in return for the man's death, and how Nor died was of little importance to him. He was not a man to savor another's torture or slow death. Dead was dead and the quicker accomplished the better. But Margaret and

Rignor and Nell, and the people of Somerstrath and Inverstrath, and William Ross, might all wish something else. Still . . . Nor dead. It was tempting.

"If you agree," Drason said, "I will tell you where Davey MacDonald is."

Gannon reached across the table and grabbed the boy's thin wrist. "Ye ken where he is?"

"I think so."

"Last night ye said ye dinna ken where he was. How is it ye now do?"

Drason looked uncomfortable. "I thought of it in the night."

Gannon made a sound of disgust and rose to leave. He'd gone three steps when the boy called out.

"Wait. Please, sir! I . . . was afraid to tell you in front of the others because I'd like to trade what I know for something."

"Which is?"

"That you must promise me that I will decide how Nor dies."

Rufus and Gannon exchanged a glance.

"How would ye do it?" Gannon asked.

"I'd burn him alive in one of his own dragonships."

Gannon blinked. He'd expected Drason to ask for mercy for Nor, for beheading or a draught of poison which would let Nor slip peacefully into death.

"Why do ye hate him so much?"

"He killed my father. He doesn't know I know, but I saw him. And he killed my uncle. He placed him, alive, in the hull of the ship that held my grandfather's body, and he set it afire and pushed it out to sea. I watched it with him, but I didn't know then that my uncle was in the ship. Nor just . . . watched while his brother was burned to death."

Gannon felt the hair on the back of his neck rise. He'd dreamed just this, a man burned alive, but he'd not tell the boy that. "How did ye discover it? Did he tell ye?"

"No. One of his men talked. Before he, too, disappeared. And our priest argued with Nor, then disappeared. And he . . . my mother is terrified of him. I'm not sure what he did to her . . . but I will avenge that as well."

"Tell me about Davey."

"He's on Skye. Take me there, and I'll show you where to find him."

"At Leod's?"

"No. But not far from there."

Gannon rose to his feet. "We'll leave now."

Drason stood as well. "Good."

The word spread quickly, and soon Margaret was running across the hall to Gannon, her face alight with hope.

"Is it true? Ye ken where Davey is?"

Gannon gestured to the corner, where Drason, under guard, was breaking his fast. "On Skye, or so he says. We're going there now, lass, to find out."

"With Leod?"

"Supposedly not."

"I'll come with ye."

"No. I dinna ken what we'll find, but if Nor is there, we'll finish it."

"Ye only have one ship."

"I'm taking *Gannon's Lady* and two of Rufus's galleys. We'll have more men than Nor Thorkelson does."

"He'll have men already there."

"Aye, but he'll not guess we'll find him."

"We have to tell Rignor."

He shook his head. "I sent men to him last night, lass, with news of the attack. If yer brother were concerned about ye and Nell, he would have been here by now. Ye'll notice he's not come."

"Perhaps Somerstrath was attacked again!"

"Then Rufus's men will bring us word of that. And in that case, Rignor willna be minding us rescuing Davey without him."

Tiernan joined them, pulling on chain mail. "Great news, aye?"

"Aye," Margaret agreed. "Will Rufus go with ye?"

"No," Gannon said. "I'll not leave ye unguarded. Tiernan, ye'll stay as well."

Tiernan's face flushed. "Ye canna mean it!"

"I do." Gannon gestured to Drason. "I'm leaving Norsemen here with my woman. Who else can I trust to keep her safe?"

Tiernan nodded, assuaged. "I'd not thought of that."

"I had," Gannon said grimly. "Watch them, Tiernan. Ye've got murderers in yer midst."

"When will ye be back?" Margaret asked.

"When Nor is dead."

The whispers found him as he was crossing the channel that separated Skye from Scotland. They spoke in breathy half words of death and horror, of revenge. He told himself that he was not hearing them, that there were no trees here, no branches for wind to rustle. He was aboard his ship in the middle of the day, in the middle of the sea. Was he losing his mind, to conjure them here? Was it a warning? Or just his fevered imagination? He looked across the water to Skye and knew he was not mad. And that it would be an interesting afternoon.

His uncle had several camps, Drason had said. The first was small, treeless, and unprepossessing, set in the back of a sea loch on a marshy meadow, moist and foul-smelling. And empty. There was not a boat in the small harbor, not a house with inhabitants. No dogs barked to herald their arrival, no one ran down to the water to see who had come. The pigsties were empty, the cattle pens bare. There were signs that people, and pigs and cattle, had been here not too long ago, but all were gone now. There was a long-house that might have been comfortably furnished, for there were tapestries on the wall and wide bedshelves fitted into wall nooks. But no one was there.

Gannon stood in the middle of the village, the hair at the nape of his neck rising. Nor Thorkelson had known they'd come looking for him, had known they would discover who he was and where he hid, that they would come after him. One of several camps, he told himself, turning to leave. And Davey was in one of them.

But not in the second either, a high spot with good views of the nearby waters, but even fewer comforts than the first. The wind blew through here constantly; the nearest fresh water was a far walk. As they returned to the ship, Gannon grabbed Drason's shoulder and whirled him around.

"If I discover ye've been lying to me, I will kill ye."

The boy nodded. "I'm not lying. I know of one more camp."

"How many are there?"

"I've been to three. They are all I know of."

"And Leod knew none of this?"

"How could he not? It's his island."

"Were ye a prisoner all the time?"

"Most of the time. My uncle has no use for men who do not enjoy killing."

"Did ye kill?"

"No. I am a disappointment to him. I was hidden away, especially when visitors came."

"Visitors? Who were they?"

"Recruits. Some Irish, some Scots, mostly Orkneymen. Some from Norway. King Haakon was said to be close by, but he never came."

"Was Nor in communication with Haakon?"

"Yes. The king was quite pleased that Nor had raised the tension between him and Alexander of Scotland. But Nor was not pleased that Haakon of Norway decided to launch a fleet against Scotland this summer, just when Nor decided to become a rich man."

"What d'ye mean? From the plunder he took?"

"That. And he had a plan—to spend one year raiding and ten collecting gold from those who would rather be robbed than raided."

"He wanted them to pay him not to attack?"

Drason gave him a withering look. "It's been done for centuries."

Gannon raised himself to his full height and gave Drason an equally withering look, pleased to see the flash of fear in Drason's eyes. "I'm beginning to see why ye were tied to the mast. I ken that it's been done for centuries. I'm just making sure I understand. Was Nor obeying Haakon's orders?"

Drason's manner was more subdued now. "Not that I know of. I don't think Nor expected or wanted Haakon to get involved, but of course that's what happened. Haakon's fleet sailed only after word of my uncle's raids reached Norway. Nor's raids were the spark that began this fire."

Gannon nodded. Whatever Drason Anderson was, he was no coward. And God help him if he was a liar.

Drason talked more as they sailed to the third camp, passing the entrance to Loch Bracadale, Leod's territory. He talked of Nor's strengths: his intelligence, courage, and ability to convince men to join him. And his weaknesses: his vanity, his arrogance, and inability to believe he could fail.

"He considers himself invincible," Drason said, his cynical tone in contrast to his youthful appearance. "He thinks no one sees the lies he tells, that no one saw what he did on Ketelsay. We did, my mother and I, and we were not alone. People started leaving, moving away in the night to other islands or even to Caithness, fearing for their lives if they opposed Nor. When droves of men came to join him, more left. My mother and I talked about leaving, but we were too late."

"Tell me of Leod," Gannon said.

Drason snorted. "Plays both sides. You'll have a difficult time pinning him down, but even if you do, he's likely to twist in the wind."

"Does Nor trust him?"

"Nor trusts no one."

"Does Leod provide Nor with men?"

Drason shook his head. "But he looks the other way.

Nor's men have angered the Skyemen. They are not . . . good guests on the island.'"

The boy said little more then except for how to reach the next camp. He hoped the boy was as truthful as he was convincing. If he had to kill Drason, he'd regret it.

Margaret was with Rufus in the courtyard, surveying what repairs would need to be made to the walls, when shouts from outside the fortress brought them out onto the field. Three men were riding Highland ponies hard toward the gates, one pulling something behind it that bounced and twisted as it hit rocks. They were Inverstrath men, men she'd known all her life, one with whom she'd wept just hours before, when his son had been among the few who had died in the Norsemen's attack. They shouted as they rode, their voices harsh with anger and something more, something that made her stop and look more closely at what they towed.

It was a man, or what was left of one. A Norseman, she thought, like the one left at Somerstrath. No mercy would be shown him.

The riders circled the field once again with their unholy burden, whooping with triumph, drawing Rufus's people from the village and the fortress to see. The three men whirled around one last time, coming to a quick stop before Rufus. And Margaret saw at last who it was they towed.

Rignor.

She fought the bile rising in her throat and took a deep breath to steady herself. Her brother was tied, hand and foot, strung to the pony by a long leather rope, his eyes covered by a band of material, his mouth as well.

But there was no mistaking him: that was Rignor's long black hair that streamed behind him, Rignor's kilt that had slid up his thigh. He was bleeding from many wounds, battered from the ride. Was it possible that they had towed him all the way from Somerstrath? He did not move; she breathed a prayer for him.

"Have ye gone mad?" She started toward Rignor, but one of the riders put a hand out to stop her, and the man who had pulled Rignor came to stand before her. "What have ye done?" she asked again, looking into his grim face.

"Justice," he said, gesturing at Rignor. "He killed my son."

"But of course he dinna," she said.

"He killed my son," the man said again. "And he might have killed all of us."

"What is the meaning of this?" Rufus demanded. "Is he alive? Move away and let us tend to him."

The first rider bent now to yank the cloth off Rignor's eyes. "Still not dead. Bastard's hardier than I would have thought."

"Why did ye do this?" Margaret shrieked. "Explain this to me!"

The third rider dismounted now and met her gaze— the man who had accompanied her from Somerstrath, who had seen the dragonships with her, who had told her of the runner's visit, of the strange visitor to Somerstrath. A terrible certainty filled her mind, and she knew, before they could say it, what they would tell her.

"He told the Norsemen where to find us," the first rider said.

The second rider looked from Rufus to Margaret. "He betrayed us all. He told them about Inverstrath, about the harbor and how many people would be here." He met Margaret's gaze. "And who would be here. And in exchange he was allowed to stay alive and keep Somerstrath."

"We had a man come, saying he was a runner from the Sinclairs, but he acted strangely, and he'd only talk to Rignor," the first man said. "And this morning he came again, asking for news of Inverstrath and who had led the defense."

"Yer brother has been drinking himself into a stupor every night," the third man said. "Sometimes he would talk, saying daft things. Mostly we stopped listening. But some of it started to make sense when the news of the attack here came. And when the runner came back, we kent what Rignor had done. . . ."

"So we asked him and it all came out," the second man said. "He traded yer lives for his own, all of us for Somerstrath."

"What did ye do to him?" Margaret whispered.

"What needed to be done. He willna live. I'm sorry."

She looked at each man in turn as the others echoed his words. There was no sorrow, no remorse, in their eyes, only a fierce anger, reflected in the faces of the Inverstrath people. She bent over Rignor, who was bloody and battered and broken. "How did it come to this?" she whispered to him, but there was no answer.

Rignor died at midday without ever regaining consciousness. He had no last words, no defense, no argument against what he'd been accused of. Margaret and Nell were by his side when he left them with a soft sigh so quiet that they'd almost missed it, as though Rignor's soul was glad to be rid of his body, as though it had another place to be. He did not see Margaret's tears fall onto his sleeve nor hear Nell's sobs.

There would be no reconciliation, no peace made between them, now or ever. Margaret had no words left. Her emotions tumbled, from regret to sadness to outrage at what had been done to her brother. To frustration because she would never know the truth. But she feared that she did already know the truth, that she'd seen it in his eyes that last day at Somerstrath. There was only one thing she knew for certain; she'd lost her brother forever.

Rignor was buried that afternoon, with many in attendance but only Margaret and Nell to mourn him. Dagmar was silent and pale and threw sidelong glances at Margaret, as though expecting to be confronted. But Margaret had nothing to say to her, knowing that nothing would change Dagmar. And Dagmar proved her right—a few hours later her laughter rang through the hall.

And a few hours after that the Norsemen came.

Margaret was alone, sitting on the berm above the beach, staring at the water, her hands in her lap, her body so weary she could not find the strength to return to the fortress and find her bed. The sea was calm, the wind brisk. No clouds marred the pristine sky. On the beach Rufus's men were repairing a mast; the fishermen had left hours before. Children ran along the shore, dancing in the waves, and she closed her eyes and bent her head to her knees, trying not to think.

The shouts roused her somewhat, the piercing screams made her look up, but still she did not move until Rufus shook her roughly. "Margaret! Sails! Norsemen!"

Everyone around was shouting and running. Rufus

grabbed her arm and pulled her along with him toward the fortress, releasing her when they both turned at the shouts behind them. The men who had been watching the sea from the northern headland were racing toward them now, mouths gaping open in terror.

"Dragonships! Norsemen! Run!"

"They're here!"

The cries were all around her. She threw a look over her shoulder and froze, saying a prayer. There, filling the harbor, which had been quiet only moments ago, were huge ships, their rounded prows topped by dragons and spirals and fierce birds, their railing lined with shields and their hulls full of armed men, who roared as they neared shore. Six, she counted. Seven. Eight. She began to run again, her heart thudding. At the fortress men were calling for the gates to be closed, and women screamed for their children.

Tiernan rushed to her side, pushing her within the walls. "Get inside!"

"Where's Nell?" she cried. "Have ye seen her?"

"No! Get inside, Margaret!"

"We'll be trapped there. We have to run for the forest."

"There's no time! They're already landing! Look!"

She followed his gaze to the beach, where the ships were sliding onto the shore, Norsemen leaping from them and running up from the beach, hundreds of them, axes and swords raised high. They shook the very ground, their battle cries like something from the Otherworld. The gates slammed shut, and Rufus's men scrambled onto the battlements. Tiernan drew his sword.

She clutched at his arm. "Come with me! Rufus, come, all of ye—there are too many of them! We canna defeat them!"

Tiernan shook his head, his jaw tight. "We defeated them before."

"There are too many this time!" *And Gannon's not here.*

"Find Nell and escape!" he shouted, and joined Rufus at the gate.

She rushed into the hall, shouting her sister's name. The hall was filled with women screaming and crying, men shouting, rushing about, some trying to escape, some wielding weapons, joining those in the courtyard.

"The garden!" Dagmar shouted. "We'll get out through the garden!"

"Nell!" Margaret cried. "Have ye seen Nell?"

Dagmar shook her head and ran toward the back of the hall, followed by the panicked people. The corridor to the kitchens quickly clogged. Margaret looked up the stairs, then took the steps two at a time, hearing the screams behind her.

"They're in the village already!"

There was chaos below as people poured back into the hall, but Margaret kept climbing. She ran down the hallway and slammed open the door to their room. It was empty, the bed tidily made, the emptiness of the room mocking her. She raced back to the hallway, calling Nell's name. Downstairs the screams were more shrill, and she could hear a loud battering, then more screams, some cries cut off far too quickly. Dear God, had they broken through already? *Tiernan. Rufus. Dear God, no.* She ran along the corridor calling for Nell, was sprinting toward the stairs when she heard the thundering sound of boots there.

She drew her short sword and turned to face her death.

TWENTY-ONE

Nell was in the village with the Somerstrath people when she heard the shouts. "What is it?" she asked, leaving her spot on the bench, moving closer to the door. She received no answer, but a moment later saw the streams of people running across the meadow, pouring from the pathway that led to Rufus's fortress.

"What happened?" Nell asked.

The first man to reach them stopped, gasping. "Norsemen! Run!"

"Norsemen! Vikings!" called a woman who did not stop. "Hundreds!"

"Margaret! Have ye seen Margaret?" Nell started toward the fortress, but one of the Somerstrath women grabbed her arm.

"She'll have gotten out!"

"She'll find us!" the others agreed, pulling her toward the trees.

"I saw her," a man said, running into the trees. "She's with us!"

"Where?" Nell cried.

The man pointed into the forest above them, to the mountains. Nell ran with them then, around the inland loch and onto the slopes of the mountain, stopping on the ledges that overlooked the glen below, affording a clear, if distant view of Inverstrath. The first to arrive were staring and pointing to the fortress, some sobbing. She did not turn, but searched though the crowd for her sister. Margaret was not there. Nor did she arrive, even with the last of the stragglers.

Nell told herself that Margaret must have escaped, that she'd simply run in a different direction, perhaps south, to the glen that Gannon had so admired. Margaret could run swiftly; she'd been outside the walls and would not have been trapped in the hall. Surely she was safe, with Tiernan and Rufus and all those—far too many—who had not joined them here. Surely they were all safe.

Nell, her heart in her throat, turned to look below. It was as she'd feared. Inverstrath was burning, the flames visible even from here, leaping from the wooden structure into the sky. In the harbor the dragonships were lined on the shore like hungry beasts, waiting to be filled. Men moved toward them, lumbering, but it was too far away for her to see what it was they carried.

"Dear God protect them!" one woman cried, and the others repeated her words, many praying aloud.

Nell joined them, sinking to the ground, fearing that her prayers might already be too late. *Keep them safe, Lord, Margaret and Tiernan and Rufus and all the others. I could not bear to lose Margaret, too. Please keep Margaret alive, Lord. Keep her safe, and I'll never ask for anything again as long as I live. And Tiernan. And Rufus and all of them.*

The third camp, on the northern shore of Skye, was neither empty nor unguarded. Drason shot Gannon a look of triumph as they rounded the headland. Dogs, barking furiously, ran toward the harbor as they neared, men not far behind, drawing weapons and shouting. There were two ships on the shore, but neither was a dragonship.

"If Davey and the others are here," Drason said, "they'll be together in a hut near the back of the camp. Nor doesn't like to be troubled by captives, and he dislikes hearing small boys weeping. We'll have to fight our way through."

"Ye'll stay here."

Drason gave him a sidelong glance, then nodded, as though he had some say in this. "You will remember our agreement?"

"I dinna think yer uncle is here."

"If he is, you will honor our agreement?"

"I dinna promise ye, lad. If we find Davey, we'll talk about it," Gannon said and slammed his helmet on his head as they landed.

There were a few fierce moments, but the Norsemen on the beach were quickly slain, as were the others who came running from the huts and tents. Not many men, and not Nor's best men, it became clear when Gannon saw some running away inland. Gannon moved cautiously through the village. It was smaller than the first, not as well placed as the second, but there were cattle here, and pigs, agitated, their noise masking all others. He smashed open doors to find the huts empty, and slashed through canvas to find abandoned tents. The animals had quieted, the silence that followed reminding him of creeping through Somerstrath. But this was not a village of the dead. They found no bodies. And no one to oppose them. Nor, it seemed, had his attention elsewhere.

In the back of the encampment, near the latrines and the pigsties, they found a small hut, just as Drason had said. It was Gannon who opened the door, sword in hand, Gannon who removed his helmet and stared back at the dozen small boys who shrank from him, Gannon who sheathed his sword and fought the wave of rage he felt upon seeing their misery and fear.

In the kindest tone he could muster, he said, "Ye're safe, lads."

They stared at him, then exchanged looks, but none spoke.

"Is Davey MacDonald among ye?" Gannon asked.

One of the boys rose slowly, his dark hair and eyes giving Gannon hope.

"He was," the boy said, "but they took him away."

"Where? Where did they take him?" At the fear in their eyes, Gannon softened his tone. "I am Gannon MacMagnus, come from Inverstrath. Margaret sent me for ye. Come, laddies, let's get ye out of here."

They quickly freed the boys from their bonds, releasing them into the sunshine, watching with grim pleasure as four of them were embraced with cries of joy by the Somerstrath men. Their story came out slowly at first, then without pause, their words tumbling over each other as the Somerstrath boys told of being loaded onto Nor's ships and shifted from camp to camp, told nothing about what their fate was to be. The other boys, from other villages, talked then, telling almost the same tale. Gannon interrupted before the Somerstrath boys could ask about their families, reminding his men that Nor could arrive at any moment.

They left quickly then, setting fire to the huts, slashing the tents until they were unusable, letting the boys help destroy their own prison. They loaded the pigs and cattle on the ship amid much laughter about it, and set sail for Inverstrath. Drason, waiting on *Gannon's Lady*, went pale when he was told Davey was not among the captives. Gannon gave him a long, measuring look, but said nothing to him. He still was not sure about Drason Anderson.

Nor was pleased. There had been no real defense. A handful of men on the beach, a score more on the rise, still more at the fortress itself, but nothing six hundred men could not easily overcome. They could see the villagers running for the forest as they neared, joined by some of the men who were obviously meant to defend the place. He sent some of his men to surround the fortress, others to chase those who thought to escape, but was content to let some live. It would not hurt for news of his revenge to reach the rest of Scotland. It might make them reach deeper in their pockets to prevent it from happening again.

His men battered easily through the gates with their axes, then struck down everyone in the courtyard, where a man, presumably the laird, led a small group of men against them. It took only a few moments to end that, a few more to beat down the door to the hall. He stood in the sunlight for a moment, triumphant, then gestured them forward. His men poured inside.

In a room, just off the hall itself, they found some of the men he'd left behind, bound and filthy. Stinking, but alive. He'd forgotten that he'd left so many behind. They struggled to their feet, hope lighting their eyes. He stood in the doorway, grinning while they cheered him.

"Did you think I would leave you behind?"

* * *

Those in the hall were mostly women, and mostly for-gettable. There was one, though, who watched him with fear, as the others did, but with something more in her gaze, something that he recognized. He let his men push her into a corner with the other women, but this one would bear further investigation. The kitchens and gardens were littered with dead, none of them his. He stepped over the bodies with distaste, then grabbed a handful of sliced grouse from a table, eating as he continued his survey.

He could hear the noise from above and climbed the stairs, licking his fingers and wiping them on his thigh. Probably women, he thought, hearing the guttural sounds. His men had their orders, had been thoroughly instructed, but he was not sure they could be trusted not to sample the women themselves. He turned the corner into the hallway; not twenty feet away his men had a woman. She was, as yet, untouched, and that pleased him.

"Sir," one called. "We found one."

He stepped closer, and his men made room for him. The woman was pressed against the far wall, holding her pitiful weapon before her, as though a small sword would protect her against axes and men who were twice as big.

"You said not to kill any women."

"Yes," he said. "Well done. This one is a prize."

And she was, a lovely creature, tall and dark-haired. She watched him with obvious fear, but, determination flickered in her eyes, too, the kind he'd seen too many times in these Scottish women.

He walked up to her, then reached to touch the torque she wore around her neck. An Irish torque. He smiled as she flinched away and reached for her again.

She flashed the sword at him, but he'd expected that and parried with a move of his own. She tried again. With a growl, he shoved her against the wall, holding the hand that gripped the sword high above her head, squeezing tighter and still tighter until at last, with a whimper, she dropped the blade. It clattered against the wood, the only other sound her ragged breathing. He leaned closer.

"I am looking for Gannon's woman."

She turned her head to the side. He felt her terror, felt her trembling against him. He stepped back from her, appraising her. Full breasts, trim waist, long legs, a pleasing face, and a man's golden torque at her neck. If she were not Gannon's woman, he would be surprised. This was a woman a man would fight for, might die for. A woman a man came back for.

And if she were not Gannon's woman? He'd find other uses for her. She'd bring a tidy sum on the slave market, more if she were a virgin, or could be sold as one. He'd look into that later; some tasks were his own. He turned to his men.

"Bring her down with the others."

Margaret tried to control her trembling as the Norsemen led her below. There were bodies at the foot of the stairs, more scattered around the hall, all of them Rufus's men, a woman here or there among them. The Vikings were rummaging through the clothing of the dead, pulling rings off fingers, killing any man who still moved. Margaret was shoved toward the cowering group of women who huddled near the wall. Dagmar was among them, but not Nell.

"Have ye seen Nell? Did anyone see Nell?"

The women shook their heads. "Many are missing," one said.

They waited then, as the Norse prisoners were released and came into the hall, as Rufus's wine and ale were opened and passed around, and the men drank heavily. Margaret closed her eyes and leaned her head against the wall. She knew what was next, why they had been spared. Images from Somerstrath came to her, and she forced herself to be calm. If she were to die today, so be it. She would face it with all the courage she could summon.

Nor Thorkelson. It must be him. He'd been too assured, too amused to be anyone but Nor. He looked like a leader, moved like a man accustomed to being obeyed. He was tall, broad-shouldered. Strong. Arrogant. He was a handsome man, his long blond hair braided back from his face, revealing a thick neck, strong jaw, and wide mouth. His eyes were a pale blue, his lashes long and blond. Women would seek him out, that she knew, but only if they did not see the coldness in that gaze, nor see the calculations that were obvious as he looked around him. This was a man who weighed everything by how it affected him.

She'd been terrified when he'd approached her, knowing she could not defeat him, knowing what he'd done elsewhere. He'd enjoyed her fear, she'd seen that, too, before his gaze had drifted lower. He'd studied her body, as though she were a horse on the auction block. And he was seeking Gannon's woman, which meant that his spies had been thorough. Or that Rignor had told them.

There might have been other spies than the monk, she realized now. Who had kept track of all who visited since the raid on Somerstrath? Any one of the runners coming with news could have been a spy. Certainly everyone who had visited had been told of the raid, and later of their success against the Norseman, and in great detail. They'd been too trusting, too open.

Nell.

Nor walked quickly through the hall, giving orders, slapping shoulders, apparently pleased. He crossed to where the women were and sat at one of the tables, relaxed amidst all the death. Most of the women looked away or kept their eyes downcast. Only Margaret and Dagmar watched him.

"I'm looking for Gannon's woman," he said in accented Gaelic.

The women were silent.

Nor's gaze touched Margaret's, lingered, then passed on to another. "I will make this simple, then. I'll kill you, one after another, right here, right now, until I'm told which one she is."

Margaret looked into his eyes. And believed him. She stepped forward.

"I am Gannon's woman."

The other women watched in horror, some stifling cries behind their hands. Nor looked at her from head to foot, then nodded. "As I thought."

He had his men bring the women forward, one by one. He said something about each of them, in incomprehensible Norse. The women were divided into two groups, Margaret put amongst the younger women, as was Dagmar. He rose then, saying something to the Norsemen and gesturing at the door. As the men herded the separate groups into the courtyard Margaret steeled herself, and it was needed. She'd known many of the Inverstrath men must be dead, but she was unprepared for what she found. She closed her eyes, but it was too late. She'd already seen Rufus, his body hanging from the fortress wall, his head at an obscene angle. And a moment later, she could see a group of Norsemen raising a body to hang next to him. A tall man, dressed like a Scot, with long blond hair that hung down his back.

Tiernan.

One of the Norsemen ripped the torque from Tiernan's neck, holding it high like a trophy. Margaret screamed at him and lunged for the torque, but was grabbed by her clothing and shoved forward while the Norsemen laughed.

There were more dead outside the gate, only a few of them Vikings. The Norsemen were bending over bodies, taking anything of value, killing those who had been only wounded. Some of the women tried to break free, to run to their husbands or fathers or brothers—or sons—but each was prevented, shoved roughly back into the group. Dagmar, pale and looking frightened, met Margaret's gaze. Both turned at the sudden screams behind them, from the older women in the other group, terrified screams that would haunt her forever.

"Dear God," the women next to her said. "He's giving them to the Vikings."

Nor's men were grabbing at the other women, tearing at their clothing, throwing them down on the ground and forcing themselves on the women, who thrashed and screamed. The women around Margaret began to scream as well and struggled to escape, but the men guarding them pushed them closer together.

And then she smelled it. Smoke.

She looked, past the dead on the ground, past where the women were being violated, past Tiernan's battered body. Inverstrath had been set ablaze.

Margaret was pulled forward. She twisted, trying to free herself from the man's grip. He yanked her toward him, spinning her around. She had a glimpse of women's frightened faces, of flames claiming Rufus's home, of the calm sky above it all. She screamed, flailing at the man who held her. He grunted as one of her blows hit home, then shook her hard, knocking her to her knees, and slapped her, then again. She tried to stand, sensed his arm drawing back.

The world went black.

Nell watched with the others until the Norsemen were gone. As their ships cleared the harbor the rains came, drenching the survivors, who clambered back down the mountain. Steam rose from the fortress as the rain competed with the flames for Inverstrath, but Nell did not look. She knew what they would find.

When she stepped out of the forest, she paused, looking at the charred fortress walls. The people separated then, some going to the village, others, like Nell, to the front of the fortress. She gasped in horror as she rounded the corner.

The field before Inverstrath was littered with its dead. She knew every one of them. Some of the women near the shore were cradling themselves and moaning, some not moving at all, some alive but staring at the sky as though senseless. But none of them Margaret. Nell left them in the care of others and turned her back on the sea, moving inland again, saying the names of the dead aloud as though somehow that was important, to say their names one last time. Here and there a dead Norseman could be found, but very few of them. And Margaret was nowhere.

When she heard the cries of the people at the fortress gates, she looked up, dreading what she would see. Rufus was dead, hanging by his neck from the fortress wall. And next to Rufus . . . was Tiernan.

Many of the women lived, some with addled wits that the older people said might never be healed, but some, although battered and aching, were able to tell what had happened. Margaret, they said, had been taken by the Norsemen, while they'd been left behind to be used here. Nell was sick when they told what had been done to them, sicker still when she realized what Margaret might be facing.

"They wanted Gannon's woman," the women said.

When one of the men tried to comfort her by saying it was a blessing that those who had died had died quickly, she could not talk to him, could not listen to his words. She stayed alone, her anger and grief threatening to engulf her. Tiernan was not in a better place. Rufus had not lived a full life. There was no blessing in their quick deaths— and no assurance that their deaths had been quick. They'd died, painfully, horribly, trying to keep others alive—and in vain. There was no comfort possible, just as there had been none when her family had been killed. How could a just God let these things happen?

She looked out to sea, wondering if Margaret were still alive, if Davey were still alive, what her family had done to deserve such fates. How long she would miss Tiernan. If this chain of death would ever stop.

And what she would tell Gannon when he returned.

The sky was clear and the wind brisk as they passed Somerstrath, the rain that had bathed them on the way now passed to the west, and while the day was waning, the evening was still bright. Gannon did not even spare it a glance, although he saw the others pointing to the destroyed village and heard the Somerstrath boys talking about it.

He'd questioned them for a good part of the journey home, asking them how many men Nor had, how well armed they were, how many ships he had with him. They were very young and could tell him little he had not known or guessed before. What was new information— which made his blood boil—was that Nor had bragged about attacking Somerstrath to his visitors, several times dragging Davey and the other boys from the huts in which they were kept, parading them before the visitors like trophies. One, the boys said, had been a monk. Another had been one of Leod's sons. On reflection, Gannon decided, he'd gotten what he'd wanted from the trip—knowledge of the man he would hunt.

Almost there. They would be in time for the evening meal. He felt his spirits rise. There was the beach where Margaret had seen the dragonships. There the last headland, where he'd kissed her before they warned Inverstrath. He dreaded telling her about Davey, but at least he could tell her that her brother had been alive not too long ago. She'd cry, of course, and perhaps he could find a way to comfort her. He stroked his hand along the smooth railing of his ship as they rounded the last head-land and sailed into Rufus's harbor, trying to find the right words to say.

He knew at once what had happened.

Rufus's galleys were burned hulks on the shingle. And beyond them, the remains of the fortress of Inverstrath lay in charred heaps. There were two ships here, neither of them belonging to Rufus, both guarded by Scots who warily watched his approach.

He paid no attention to his ship as it slid high onto the beach, nor to the dead that lay on the bloody ground, except to glance at the blond men among them. He did not hear the cries of distress from the others behind him, did not look long at the women who had been slain. None of them were Margaret.

He moved on, seeing the bodies hanging from the remains of the fortress wall, telling himself he was wrong, that it could not be. He did not listen when Nell ran toward him from somewhere, her small face ravaged, her eyes red from weeping. He gripped her shoulders.

"Where's Margaret?" he cried. "Where's Tiernan?"

"They took her, Gannon! The Norsemen took her!"

"No. And Tiernan?"

"Oh, Gannon!" Tears streamed down her face as she pointed.

He did not hear what the others were telling him; the roaring in his ears was too loud. He did not turn to see who it was who clutched at his sleeve, which men were telling him not to look, saying things he could not under-stand. He walked forward, stopping only when he reached his brother's body, staring at what was left of Tiernan.

And then he sank to the ground with a cry of despair.

* * *

Margaret woke in a heap in the bottom of a ship. Some of the other women were piled around her, huddled together, some weeping, some simply watching, terrified, as the Norsemen plied the oars next to them. Her head throbbed, her neck ached. Her entire body felt pummeled. Her mind was filled with what she'd seen.

Nor was not here; Dagmar was not among the women. The sky beyond the men was blue and cloudless, and the ship rocked beneath her; they must have reached the open sea, she thought, for the men were putting up their oars, and the sail was being lowered.

"They're taking us away, Lady Margaret," a girl said,

"Aye," she said.

The girl bit her lip and began to cry. "They killed my mother."

Margaret had no answer. She patted the girl's arm.

"They're going to kill all of us, aren't they?"

"I dinna ken," Margaret said woodenly, not saying the obvious. If Nor had wanted them dead, he would have killed them already. Which meant he had another plan for them, and that one she could guess. She closed her eyes, ignoring her roiling stomach and her aching body. There were only two things to concentrate on: Nell was not here with her. And Gannon was still alive.

Nell. Gannon. Tiernan. Rufus. Dear God, let me wake from this nightmare.

She did not know how long they sailed, nor which way they went, for she could not see over the shields that lined the railing. It seemed like forever, and she closed her eyes, letting the motion of the ship lull her into a trance. She opened her eyes occasionally, but could only see the red sail, stretched full with wind above her, and the men who watched her and the women around her. No one touched them; no one spoke to them. She searched the men's faces, but saw no compassion, no kindness, only a tense excitement that terrified her. She expected no mercy from them, not from men who could kill as they had, who could rape and murder and plunder and laugh at it. They talked among themselves; she could not understand their comments, but realized what had been discussed when she heard the low, predatory laughter that followed.

The ship was not alone. There were others with them; she could occasionally see the top of masts and the banners that flew there, banners she did not recognize. From Orkney, she wondered? Or had that been a ruse? And was Drason's story a ruse as well? Had he lied, luring Gannon away from Inverstrath with stories of knowing where Davey was, while Nor waited out of sight, ready to pounce? Was Davey even still alive? And was she now the bait to bring Gannon and the rest of his men—and hers—to their deaths?

Gannon, love, I am so sorry. When you find Tiernan . . .

The men hurried to adjust lines, and the ship turned suddenly, swinging to the right, shivering before leaping forward. She could see the tops of cliffs, barren and dark against the sky, on both sides of the ship, as though they sailed down a long narrow channel. Then nothing but sky as the men lowered the sail and raised their oars. And then cliffs again, these manned, the men on them waving and calling greetings. Dozens of men, it seemed, all Norse. The ship slowed, then stopped. A Norseman gestured for her to rise, and she stood unsteadily, grasping the railing as she looked around.

They were in a sea loch, surrounded by tall cliffs except for directly before her, where a rocky meadow led up to a crude sort of camp. She could see tents and two wooden structures. The loch was filled with longships, dragonships, galleys, and shore boats of every size, not enough to be Haakon's fleet, but more than she'd expected. Nor was no lone marauder; he was a warlord.

Milling on the shore, catching lines to the arriving ships, were more Norsemen, grinning and whistling as the women were lifted from the ships and deposited on the shingle. The women huddled together, casting fearful glances at each other. Only Margaret looked around her. And Dagmar, who appeared now, in the ship that was next to them. With Nor.

Nor leapt gracefully from his ship to the ground and called to the Norsemen, who listened intently as he swept his hand to indicate the women, then said "Gannon." The men cheered. Nor then pointed to her, unmistakably saying that she was Gannon's woman, and the men cheered again. What else he said was lost on her; she was watching his glow of triumph and the hungry looks his men were giving the women.

Nor stalked over to her, offering her his elbow and smiling. "Welcome, Lady Margaret MacDonald."

She glanced behind him, at Dagmar, who no doubt had supplied her name.

"I trust you'll find it interesting here," he said.

He led her up the gentle slope, talking as though they were at a social gathering, as though he were not leading her to a barren stretch of flat land, as if he were not stopping before a grimy wooden hut and gesturing for his man to push the low-slung door open. The wind was brisk here and behind him, towering above his encampment, the majestic Cuillins rose high, dwarfing all beneath them, the unmistakable mountains of Skye.

She looked into his pale blue eyes, then away before he could see her sudden excitement. She was on Skye. In a small boat she could sail home. There were people here on this island who might help her, who might send word to Gannon or to Uncle William of all that had happened. She kept her gaze averted from him, looking instead at the encampment. It looked recent, but was well supplied, for there were horses and pigs, and cattle penned at the far side of the camp. There were women, too, a few at least, brazen camp followers, dressed in the Norse fashion, strutting among the men and watching the new arrivals.

"You will dine with me tonight," Nor said, drawing her attention back to him. "I'll send for you later."

"No," she said.

He blinked, then threw his head back and laughed.

"Yes," he said, and strode away. Behind him, guarded by two men, Dagmar followed him. They went higher up the hill, disappearing into the only other wooden structure.

Nor's man pushed her inside the dark hut. She was soon joined by the other women. Margaret sat in a corner, silent, while some of the others sobbed. The guards were many, the location remote. How could she escape? How could she take the others with her? It seemed impossible. But she was on Skye, and that alone was comforting.

Gannon. Nell, dear heart, be safe.

TWENTY-TWO

Gannon buried his brother himself, refusing all aid except to bring Tiernan down from the wall where he'd been strung like a prize. He dug the grave in the fading light while the others watched, and placed Tiernan within it, then filled the hole. When the others came forward with the small stones for his brother's cairn, he stacked them himself. He stood silently while they prayed over the tiny plot of land that held Tiernan then moved on to the other graves.

How was it possible that Tiernan was dead, that he would never hear that merry laugh again, never be teased by him? Never argue with him again? How was it possible that he'd left his brother to face death without him, knowing what Nor was? He'd not been here to protect him. He'd been chasing across the sea, looking for a monster. And the monster had been here, taking his revenge. Taking Margaret. Once again, as at Somerstrath, he helped bury the dead. Here, now, he buried his own, working with a growing determination. Nor Thorkelson might have started the raids, might indeed have started a war. But Gannon vowed he would finish it.

Nell was alive, and for that he was grateful. She'd told

him everything she knew, and he'd wrapped his arms around her, telling her that he was glad she'd survived. He'd held her while she cried for Tiernan, his own tears mingling with hers. When he'd told her about the boys he'd brought home, she'd brightened for a moment, then slumped again when he said that Davey was not among them.

He could think of little else than that Margaret was gone. Dagmar had been taken as well, along with the youngest of the women. And Rignor . . . was dead, killed by his own men. He heard the story, but not from the men who had killed Rignor, for they, too, had died in the attack. He buried them next to Rignor, finding a grim satisfaction in it. He'd never liked the man, that was true, but he'd never imagined that Rignor would tell murderers where to find his sisters—or the woman he'd loved for most of his life. Or the people he'd been entrusted to lead. Had his wrath been directed only at Margaret or Dagmar? Or was this, his final act, as undisciplined and poorly thought through as all his other actions? It was a contemptible legacy for a man to leave.

The ships in Rufus's harbor belonged to the next clan, whose chieftain, a hardy man named MacDougall, had filled his two ships with armed men and come to assist when the Inverstrath runner brought word of the attack. They, too, arrived too late to do anything but help bury the dead, but they offered safe haven to Inverstrath's survivors. Gannon encouraged Rufus's people to go with the MacDougalls, but refused the shelter for himself.

"I'm going to Skye," he told them, "to find Margaret and bring her home."

MacDougall pledged his aid, and Gannon was both

surprised and pleased when many volunteered to join him.

"Ye are one of us now," one of the Inverstrath women told him.

He had to turn away from her before she saw his eyes filling with tears. How could it be, when he'd lost everyone dear to him, when he'd failed to protect them, that they could have faith in him?

After a hurried meal, a hurried conversation with Nell and an even more hurried one with MacDougall, Gannon and his fleet left. He had three ships now and 150 men. It would have to do. He'd ignored the worried questions about sailing through the night, about how they would find Nor's encampment. He'd looked at Nell, who would stay behind, embracing her, then gently pushing her away when she clung to him, telling her to be brave a bit longer. And he looked at Drason Anderson, unbound now and sitting among Gannon's men. Drason, who had expressed as much horror as the others at what they'd found at Inverstrath, and who, eyes burning with anger, told Gannon they would hunt Nor down if it took forever. He believed the boy.

Gannon's Lady slipped back into the sea, catching the night wind eagerly, and headed back the way she'd come. He'd find Nor. But first he had a stop to make.

She heard his laughter in her dream, the low chuckle that rumbled through his chest, the one she'd been delighted to discover when they'd made love. He'd been a different man that night, tender and almost carefree, the fearsome warrior gone and in his place a man she could well imagine spending the rest of her life with, one who teased and smiled, who gave pleasure as he took his own. She'd slid her finger across his chest, feeling his laughter, the crisp golden hairs that dusted his skin, had run her hand the length of the scar the Norsemen had given him, suddenly aware of a cold wind coming from somewhere. And then her dream changed, from a candlelit room to a cold beach, where a severed head was slammed onto the sand by angry waves, and small boys looked at her for an explanation.

Margaret opened her eyes at the rough shaking. Above her a familiar and hated face loomed, that of the man who guarded the women, a foul man who had taken more than his share of liberties with them. He gestured for her to rise, not bothering to hide his smirk, and she knew where she was headed. The women around her cowered, their wide eyes revealing both their fear and their relief that it was not them being summoned. The last girl to leave had been given to Nor's men. They'd heard her screams, then the laughter of men. She had not returned.

She was too slow to rise for the guard, for he grabbed her and shoved her toward the door. She stumbled out into the predawn light.

Nor had not called for her last night. And Dagmar had not joined the women; it did not take much imagination to know where she'd been. The man led her up the path, along the edge of the cliff, to the longhouse. Below her in the harbor men were already moving about on the ships. One ship was arriving, gliding in silently from the long channel that led to the sea. Two more were leaving. More raids, she wondered, shivering at the thought. Was Nor with them? Was she being brought to the longhouse to serve another purpose than the one she anticipated? She thought of the older Inverstrath women thrown to the Norsemen like scraps to starving wolves. She would endure it. Whatever this day brought, she would endure it.

The guard stopped before the longhouse. It was well named, for the building was long and squat, huddled against the ground. Crude, she thought, fitting for the man who held court there. The guard knocked. She could hear Nor's answer, curt and tinged with humor, but could not understand his words. The guard pushed the door open and gestured her inside.

The room was low, built of dark timbers without decoration. There was a fire of sorts thrust into a brazier that looked almost Roman, but no chimney. The smoke escaped through a ragged hole cut in the roof. On the floor was a rug from Persia and on a low, ornately carved chest, was the silver candlestick that had once been her mother's, the one that Lachlan had brought with him to Fiona's on that fateful night. It steadied her, the sight of the candlestick, reminded her of all this man had done, of all he was, and that the only way to defeat him might be to die with him. She had no weapon but her mind, and she must be prepared to use it.

Nor watched her from a large chair across the room, like a king overseeing his domain. At the other end of the room was a beautiful bed, stolen, no doubt, from one of the raided villages, for the turned bedposts were carved with Celtic symbols, intertwining animals and plants. It was empty, but the coverings lay clustered at the foot of the bed, as though someone had just risen. Dagmar? There was, blessedly, no sign of her.

Nor smiled now, gesturing for her to stand before him, his pale blue eyes noting every detail of her. "Come in, Lady Margaret. I trust you are well today."

"Aye," she said.

"As am I, although you have not asked."

She did not answer.

"Dagmar has been an interesting companion."

"All the men say that."

He gave a bark of laughter. "She's told me much about you, about your history and your family. You are the niece of the Earl of Ross, which is most interesting. And Somerstrath was your home. So sorry to have destroyed it. Had I known you would return, I would have waited for you. And you are the reluctant wife of Lachlan Ross, married by a monk, who was not a monk. You were wed and not wed." He leaned forward, his smile wide. "I have rarely enjoyed anything more than thinking of you married by a man from Caithness who would sell his mother for silver." He laughed aloud. "And now you have an attachment to Gannon Magnusson, MacMagnus, as you Scots call him."

She met his gaze, but said nothing. He smiled again, appearing for a moment to be nothing more than a genial, handsome man.

"And this Gannon, I've discovered, is kin to the laird of Ulster. Pity about his brother. No doubt his uncle in Antrim will be displeased with me. But none of this is news to you." He paused, rubbing his hand along the arm of the chair. He tossed his hair over his shoulder, raising his chin as he studied her.

"You are beautiful, which is fortunate. I could ransom you." He spoke as though he were discussing the weather. "Gannon would probably pay to have you back, even if your 'husband' would not. Or perhaps your uncle would. Or perhaps you're thinking that they will come for you, that I've killed a lot of people, and they will come for revenge. But let's consider. Lachlan Ross will not come for you, not after the way you treated him. Your uncle is very busy with other things, with Haakon's fleet off Scotland's shores and King Alexander's request that your uncle bring an army to aid him. William might be too busy with all that to arrange a ransom just now. With Norway and Scotland at war who has time to consider the fate of one insignificant woman?"

She watched him move, but did not speak.

"So now," he continued, "we have only Gannon, who is burying his brother. But even if Gannon wanted to come for you, he cannot. I left no ship whole at Inverstrath and very few men. He has only one ship and a handful of companions." He shook his head. "Gannon will not come for you."

"He will. Perhaps not soon, but he will come and make you pay for what you've done."

He smiled slowly. "Ah. How certain you seem that he'll come. Perhaps you're right. But let me assure you, that if Gannon comes here, we will be ready. And our hospitality will be unlike anything he's ever known."

"He will not come alone. He will find ye and destroy ye."

He went on as if she'd not spoken. "If no one meets my price, I could sell you in Norway, where many men might like to bed the niece of the Earl of Ross. Or send you even farther away, places where white skin and a face like yours would bring me a nice sum." He slid from the chair and paced the room. "I could give you to my men, who would use you up in a week. But that would be wasteful when I have the others to pass along when I'm finished. Or I could keep you for myself if you prove interesting enough, if you are as inventive as Dagmar."

"I assure you I am not."

"It would please me to have Gannon know I had you. Shall we wait until he comes and have him watch?"

"Ye are disgusting."

"And you, madam, are predictable."

"As ye are."

He smiled coldly. "I am not predictable."

"But ye are. At every turn ye take the brutal course. It doesna take a fine mind to mistreat people."

"Are you trying to win me over?"

"If I were, I'd be obsequious and tell ye that there's never been anyone like ye, as Dagmar has. Or will. She says that to all the men."

"And how would you know that?"

"The walls are sometimes thin."

He laughed. "I have your brother David. He's being held not far away."

Her heart lurched.

"You may see him. In return for . . . certain favors."

Here it was, just as she'd expected. Actually more civil than she'd expected. She told herself it did not matter what he did to her, that despite his talk of selling her as a slave, he was far more likely to keep her alive to hold for ransom. Her value to him was as a pawn with which to bargain. And no one pays well for a dead woman. Nor Thorkelson might be intelligent, but he'd backed himself into a corner; she might be his path out of it. If Haakon of Norway won the war, Nor would never be asked to account for what he'd done. But if Alexander of Scotland won, Nor would be hunted. It was a gamble, and she was willing to bet that he'd take the safest route, that he would take the road that would keep them both alive.

She trembled as he came to stand before her, lifting her chin, moving her face side to side as though studying it. He brushed her hair back from her face, his touch gentle and caressing. *Let him do what he wants. Live through this. Don't think.*

He slid his hand into the neck of her bodice, the backs of his fingers cold against her skin; she tried to control her flinch. He smiled slowly, thrusting his hand deeper, to rest between her breasts. And then he yanked, tearing her clothing from neckline to waist, pushing her back until she met the wall. He stripped what was left of her bodice from her, then stepped closer, lifting one breast, then the other.

"Gannon's woman." He leaned even closer, nuzzling her neck, his hips against hers, his arousal hard against her stomach.

I will bear this.

"Do you want your brother to live? He's so young . . ."

"Aye."

His lips moved to her shoulder and his hand tightened on her breast, then slid down to her waist, slipping under the edge of her skirts. "What are you willing to do?"

"What do ye want?"

He pulled his hand back, tearing her skirts open. She froze, closing her eyes, refusing to look at him as the air met her skin. He tore again. The last of her skirts fell, and she was naked.

"Open your eyes, Margaret!"

She did. His gaze was fevered, his eyes glowing.

"I want Gannon. And you're going to deliver him, aren't you? In exchange for your brother's life, you will lure Gannon to me. But that's not all. I want this," he said, painfully tightening his grip on her breast.

I will bear this.

"And this," he said, thrusting a hand between her legs, his fingers on her, then in her.

She gasped, jerked away from him, but he held her pinned against the wall. He pressed his mouth against hers, forcing her lips open. He thrust his tongue into her, probing, one hand on her breast again, the other, inside her, moving in rhythm with his tongue. She moaned and tried to break free, but he leaned against her now, her shoulders and back pressed into the rough wood of the wall. He lifted his head and looked at her.

"You are not enjoying this. Perhaps you like other things better."

He stepped back, withdrew his hand from her, and grabbed her wrist, jerking her behind him toward the bed. "What does Gannon do to entertain you, sing to you? Write poems in your honor, like some Norman knight? And this is the man who . . ."

Defeated ye, she thought, but knew better than to say it.

". . . beds you," he finished. "I'll show you things you've never imagined."

He tossed her on the bed, threw himself atop her before she could move; he fumbled with his clothing with one hand while he held her down with his other. When he straddled her and pulled his tunic over his head, she struck him between the legs with all her might.

He groaned. His lips twisted into a sneer, and he hit her, hard, across the face, then again with the back of his hand, knocking her from the bed to the floor, his breath rasping. She put a hand to her mouth; it came away bloody.

"Sir." The voice came from the doorway, but no one entered.

"What is it?" Nor shouted.

"Sir, there's a messenger. Will you come out? Shall we come in?"

"What is the news?"

"Sir? You might want to . . ."

"Tell me!"

There was a slight pause, then the guard spoke again. "The Scots raided the northern camp. They killed all of our men. They took the boys. They even took the pigs and cattle. Our men just arrived with the news, sir. All the boys are gone."

Nor's laugh was low and bitter as he returned to the bed, pulling his tunic on with rough, angry motions. He called loudly for his guard, who entered at once, his manner diffident. He did not look at Margaret.

"Get her out of here. And be sure no one—no one—touches her but me."

"Yes, sir," the guard said.

Nell and a handful of Inverstrath women whose men had accompanied Gannon took turns watching the shore for sails, even though they could do nothing but run inland to warn the others if the Norsemen returned. But still they watched. Nell watched most closely of all. Late in the day after Gannon left, the Ross ships arrived. Uncle William was not with them, but his captain, a thin, wiry man she'd met several times before, told her that William was bringing troops to support the king and could not come, but he sent his love. William, the captain said, had heard of the attack and of Gannon's brilliant defense of Inverstrath.

"But not this!" the captain said, looking at the ruins of Rufus's fortress. "No one's yet heard that they came back and took their revenge. Lord, God, I'm so sorry."

"They took Margaret," Nell said. "They killed Rufus. And Gannon's brother. And Rignor's dead."

"Ross willna like that ye're here alone. Ye'd best come with me."

"I'm not alone, sir, and I willna leave until Gannon comes back with Margaret. But I thank ye, sir."

The man sighed. "It may be for the best, lassie. The whole country's in an uproar, Lady Nell. Yer uncle is bringing his army south and he's not alone. All the clans and the Border Lords are collecting men to join King Alexander. Have ye heard all the news, that Haakon of Norway's men pulled ships overland to Loch Lomond and sacked everything there? Pulled their longships overland! It's war, lass. The king is still parleying with Haakon, but where else can it go? Most I've talked to think it's time for the islands in Scotland's waters to belong to Scotland, for us all to be united. Haakon's an old man, Alexander a young one. It's time for Haakon to give over the reins. And to stop things like what happened here and at Brenmargon Abbey."

Nell's heart sank. "What happened at Brenmargon?"

"Ye'd not heard? Dead, all of them. Abbess Judith and everaone of the women. Hard to understand men who do such things, aye?"

Nell thought of Judith and her warmth, her faith, her laughter and hospitality. The world, it seemed, had gone mad.

"Did ye ken them, Lady Nell?"

"Aye," she whispered. "We did."

Gannon shaded his eyes as the sun rose over Leod's loch, turning the gray water to silver. The rest of Skye was already bathed in light, but dawn came last to the north-western waters. He shifted his weight as his ship rolled with the swells that raced past him and through the arms of the headlands that guarded Loch Dunvegan. The tide was coming in. And somewhere above, no doubt still in his warm bed, Leod would soon learn that he had visitors.

They'd sailed all night, *Gannon's Lady* and MacDougall's two galleys, aided by a lively wind and a full moon, reaching Skye before dawn. They used the early light to sail past the camps he'd visited with Drason, not expecting Nor to be there, but, on the off chance, they'd checked and found nothing. And then he'd come here.

Margaret was here, somewhere on this island. He could feel it in his bones. Every hour that passed increased his determination and his rage. If Nor had harmed her . . . he would not be responsible for his actions. And Tiernan had died at the man's hand.

Hurry.

He whirled around, causing several of his men to look at him in surprise, but there was no one there, and he realized that the whispers had found him again.

Hurry.

"Let's go," he said, willing his heart to slow. Around him his men roused themselves and began to lift their oars. He gave the signal to MacDougall. The other man nodded, and his men, too, began to move. "Ye'll come with me," he told Drason. The boy nodded.

Gannon watched as his men raised the sail and waited for his signal. He told them to keep their shields on the railing and their weapons hidden. It would not do to look aggressive when arriving at Leod's door unannounced, especially since his message might not be welcome. MacDougall had brought news of the outside world, of the turmoil Scotland was in. His conversation with Leod would be illuminating. And, God willing, he'd live through it.

As *Gannon's Lady* moved toward shore, the two Scottish galleys moved in the opposite direction, south on the open sea, carrying letters Gannon had written before he left, to Rory, to William Ross, and to King Alexander. If Gannon had not joined him in two hours, MacDougall would sail for home and spread the news.

As he had last time, Gannon waited at Leod's dock, sending word of his arrival up the hill. There were no dragonships here, no longships even, except Leod's, sporting his distinctive lion prow. There was no sign of preparation for war, no groups of armed men waiting for orders, no bustle that was unseemly. He glanced at Drason, sitting where Tiernan had sat, and thought of all that had happened since his last trip here.

Last night, in the dark, he'd almost turned to Tiernan with a comment, only to remember that he could never do that again. He'd been glad of the darkness then, welcoming it to hide his emotions. By the time the moon had risen, he'd been more under control, or as much as he could when his rage was simmering just under the surface. There was no reason his brother had died other than Nor's greed and rapacity, his darkness, which must be obliterated. If Nor had touched Margaret, he'd make the man pay. If he'd hurt her, Nor would suffer every torture Gannon could imagine, and just now his imagination was quite fertile.

When Leod's message came for Gannon to join him, he left his men without a backward glance. They knew what to do—he'd given them the same orders he'd given Tiernan when last they were here. Wait two hours. Then sail like hell and raise the alarm.

Like last time he was shown straight to Leod, and like last time the man was not surprised to see him. He was offered ale, and bread and cheese to break his fast. He accepted it all, eating slowly as he sat opposite the older man.

"Winter's coming," Leod said, rubbing his thigh. "I can always feel it in my legs. It was cold last night."

"Was it?" Gannon asked mildly. "I dinna notice."

"That anxious to visit me again, were ye? I'm flattered."

Gannon smiled tightly. "They'll be plenty of others behind me. I'm told that the clans have risen to join King Alexander."

"Haakon's said to have eighty ships."

"Haakon's an old man a long way from home."

"Alexander's untested."

"Alexander has the backing of the entire country. Scotland's united behind him in this, especially after the raids around Loch Lomond. Haakon should have been more prudent. The old ways are gone, Leod. Raiding is no longer going to be tolerated."

Leod took a large bite of bread and chewed thoughtfully. Gannon waited.

"It's been successful for centuries," Leod said at last.

"Those days are over. The Nor Thorkelsons of the world will be defeated."

"Alexander's a bit busy just now. Who will defeat Nor?"

"I will."

Leod raised his eyebrows. "With one ship?"

"I'm not alone. And lest ye think to simply kill me and be rid of the problem I'm bringing ye, let me forestall that. Before I came, I wrote to Rory O'Neill and to William Ross and Alexander of Scotland, telling them what I mean to do. If I die here with ye, I will be avenged."

"I'm not a murderer."

"Ye harbor them."

"I do not."

"Ye've offered them land, bases from which to attack Ireland and Scotland. They come here for women. And, I'm told, to visit with ye. I'm offering ye a chance to redeem yerself. Join me."

"In?"

"Tiernan is dead. Rufus of Inverstrath is dead. A lot of good men are dead because of one man. Now he is holding Margaret MacDonald hostage. I mean to take her back."

There was a flicker in Leod's eyes. "He has Ross's niece?"

"Aye."

"I thought she married elsewhere."

"The marriage wasna valid."

"I've heard otherwise."

Gannon spoke coldly. "We'll not debate it. Look, I'm being as direct with ye as I can. Join me and survive. If ye harbor Nor, ye'll share his fate."

"Which will be?"

"I'll find him. I'll kill him."

"Are you threatening me?"

"I'm warning ye. The old days are over. If ye wish to keep yer home and yer power, join with the ones who will triumph. The Haakons and the Nors of this world are from a time past."

"What do you ask of me?"

"Ships. Men. Directions. I have Nor's nephew with me; the boy kens much, but I'd rather it was ye who told me where to find Nor. That way, when I'm telling the story to King Alexander, I can say that ye came with me as an eager ally. As an old friend who remembered my father."

Leod pushed back his chair and crossed the room to stand in front of his window overlooking the water below, his back to Gannon. *Hurry.* Gannon fought the sudden chill of fear that claimed him. She was here, he could feel it. Moments passed. He clenched his hands beneath the table and kept his face impassive.

"It's a new day, Leod."

"I was just looking at that," Leod said.

"Winter's coming. It could be cold out here all alone."

"Aye."

"I'd argue for ye to keep yer lands."

Leod faced him. "Tell me again why I should be listening to ye."

"My cousin is the laird of Ulster, my uncle the leader of Antrim. And my woman is the niece of one of Scotland's most powerful men. I have the ear of Ireland and Scotland. I'd make a better ally than an enemy. And I'm not leaving Skye until I have Margaret back."

"She's that important to you."

"She's that important to me."

Leod moved slowly back to the table. "How many men do you need?"

"How many are ye offering?"

TWENTY-THREE

Margaret was separated from the other women, put into a tent with guards all around her. She lay back, still wrapped in the plaid that the guard had thrown at her. Later, when her hands stopped trembling, she would fashion some sort of gown from it. It didn't matter, none of it. She was alive. *And Davey is free.*

She'd meant to be calm, to let Nor do as he would, telling herself that Davey's survival might rely on it. But when he touched her, he'd unleashed something fierce in her. Submitting to him would have meant that she had assisted him in dominating her. When she saw the pleasure in his eyes, saw that he enjoyed her fear, she'd chosen to battle instead. She touched her face, swollen from his blows. Davey was free. She'd not known that when she struck Nor, but now, thank God, it did not matter what she'd done. And God willing, Nell was safe.

It was Gannon who mattered now. Gannon, who probably had already returned to Inverstrath, had found Tiernan dead. Her heart ached for him, for his pain at the discovery. He'd talk to the Inverstrath people and learn that Nor had taken her. Gannon would come for her as Nor had known he would. She was terrified for him. Gannon would find this place, and Nor would be waiting for him, like a viper.

Almost there.

Gannon lifted his head and smiled. Whatever the whispers were, he was glad of their company this fine day. He watched the coastline, looking for the passage. And then there it was, just as Leod had said, a small opening in the sea cliffs, easily missed if one was not searching for it, a finger of water that led inland, through the tall cliffs that guarded the entrance. He felt his blood rise and gave the signal to the others.

Leod had given him three ships, full of armed men, and given them orders to destroy Nor's camp and Nor himself. It had taken hours for them to prepare, but the time had been worth spending. Gannon had used it well, leaving Leod's stronghold to find MacDougall offshore, who was waiting as planned. And with MacDougall were two of William Ross's ships outside the entrance to Loch Bracadale—a most welcome sight. Gannon now had eight ships and five hundred men with him. Cities had been flattened by fewer.

But that was not the best of it. Leod had provided maps and men who knew this island better than any. Some had gone overland from the north, would wait for Gannon's arrival. The rest were with him now.

Nor had chosen his camp well, Leod's men had said. It was a perfect trap for Nor's enemies. The sea loch entrance was long and narrow, and while it was deep, there was not enough room for a ship to turn. From the steep cliffs towering overhead men could easily launch a hail of arrows, or worse, on any ship trying to enter. At the end of the passage was a large inner loch, mostly ringed with cliffs, but with flatland near the eastern side of the water, where Nor's ships were beached, where, behind a low-slung wooden wall, the gentle rise was filled with tents. And where Nor—and Margaret— would be. He knew Nor would be expecting him to come after Margaret and the other women. But he would not guess how.

Gannon climbed out of *Gannon's Lady* and into one of Leod's ships, giving his own ship's painted railing a pat, perhaps for the last time. It did not matter if he lost her; he had more important goals now. He gave the signal for the other ships to wait here, outside the passage, then sailed south with another of Leod's ships, to the next bay. He left the two ships there with a handful of men to guard them—their escape route if all went astray—and with fifty of his Irish and Inverstrath men, climbed the cliffs of the bay. There was no one to oppose them atop the flat headland, and they loped northward, toward Nor's encampment.

He left most of the men in a sheltered spot, with orders to wait for his return. Then he, with five others, crept westward, quickly finding Nor's men who guarded the cliffs above the passage from the sea. There had been only three, just as Leod had said. They were quickly dispatched. And there, on the cliffs opposite, he saw Leod's men come from the north and remove Nor's guards on that side. Gannon breathed a little easier. He'd not been sure Leod's information would be accurate, nor that the man would actually send his men. But there they were.

Gannon, at the edge of the cliff, waved the signal to the waiting MacDougall and Ross's ships below, *Gannon's*

Lady with them. Nor would have little warning of their arrival. He watched the six ships, safe now from attack from above, glide into the passage, then ran back to his men.

Nor settled himself between Dagmar's legs, thrusting inside her without preliminaries. She was lovely, this Scottish woman, and would be, at least for another few years before her sharp features grew shrewish and her words irritated more than her tongue pleasured. She was artful and imaginative, he thought, withdrawing, then sliding deeper into her, ignoring her gasp, quickly followed by her wide smile. Dagmar was more than willing; she was ambitious. At first she'd been content not to be raped, suggesting, when he'd started to force her, that he would be far better pleasured if she was allowed to participate. She had caught him off guard, for he'd become accustomed to terrifying women.

She'd been an energetic lover, never refusing him, always praising and cosseting him, so much so that it began to be cloying, her words ringing false now that he'd heard them so often. She did not shrink from his touch like Margaret MacDonald.

Dagmar, her back arched and head thrown back against the pillow, squirmed beneath him. "Oh, Nor, ye are amazing. Ye're so big; ye fill me so completely."

"You told me that Margaret was passive. She's not."

"Then teach her to be. Ye terrify men. Surely ye can subdue one woman." She wrapped her arms around his neck and bit his lower lip. "Ye misunderstood."

He watched her for a moment. He did not like that tone from her. From anyone. "I misunderstood?"

"Aye." She arched higher.

He thrust deeper. "Tell me again that there's never been anyone like me."

"There's never been anyone like ye."

He slipped his hands around her neck. "Tell me again."

"There's never been anyone like ye," she gasped, as he drove into her.

"And again," he said, tightening his grip on her throat, then tighter still.

She tossed her head from side to side, her legs thrashing now. He climaxed, his grip on her neck relaxing with the rest of him. She lay gasping, staring at him, her eyes huge. He was quite sure she would not use that tone again.

"Get out," he said.

He expected her to scramble to collect her clothing and run naked for the door. Instead, she stretched languorously, like a cat, then turned on her side. "Again," she said. "Do it again, Nor. If ye can."

He slid a hand along her sleek side, feeling the softness of her skin. She looked over her shoulder and smiled a sly smile, and he felt his anger rise. It was time that Dagmar learned not to make demands, that he decided their actions, not she.

She pushed back against him. "Not yet, aye?" She laughed. "I can wait."

He turned her to see her face and put a hand on her neck, trying to think if there was anything else he might need her for. There were always willing women. He tightened his grip.

"That hurts," she complained, batting ineffectually at him.

He put a second hand on her neck.

"Nor!"

"Farewell, Dagmar," he said softly, then tightened his grip.

She thrashed a bit, arching against him with both hands pulling at his, her nails digging into his skin. When at last she lay still beneath him, he gave a low laugh. He lay on his back and looked away, then tossed a cover over her, so that her face could not reproach him again.

"Sir! Sir! Come at once!" The guard's tone was shrill as he burst through the door, his eyes widening as he looked from Nor to Dagmar.

"This had better be important," Nor said, sitting up.

"Is she dead?"

"Yes. Have someone take her away. What is it?"

"Ships, sir. Six of them in the passage!"

Nor stood, naked. "Not ours, obviously."

"No! Sir, the men . . . what should we do?"

Nor pulled on leggings, then his shirt. "Calm down. We knew they were coming, we just didn't know when. Get Margaret MacDonald on her way."

As the guard scurried to do his bidding, Nor pulled his chain mail over his head, strapped on his leather armor, and, grabbing his helmet, strode outside. His men, gathered and armed, were anxious to board their ships and confront the invaders.

"Wait," he told them. "They will come to us."

A moment later he was proved right. From the dark passageway at the far end of the loch came six ships, Scots, built the best way, in the Norse fashion. Each was full of men, shields at the railings, helmets on head. Men who had come for battle, not negotiations. At the head of this fleet was a graceful longship, dark wood with a red sail. Gannon's, he would wager—and as anticipated. And Margaret had thought *him* predictable. William Ross's banner flew above another ship, but Nor was quite sure Ross was not here himself. The others looked like Leod's ships, but that could not be.

There were more ships than he'd expected. His anger grew. The men he'd had stationed on the cliffs were supposed to shower arrows on any enemy ships entering the loch, but there was not even one arrow visible, no dying or dead men to be seen. He swore and counted his opponents' ships, then swore again. How had even six ships arrived unharassed? Had the men he had stationed there abandoned their posts? Or had they somehow been attacked?

He was angry, but not alarmed. His men should be moving even now to seal the only exit from the loch, as they'd been trained to do. He grunted with satisfaction as two of his ships moved to do just that. His visitors would be staying for a while, enjoying his own special brand of hospitality. But wait . . . two of the enemy ships were turning to face his, preventing the passage from being sealed. He watched as they became engaged in battle, and the rest of the enemy fleet moved closer. He cursed silently, refusing to let his men see his agitation.

"Let them come to us," he said, keeping his manner calm while his heart pounded in his chest.

Gannon's men were waiting for him, gesturing him to the new vantage point they'd found. Nor's encampment was laid out before him. The loch was oval, tents strung along a flat stretch of land above a gentle slope on the eastern shore to his right. There were a few huts among the tents, signs that someone had once lived here permanently. And where Margaret and Davey would be hidden. Nor's ships were on the beach, men working nearby.

From the left of the loch the MacDougall and Ross ships slid out of the passage, followed by Leod's. And *Gannon's Lady*. Gannon allowed himself a moment to admire her beauty and regret that she might not survive this day. Then he turned his attention to the Norsemen on the beach, who were going mad, shouting and arming themselves, more pouring from the tents above and running toward the beach. All was going according to the plan he'd worked out with MacDougall and Leod and the Ross men, who'd proved surprisingly willing to follow his plan. They'd been unconvinced at first, but agreed; and now proved as good as their word.

And there, in the camp, stood the man who must be Nor Thorkelson.

There was no mistaking him. He strode out of the most substantial hut with a battle-axe in one hand and a helmet in the other. His walk was a swagger, his shoulders were wide, and his stance arrogant. Long blond hair streamed down his back. Nor walked quickly to the shore, watching two of the Scottish ships take on his sentry ships stationed at the neck of the passage, then donned his helmet.

Gannon watched for a moment more while the four ships struggled, pleased to see that at least one of Nor's ships was getting the worst of it. The MacDougall and Ross ships slid closer, Leod's ships just behind, almost at the shore now and still untouched, while Nor's men struggled to get their ships in the water. Gannon waited, knowing what would happen next, then smiled grimly as the rain of flaming arrows flew from the Scottish ships, landing on the beach and in Nor's ships, setting at least one of the sails aflame.

The Scottish ships moved closer and let off another volley, these landing farther up the shore, igniting the tents and scattering the defenders. Gannon jumped to his feet then, giving the signal for his men to follow. He smelled the burning canvas and ran even faster. If he'd been wrong, and Margaret was in one of those tents, he had only moments to save her. He could hear the bellows of rage from the beach, followed by orders given in a harsh shout. Nor, it seemed, objected to his brand of warfare. Gannon spared a glance at the shore, pleased to see the sails of two of Nor's ships were aflame and the Scottish ships landing, men pouring from them.

He ran toward the women's screams, shouting Margaret's name. Overhead the third and last volley of flaming arrows hit the encampment, and he watched the sky lest he be hit. No more would be coming. And none needed, for the camp was fully on fire. He slashed through the tops of the first two tents he reached, finding them empty. Behind him his men were doing the same. He left them there and ran toward the crude hut where the women were held, their screams loud, their hands thrust between the tree limbs that served as walls.

"Margaret!" he shouted, reaching for the door.

From nowhere a huge man leapt atop him, the women's guard, he realized as he fell, the giant atop him.

"No!" Nor shouted, as the tents behind him burst into flame. He cursed the rock below them, which provided no defense, and the constant wind that had sucked all moisture from the oiled canvas. They were like torches now, the tents. The huts were slower to burn, and his own shelter was still intact. Nor's men ran to douse the flames. The women in the prisoner's hovel screamed as the structure was hit.

"Let it burn!" Nor shouted. "Let it all burn!"

They could rebuild shelters and get more prisoners. It was the attackers who needed to be faced. They were pouring from the ships, shields held before them, far more men than he'd ever thought the Irishman could have mustered, far more men than he had himself. Scots in their ridiculous skirts, the Irish in their long tunics and trousers, and Norsemen, for they could be nothing else. Well-armed men with spears and swords and battle-axes, many dressed in chain-mail shirts or leather-padded armor. Somehow, in hours rather than the weeks he'd anticipated, an alliance had been formed. He'd not thought they could accomplish that until the war between Haakon and Alexander was over—when he'd planned to be far away. Damn the man who had accomplished this.

Nor shouted for his men to gather behind him, heard the clink of metal on metal, the thud of wooden shields. Up the slope the women were screaming, horses shrilling and battering against their pens, and above all was the crackle of flames. Below him Gannon's force moved steadily through what was left of his men on the beach. Damn the man. He raised his axe and gave the order, then led the charge. Apparently he would have to dispatch Magnusson himself.

* * *

Outside the hut, Gannon pushed the man's weight from him and rose to his feet. The guard, his throat slit, hit the ground with a thud.

Drason Anderson grinned and wiped his bloody sword on the man's clothing. "I never did like him."

"Thank ye," Gannon said, and yanked the door of the hut off its straps. The women poured from the enclosure, wild-eyed and crying. He handed them past him to his waiting men. "Margaret! Where's Margaret?"

A girl pointed up the hill, to the one structure still standing. "He took her there yesterday. We've not seen her since."

Gannon sprinted up the hill, hearing his men at his heels. He burst through the door and was greeted with silence.

"Margaret!"

There was no answer. But at the far end of the room, atop the bed there, lay a naked woman, unmoving, her face turned away, her head covered. The room stank of death.

He prayed as he moved closer, and for once his prayers were answered. Dagmar, not Margaret, lay dead on the bed. He stared at her for a moment, then threw the bed-covers over her before he left, wondering if the gods thought this a fitting death for her.

Margaret was not in any of the tents—all burnt or slashed open now—not in the few huts that were not burning. Pigs ran by him, squealing their panic, and he could hear horses somewhere in the smoke that was already clearing.

Down in the water, the Scots had done their jobs well. Four of Nor's ships were ablaze, pushed into the middle of the loch, where they drifted with the tide, headed for the rocks at the bottom of the northern cliffs. And on the beach the Scottish forces had almost subdued the Norsemen, who were retreating up the hill to the encampment, rushing headlong into Gannon and his waiting men. He whirled to avoid a blow from one of them, then sank his sword into flesh.

He was surrounded then, by his own men and Drason, who somehow managed always to be at his side, and by Nor's men, some of whom he recognized from their imprisonment at Inverstrath. He killed one, then another who had targeted Drason. He worked his way through them like a scythe through barley. And suddenly there were no more to fight, at least not here.

Drason gave him a ferocious grin and lifted his sword. "Let's find my uncle."

Margaret smothered her cry of pain as the men cinched the rope that bound her hands tighter; her arms were pulled behind her and the rope secured again. She'd fought, kicking and screaming and even biting, when they'd pulled her through the camp, past the hovel that held the women, and toward the path that topped the cliffs. She tried wrenching herself from their grip, but had failed. One had hit her then, and again when she'd risen. He threw her over his shoulder and carried her far beyond the camp, up to the windswept bluff above the loch.

Still she resisted, and eventually he tossed her on the ground before an isolated standing stone that overlooked the loch, the sort that women long ago had offered sacrifices to in order to ensure fertility. For a wild moment, when they lashed her to the gray stone, whose surface was carved with fantastical animals, she thought they meant to sacrifice her, but the Norsemen were cursing her in their strange language.

No, they weren't cursing her, for they were staring down into the loch, where ships were pouring in from the passage to the sea. Two of Nor's ships had moved to close the entrance, but one had been so damaged that it was sinking, while the other drifted slowly around the loch, empty, its sail aflame. On the shore near the camp some of Nor's ships were burning. And on the slope above, men fought in hand-to-hand combat.

Gannon.

She could not tell if he was among them. There were Scots and Irish, she could tell by their dress, but it seemed as though Norsemen were fighting on both sides and so many men were blond or wore helmets that it was impossible to be sure. The shouts and sounds of battle could be heard even here, and she watched, but had no idea whom she was watching.

Her captors turned to the rocks on her right. Norsemen were pouring over the rise, their cries harsh and axes raised as they rushed toward her. She screamed, expecting to be cut down, but was left untouched as they passed by her without a glance and attacked Nor's men. The struggle was brief; both men were cut down quickly. Then the Norsemen turned to her, and the world seemed to stop.

Let it come, she told herself. But despite her brave thoughts, she shrank back when the closest man moved toward her with a drawn knife.

Her bonds were cut and tossed on the ground.

"Leod sends his regards, miss," he said with the unmistakable accent of a Skye man. "Go north. Ye'll be given shelter at Dunvegan." He raised his arm to his companions, leading them toward the melee without a backward glance at her.

She followed them, running as quickly as she could, faster when more arrows rained flame on the encampment. She could hear the women's screams from here, and darted to the left when cattle rampaged past her, their eyes wild with fear. A horse ran toward the mountains, whirled to face the water, then whirled again, neighing shrilly as it raced away. She ran on, panting now, passing camp followers who stared at her as though she were mad to be returning instead of running, and perhaps she was, but she would not stand and watch.

The Inverstrath women running toward her tried to stop her, to get her to run inland with them, but she shook herself free. "No! Gannon is there," she cried. "And Davey! Have any of ye seen Davey?"

They shook they heads and tried again to persuade her to go with them, but she ran on, toward the burning encampment.

Gannon reached the water, then turned again and fought his way back up the slope, looking for Nor. He could no longer count the men he'd killed. Nor's forces were whittled away to small spots of resistance, many of the others left fleeing up the slope.

It was then, when the ranks had thinned and the battle was all but over, that he saw Nor. The Norseman stood above him on the edge of the encampment with what was left of his troops. He looked exactly as Gannon had imagined him, in his middle years, lean and strong, battle-axe in hand. He looked both fit and ruthless, his eyes narrowing as he watched the fighting on the water.

"Is that Nor?" he asked Drason, who was still shadowing him.

"It's him," Drason said, a strange note in his voice.

Gannon raised his sword high. "Nor Thorkelson! I await ye!"

Nor shifted his gaze and looked down at Gannon with a wolfish grin. "And I you, Gannon Magnusson. And Drason at your side. Of course."

"Uncle," Drason said defiantly.

Gannon gave the boy a sharp glance, no longer doubting that revenge was what drove him; he'd seen that look before. He turned back to Nor. Drason might justifiably lust for Nor's blood, but the honors would be his own.

"Are ye," Gannon called, sensing his men gathering behind him, "the same Nor Thorkelson who ran from Inverstrath?"

Nor's grin faded a bit. "Who burned Inverstrath to the ground."

"Who murdered innocent people at Somerstrath?"

"Who killed your brother. He begged for his life before he died, Magnusson. Did you know that? Your brother shamed himself and your line with his groveling."

It was not true; Gannon knew it. Still, it took a moment for him to control his rage. It would be so easy to rush forward, blinded by his thirst for this man's blood, but he would not be so easily manipulated. There was a sudden silence as Gannon and Nor stared at each other.

They gave their signals to their men at the same moment, steel meeting steel. Steel meeting flesh. Men died quickly. Gannon shouted to his men as he moved forward again. Their battle cries echoing off the cliffs. He met Nor in the middle of the melee. Nor wasted no time, leaning into a wide swing. Gannon leapt back, and the axe cut only through air. They circled each other then, ignoring the fighting raging behind them, the shouts of triumph from the beach.

Gannon leaned into his thrust, his blade clashing against Nor's, the impact shivering down his arm. He struck again, his blow met again, the sound of metal on metal shimmering above them. Again, this time lower, slashing through the leather padding that covered Nor's thigh. And drawing blood at last.

"That was for Tiernan," Gannon said. "One of many."

Nor did not even look at his leg. He didn't need to; he could feel the wound, could feel the warm blood that seeped through his trousers. But he would be damned before he'd let this Irishman see that he was in pain.

Both he and Gannon stepped back, breathing deeply, then rushed forward again. This time Nor's axe grazed Gannon's shoulder, laying the flesh open. Gannon slashed low again, meeting Nor's thigh for the second time, but still Nor managed to keep his feet, willing himself not to feel the pain.

"Where is she?" Gannon demanded. "Where is Margaret MacDonald?"

Nor grinned. Predictable. "Gone." He stepped forward, but Gannon jumped out of range of the swing that would have decapitated him.

"Where is she?"

"I used her. Then gave her to my men. They buried what was left."

Gannon's mouth drew back in a snarl and he leapt forward, delivering blow after crashing blow. It took all of Nor's strength to defend himself. He felt himself weakening. But then, above from the encampment, Leod's battle cry. Reinforcements, Nor thought, his strength returning. He'd have Gannon's head on a spike yet. His heart stopped as he realized that Leod's men were not coming to aid his men, but to murder them.

The battle here would soon be lost. He would have to be swift.

Leod's men ran through the middle of the knot of fighters, forcing Gannon and Nor back from each other. When they'd passed, Gannon was on the other side of the fighting, his attention caught by one of Nor's best.

Nor stepped back and looked around. His ships were afire, burning on the beach. His camp was in ruins, and, more important, so were his troops. How could these be the same men who had fought so well at his side in earlier battles? How could they have collapsed so quickly under this siege? They'd failed him. He owed them nothing. He spun around and battled his way up the hill. And then, standing directly before him was Gannon.

His rage exploded. This man had thwarted him at every turn, and here he was again. Nor stepped forward, felt the gash in his thigh burn, and swung blindly. His axe met only air, and he called to one of his men for help. Miraculously, the man did as he was bidden, attacking Gannon from the back. As Gannon spun around, Nor took the chance the gods offered, sprinting up the last of the slope.

He skirted the ruined tents and hut, did not even give his own shelter a glance, but hurried along the path that ran along the cliffs. He'd get to Dunvegan overland and abuse Leod's hospitality one more time. Or, he thought, remembering that Leod was now the enemy, he'd steal one of Leod's ships and spread the word throughout the Norse world. Leod would pay dearly for his perfidy. Before Nor was finished, Haakon himself would avenge Leod's betrayal.

Margaret ran through the deserted camp. All was in ruins, not a tent still standing, the pens that had held the pigs and cattle and horses all broken open. The hut where the women had been imprisoned was doorless and empty, the guard dead just outside. She'd passed more of the Inverstrath women—and some of Nor's men—fleeing inland.

But no Gannon. No Davey. There was only one structure left standing—Nor's—and she hurried up the hill toward it.

The door hung open, swaying in the sudden wind that came from the north, pushing the last of the smoke away from the encampment, letting her see the destruction. Nothing moved there, no man or animal left alive. The fighting continued on the slope below, only a small band of men remained, none she recognized. But there, on the path that ran along the cliffs, a man hurried northward, limping, an axe hanging from his hand. Nor? But no, surely Nor was not running from his own battle. She hurried up the steps and into the hut.

"Davey?"

There was only silence in answer to her call. No small boy came out of hiding; there was no sign of him here. The chair where Nor had sat like a king was empty. But the bed on the far side of the room was not.

Dagmar had died struggling, that much was obvious. Her throat was mottled, her eyes bulging, and Margaret's stomach heaved. Despite all the times she'd wished this woman ill, she'd never have chosen this. Margaret leaned over, her breaths coming in huge, gulping gasps. Then she straightened. Davey was not here, not anywhere in the encampment. No one had seen him.

And with a sudden certainty, she knew he'd never been here, that he'd been a lure Nor had used to try to gain her cooperation. And that it had been Nor running along the cliffs. She spun on her heel.

Gannon pulled his blade from the man's throat and whirled around, looking wildly for Nor. He was not here among the dead, not among those held at sword point by Gannon's Irish.

"Do ye see him?" he called to his men. "Nor? D'ye see him anywhere?"

"There!" One of the men shouted, pointing to the pathway that ran along the top of the cliffs. "He's leaving, the swine!"

Gannon followed the man's gaze. Nor was limping, he saw with savage delight, but still moving quickly. *Bastard's deserting his own men.* Gannon ran past the last of the tents and along the rocky top of the cliffs. The path was well-defined, but old, rutted, dotted with sparse clumps of plants, showing how seldom it had been used. Ahead was the guardian standing stone of the loch, and beyond it, on the northern rim, Nor still ran. Gannon increased his speed, feeling his shoulder wound burn as he hefted his axe in one hand, his sword in the other. One of them was about to die.

He could hear footsteps behind him and threw a glance over his shoulder, not surprised to see Drason following him, the boy's jaw clenched in fury.

"He's mine!" Drason shouted, lifting his sword arm high. "Let me kill him!"

Gannon concentrated on catching Nor. If possible, he'd let the boy have a swing at his uncle, but he himself would see the Norseman dead. Below, the water rippled in the sudden breeze, Nor's ships, one still burning, were spun closer to the rocks beneath the cliffs.

He could hear Nor's breathing now, labored but still strong. And then he was there, just behind Nor, who turned to meet him, lips drawn back in a feral smile. Nor raised his axe, swinging at Gannon with surprising speed. Gannon jumped out of the way and whirled around, delivering a blow to Nor's side. The angle was wrong, and the blade bounced off Nor's chain mail instead of going through it, but the Norseman staggered backward.

"Nor!" Drason shouted, racing past Gannon. "You filthy swine! You killed my father and Thorfinn. And you thought no one knew. But I did."

Nor's smile was self-satisfied. "And who is left to challenge me now? You? A boy too afraid to do battle?"

With a roar, Drason lunged at Nor, his blows raining on his uncle's shoulders, but deflected by the chain mail. The boy, Gannon realized, was not able to deliver enough force to pierce the mail. Nor raised his arm, and Gannon shoved the boy aside, stepping forward to intercept Nor's blow with his own. The shock of the impact sent them both reeling, Nor spinning close to the cliff edge, silhouetted against the blue of the water behind him.

* * *

Margaret looked at the men on the beach, but did not see Gannon there; nor was he among those who stood on the slope, where the battle was now over. And he was not, she breathed a prayer of thanks for it, among the dead being laid out on the shingle. She looked along the cliff path, where Nor was—no longer alone. Nor stood, his back to the cliff, facing Gannon. To Gannon's right Drason was climbing to his feet. Nor slashed at Gannon, the diagonal swing of his axe catching the sun; Gannon's blade met Nor's above their heads. The men leaned forward, each trying to break the other's grip, then staggered backward as the blades slipped apart.

Gannon was alive. She ran to him, through the last of the encampment and up the path to the cliffs. She was praying out loud when she passed the standing stone, and pressed her hand on it, praying to its spirit as well, just in case the old gods lingered here. And then she ran on. Gannon and Nor were of a height, both strong men. Gannon was younger; Nor was heavier. More ruthless.

The two men faced each other, but they'd shifted positions, their sides to the cliff now. Gannon raised his arm. And saw her. He paused. And Nor moved.

"Gannon, look out!" she screamed.

It happened all at once. She reached them just as Nor's arm swung up, his blow catching not Gannon, but bouncing off the shield that Drason, darting between them, held high, using it to shelter himself as he struck at Nor's middle with his sword, his shout of triumph ringing across the loch. He stepped back, glaring at Nor.

Nor staggered backward. Then, with a visible effort, raised his arm again. Gannon pushed the boy aside, thrusting at Nor. The blade hit home, piercing the chain mail just below Nor's arm, and again. Nor gave a grunt of surprise and stared at Gannon, his arm falling slowly and all color leaving his face. Gannon held the blade to the tender skin of Nor's neck, above the chain mail.

"May ye burn in Hell for yer evil deeds, Nor Thorkelson," Gannon said.

"Only in your dreams, Irishman," Nor grunted, his voice weaker. He dropped the axe and clutched his side, blood streaming down him now. "Damn you."

With a snarl, Drason gave Nor a shove, to the rim of the cliff. "Damn you, Nor!" he shouted, and shoved again.

Nor swayed. Margaret could see the realization in his eyes that he was about to fall. Nor's head tilted back. As he tumbled into the air, he grabbed Gannon's shirt and pulled him forward.

They fell over the edge together.

The last thing Gannon heard before the water closed over his head was Margaret's scream. And then all was cold and dark as he struggled. Alone, for Nor was not here. He stretched his arms wide, kicking and pushing toward the surface, but sank deeper.

He'd failed and death was at hand. Water seeped beneath his clothing, heartless liquid fingers sucking the last of his breath from his lungs and catching at his legs, the weight of the chain mail he wore pulling him relentlessly down. His limbs were too heavy to raise. He looked up at the light one last time. *Margaret.*

TWENTY-FOUR

Margaret did not know how many times she screamed, nor how she got to the edge of the cliff, but she was there, leaning to look, Drason clutching her back from the rim. They stared down together and she screamed Gannon's name again.

There was no answer, no reassuring call from him, just a groan from Nor and the raucous cries of the seagulls circling overhead.

"Gannon!"

Nor was still not dead. He would be soon, though, for no one could live impaled on a mast. One of Nor's own ships had drifted beneath the cliff, its mast tapered at the top, the wood piercing his middle. Nor was moving, his arms flailing slowly, his head lifting to stare across the water. She screamed again at the horror of it, at the realization that Gannon was not on the ship but gone under the water.

Drason released her, dropping his sword, and without a word, dove into the icy waters next to the ship, the wave closing over him as it must have over Gannon. Suddenly there were men everywhere, next to her, and on the shore to her left, and in *Gannon's Lady,* being pushed off the beach, men pointing to where Gannon had disappeared beneath the waves. She fell to her knees, tears streaming down her cheeks, praying.

It is not your time, the whispers said. *Go back. It is not your time.*

Gannon gained another foot, then another, rising toward the light. But the chain mail dragged him back down. He ached with every movement. It would be so simple to just let himself sink, to find sweet sleep and to rest.

Margaret is waiting, the whispers said. *Go back.*

He fought the weariness and the cold, yanking the mail over his head with a strength he did not know he still had, ignoring his burning lungs and the stabs of pain from his shoulder. He let the chain mail fall from his hand; it sank immediately from sight. He pushed himself toward the surface.

His hand broke through, then his head. He filled his lungs with air.

"Gannon! Here!"

It was Drason's voice. He turned to see the boy in the water with him, gripping the side of Nor's charred ship, reaching his hand for Gannon to grab. And above Drason, impaled on the mast, was Nor, dropped against the wood, his body swaying with the motion of the ship.

"He's dead," Drason said unnecessarily, towing Gannon toward the ship.

"Gannon! Gannon! Dear God, thank ye! Gannon!"

He saw Margaret at once, leaning over the edge of the cliff, one of the Inverstrath men holding on to her arm. She waved frantically, and he raised his arm in a weak salute.

"Margaret!"

She was running toward the harbor. He was too weary to call to her again, too weary to do anything but hang on to the railing and be grateful for each breath of air. Drason pointed, and he followed the boy's gaze, to see *Gannon's Lady* approaching, full of his men. He looked from the ship to Margaret, running. *Gannon's Lady* and Gannon's lady. He lay back in the water and stared at the sky. And laughed. Nor was dead. And they were alive.

"Gannon! Sir!"

His ship was alongside him now, hands reaching to haul him aboard. And a few moments later he was delivered to the beach, to Margaret's waiting arms. He clasped her to him, breathing prayers of thanksgiving, catching sight over her head of the guardian stone at the end of the loch, hearing faint traces of whispers on the wind. To whoever, whatever, had protected them, he was grateful. He held her tighter, let her sob into his shoulder, his thoughts making him speechless. His near drowning had happened almost exactly as he'd dreamt it. In his dreams he'd failed. In life he had not. He had triumphed over death itself, and every breath seemed precious now.

Margaret turned in his arms. "My love," she said, and kissed his neck.

His heart was too full to speak. He pulled her hand to his mouth and kissed it, then held it in his own. She would heal him. And he her. They'd spend their lives together. He pulled her closer, and said a silent prayer of thanks.

Their homecoming at Inverstrath was bittersweet. Nell was waiting at the headland when they sailed into the harbor and met them on the beach, dancing with excitement, throwing her arms around Margaret, then bursting into tears when they told her they'd not found Davey, and worse, the news they'd learned from Nor's men, that Davey had disappeared.

"He could still be alive," Margaret told her, seeing in Nell's eyes that she found as little comfort in that as Margaret did.

The Inverstrath women, most unharmed, were delighted to be home, and the Inverstrath men proud of their part in returning them and destroying Nor and his fleet. Drason was hailed as a hero, the boy's delight in it obvious. But Inverstrath itself was gone, and the mood quickly sobered as they all realized that the simplest of things, like a warm bed and a supply of food, might be beyond them for a while.

MacDougall offered them shelter, and the people thanked him, but refused, saying they would stay. They waved to him and to the Ross ships as they departed, then turned to Gannon for direction. He told them that Inverstrath's village could be rebuilt and started on it at once with most of the men, sending others into the forest to hunt for food. And a runner to find a priest, for Margaret and Gannon intended to marry at once.

For four days all was quiet. On the fifth day a visitor came—not the anticipated priest, but a messenger from the king. Alexander's message was simple. Gannon was to come to him at once. And bring Margaret and Nell.

It took over a week to reach the king. They sailed south on *Gannon's Lady,* through the Sound of Mull and the Firth of Lorne, landing in a tiny village on Kintyre. From there they made their way overland and on small boats, skirting the waters where Haakon's fleet might be anchored, arriving in the early evening of a cold and rainy day in October. The king was billeted in the home of a local laird, the troops sent to him by the seven earls camped around him in a great circle.

Gannon had argued against going to Alexander, for he could think of only two reasons that they had been summoned: Margaret's betrothal and her family's deaths, and he'd not wanted to discuss either with the king. He feared that he was about to lose the woman he loved to Lachlan, that Alexander would order Margaret to marry him and Gannon to watch it yet again. He'd had no nightmares since their return to Inverstrath, and for the first time in years the whispers were silent. He felt unguided, wondering if his wishes that the dreams and whispers would leave him alone had at last had been granted. And if that was for the best.

He missed Tiernan. Life would never be same. He gave Nell the golden brooch that had been Tiernan's, telling her that it had been hammered by Thor himself. When she protested, sobbing, that he should keep it, he put a hand over his heart, telling her his brother would always be there. And that he knew Nell had loved him, too. She clasped the brooch in her hand and nodded, and he leaned to kiss her forehead.

He tried to be sanguine, telling himself that Alexander of Scotland held no authority over him, and that if need be, he'd steal Margaret off in the night and together they'd make a life in Ireland. He'd had to be content with that.

Alexander's encampment was large, a city of tents outside the home the king was using as his base camp. Queen Margaret had stayed at Stirling, but many of the courtiers had accompanied the king. Uncle William received them at once, telling them that Lachlan was there. Margaret's mood, already low, plummeted further. Gannon said nothing, but his expression gave his thoughts away, and she wondered yet again if they'd been foolish to come. How simple it would have been to slip away to Ireland and pretend never to have received the message. What had made her believe that putting them all in Alexander's power was wise?

The king sent word that he would receive them the next day, which did little to allay their anxiety. They stayed with Uncle William that night, in his camp, comfortable, but far from luxurious, talking for hours of all that had happened since they'd parted. William told them that Gannon was being hailed as "the hero of Inverstrath," the only man to have fought off the Norsemen and lived to tell of it, and Margaret's mood lightened. Surely the king would not force her now, not when all the talk was of Gannon's prowess.

They talked then of the seemingly endless rounds of negotiations between Haakon and Alexander.

"This is intentional on Alexander's part," William told them. "If the king wanted to end this, it would have been settled long ago. I think Alexander's waiting for the winter storms."

"Or for Haakon to die," Gannon said.

"Or for Haakon to die," William agreed.

It was midafternoon before they were summoned to the king, their nerves stretched taut with the wait. The audience was not private, as Gannon had hoped. The hall was filled with more than fifty people who strained to see him, Margaret, and Nell enter. Gannon looked across the gathering, finding Lachlan, as he'd known he would.

King Alexander was younger than Gannon had realized, not much older than Gannon himself. He greeted them cordially, which allayed some of Gannon's fears.

"We have heard of all you have suffered," Alexander said to them, "and are sorry for your losses."

Margaret and Nell thanked him. Gannon nodded.

"Gannon MacMagnus," Alexander said. "You come well recommended as a cousin of Rory O'Neill and a favorite of the Earl of Ross. Either man's endorsement would have been enough for us to take notice. Both means I need to discover more about you. No one else has defeated the Norsemen. You've done it twice. Tell me how."

Gannon described the battle at Inverstrath, then what happened on Skye, keeping the details sparse. But the king wanted to know more, questioning Gannon at length, asking for diagrams and maps, coming to stand at Gannon's side as he explained the victories. It took hours—and bored many in the court—but when the last question of the king's had been answered, Alexander smiled.

"We are grateful for your courage, and your service to Scotland," Alexander said, handing a scroll to Gannon. "I give you this as a token of that gratitude."

Those watching craned to see. Lachlan frowned. Margaret and Nell exchanged a look, and William Ross looked smug, as though he already knew what the scroll held.

"You can read?" the king asked, when Gannon did not unroll the parchment.

"I can, Yer Majesty," Gannon said. "And I am grateful

for your generosity. But I dinna want whatever this holds. There is only one thing I desire from ye."

"You are refusing my gift?"

Alexander's words were quiet; the murmur through the crowd was not.

"It is only a small gesture," the king said. "A grant of land on Skye, on the Trotternish Peninsula. Fitting, I thought, for a man who defeated the Norsemen there. And lands in Ayreshire. My motives are not pure. I understand you wished to have land of your own and had hoped with this gift to keep you here in Scotland. I'm sure Rory O'Neill will forgive me in time."

Gannon paused, then nodded. "It's true, Yer Majesty, I have dreamed of my own land. But I ask that ye keep the land and grant me something else instead."

There was silence in the room. Margaret put a hand to her throat. William Ross looked worried. Lachlan was smiling.

The king studied Gannon for a moment. "What is it you desire?"

"I ask ye to release Margaret MacDonald from her betrothal to Lachlan Ross."

The silence stretched longer this time. Margaret swore she could hear her heart beat.

"I love her," Gannon said. "I would marry her."

He ignored the murmurs that followed, the smiles of the women who listened, the speculative glances thrown at him and Margaret. He ignored all of it.

As did the king.

Alexander nodded thoughtfully. "I have heard this. Lady Margaret," he said, shifting his gaze, "you do realize that you are now Somerstrath? Your father and brothers are dead. The title and the lands are yours now, and I would see you well married."

Margaret nodded. "I will marry no one but Gannon, my lord."

The king looked at Gannon again. "If you were to marry her, would you stay in Scotland?"

"If she wishes it, my lord."

"Then it's done," Alexander said lightly. "Have both, MacMagnus, the land and the woman. I wish you well of them. I will have the papers drawn up immediately. I ask that you wed at once, but stay and talk with me and my generals in greater detail about fighting the Norsemen. And when this war is over you'll come to court, both of you." He looked at Nell. "All of you."

Gannon thanked him profusely. Alexander smiled and waved his words away. "Be gone, MacMagnus. I have a Norse king to irritate before the day is done. But don't go far. Lachlan Ross, don't look so glum. There are other women." He rose and ended the audience.

Outside the hall, Gannon lifted Margaret into his arms and whirled them both around, laughing. "Marry me now, before I wake. Will ye, lass?"

Margaret laughed again. "Aye and aye and a thousand times aye."

She kissed him while the courtiers smiled and clapped. And again when Nell wept with joy. And again.

Gannon and Margaret were married the next morning, in a simple service given by a proper priest, with Nell and William Ross, who had given his blessing, in attendance. There was a third uninvited guest—an ancient woman who smiled on their union.

Margaret, who thought the day could not be improved, smiled and embraced the woman. "Ye told me at Stirling this would happen, d'ye remember? Ye said we would meet at a court that was not a court."

The old woman smiled and lifted a cup in their honor. "May your union be blessed. May it be happy and fruitful, for in your children lies the future of Scotland. May your home be filled with the laughter of children and of your children's children, and may you have the wisdom both to treasure those days and prepare for others. May you find solace in each other when the wind blows ill, and joy when the sun shines upon you. May you never forget this moment, when love is your prize for courage. May your line continue into the future, to bring honor and love to other peoples and other lands, but may they never forget from whence they came. It is through them that you will live forever."

"Amen," William said, and they all laughed, then drank deeply.

With a wink to Nell, the woman left them staring after her.

"Another toast," William said. "To love."

They drank deeply again. Margaret looked at the splendid man who was hers. I've found it, she thought, the love of legends.

We dinna choose what God sends us, child, any more than we choose our own name. Margaret you are, and Margaret you will be, and your life will be formed by that. You'll face dragons.

Margaret smiled. She had. And won.

EPILOGUE

After being defeated at the Battle of Largs later that month, Haakon of Norway's fleet retreated, never to return. Three years later, in 1266, the Treaty of Perth was signed, making the Isle of Skye and the other Hebrides Islands part of Scotland, as they still are. Haakon sailed only as far as the Orkneys, where he died in December.

Leod lived to a great age, founding what became the Clan MacLeod. His home at Dunvegan on the Isle of Skye became in time a castle, which still stands. William Ross lived to see his grandchildren. His line still prospers.

Neither Somerstrath nor Inverstrath was ever rebuilt. The Inverstrath and Somerstrath people were delighted that Margaret inherited the title and welcomed Gannon with joy. Most of Gannon's men stayed with him in Scotland, marrying and building new lives, and Rory O'Neill eventually forgave Gannon for leaving Ireland.

Gannon and Margaret thrived in their new home and lived a full and peaceful life. Their love grew with the decades, and their descendants roamed the Earth, but never forgot their origins. They built a stone fortress that stood for almost five hundred years, and a small stone chapel in which to baptize their first child, a healthy boy they named Alexander after the king. The name stayed in the family for centuries. In time the fortress became known as Kilgannon, or Gannon's church.

And Davey and Nell . . . but that's another story.

AUTHOR'S NOTE

I mixed factual and fictional events, places, and people freely in this story and have done my best to make my depiction close to the spirit, if not the letter, of the past. When faced with diverging records of the same event or person, I shamelessly used the one that best suited my story.

William Ross, the third Earl of Ross, did exist, and in 1263 was one of Scotland's most important leaders. He was married to Jean Comyn and oversaw the western coast of Scotland. He led the right flank of King Alexander's army at the Battle of Largs and was less favorably known for invading Skye a few months earlier than I placed it (reports vary, both of the timing and the severity of his attack). The William Ross who emerged from my research proved to be far from the ruthless and cruel man often depicted. It seemed entirely plausible that William might have a sister and nieces and nephews, and that he might have invaded Skye for what he thought was an excellent reason. I have provided my own reason for him, entirely invented. William took the blame for that raid, although we all know it was Gannon's doing.

The MacDonald clan then controlled the area in which Margaret and Nell and their family lived. Somerstrath and Inverstrath are compilations of some of the beautiful coastline of western Scotland. The Isle of Skye and the Orkney Islands are real, as was Leod, reported to be intelligent, wily, and unpredictable. He was half-Scot, Half-Norse, which served him well all his life. He founded the Clan MacLeod, the home of which is still Dunvegan Castle on Skye. In 1266 the Treaty of Perth was signed, placing the control of the Hebrides Islands, including Skye, into the hands of the king of Scotland. Leod's son married William Ross's granddaughter Dorothea.

Harald Hardrata, from whom Gannon and Tiernan are to have descended, was real, a notoriously ruthless king of Norway, and his descendants settled in several parts of Ireland. The O'Neill who led Ulster in 1263 was said to be fair, courageous, and closely allied to Scotland. I found conflicting first names for him and chose Rory simply because I liked it. Whatever his name, his bloodlines still run through those in Northern Ireland, both green and orange.

Men like Nor did roam the seas at that time, and there was a brief, cruel, and short-lived series of raids on Scotland and Ireland in 1262 and 1263, which ended, never to be repeated, after the Battle of Largs. King Alexander III of Scotland and King Haakon of Norway both are factual, and the real events of Haakon's invasion of Ayrshire and Alexander's repulsion of that attempt were perfect for my story. After his defeat in Scotland, Haakon limped back to Kirkwall, in Orkney, where he died. He never saw Norway again.

Alexander inherited the throne in 1249, at the age of

eight. He reigned under regents, then on his own. He out-lived his wife and children and died tragically in 1286, plunging Scotland into the turmoil that would later lead to King Edward of England's seizure of Scotland, William Wallace's rebellion, and Robert the Bruce and an inde-pendent Scotland.

ACKNOWLEDGMENTS

My thanks go to Maggie Crawford, Louise Burke, Anne Dowling, and the entire Pocket team for making the process so painless. To Russ and Cheryl, for reading every generation of this novel with their usual thoroughness and gentle guidance.

To Forrest, MJ, Enrique, Michael, Matthew, Ron/Nor, and Valerie, who cheered me on through some interesting times. To Joe Markowitz, Bill Halle, and the flawless Dr. Michael Kinsman for their integrity, friendship, and support above and beyond. To Sherri, for reading and encouraging me, and Dinah, who helped me keep perspective. To Pam, who said it would be like this, and Bob, Gwen, Nikki and Kim, Bev, and all the kids, for the good times. To Rick and Mary, Jeanne and Don, Jeanne, Susie and Mike, and The Lunch Bunch, for their insight into human behavior and a ready shoulder when I needed it.

To Dick Francis for his encouragement and kind words, and to Barbara and Ed for their amazing hurricane stories and for being survivors as well as great book people. To Nancy and Charles for all the Tea and

Sympathy. To Monica McCarty, for being my personal shopper in Scotland.

To Ann McKenzie Stansbarger and Barbara McKenzie of the Clan MacKenzie Society in the Americas, and Alan McKenzie, of the Canadian Chapter of the Clan McKenzie Society and Lieutenant to Caberfeidh, and to the Clans MacDonald and Ross, for their assistance in research. And to the memory of Steve McKenzie, Past President of the Clan McKenzie Society, a wonderful resource, gentleman, and friend.

To all those readers with generous hearts who wrote to encourage me: I thank you profoundly.

Pocket Books proudly presents

RIVALS FOR THE CROWN

KATHLEEN GIVENS

Coming in July 2007

**Please turn the page for a preview of
Kathleen Givens's enthralling new
historical novel featuring the next
generation of the MacGannons and
the MacDonalds. . . .**

Rory MacGannon waited in the rain at the Tower landing, where the ferryboat would bring Isabel from Westminster. Two boats arrived, then a third, with her on none of them. He felt like a fool and stepped back under the cover of the nearest shop, telling himself that if she were not on the next boat, he would leave.

When the next boat came, she was on it. But not alone.

Henry de Boyer leapt to the dock, reaching back to help her out instead of the ferryman, who watched them with a crooked smile. She smiled at de Boyer and let him lead her to the small square near the street, where she stood in a pool of sudden sunshine. She pushed the hood off her head and looked left, then right, her simple skirts swaying from her hips as she moved, her light brown hair gleaming in the sunlight. De Boyer said something to her that made her laugh, and Rory peeled himself from the shop wall, striding quickly forward.

He stopped before her and bowed. "Mistress de Burke, I thought perhaps ye had forgotten."

She whirled to face him, her face brightening as she saw him. "Oh! Good! I thought I was too late and that you had gone. Or perhaps not come at all."

"I would not have missed this, demoiselle."

"I am so very sorry to have been delayed," she said, her words rushed. "I was asked to do several tasks, and everything seemed to take forever. I came as quickly as I could."

"I'm glad of it, mistress. And dinna worry about yer letter. I'm sending it north with John Comyn. He assures me it will be delivered to your cousin in Berwick."

"Even better news," she said. "You here and my letter on its way."

"A cousin in Berwick, demoiselle?" de Boyer said. "One of your father's relations?"

She gave de Boyer a wary glance. "Yes," she said, then turned back to Rory. "You do remember Sir Henry de Boyer, sir?"

"No," Rory said. "Nice to meet ye, de Boyer."

Henry de Boyer nodded. "We met at the palace, MacGannon. I would have thought you on your way north already. Scotland is very far from London."

"Och, no, I'm staying all winter. Is that not grand?"

Isabel's smile was delighted.

De Boyer's smile was slow and appraising. "Why do you stay, MacGannon? Does John Comyn always keep his lackeys here in London?"

"I dinna ken. I'll ask him. I am here to see the sights, sir. And are they not magnificent?" He smiled at Isabel, then turned back to de Boyer. "D'ye mean to spend the afternoon with us? I am delighted, of course, if ye are. But I am surprised that ye keep seeking me out."

De Boyer laughed. "I assure you, sir, that it is not your company I seek. No, I have an appointment elsewhere. Demoiselle, I will meet you here for your return as we agreed." He met Rory's gaze. "We see each other daily, of course, living as we do so close together at court."

"Do ye now?"

"We do." De Boyer bowed over Isabel's hand. "Until later."

She smiled. "Enjoy your tryst, sir."

De Boyer looked startled, then smiled. "Enjoy your walk, demoiselle."

"I am sure I will."

They stood together, he and Isabel, watching de Boyer walk briskly away. Rory wondered briefly if Isabel was using him to make the other man jealous. And how he could make the most of that. He turned to her with another smile.

"Good to see ye, lass. I was afraid ye'd been warned away from me."

"We made a bargain, sir, and I always keep my word."

"Do ye? Good to ken that. Ye look bonnie. I like yer hair loose like that."

"Thank you, sir. Now, tell me, why will you stay in London?"

"I'm being hunted in Scotland and am here for my health."

"I do not understand."

"Nor do I, to tell ye the truth. But tell me, lass, how is it Henry de Boyer appears every time I see ye? Ye seem to be well-acquainted."

"Henry is one of the king's household knights, and I was one of the queen's ladies. There is nothing more between us."

"Ah. I'm glad of it. But he is escorting ye back to Westminster."

"There is nothing to that, sir. We were on the same boat coming here and he asked me what time I would be returning."

"And is he truly off to a tryst? Do the two of ye talk of such things?"

Her laugh was brittle. "It was my poor attempt at wit, sir. I have no idea of his plans, nor who he is meeting."

Rory nodded, but was not convinced. He'd seen the looks thrown between the two of them, seen the surprise on de Boyer's face at her remark, the caustic note in her voice. There was something between them, perhaps something unrealized, but still there.

"Tell me," he said, "how can ye still have duties if the queen is dead?"

"I've been asked to do small things. To start packing her clothing. It won't last. One day I'll be told my services are no longer needed."

"And ye'll go home to yer family?"

"My family is here, my mother, and my grand-mother."

"And yer father?"

"Dead. And you?"

"One brother, many cousins, of which Kieran is one. Two parents, two aunts, two uncles. That is my family. So what will ye do, when yer services are no longer needed?"

"I have no idea. Where shall we walk, sir?"

He smiled at her. "Ye ken the city and I'm the stranger. What should I see?"

"What have you seen already?"

"We were at Westminster Abbey for the funeral, as ye ken. And we were at the funeral banquet afterward."

"Were you? I didn't see you there."

"Why would ye? Ye were dining with the king's party and we were among the invisible Scots."

"I'm still surprised I did not see you. You are . . . notable, sir."

"Am I? Trust me, lass, I am of no significance here in London."

"Nor I." She shivered at a sudden blast of wind. "Now, where shall we go?"

"Somewhere within walls? Could ye show me the Tower, at least from the outside? Then we'll find somewhere warm."

"Oh!" She seemed to ponder something, then nodded. "Of course. But we'll go into the grounds. I'll be pleased to show it to you."

She led the way up the slight hill from the water, then along a narrow and cramped street, keeping under the shelter of the houses that leaned toward each other from either side, lifting her skirts high to step over a puddle. He enjoyed the view of her leg above the short leather boots she wore, then took her arm to pull her against the wall while a cart laden with fish rumbled past them, enjoying the feel of her next to him. He looked down at her, at the curves of her body, soft and desirable. No wonder de Boyer was attentive.

"How is it," he asked, "that ye and Rachel Angenhoff are friends?"

"Her family lived near my grandmother. We met as small girls and played together, and we continued to be friends as we grew. What did she tell you?"

"The same thing. And that she had to leave London suddenly. They were expelled, aye?"

"Yes." Her face flushed with color. "How horrid is that, that they were driven from London because they are Jews! I was going to ask the queen for her help in rescinding the expulsion, but, of course, I cannot now."

"Probably wise that ye dinna, and I wouldna put it to the king, were I ye."

"No. Nor will I have the chance."

"I'll probably see him before ye do."

"Why, sir? Are you acquainted?"

"No. But I think yer king wants my country and I think he means to have it."

"Surely he simply means to help you find a king. And why is it that your people have not been able to do that?"

"We have two factions and everyone has chosen sides and willna relent. Neither side is willing to let the other rule, and can ye blame them? There's a throne at stake, and a great deal of money and power. And that's why yer king is 'helping.' He's put his own name on the list of competitors, has he not? If he thought the Scots would accept him, he'd be ruling us now."

"Would that not at least bring peace to your country? I mean no insult, sir, but would it not be better for all if our countries were united?"

"Let me ask ye this, lass. What would happen to yer friend if England and Scotland were united? Would she and her family then be driven from Scotland as well?"

"No . . . I don't know," she said hesitantly. "But, sir, may I remind you that King Edward generally gets what he goes after."

"Aye. Ask the Welsh, right?"

She nodded. They talked then of their families, of the

differences between Scotland and London. She told him of her grandmother's illegitimacy, and of the lady-in-waiting named Alis, who had betrayed her trust. And her fears for the future, that she and her mother might be turned out into the street.

"For what need does a king have of a queen's lady, or a queen's seamstress, if there is no queen?" she asked.

"Now," he said. "Perhaps, King Edward is planning to marry again and he wants all of ye to stay to attend his new queen."

Her eyes widened. "Oh, no! Surely he won't remarry! I may despise what the king did, but he was devoted to Eleanor, and to his daughters. And he has a son and heir. He does not need to remarry. How could he? They were married for thirty-six years. He loved her. And she was devoted to him. You've heard the story of how she saved his life in the Holy Land?"

"No." Rory looked over her shoulder. Had he not seen that same man at the dock earlier? The man was of middle height, middle weight, and middle age. Rory almost laughed at himself, but what better person to spy on another than a man easily lost in a crowd? He would look for the man again later, he thought, and turned his attention to Isabel once again, enjoying her bright eyes and lively tone.

"It's such an amazing story! King Edward was struck by a poisoned arrow and he was dying. No one knew what to do, but Eleanor pulled the arrow out of him and sucked the poison from the wound and saved his life! Is that not the most romantic story?"

"Ye think it romantic when a woman sucks the poison out of a man? So would most men."

She took two steps, then stopped and faced him, her cheeks scarlet.

He felt coarse. "I'm sorry. That wasna a proper thing to say. I dinna mean to offend ye."

"I'm . . . I'm not offended. I've been at court all my life. There is not much that can be said that I've not heard."

"I'll wager ye're wrong, mistress. We men are base creatures."

"Not all, certainly."

"Most. But probably not yer Sir Henry."

"He is not my Sir Henry. If he belongs to anyone, it is Alis de Braun."

"The lady-in-waiting who betrayed yer trust?"

She nodded.

"Ah, so that was it then, she and he . . . I take it then, that I am to be the instrument to bring his attention back to ye?"

"I never had his attention."

"But ye wanted it."

"I . . . admit I found him handsome at first. And charming. But . . ."

Her gaze went to his mouth and he felt his body respond. God's blood she was beautiful. Her smile was admiring and his body stirred again.

"I have discovered that there are men whose charms are equal to Sir Henry's. Or far exceed them. I would not use you as an instrument, sir."

"Not even if I begged?"

She laughed. "It depends upon how prettily you beg, I think."

"That could be difficult. We speak what we mean in

the Highlands and not in riddles, nor with pretty language."

"You could put it in a poem, perhaps."

"Me? Write a poem? Like one of the king's courtiers?" He laughed. "Ah, lass, that I cannot do for I know nothing of courtly love. Perhaps ye can explain it to me."

And this she did as they walked through the streets of London.

When they reached the crest of a hill, Isabel said, "There, below us, is the Tower."

He followed her gaze to the immense walls of the fortress called simply the Tower, which was surrounded by a moat linked to the River Thames. Above the walls, the large and impressive White Tower rose high to dominate the skyline. And ahead of them, built of heavy gray stone lay the Lion Tower, the formidable entrance to the fortress. She moved toward it and he followed, throwing a glance over his shoulder. No man of middle height crossed the empty space behind them.

"William the Conqueror built the White Tower," she said, "after defeating Harold the Saxon at Hastings, in 1066, over two hundred years ago."

"Were yer people in England then?"

"My mother's people came over with William. When William stayed, so did they. We've been in London ever since. King Edward's father, Henry III, enlarged and improved the Tower, which was not popular with those who lived on the land he confiscated. And King Edward has done the same, only tenfold, pushing the outer walls into the city, and building new towers and creating the new entrance."

She moved forward to speak to the guard at the first

barrier, who greeted her by name. " My companion is Rory MacGannon, of Loch Gannon, in London for the queen's funeral. We have business within."

"Of course, Mistress de Burke. Mind your step, there's still ice from last night on the stones."

Isabel thanked the man, leading the way across the first drawbridge. "There, you can see where the land gate was. And this," she said as they entered the first structure, "is the Lion Tower."

He jumped as the air was suddenly filled with a sound he'd never heard, as though she'd conjured demons from hell. He reached for the sword at his hip.

"Lions, sir," she said with a smile. "Have you not heard lions before?"

He smiled at her, feeling foolish as he took his hand from the hilt of his sword. The lions roared again. And he might do the same, imprisoned in these dank stones rather than roaming free in Africa. "Nay, but it's a sound I will remember. I'd heard the king had a menagerie."

"Not a large one now. He did have elephants once. They died, but the lions have thrived. They remind visitors that this is the home of the lion of England."

"Outside of England your Edward is often called a leopard."

She arched an eyebrow. "And within England he is called king."

He laughed, following her across another drawbridge and within the walls of the Tower. She showed him the palace that Edward had built overlooking the river, where she'd slept when she'd stayed here with the queen. And the water gate Edward had constructed, and the rest of it.

But he did not retain all her words. He was too busy watching her, enjoying the graceful way she moved, the way her eyes lit when she looked at him, the soft curve of her smile. He was not the only one to notice her, he saw, as the king's household knights greeted her, and even the guards smiled at her on this cold wintry day. The sun had stayed with them, but it was dank and chill within the Tower walls.

"And that building?" he asked her as they made their way to leave.

"The Wardrobe Tower," she said, an odd note in her voice as she glanced up at it. "Come, Rory, it grows late."

"Isabel."

The voice came from above them and she stopped moving at Rory's side, her expression suddenly wary. He looked up to see a man leaning through a window, watching them. He was richly dressed, the gold on his fingers and clothing visible even in the dim winter light. Isabel sucked in her breath.

"My lord bishop," she said, bowing. "I had heard you were in Greenwich."

"You heard incorrectly," he said. "Bring your friend up to see me."

"I'm so sorry, my lord, but we must hurry. I must have him at Westminster before dark and we have little time."

"Who do you take him to see at Westminster, Isabel?"

Rory put a hand on Isabel's arm. "Who is it who's asking, sir?"

"Your friend is a Scot, Isabel. Who do you take him to see at Westminster?"

"Bishop Bek, my lord," she said, naming the first powerful man she could think of.

"Your friend is a Scot, Isabel. Are the Scots wooing Bek now, my dear?"

"This Scot prefers to woo women, sir," Rory answered.

The man's smile was not amused. "Bring him up, Isabel."

"I thank ye for the invitation," Rory said, then lowered his voice. "Do ye wish to see him, lass? I'll go if ye wish it."

"Oh, no! Please, let us leave."

"Aye, then we will," Rory said quietly. "Farewell, sir," he called and hurried her forward. The man withdrew, slamming the window behind him.

"Hurry!" She turned to look at him, her face now pale and fearful. "We need to leave before he comes down to find us!"

"Lass? Who is he? Why does he frighten ye so much?"

"Please! Let us leave here and I will tell you."

Rory followed her, through the large gate, past Edward's palace and water gate and through the Byward Tower. This time the lions were silent as they passed through that tower, and Rory was grateful for it. She hurried him across the drawbridge and through the first gatehouse. He let her lead them past All Hallows Church and around the corner before he stopped her, grabbing her arm and turning her to face him.

"Far enough. Who is the man and why are ye so afraid of him?"

"He is Walter Langton, Bishop of Lichfield, Steward of the Wardrobe."

"He terrifies ye. Why?"

She looked close to tears. "He . . . he looks at me . . . he says things that make me . . . feel . . . soiled."

"Has he harmed ye? Has he touched ye?"

"No. But I fear . . . if I were to be close to him . . . I fear him."

"Can ye tell no one of this?"

"Who? He is among the king's closest advisors. I am alone in this."

He did not think then, but pulled her into his arms, ignoring the glances and smiles of those who passed them. "No, ye're not, lass. Say the word and I swear I will protect ye."